Praise for Tyler R. Tichelaar's Children of Arthur Series

Arthur's Legacy: The Children of Arthur, Book One

"If you love the mystical magic of Camelot but thrive on the excitement and tribulations of *Game of Thrones*, this book is for you. Tichelaar encompasses the familiarity of contemporary times and skillfully interweaves history and mysticism into the Arthurian legend that has withstood the test of time, and brings the characters all to life."

— Rowena Portch, award-winning author of *The Spirian Saga*

"Tichelaar's engaging writing and deep knowledge of his subject keeps the work from ever dragging. It's never less than a page-turner: and the modern section is also filled with deliciously knowing nods to the legendary material—some deliberately obvious, others very subtle.... Tichelaar's years of research shine through without ever compromising his storytelling: his ingenious use of throwaway snippets and very obscure sources combines with a powerful imagination to make the old, old story fresh.... The finale brings the two strands of the novel together, at the same time synthesising its pagan and Christian elements into a Blakeian, poetic pantheism."

— Marcus Pitcaithly, author of *The Realm of Albion*

"Tichelaar weaves a tale of druids, witches, conspiracy, evil versus good, romance and action with all the elements of good storytelling. Careful character development and engaging dialog help in creating a back story and natural flow to an otherwise complex plot."

— Richard R. Blake, Reader Views

"So much is asked of saviors that we can forget the beating heart behind the legends. Tyler Tichelaar understands the contradiction between our expectation of heroes and their lonely destiny. In exploring the Arthurian legend, he shows himself once more the master of the complexities of the human heart."

— Diana M. Deluca, Ph.D., and author of *Extraordinary Things* and
A Dream of Shadows

"If you like medieval fiction, then this story should be right up your alley. It certainly was mine. The author knows how to turn a phrase. His characters are well-developed and interesting. Highly recommended."

— Sara Knight, The Drunken Druid

"*Arthur's Legacy* is a fresh new take on the ancient and wondrous myth of Arthur. Works of this kind are hugely important because they keep the legends alive and bring them into the 21st century. Strongly recommended for all who love the old and the new in mythic fiction."

— John Matthews, author of *King Arthur: Dark Age Warrior and Mythic Hero*

"What if the story of King Arthur was not quite what you thought? And what if its repercussions echoed down the centuries and across the seas? Casting a fresh, inventive and sometimes controversial eye over the rich tradition of Arthurian legend, especially its Welsh roots, in *Arthur's Legacy* Tyler Tichelaar has crafted an intriguing blend of action-packed time-slip fantasy adventure, moving love story, multi-layered mystery, and unusual spiritual exploration."

— Sophie Masson, editor of *The Road to Camelot*

"Tyler has clothed the stereotyped characters of myth with real, three-dimensional personalities, and has given strengths and faults to each. This is what makes the story so engrossing."
— Bob Rich, Ph.D., and author of *Ascending Spiral*

"*Arthur's Legacy* will electrify true fans of the Arthurian legend. Tichelaar's research and his weaving of the Arthurian mythos into a cohesive story for the contemporary reader is second to none. *Arthur's Legacy* will surely take its rightful place among the canon of great Arthurian literature."
— Steven Maines, author of *The Merlin Factor* series

"*Arthur's Legacy* by Tyler Tichelaar is a unique blend of medieval fantasy and modern day situations that will hook readers from page one. Part Three illustrates the depth of Tichelaar's knowledge about Arthurian lore and will test the most devoted Arthurian fan. Added to this are Tichelaar's own twists on the lore that will keep readers engaged and questioning until the very end. The story was excellent. Makes me wonder whether someone deliberately made Mordred evil all those centuries ago! Plenty of excitement and intrigue for any mystery reader. Discover a King Arthur as he has never before been portrayed. Before *Arthur's Legacy*, Arthur was seen as a shell of a man; Tichelaar shows us a human being with faults and desires."
— Cheryl Carpinello, author of *Guinevere: On the Eve of Legend*

"Author Tyler R. Tichelaar has performed impeccable research into the Arthurian legend, finding neglected details in early sources and reigniting their significance. His depiction of what might have really happened at Camelot is both refreshing and enticing."
— Debra Kemp, author of *The House of Pendragon* series

Melusine's Gift: The Children of Arthur, Book Two

"What if you discovered the famous legends you'd heard and believed all your life didn't happen the way they'd always been told? In *Melusine's Gift*, readers will join Adam and Anne Delaney as they hear the truth right from the mouths of the characters who lived the tales. Readers unfamiliar with Melusine's place in history will be drawn into her world, while the captivating web of multi-layered stories within stories combine and complement to obliterate the preconceived notions of those who consider themselves experts on her legend. I loved *Melusine's Gift* even more than *Arthur's Legacy* and can't wait for the twists and turns of *Ogier's Prayer*."

— Jenifer Brady, author of the *Abby's Camp Days* series

"Like a nested egg, rich, medieval version of Scheherazade's tales, the hypnotic story-within-story-within-story structure of *Melusine's Gift* spirals you into its center to discover the surprising twist to its one-of-a-kind treasure—a moral that takes you beyond conventional notions of good versus evil to the heart of humanity's ultimate and enduring challenge—that of choosing love over fear. Its finale then pops you back out to modern times with a gut-wrenching example of such a challenge in the lives of its contemporary main characters, one that will leave you hanging on the edge of your seat for the next and third installment of Tichelaar's Children of Arthur series."

— Roslyn McGrath, author of *The Third Mary: 55 Messages for Empowering Truth, Peace & Grace from the Mother of Mary Magdalene*

"Once again Tyler Tichelaar weaves a riveting story that mixes Arthurian lore with fact and fiction. *Melusine's Gift* is skillfully written and is reminiscent of those ancient tales from the *Arabian Nights* where one story flows into the next one and that into the next and so on. In this case, the stories reveal how the descendants of King Arthur are connected through the isle Avalon."

— Cheryl Carpinello, author of *Guinevere: On the Eve of Legend*

OGIER'S PRAYER

OGIER'S PRAYER

THE CHILDREN OF ARTHUR: BOOK THREE

BY

TYLER R. TICHELAAR

"If thou shouldst never see my face again,
Pray for my soul. More things are wrought by prayer
Than this world dreams of. Wherefore, let thy voice
Rise like a fountain for me night and day."
— Alfred, Lord Tennyson, "The Passing of Arthur"

"Work out your own salvation. Do not depend on others."
— Buddha

CONTENTS

PROLOGUE

803 A.D.
YEAR 187 BY THE MUSLIM CALENDAR

HAROUN AL-RASHID—sovereign over half the known world as ruler of the Abbasid Caliphate, which stretched from Arabia's southern deserts to the great Caspian Sea, and from the Mediterranean's easternmost reaches to the borders of India, so that all the world knew his fame and feared him, yet marveled at his magnificence and admired his wisdom and prowess—was terribly bored.

The mighty caliph sat in his sumptuous palace in his glorious capital city of Baghdad and wondered whether there was anything at all left in the world that could possibly give him a few hours' amusement. He had engaged in all manner of sport, warfare, and love during his youth. He was honored and esteemed above all in his domains and over all princes and heads of state outside the borders of his empire. Not even Charlemagne of the Franks himself could rival the caliph in any way. And now as the great caliph approached his fortieth year, he felt that everything there was to see and do, had been seen and done, and so being a great ruler was a sorry position to hold in life, for all manner of amusement had always been readily available to him, all his desires quickly and easily fulfilled, and only great boredom had resulted from all his prosperity and success.

Today, this mighty potentate was in a miserable, listless mood that not even wine nor song nor women nor games could dispel. Such was his mood when Giafar, the grand vizier and Haroun al-Rashid's old and tried friend, entered his chamber. Bowing low, Giafar waited, as was his duty, till his master spoke, but Haroun al-Rashid merely turned his head and looked at his friend, and then he sank back into his former weary posture of being slumped in his chair. After a moment, he sighed in a manner that asked Giafar, without the actual use of words, "What is it this time?"

Now, Giafar had something of importance to say to the caliph, and he had no intention of being put off by mere silence, so taking Haroun al-Rashid's sigh for permission, he made another low bow in front of the throne and began to speak.

"Commander of the Faithful," said Giafar, "I have come to remind your eminence of how you have undertaken to observe, secretly and for yourself, the manner in which justice is done and order is kept throughout your great capital city. For that very reason, you came to Baghdad from your palace in Ar-Raqqah. And today is the day you have set apart to devote to this purpose, and perhaps in fulfilling this duty, you may find some distraction from the melancholy that I perceive is so strongly overpowering you."

"Giafar, you are right!" exclaimed the caliph, suddenly stirred with a renewed interest in life. "Thank goodness you reminded me. I always find my people amusing, and at times, I have been able to right a wrong, punish an evildoer, and even gain some wisdom from the common folk. But what are you waiting for? Go, find our disguises, and we will walk among the common people as if we were one—or rather two—of them."

Giafar bowed and quickly obeyed. Five minutes later, he returned with two disguises, and after assisting his master, within a few moments, they were both dressed as foreign merchants.

And in another minute, the caliph and grand vizier had passed through a secret door in Haroun al-Rashid's private chamber that took them through a long and twisting tunnel beneath the palace. Soon they emerged outside through a hidden door in a city wall covered by a great shrubbery. Quickly, they merged with the crowds, as if it were an everyday ordinary activity for them to walk the streets of Baghdad, bartering in the bazaar, giving alms to beggars, and stopping to kneel when the call to prayer was sounded.

So disguised, Haroun al-Rashid was able to find some pleasure in this great joke that freed him from the burdens of statecraft. Often, he considered that he might so remain in such a disguise, with the intent to slip away from the palace and Baghdad and his own high position so that he might forget all his cares, for the ruling of an empire was no light matter. But he also knew that his wife, Zubaida, and his children, as well as the many millions of his subjects, depended on him. Should he disappear, his absence would cause all manner of problems for the empire and lead to rumors of his death, suspicions of foul play, and even civil war. No, he had a duty to his people and could not forsake it, but it did not hurt to fulfill that duty now and then by pretending to be one of the people so he could better understand those whom he ruled.

Despite the diversion of pretending to be a foreign merchant, today the great caliph found no amusement in the streets capable of diverting him from his melancholy and boredom. He was pleased to see the peace and good order of the city; his people appeared content, and he could observe that the city was prosperous. Even the blind beggar he passed had a smile on his face.

"Blind one," he stopped to inquire, "what reason gives you cause to be smiling?"

The beggar's smile only widened at the question, and looking over the caliph's shoulder, he pointed up into the sky.

"He is not blind!" exclaimed Giafar. "Blind men do not point at the sky!"

But the blind man continued to point, and his dishonesty was quickly forgotten when Giafar and Haroun al-Rashid both turned to discover what so commanded the beggar's attention.

Soon everyone in the street was also staring—and pointing, and gasping, and exclaiming, "Is it a genie? An evil sorcerer? It can't be real! Am I seeing things?"

Haroun al-Rashid had never in his life doubted his own vision, but at that moment, he came very close to it.

"A genuine magical flying carpet!" exclaimed Giafar.

"It is indeed!" Haroun al-Rashid agreed. "The stuff of genie tales."

The carpet was floating over the city, just perhaps fifty feet above it, slowly growing closer and gently descending. For a good five minutes, everyone in the streets of Baghdad stared up at it, murmuring in astonishment, and children crawled up onto their parents' shoulders so they might see it better.

In a little while, the carpet descended so that it landed on the flat roof of a house. And when the man, who had previously sat cross-legged upon it and whose appearance had been difficult until now to see clearly, stood up, even more gasps filled the street.

This man was no native of the city, nor even of any city or property in all the great Abbasid Caliphate. This man had a light complexion like no one in Baghdad had ever seen. His hair looked to have been spun from gold, and he was clad in shining silver armor that sparkled in the sun.

"Is it a god?" cried one woman.

"Blasphemy!" a man replied.

"It must be a Christian," said another man. "For look at his pale skin—and a Christian is the farthest thing from a god that anyone could be!"

The golden-haired man was beautiful, however, and tall and finely formed, and dazzling even without a smile, for he looked uncertain, looking down first upon the crowd, and then at the magic carpet beneath his feet, as if willing it to fly back up into the air.

And then the magic moment was broken as three soldiers stormed into the house, upon the roof of which the golden-haired man stood.

In another minute, the soldiers had arrived on the roof, and the Christian knight, if that is what he was, had drawn his sword, ready to do battle.

"Drop your sword!" cried one soldier. "You are under arrest by order of his great majesty, Caliph Haroun al-Rashid!"

The caliph heard his name invoked, but he made no move, not wishing to reveal his true identity, but even more so, wishing to see how this fight would turn out.

The golden-haired stranger, instead of dropping his sword, charged toward his assailants, and within a minute, the three soldiers found their own weapons struck from their hands and sent flying into the street, the crowd quickly dodging them. One man, in the fight that ensued, stumbled over the roof's edge and went crashing into the crowd, causing a bystander a broken arm. Another, in fear, jumped onto a neighboring roof, while the third soldier fell to his knees, begging mercy from the golden-haired, godlike warrior who had so mysteriously appeared in their city.

"Now!" exclaimed the stranger, "you may take me to your king, but I go as his guest, and not as a prisoner to any man."

After recovering from his astonishment, the kneeling soldier regained his feet and did as he was bid, leading the way back down through the house. The stranger stopped a moment to put his sword back into its sheath; then he bent down to gather up the magic carpet, roll it, and tuck it under his arm, before descending through the house.

As the crowd waited in astonishment to see this amazing warrior enter the street, Haroun al-Rashid said to Giafar, "Quickly. We must return." And elbowing their way through the clamoring crowd of men, women, and children, all seeking to get a glimpse of, or even better, to touch the mysterious stranger, the caliph and his grand vizier made their way back to the secret tunnel that would allow them to return to the palace.

Within half an hour, they were once again in the caliph's private chamber, and immediately, they heard a rapid, insistent pounding on the door from the servants who repeatedly cried, "My caliph, are you there? Please, a great marvel has happened. Come quickly!"

"I will be there in a moment!" the caliph shouted, perturbed by his servants' impatience; they should know better than to harangue him.

Then there was silence, for once confirmation was heard of their master's presence, his servants dared not anger him.

Giafar quickly helped his master change out of the merchant's clothing and back into robes suitable for a great ruler to receive an esteemed visitor.

Then Haroun al-Rashid stepped toward the door and placed his fingers around the handle to open it, but first he turned back and said to Giafar, "Have that deceitful blind beggar found and thrown into prison for his falsehood." When the caliph did open the door, dozens of servants, his wife, children, and ministers all bowed before him and created a path so he could pass through. Haroun al-Rashid ignored them all and strode through the palace to his throne room where he intended to receive his illustrious guest.

Once seated, with a wave of his hand, the caliph ordered the guards to open the door. Then in strode the golden-haired man, taller than everyone else in the room, and escorted by six more soldiers, whom no doubt he could have easily divested of their swords if he had so wished, but instead, he had willingly given up his own sword, his air of confidence and bearing declaring he felt no need for it.

The mysterious stranger came to a stop a few feet before Haroun al-Rashid's throne, and after bowing, he awaited permission to speak.

"Stranger," said the caliph, "we have seen with our own eyes your amazing entry into our great city. We would know your name and your purpose here."

"Great Caliph," said the golden-haired giant of a man, "I am Ogier the Dane, one of the paladins to the great Charles, King of the Franks, and in my own right, Prince of Denmark. I am a stranger here in your domain, it is true, but I come in peace on a mission I can share with your ears alone. I beg a private audience with your majesty."

By then, the multitude of the royal household had crowded into the throne room. They now all gasped at such a bold demand from a stranger.

Haroun al-Rashid waited a moment as everyone reacted to this unusual request, and then, clapping his hands together, he ordered, "Silence!"

The room became still as Haroun al-Rashid looked deep into Ogier the Dane's eyes, searching as if to read his very soul. After a moment, he rose from his throne and stepped forward.

The silence was broken when he placed his hand on Ogier's shoulder, a familiarity he had never shown in public to any man, not even to Giafar.

"Come," said Haroun al-Rashid. "I have been sorely bored, and you have brought me pleasure in the unexpectedness of your visit. Your words speak truth, for you look to be one of noble breeding, and your eyes bespeak suffering but also wisdom. I will hear your tale, but first, we will have you properly bathed and fed."

And then leading the way, Haroun al-Rashid personally escorted the stranger to his own private bathing pool where he left him under the care of his servants, saying to Ogier, "Please refresh yourself, and then my servants will bring you to me to dine. Over our meal, I will hear with great pleasure all you have to say."

And so it was, in an hour's time, that Ogier the Dane, Prince of Denmark, thousands of miles from the cold northern climes where he had been raised, found himself dining with Haroun al-Rashid, the Caliph of the Abbasid Empire, the most powerful man in the world.

Seated at a table, the caliph ordered wine for his guest and also all manner of sweetmeats and fruits and vegetables, every delicacy known within his great empire, and as they began to eat, the caliph said, "Now, I wish to hear your tale for I have no doubt it is a marvelous one."

Ogier the Dane nodded in agreement and said, "My lord, I will be most pleased to tell you my story, and perhaps when I have finished, you will be good enough to aid me, though I am but a humble knight of Charles the Great, King of the Franks."

"We are good friends with King Charles," replied the caliph, "although he now calls himself an emperor, so I am surprised you do not show him the respect he deserves with that title."

"Emperor?" muttered Ogier. "Emperor of what?"

"He was crowned as Holy Roman Emperor by the Pope. Did you not know this? It has been two or three years now since it happened."

"No, I...I—"

"It seems you have been journeying far from home for a long time then, Prince Ogier."

"I believe so, your majesty," replied the Dane.

"Come. Tell me all about it. When did you leave King Charles' court, and how did you come to be in my domains?"

"That is a long, long tale, Great Caliph, and I find it not easy to know where to start. I do not wish to weary you, but I fear we must begin just a few days after my birth."

"I am prepared for a tale as long as you have to tell," Haroun al-Rashid replied, "and we have all night for the telling."

"I suspect it will take at least that long, if not longer," Ogier began, "but I am happy to obey your command to hear it, and I hope that in my words you will find the entertainment you seek."

PART I
DELANEY CASTLE, ENGLAND
1995

CHAPTER 1

"**I**T'S THE TWINS! Oh, God. Adam, it's—they—they took them. I don't know who or how, but someone kidnapped them. Lance and Tristan, your precious boys, they're—they're gone. I don't know how this happened. Who could do it?"

Hours later, his mother's panicky screams still rang in Adam's ears. He and his wife Anne had been vacationing in France on their long overdue honeymoon while leaving their infant twin sons in the care of Adam's mother and grandmother for a few days back at Delaney Castle. And then the phone had rung with the horrible message—turning a parent's worst nightmare into reality.

Adam and Anne had quickly hopped in the car and driven all night back to England and their home at Delaney Castle, arriving late that afternoon. By then, the Bordenshire police had arrived and started an investigation. Detectives had placed the property under surveillance, the police had blocked off the roads, missing children alerts had spread across Britain, and the BBC evening news had carried the story that the Earl of Delaney's twin sons—not yet five months old—had been kidnapped.

Adam was not at all happy about the publicity—in fact, he and Anne had heard the story on the car radio while they were still two hours from home.

They arrived at Delaney Castle to find Adam's mother, Mary Morgan, a nervous wreck, his grandmother, Elizabeth Morgan, crying in the library, and Anne's father, Cedric Harker, slamming the front door in the face of reporters wanting an interview. Anne and Adam had managed to sneak through a back garage door to avoid the reporters, but they could not avoid the police and were subjected to hours of questioning, within two minutes of stepping into the house. Repeatedly, they were asked, "Who could possibly wish to kidnap your children?" and "It's possible it was done solely for ransom money, but do you have any enemies?"

"There was a man who broke into our motel room in France last night," Adam told Detective Harris, who was heading the investigation. "I chased after him, but he got away. Do you think he could be connected to the kidnapping?"

"Perhaps, if it were thought you had the children with you and kidnapping was intended," mused the detective, "but no, whoever kidnapped the children knew they were here, so more than likely, it was just a coincidence. Someone who probably doesn't even know who you are, more likely, was simply trying to rob you. Still, we can investigate with the French authorities. Did you report the incident to the police?"

"N-no," said Adam, faltering because he didn't know how to explain why he had not reported it. The truth was that he had been in the middle of looking for Anne, who had wandered off in the night, and together, they had experienced a strange sort of time-travel dream that Adam now pushed to the back of his mind to focus on his children's disappearance. That experience was all too much to explain right now, so he simply told Detective Harris, "My mom called right after it happened, so I didn't have time to pursue it. My first thought was to get home."

"Understandable," said the detective. "We'll contact the local French police, however, to ask questions at the motel and find out if anyone saw anything further that could help us."

Adam gave Detective Harris the name of the motel where he and Anne had stayed, and after thanking the detective and several other members of the police staff, they were relieved to be left alone with the family. They were both exhausted and starving, so they had a quick meal with Adam's mother and Anne's father. Adam's grandmother had been so upset that she had gone straight to bed once the police left, saying she had no appetite. After eating, they all felt ready to retire for the evening, knowing they were too upset to sleep very well, but also realizing they needed to rest to keep up their strength.

"We'll all feel better in the morning," Mary assured everyone.

Cedric talked Anne into taking a sleeping pill because she was so upset, and he went upstairs with her to find her one. A guest room had been prepared for Cedric, who lived a few miles away, so he could be present if any news arrived. Although he and Adam had not seen eye-to-eye at first, Cedric was putting aside old prejudices in his concern for his grandchildren.

"He's been so strong through it all," Mary told Adam once Cedric had gone upstairs with Anne. Mary and Adam had sent Mrs. Deneker, the housekeeper, to bed as well while they sat together in the library, trying to catch their breaths after the past horrid twenty-four hours. "Cedric really got me through the day until you arrived. He made sure Mother and I ate and he dealt with the media and talked to the detectives with us. He's been a tower of strength. He must really love those boys, and I'm not surprised since he's seen them more than I have. I should have come to England for their birth."

"You're here now, Mother," Adam said. "That's enough. Let's go get some sleep."

"I don't think I can sleep," Mary replied. "I feel like this is all my fault."

"It's not your fault, Mom," Adam said, putting his arm around her. "You couldn't have known anyone would try to steal the children."

"I never should have let them out of my sight," Mary replied, trying to hold back her tears. "I should have slept in the room with them, but what do I know about being a mother, much less a grandmother? I was never a mother to you, and now I'm being punished for it."

"That's all in the past, Mom," he replied.

"I wish it were, Adam," she said, "but I fear it's not. I love you dearly; I always have, but I just couldn't be a mother to you."

"I know," said Adam, pausing to give her a tissue. "I understand about the shame you felt having a child out of wedlock back when people still thought such things mattered. I understand all that, and Grandpa and Grandma did a good job of raising me. It's all long forgiven now, if there ever was anything to forgive."

"It's not just that," Mary said. "I have other reasons I haven't told you—I—" She hesitated, stopped to wipe her tears, and then added, "Well, I'll explain it to you some other time, but I shouldn't worry you with my troubles right now. I don't know how I'll sleep, but I do want you to sleep tonight. Come on; I'll walk you up to your room. There's nothing more we can do tonight."

Adam stood up at the same time as his mother and gave her his hand. She kissed him on the cheek and repeated, "Adam, I'm so truly sorry. I love you and I love those boys far more than I can tell you."

"I know, Mom. It'll all work out. We just have to be patient." He said the words to comfort her, though he could not believe them himself.

They walked together into the hall, their arms around each other's backs, and then they went up the stairs to the second floor.

"Poor Anne," said Mary when they stopped in front of Adam and Anne's bedroom. "It was terrible enough for me to leave my child; I can't imagine what it must be for her to have this happen to her sons. I hope she can sleep tonight."

"I'll look after her; don't worry," said Adam.

"I know you will. You're a good man, Adam. I'm so proud of the man you are, even if I had nothing to do with raising you. Your father would be proud of you, too."

Adam now felt a bit teary-eyed, but he shook it off and said, "Sometimes, it seems like I can still feel Dad's spirit in this house. I felt it the day you came, as if he were happy to have you here finally."

Mary smiled at the thought, then kissed Adam on the cheek.

"Good night," she said.

"Good night," Adam replied, and then he opened his bedroom door. He found Anne lying in bed with the light off. In a couple of minutes, he had changed into his pajamas and crawled into bed beside her. But before he could wrap his arms around her, she rolled over to face him.

"I thought you were asleep," he said. "I was trying not to wake you."

"I slept for a few minutes, I think," she said, "but the sleeping pill doesn't seem to be working, and I just want to hold you for a little while."

He let her cuddle her head against his chest as he wrapped his arm around her, stroking her hair and kissing her forehead.

"I love you," he said. "We'll get the boys back somehow. We have to believe only the best will happen and that there's a reason for all of this."

"I sure hope so," she said. "I—" She hesitated, then said, "Adam, I know the twins are more important, but you know that strange dream I told you I had just before you told me the boys were gone—you said you knew about it—that you'd had the same one."

"Yes," he said. "The dream about Roland and Melusine."

"Yes, but how is it possible that we had the same dream? And do you think it has something to do with the boys? I haven't had time to process it all yet, but I think maybe—well, I don't really understand it all, but I thought I was told in it that we were all descended from King Arthur or something like that, and Merlin told Roland there was some plot against his descendants by someone—Ganelon or Constantine or someone. Do you remember that? Am I remembering it correctly?"

"Yes," said Adam. "I don't know what it has to do with our children, but it might be connected. I don't know...." Adam felt he should say more, but he wasn't ready yet to tell her all he knew.

"It must be connected somehow," Anne continued. "I just can't stop thinking about it. What does it mean? Do you think it could be true? How can I have a dream like that with so many details in it? Even as I was listening to Roland and Raimond and all the others telling the tales, I was seeing the images before my eyes. I can even remember Melusine scratching her ear while she talked about her life in Avalon. It's just—it's so crazy, Adam, and even more so since you dreamed it, too! How is that possible?"

Anne sat up in bed, the comfort of being with Adam now being replaced by disbelief.

Adam pulled her back down beside him and again stroked her hair.

"Anne, darling," he said, digging up his courage, "I love you so much, and I would never want to keep anything from you because I firmly believe you're my one and only soulmate. But there is something I haven't told you—only because I was afraid you would think I was crazy, but once before I had a dream like the one we had last night, and Merlin was in it, only it was about Camelot, and in the end, Merlin told me I was descended from King Arthur, and—"

"Oh my gosh!" Anne exclaimed, sitting up. "Remember the manuscript we found, too!" She propped herself on her elbow, still facing Adam, who rolled onto his side to face her. "The manuscript we found in the ruins of the original Delaney Castle right after we first met—remember how it said the Delaneys were descended from King Arthur? Then, maybe it's true. Maybe we aren't crazy—or maybe, maybe we're schizophrenic or something and having that idea planted into our brains of being descended from King Arthur has made us crazy."

"I thought that might be the case when I had the dream about King Arthur," Adam admitted, looking into her eyes, "but even the craziest people can't dream the same dream simultaneously. There has to be something more to it than that."

"But what?" Anne asked. "And what does it have to do with our boys?"

"I don't know," said Adam, "but I'm determined to find out."

Anne sighed and lay back down on her pillow beside Adam.

"I think the sleeping pill is catching up with me now," she said. "I can feel it making me drowsy."

"You need your rest," said Adam. "We'll sort it all out in the morning when our heads are clearer."

Anne rolled onto her stomach. "Maybe I'll dream again and find the answers."

"I hope so," said Adam, turning onto his side to place his hand gently on her back until he heard her breathing change so he knew she was asleep.

Adam lay then for an hour, cursing Merlin, whom he blamed for bringing all this grief to them, but in time, exhaustion also overcame him and he closed his eyes.

CHAPTER 2

ADAM WOKE TO the sun early that late June morning. It was barely six o'clock, but after a few minutes, he knew he would not fall back asleep. For a second, he lay there quietly, and then he remembered his children were missing and a knot tied itself in his stomach. Anne was sleeping peacefully beside him, and he knew she must still be exhausted. It was unlikely there would be any news for hours to come, so he might as well let her sleep.

He got up, put on his pants and a shirt, and walked downstairs to the kitchen to make some coffee.

When Adam reached the dining room, he saw the door to the kitchen was open, which was unusual since Mrs. Deneker always insisted the servants were not to be seen in their natural environment, as she believed the kitchen to be. She never could seem to get used to Adam entering the kitchen and helping himself to coffee, but he had been raised as a middle class American boy, not a future English earl, so he preferred to wait on himself. Now as he stepped closer to the kitchen door, he heard voices, and as he came into the doorway, he heard Cedric say, "You have to tell them. They have a right to know."

"It's not time yet," Mary replied.

As he passed through the door, Adam was about to ask, "Tell me what?" But the sudden sight of Cedric's hands clasped over his mother's, as the two sat across from each other at the table, made Adam momentarily silent.

"When would be the right time if not now?" Cedric asked Mary.

"Good morning," said Adam, not wanting to eavesdrop. He walked toward the coffeepot, which he saw was already full.

"Did you sleep at all, Adam?" asked his mother, turning from Cedric to him.

Out of the corner of his eye, Adam saw Cedric withdraw his hands and place them under the table. *It's nothing*, Adam told himself. *She's just upset and he's trying to comfort her.*

"I slept a few hours," he said. "But when I woke up, I knew I wouldn't fall back asleep, and Anne was resting peacefully, so I didn't want to disturb her."

"The poor thing," said Mary. "I can't imagine anything worse than this happening to us all."

"I don't have much faith in the local police," Cedric said. "We should have Scotland Yard called in. They're the best in the land."

"I don't even know how the kidnappers managed to get in the house," said Mary. "The police think they came through the upstairs window, but how? No one could have climbed up the wall, and if they did, there'd be some mark, but the detectives said they could find nothing, not even a footprint of any sort around the shrubs beneath the windows."

"They'll find out what happened," Cedric insisted. "They just need time."

His coffee poured, Adam sat down at the table next to his mother, who was sipping her own coffee. Apparently, like her son, Mary preferred the kitchen to the austere dining room, and the circles under her eyes told Adam she'd been seated there for some time. After a moment of awkward silence, Cedric glanced toward a window and commented, "The police have had the house surrounded all night."

"A lot of good that does," said Adam, "when the kidnappers already have what they wanted to steal."

"I don't understand," said Mary. "Why would they take the boys? I mean, they didn't leave a ransom note or anything like that. Isn't that why children are usually kidnapped—for ransom? But the inspector said if that were the case, we would most likely hear from the kidnappers within twenty-four hours, just as soon as they were far enough away to feel safe, but it's been over twenty-four hours now. Why couldn't they have just broken in and stolen money or a valuable painting or something like that? The house is full of priceless items they could have taken much more easily, considering how quietly they performed the operation, and it would have been less dangerous for them than risking the twins screaming and alerting the whole household."

"You never heard anything?" asked Adam.

"No, not a thing, but it's such a big house, you know. I put the boys to bed around eight, and I had the baby monitor with me. They were so very quiet, and Mother and I were watching television, but during the commercials, I kept putting the TV on mute so I could listen for the boys' breathing. And then around ten o'clock, I went up to check on them because they'd never been quiet for two full hours during the couple of nights before that. That's when I discovered they were gone, and then I realized the window was wide open. I never even heard a sound, though—not even with the baby monitor. I just...." Mary began to cry again. "I should have...."

"Mother, it's not your fault," Adam snapped, irritated more from lack of sleep than at her. "Please stop blaming yourself. It won't help anything."

"Adam, I—you don't know that it isn't my fault—you don't."

Mary covered her face with her hands.

Cedric looked at Adam and said, "Don't yell at your mother. You don't know what she's been through."

Now Adam felt like yelling at Cedric. If the man weren't Anne's father, he would have, but he bit his tongue, and after a second, he said, "I'm sorry, Mom. But there's no way it can be your fault. It's just some greedy bastards who, for whatever reason, decided to target us."

"That's the thing, Adam," she said, sniffling and wiping a tear from her eye. "You don't know that they don't have a reason. You don't...well, you don't know everything about me...and well, maybe...."

"Shh," said Cedric. "Not now. Let's have some breakfast before the detective returns. He wants to question everyone again to see whether we'll remember anything else, and—"

"There's nothing to remember," said Mary, accepting the handkerchief Cedric handed her. "There's just the past, the guilt I feel, and—"

"Mom, I've told you I've forgiven you for all that," Adam said, shaking his head. Then he quickly swallowed down his cup of coffee and got back up to refill it, hoping more caffeine would make him less irritable.

"I know, Adam," Mary continued, "but you don't know what you are forgiving."

"We've all made mistakes," said Cedric, again reaching across the table to take her hand. "Myself included, and as much or more than you, Mary. But Anne should know everything too; let's wait until she's awake before we start making any confessions."

"What are you two talking about?" asked Adam, setting his coffee cup down on the counter so hard that the coffee spilled over the rim. "I keep telling you it's all in the past. Neither the fact that my mother wasn't around when I was a kid, or that you, Cedric, lied all these years about being Anne's father has anything to do with my sons being kidnapped. Right?"

Mary looked Cedric in the eye, but he just shrugged his shoulders.

Not being able to make any sense out of his mother and Cedric's behavior, Adam shook his head and said, "I need a walk and some fresh air."

"Don't you want breakfast?" asked Mary.

"I need to burn off some frustration first," Adam replied, heading to the back door. "I'll be back in a little while. I just need to calm down and clear my thoughts. Anne will be up soon and then I'll eat with her."

"That sounds like a good idea, son," said Cedric.

Adam felt like punching Cedric for calling him "son." Who the hell did he think he was? His father? He might be his father-in-law, but in the little more than a year that they had known each other, neither had grown to like the other, and now Adam wanted to know why the hell the man was holding his mother's hands.

Adam went through the back door—the servant's entrance, according to Mrs. Deneker—then down the drive and into the gardens that stretched on for acres and provided full-time positions for two men. Adam never ceased to marvel that he was employing a staff of twelve—Mrs. Deneker was the housekeeper, and then there was the butler, Robert, plus two gardeners, and the maids—there was a parlormaid or a chambermaid or some such title—and a manservant, whom Adam refused to allow to dress him, and a cook and her helper, and a chauffeur, and a security guard, who apparently was useless since he had seen or heard nothing the night of the kidnapping, and of course, the accountant, who handled all the bills and told him the staff was necessary for the upkeep of the house to keep it looking good for the tourists, although Adam doubted they had enough tourists to cover the wages for all these people. He knew his father had money in all sorts of stocks and bonds and various business interests as well as in Swiss bank accounts and who knew all what—Adam knew all this because the accountant had explained it to him, but he had never fully comprehended it all. Cedric had assured him not to worry—that all the servants had been with his father for a long time, save for the parlormaid who had been replaced that past winter, but Mrs. Deneker would keep an eye on her, and they had all been devoted to the late earl and would be devoted to him and Anne as well. Adam was still trying to become comfortable in his new role that made him feel like the medieval lord of a manor, and he couldn't even wrap his head around all the other property, homes, and businesses he now owned, much less how many people were employed by all of them. In fact, he wasn't even clear how many millions of pounds he was worth, nor did it seem to matter since the accountant had told him that unless he wanted to buy an entire country, it was unlikely he could ever exceed his annual income and need to touch the principal. Mind-boggling!

How was it possible that he, formerly Adam Morgan, a simple boy from Michigan, could have inherited all this wealth from his father, whom he had never even known until a little over a year ago and who had turned out to be an English earl? It was still all so surreal to him.

The house and the gardens were enormous, and the money more than he and Anne or their sons or grandsons would ever be able to spend—and after having inherited it all a year ago, and having had to deal with lawyers and courts so he would be recognized as the rightful earl as Anne's husband, Adam still had not come to terms with it all. Anne was much more comfortable with it, having grown up in this lifestyle, but Adam had felted tempted to sell everything and donate the money all to charity while they just kept enough to buy a simple house and have whatever money he and Anne would need to be comfortable for the rest of their lives. Now he wished he had.

"Money just brings worries," he muttered to himself as he walked past wisteria vines strung along the side of the house, and then amid perfectly manicured bushes and countless flowers whose names he would never be able to learn. "The boys never would have been kidnapped if I didn't have money."

"You don't know that," said an unexpected voice.

Startled, Adam swung around, but no one was behind him. He had thought the speaker might be one of the police watching the property, but he could see no one.

"Who's there?" he called, looking around until he lifted his head and saw a man perched up in a tree. Adam couldn't see the man's face yet, but he knew right away whom it had to be.

"Damn it, Merlin!" he yelled. "What the hell is going on? Are you involved in all of this?"

"Such language," said Merlin, hesitantly stretching his foot onto a branch so he could begin to climb down. "I never heard King Arthur talk—ayyyy!" The wizard had missed his foothold and gone crashing down into a hedge.

Adam grabbed the bumbling old man, who had squashed the hedge into more of a mattress, and helped him to his feet.

"Ha, ha!" Merlin laughed, brushing twigs and pieces of shrubbery out of his long white beard. "I just thought I'd 'drop in' on you." He grinned gleefully at Adam.

Adam was not amused.

"I'm just trying to lighten up the moment a little, my boy," the wizard said. "I thought a dose of humor might help considering how stressed out you look right now."

"My sons have been kidnapped!" Adam exclaimed. "Don't you know that? I thought you knew everything!"

"Well, now," said Merlin, putting his finger in his mouth to pull out a leaf, "*everything* is more than anyone can possibly know. I mean, I am only human, even though not exactly mortal. I do know a lot, about thirty-seven times as much as you do from my best calculations, but that's not really all that much to brag about considering I've been around for over twenty centuries. I've really been quite lazy with my learning at times."

"Cut the bullshit and tell me what's going on," Adam demanded, getting in the old man's face.

"Well, I can see there's no talking to you right now," said Merlin, taking a step back. "I have plenty to tell you, but you need to calm down first, and besides, if you look to your right, you'll see the police detective is pulling into the drive so you better go talk to him. We can talk later. Plus, your mother also has something she needs to tell you. I'd just be in the way, so why don't I come back this afternoon? That should also give you time to tell Anne about your dream of Camelot—I don't know what kind of a husband keeps such things from his wife for so long. Why don't you and Anne take tea in the privacy of your room this afternoon, and I'll come by to talk to you then."

"I want to know—" Adam began.

But before Adam could finish his sentence, Merlin literally

dissolved into a mist that quickly vanished in the morning sun. If he weren't so angry, Adam would have been completely unnerved by the scene.

"Your lordship!"

Turning, Adam found the inspector beckoning to him from the drive, so he turned back toward the house, relieved that the inspector had apparently not noticed Merlin's vanishing act.

"I knew the old bastard was involved in this," Adam muttered to himself. "Why the hell did I ever have to get mixed up with that lunatic?" But he actually felt relief that Merlin knew something about the kidnapping. Hopefully, the crazy wizard would be able to help them locate the children—and probably sooner than the inspector would with his dozens of questions that no one could answer.

The inspector stood by his car, waiting for Adam, who was by his side in a minute.

"Hello, Inspector," Adam said, shaking his hand.

"It's detective, your lordship. Technically, detective superintendant, but if you want to call me Detective Harris, that will be fine."

"I'm sorry, Detective. You know I'm American, so I'm still getting used to the different titles used in England. I can't even get used to my own."

"Not a problem. I'm sure you have far more important things on your mind."

"Do you have any updates for us?" Adam asked. It was almost on the tip of his tongue to tell the detective that Merlin might be able to help with the investigation, but then he stopped himself, realizing that to mention Merlin would cause the detective to wonder whether he himself was crazy. Adam still wondered sometimes himself.

"I'm afraid not," said the detective, "but we are doing our very best.

Your lordship, I have to question all the family and the staff. I did speak to your mother, grandmother, and your family solicitor, Mister...."

The detective paused to look in his notepad, which he drew from his pocket, but Adam supplied the name for him. "Mr. Harker, Cedric Harker."

"Yes, Mr. Harker. Thank you. You understand, of course, that everyone is a suspect until we find out what actually happened. I was hoping I could conduct some more interviews today, both with the family and the servants."

"By all means," said Adam, walking with him to the house. "Come on in. You can use the library, and you can speak to anyone you want."

"I know also that you were just in France," said the detective, nodding his head, "but I must ask that you and all your family not leave England again until I give permission, and preferably not leave Bordenshire County without informing me."

"You have my word," said Adam, "that neither my wife, nor I, nor any of our family or servants will do so. I'm sure we're all innocent and will do anything we can to aid your investigation."

"Thank you," said Detective Harris, again nodding his head and waiting for Adam to open the door and lead the way inside.

"Come in," Adam repeated, stepping up to the back door and taking the handle in his hand. "It's awful early. Have you had breakfast yet?"

"Yes, but I wouldn't mind a cup of tea," Detective Harris replied.

"I'll have Mrs. Deneker make some right away. I'm afraid we're all coffee drinkers, save for Anne and Cedric, since we're American."

"Understandable," said the detective. "I hope I'm not intruding too early. I was just going to look around the property before I questioned you all, and I can wait if need be."

"Most of us are already up," Adam replied. "I'll go wake my wife. My grandmother might still be in bed, but my mom and Cedric are both up."

Detective Harris followed Adam in through the kitchen door. Cook and her assistant were both busy making breakfast now. Mrs. Deneker was also present and told Adam and the detective that Cedric and Mary had gone into the dining room. Adam explained that Detective Harris had more questions for everyone. Mrs. Deneker said she would fetch the parlormaid, and he could start with her while the rest had breakfast. "I'll have tea brought to you in the library," Cook added. Detective Harris thanked both women and then followed Adam into the dining room.

"Mother, Cedric, you remember Inspector Harris," Adam introduced everyone. "He has some questions for all of us. He's going to be in the library, at least for the morning, and take turns interviewing all of us."

Mary nodded in acknowledgment. Cedric said, "Thank you for coming, Detective. I don't know what we can tell you that we haven't already, but I guess you know what you're doing."

"This way, Detective," said Adam, again feeling irritated by his father-in-law and also with himself since he had again used the wrong title for the detective. He led his guest into the hall and to the library. "Please make yourself at home, Detective. Mrs. Deneker is very efficient so I'm sure the parlormaid is already on her way. I'll go up to wake Anne so we can have breakfast before you need us."

"Thank you, your lordship," said Detective Harris.

Two minutes later, when Adam entered his bedroom, he found Anne already dressed and sitting in a chair by the window. He told her about the detective's visit and that breakfast was almost ready.

"I'm not hungry," said Anne.

"You have to eat, dear," he replied.

"Adam, I need to know," she insisted. "You told me you had the same dream that I did the other night, and then before we fell asleep, you were telling me something else, about a dream of Camelot that you'd also had. I was so tired I'm not sure whether I'm remembering that or I dreamt it."

Adam sighed and sat down on the small sofa in their room. "Yes, you're remembering it correctly. Do you want me to tell you about that now? It will take a little while."

She got up from her chair and came to sit beside him.

"I don't know where to begin," he said, looking her in the eye and seeing how anxious she was to hear what he had to say. "You know how much I love you, but you also know there was something very strange about the way we met and how you got pregnant right away, and then how it just so happened that we should be brother and sister, or so we thought until my father confessed that he wasn't your father."

"That did seem like too much of a coincidence," Anne admitted, "but it's all worked out. I don't know that it was anything more than a coincidence, although...."

"Although what?" asked Adam.

"Well, in the dream I had, I saw my friend Morgan, and she—well she was with me the night I met you, remember? And you were with that Merle chap, and then you told me later that when you tried to find me, you went to Morgan's apartment and found him there, like they were living together as lovers or something—I just couldn't believe that!"

"Yes, that's just it, Anne. It wasn't a coincidence. That dream told you that your friend Morgan is really the famous sorceress Morgan le Fay, King Arthur's sister, and that fellow Merle is really Merlin, Arthur's court magician. I know it all sounds crazy, and I don't know how it's even possible, but the two of them are alive and living in the twentieth century, and I'm sure they somehow manipulated things so we would come together; I mean, they obviously orchestrated the dream we both had the other night."

"But what does it all mean?" asked Anne, her eyes growing wide with wonder and a tinge of fear.

Adam was silent a moment. "I think—"

"Do you think," Anne interrupted, putting her hand on his shoulder, "that they have something to do with the children being kidnapped?"

"I don't know what to think," said Adam.

"But, well, I've known Morgan for years. I don't think she...."

"Kidnappers usually are people you know," said Adam. "But she and Merlin were in France with us when the boys were kidnapped. Still, they could have.... Oh, hell, I don't know. This whole situation is crazy!"

"Well, we have to tell the police then that they could be suspects," said Anne, nervous and now moving both her hands to her lap.

"That's the thing," said Adam. "If they really are Morgan le Fay and Merlin, we can't tell the police that. They'll think we're lunatics, and if Morgan and Merlin really have magical powers, what good would the police do?"

"But I don't understand why they would take our boys," cried Anne.

"I don't either," said Adam, squeezing her shoulder, "but they must be involved—I saw Merlin in the garden just a few minutes ago."

Anne gasped.

"It's okay," said Adam. "He said he has something to tell us and he'll be back this afternoon."

"Then he is involved, or at least he knows something." Tears sprung to Anne's eyes. "But why is he tormenting us by keeping us in suspense? Why didn't he tell you what's going on? Why would anyone steal our children or wish to harm them?"

"The obvious answer is money," said Adam, "but if Merlin is involved, I'm sure it's not money that motivates him, and despite his odd behavior, I can't imagine he would ever harm our children."

"I don't think Morgan would harm them either," said Anne. "As scary as this situation is, I just can't believe that of her. She was my best friend in college, or at least that's what I thought."

"There must be some reason why they're telling us these stories," said Adam, "even though I'm not clear what it is. Still, as strange as they're behaving, I feel they are benevolent and mean to do well by us."

"And you say you already heard another long story like the one I experienced the other night?" asked Anne.

"Yes," Adam replied, stroking her hair. "I never told you because I was afraid you would think I was crazy before."

"I'm ready to believe just about anything now," said Anne. "Tell me what it was about."

"It happened that day Devin and I went to London and we stopped at Cadbury Hill—the same day Dad died. Merlin appeared to me there, and he put me to sleep somehow, and suddenly, I dreamt I was back in Camelot—not like I was really there, but more like I was watching a movie, only it was more vivid than a movie, like I was really on the streets or in the rooms of the castle, sitting in a corner or a room and watching everything that happened—like a 3-D movie, but ten times more real. I dreamt the whole story of Camelot's end, really, and how

Arthur and Mordred really didn't fight, but Constantine was the villain along with the evil witch Gwenhwyvach, Guinevere's half-sister, and... well, there's so much more that feels all muddled in my head now. But I think the important part was that King Arthur was human, flawed, and yet still noble, and that Mordred loved his father, and Mordred's sons died by Constantine's sword, and...and Rachel, who was married to one of Mordred's sons, she had a child, and from what we learned from the dream we both had the other night, that child's descendants included Raimond. So Melusine married Raimond because he was Arthur's descendant, and so then, all of their descendants are also Arthur's, which would apparently include us."

Anne had tried to follow this explanation, but with all the confusing names mentioned, the best she could do was ask, "But what does all that have to do with us?"

"I think—well, I got to talk to King Arthur at the end of my dream, and he told me I was descended from him, but I don't know what that has to do with you because we're not related to each other, at least not as far as we know."

"You actually talked to King Arthur!" exclaimed Anne. "If it were anyone but you telling me that, I would think you were crazy."

"I know," said Adam. "So do you forgive me for not telling you sooner?"

"Of course," she said, kissing him on the cheek. "But it still doesn't make sense why I had the dream because even if the Delaneys are descended from King Arthur, I'm not a Delaney by blood. Maybe Merlin and Morgan just included me in this dream now because I'm the mother of your children and they're King Arthur's descendants?"

"I don't know," said Adam, "but there has to be a reason for it all, and...."

"And what?"

"I think it has to do with the children. I know twins aren't that uncommon, but isn't it funny how we picked out their names? You liked Tristan because that was the name of Brad Pitt's character in *Legends of the Fall*, and then when I said I liked Lance, you said, "Like Sir Lancelot?" I had never thought of that until you said it, but it somehow seemed fitting, and so both of the boys are named for Knights of the Round Table, although that's not why we picked those names."

"Yes," said Anne, "although then your cousin Devin told us they really weren't true Arthurian names because there was no Tristan or Lancelot in the early versions of the Arthurian legend; their stories were just tacked on later."

"Still," said Adam, "I don't see how that can be a coincidence."

"No, I'm starting to think it isn't either."

They were silent for a minute, holding hands, but staring at the floor now, as if trying to figure it all out, but no answers were coming to them until Adam finally said, "I think I remember something about King Arthur's return. That maybe we were supposed to help in bringing that about, but...how can that be?"

"I've heard King Arthur is supposed to return in the hour of Britain's greatest need," Anne replied, "but I don't know what that has to do with us either."

They both sat silently pondering this idea for a moment, but then Adam shook his head and said, "I think we should go downstairs and eat something. You need to keep up your strength. Plus, Detective Harris is back and might want to ask you some more questions."

Anne smirked at the thought of another interrogation by the detective, but she said, "I do feel like I could eat something now. I want my boys back desperately, but I'm starting to think there must be a reason for all these coincidences."

"I hope so," said Adam. "I hope that means we'll understand it eventually. Anyway, I oddly feel less worried than I did yesterday."

"Yes, yesterday was a terrible nightmare," said Anne, "but I feel a little hope now."

Adam stood up and took Anne's hand. In a couple of more minutes, they had made their way to the dining room.

Anne said good morning to the rest of the family, then went into the kitchen to let Cook know she was ready to eat so they wouldn't keep the detective waiting. Cook told Anne that Detective Harris was now interviewing Mrs. Deneker, and the head gardener had arrived for work and was to go in next; then she herself would go in before the family was questioned.

Once Anne returned to the dining room, she seated herself and the whole family had breakfast together. Conversation was lacking, but they all felt some comfort in each other's presence. Regardless, for the most part they all stared at their plates, caught up in their own thoughts as they slowly ate, although a couple of times, Adam was sure he saw meaningful glances exchanged between Cedric and his mother; he was starting to fear something more than friendship had evolved between them while he and Anne were in France—feared because he still felt he could not wholly trust Cedric. But then he saw his mother give his grandmother a similar look. What could it possibly mean? Adam couldn't imagine the three of them were in on a conspiracy to kidnap his children.... They would never do such a thing—would they? Well, maybe Cedric, but certainly not his mother—but then again...well, how well did he really know his mother? But certainly his grandmother, who had raised him and whom he knew like the back of his hand, would never allow such a thing to happen; he had never known anything but love from her, even when he had least deserved it. Still, the three of them seemed to be keeping something from Anne and him. He didn't want to make a scene at breakfast, but maybe he could try talking to each one individually later, after Detective Harris left, to find out what they weren't saying.

CHAPTER 3

DETECTIVE HARRIS REMAINED all morning and through most of the afternoon, and it was nearly tea time before he prepared to depart, promising he would let them know of any new developments in the case that evening. The family had all assembled in the parlor, and Adam politely asked Detective Harris to stay and have tea with them, but he declined, having already put in more than an eight-hour workday and still having some paperwork to do back at the office.

"We certainly don't want to keep you from the investigation," Anne told him. "We appreciate your help so very much."

"Rest assured, your ladyship," he replied, "that we will do absolutely everything we can to find your children and bring their abductors to justice."

"We know you will," said Anne. "Thank you."

As Adam walked him to the door, Detective Harris added, "There will be police guarding the house around the clock. Criminals often return to the scene of the crime. During the evening hours, my men will do their best to be concealed and not noticeable, both to catch the criminals unawares and so they do not disturb your family in any way."

"Thank you," Adam repeated. He waited for the detective to climb into his car, and then Adam returned to the family in the parlor. It had been a long day and he was exhausted, and although he remained a coffee drinker, he found himself now looking forward to a cup of tea to reinvigorate himself. But he was not prepared to find his mother again in tears.

"Adam, dear Adam, it is all my fault," Mary said as soon as he'd entered the room. "I know it is. Only, I couldn't tell the detective. He would think I was crazy. There are things I need to tell you, and when I do, you and Anne will think I'm crazy, too, but Cedric and Mother can verify for you that everything I have to say is true, no matter how crazy it sounds."

"What are you talking about, Mom?" Adam asked, and then before she could answer, Adam could almost feel his jaw drop when Cedric quickly rose from his chair and went to sit by Mary on the sofa, again taking her hand in his.

Adam's grandmother, sitting in a chair adjacent to the sofa, handed her daughter the tissue box on the coffee table.

Adam sat down with Anne on the other sofa across from the coffee table. He could sense how nervous Anne felt, so he put his arm around her as his mother spoke.

"I don't even know where to begin," said Mary, wiping her eyes.

"Please tell us," Anne said. "You might be surprised by what we already know—I guarantee that nothing seems crazy to us anymore."

Adam had not been prepared to reveal his and Anne's own secrets yet, and he felt disconcerted when his mother, grandmother, and Cedric all stared at them in surprise.

"What do you mean?" asked Cedric.

But before Adam could reply, the library door opened and Robert, the butler, brought in the tea. Anne thanked him as he set it down, and then they all sat quietly waiting for him to leave since none of them, save Anne and Cedric, were used to talking before servants.

Finally, when Robert had made his exit, Adam answered. He'd had a moment to think about his words and wanted to avoid telling them what he and Anne knew until he heard what his mother would say.

"I just mean," said Adam, "that we won't blame you for whatever you want to share because this whole situation feels unbelievable; anything you can tell us to help solve this mystery will be appreciated."

"Adam," said his mother, pausing to look him straight in the eye, "I've told you that I worked as a secretary during all the years I was separated from you, and that I've lived in Washington State, and that I left after you were born because I lived in a small town and I was ashamed to have an illegitimate child."

Adam nodded, encouraging her to go on.

"I'll pour the tea," said Elizabeth, who apparently knew what Mary had to say so she didn't need to listen closely to the story. For a moment, Adam remembered he and Anne should have had tea in the privacy of their room so Merlin could visit them, but he trusted Merlin would know enough to wait. First he needed to hear his mother's story.

"But that's not really all true," Mary continued. "Well, none of it is true, actually, and I certainly don't want you to think any longer that I was ashamed of your birth."

Adam didn't know what to say. He was relieved that she hadn't felt shame over his birth, but he was alarmed that after all these years, she still hadn't been honest with him. He simply replied, "Go on."

"The truth is," said Mary, "that I always thought you were a golden child, the child I longed for and sought to have, and I knew the night I was with your father that I would conceive a child by him. In fact,

I knew the moment I met Bram that I was destined to be with him. You see, there are things about myself and your father—and your grandparents—and even Cedric—that you've never known and that we've always kept from you, not because we wanted to keep secrets, but because we wanted to wait until you were old enough to understand and accept these things that are almost unbelievable. You're so very young, Adam. Why, you're only twenty-three. We had thought we would wait until you were twenty-five at least, but when your grandfather died so unexpectedly, it changed our plans, and then you were so gung-ho to go find your father that it set everything into motion faster."

"I don't understand," said Adam. "Are you telling me that everything you told me about how you met my father isn't true?"

"No, not exactly. I didn't know your father would appear that night, but I sensed who he was the moment I met him. Only, I didn't sense who Cedric was as well. I just knew somehow your father was the chosen one for me—the one I was meant to be with. Your grandmother, well, she had told me I would meet him someday. She had had a dream about it, and she had told me what he looked like in detail—you're probably not aware of it, but Devin gets his gift of premonition from her." At this point, Elizabeth handed Adam his tea cup with a wink that surprised him, but he kept listening to his mother's tale. "Anyway, when Bram arrived at our hotel, I sensed immediately who he was, and I was determined, well, I'm not sure how to put it, but I immediately knew he must be the father of my child. What I didn't know was that Cedric had arranged for them to be there that night for the same reason—so he could be with—well...but my sister...."

"You're losing me," Adam said.

"I'm sorry," said Mary. "You see, we are a special race of people, your father, and Cedric, and my sister and me, and my parents."

"Mother, are you saying that you intended to sleep with my father and that Cedric wanted to sleep with your sister?"

"Actually," Cedric clarified, "I wanted to possess your mother herself."

"Possess!" exclaimed Adam.

"Just let me finish," Cedric snapped. "Yes, possess. That's why I was so upset. I never should have brought Bram to America with me, but I didn't have the money to be traveling, which is why I convinced Bram to take the trip with me—so he would pay for it all—never telling him my real purpose. I figured I would find Mary and conquer her, since she was the oldest, but she found Bram and conquered him before I could conquer her so I had to settle for her sister, Martha."

"Conquer!" exclaimed Anne, disgusted by the term. "What do you mean? You sound like you were at war with her or something."

"Well, it has been a war," said Cedric. "You see, we are all the products of long and ancient bloodlines, and over the centuries, we have sought out one another to destroy, or control, or benefit from those bloodlines. Your mother, Adam, is of a very special bloodline, an ancient and sacred one, and so, consequently, I wished to mate with her, but Bram's bloodline is equally great, and to my eternal regret—and at the time, my great anger—he won her first."

"I'm confused, Dad," said Anne. "You're saying you're from one of these bloodlines, too?"

"Yes," said Cedric, "but my bloodline has always been at war with the bloodlines that Bram and Mary belong to, at least to a degree; the bloodlines are so intermixed from our families continually trying to breed and gain power over one another that we're all really branches of the same family."

"I'm still confused," said Anne.

"I'm not," said Adam, his face glowing, as if a lightbulb had gone off in his head, "not wholly anyway. I think we can tell them what we know, Anne. That might help us all to make sense of it."

"What do you know?" Mary asked.

Adam looked at his mother and grandmother and then at Cedric. Then he took a sip of his tea, sighed a deep breath, and began.

"Anne and I have had some strange dreams—dreams that have led us to believe we are descended from King Arthur—does that have anything to do with what all of you are trying to tell us?"

"Dreams..." muttered Elizabeth.

"What kinds of dreams?" asked Mary.

"Dreams that made us seem like we were living back in the Middle Ages—in Camelot and in another place called Lusignan."

Adam watched as his mother and grandmother exchanged astonished looks.

"And," added Anne, "we think we've met some legendary people."

"Who?" asked Cedric.

"Merlin, for starters," said Adam.

"And Morgan le Fay," added Anne.

"Morgan le Fay," muttered Mary. "Then perhaps it is true. I always hoped, but—"

"Then you don't think we're crazy?" asked Anne.

"No, no more than I am at least," said Mary.

"My mother," added Elizabeth, "was the most honest person I ever knew, and she once told me that she had met Morgan le Fay. I've always wondered why I've never met her myself, but I guess the time was not right until now for her to reappear."

"But how or when did you see them?" Cedric asked.

"I met Merlin when I first arrived in England," said Adam,

"although I thought he was just a regular person at the time. I was with him when I met Anne, and she was with Morgan. And we believe that somehow Merlin manipulated us that night so we would end up together."

"I went to college with Morgan," Anne added. "All those years, I thought she was just a regular person like me."

"And then," continued Adam, relieved now to get it all out, "just before Dad died, Merlin appeared again and put me into this sort of trance in which I had a dream of King Arthur, and then when Anne and I were in France, the same thing happened, only Anne and I both dreamt the same dream, and this time it was about a fairy named Melusine and about Roland, Charlemagne's nephew."

"Why have you kept all this from us?" Cedric asked, scooting forward on the sofa as if demanding an answer.

"Because we feared you would think us crazy!" Adam replied. "And it was hard for us to know what to think about it all once the boys were kidnapped."

"No, we wouldn't have thought you crazy," said Cedric, relaxing back against the sofa again, "but I don't understand why the two of you get to know these things, and from the lips of Merlin and Morgan le Fay themselves, when all our lives, Mary and I have been wondering whether the stories we were raised on about our destinies were really true or just a bunch of fairy tales made up by our ancestors."

"No," said Mary, starting to feel relaxed enough to bite into a biscuit and then say with her mouth full, "I never doubted the stories; not once I was given my mission."

Anne was just about to ask what she meant by "mission," but first, Adam burst out, "Grandma, why after all those years I lived with you and Grandpa, didn't you ever tell me all this? Did Grandpa know all this, too?"

"Yes," said Elizabeth. "Your grandpa and I were both of the bloodline. That's why our surname is Morgan. We are descendants of Morgan le Fay, although not of King Arthur."

"But how can that be?" asked Adam. "I didn't know that she had any children other than Mordred."

"She did," said Elizabeth. "She had—"

"A genealogy lesson isn't appropriate right now," Cedric interrupted. "Lance and Tristan have been kidnapped and we need to find them. We could spend months trying to sort out our confusing genealogies. It's enough to know we all have links back to either King Arthur or Morgan le Fay or to...."

But here his voice trailed off. This time, Mary took his hand into hers. "It doesn't matter to me, Cedric. Perhaps it did when I fell in love with Bram, but it doesn't matter now."

"I'm becoming more and more confused," said Anne. "Is there something else you need to tell us?"

"I think I should leave," said Cedric. "Now that the secret is out, perhaps it's best if I'm not here while you explain my role in this drama."

"No, dear. Stay," said Mary, putting her hand on his arm.

Adam and Anne looked at each other with raised eyebrows when they heard Mary address Cedric as "dear."

"He blames himself," Mary explained to them.

"I am partly responsible," Cedric admitted.

"Cedric, it was so long ago," Mary continued. "It's all forgiven and in the past. We know you want to make it right now; that's what matters."

Adam noticed how his grandmother bit her lip at these words, as if doubtful about Cedric's intentions, but Cedric replied, "If only I can make it right. I fear it's too late now."

Mary patted his arm and then said, "I mentioned a minute ago that I was given a mission, which is why I believe these stories are true. As I said, I didn't really work as a secretary. I work for—well, for the good of mankind, I hope."

"Go on," said Adam as his mother searched for the right words.

"Adam, I love you dearly, and there is nothing in this world I ever wanted so much as to be your mother. You see, Merlin prophesied that I would give birth to you. He made that prophecy generations ago, and my parents raised me to know I would fulfill it. That's why my sister Martha and I were always at odds with one another. She was always jealous of me—jealous that she would not be mother to a hero, so to speak, for you are a hero, Adam, or at least you will be. It's important that you understand that. I was destined to be mother to a hero, and that could only happen if I mated with one descended from King Arthur in the paternal line, just as we Morgans are descended from Morgan le Fay in the female line.

"Now, I am not the keeper of the Holy Grail—theories of the sangreal, some royal bloodline or cup passed down through generations—are really just fantasies made up by medieval authors, but in some respect, you can say that I carry the bloodline of Morgan le Fay while your father, Bram, carried the bloodline of King Arthur. However, the Delaneys had long ago dismissed their descent from King Arthur as just a fairy tale, and by Bram's time, the family had forgotten all about it, I suspect. Nevertheless, we Morgans had kept track of their family line, which is why I knew Bram Delaney was the man destined to be my husband and partner in life. What I didn't know was that I would only get half of what I expected—his love I did receive, but I never knew the full comfort of having him as my husband because he deserted me so quickly once Cedric convinced him to leave the hotel the morning after you were conceived...and Cedric did that because he had his own agenda and role to play, as I'll explain in a minute."

Mary stopped to sip her tea as Cedric's face went white. Her throat was still so dry from crying that she drank the entire cup, even though the tea had long gone cold. Then she cleared her throat as Elizabeth picked up the teapot to refill her daughter's cup.

"Mother, can you fill in for me for a minute?" asked Mary. "Tell them about my mission. I'll just go on too long about it, and I need to catch my breath."

Elizabeth nodded, thinking a moment of what to say before she began.

"Humans simplify everything in their stories," she said. "They cannot always remember what truly matters, all the details. They dumb down—perhaps that's not the right way to say it—but they dumb down everything, even their greatest stories and tales. They find it sufficient to categorize everything as black and white, and then they make it all into a great battle of good and evil. And when they do that, they leave out the subtleties, the texture, the nuances, and the details that make it not really about good and evil, but about the different levels of human evolution—and I don't mean evolution in terms of DNA or survival of the fittest—I mean the human soul's evolution over centuries and millennia. They have made everything, especially in the Judeo-Christian religions, into a linear tale with a beginning and an end, and that has served them well in many ways—it is, after all, how a good story is told—but the truth is that the boundaries of a traditional storyline, as we humans have come to tell it, are not capable of holding within it the truth of human history any more than any language is adequate in describing God and the mysteries of the universe."

"Mother," Mary broke in, "all you say has its merit, but you are certainly taking the long route about it. I thank you for your prologue, but let me tell the rest."

Mary had a look of peace on her face now, as if she had just needed a proper cue before speaking her own lines in a dramatic play.

Elizabeth simply nodded and allowed her daughter to continue.

Adam and Anne looked at one another, hoping this would not be another long story when all they truly wanted was to have their children back.

"Mother says people simplify everything," began Mary, "but all those complications of the story we can go over later. The truth is that there is good and evil within this world, for I have seen it myself, and all of us in this room have witnessed it, except perhaps the two of you because you are too young to understand it yet—although you may think that since your children have been kidnapped, you now have a sense of what evil is. But evil is not that simple, and it is not even truly evil. After all, even some of your Christian theologians will argue that Satan secretly seeks reconciliation with God, or at least, a sense of self-worth—all his evil being performed in a quest for self-value. Although, let me be clear that Satan doesn't really exist anyway—the idea of him is just another way humans have tried to simplify things, looking for a mythical scapegoat to blame for their own failure to be responsible for their behaviors."

"Now who's taking the long route in telling this story?" asked Elizabeth, smirking.

"Mother," broke in Adam, "you said you would tell me where you've been all these years. Will you just explain that to us?"

"Yes, I've been trying to get to that, but worrying over the twins is making me a bit convoluted in my speech, I guess."

"That's understandable," said Cedric, squeezing her hand.

"As I said," Mary continued, after taking a deep breath, "I am a keeper, not of the Holy Grail, but of one whom you would consider evil, although the full truth is that she is just badly misunderstood, but no less dangerous because of that misunderstanding. You know, of course, the tale of Adam and Eve in the Bible, but perhaps you have not heard that Adam had a first wife, named Lilith."

"Yes," said Anne. "I heard about her in a feminist studies class. She's not mentioned in the Bible, but Jewish tradition says she was Adam's first wife. She refused to let him be on top when they had sex, so she was cast out of the Garden of Eden, and God created Eve for Adam to replace her. It's a male patriarchal story intended to demean women and prove that men are supposed to be dominant, using God as an excuse to support it."

"Well," said Elizabeth," I'll agree the story is misogynistic, but you may be surprised to know that the story does have some historical basis."

"Isn't it just a myth?" asked Anne. "I mean, Adam and Eve, they weren't real people."

Before Elizabeth or Mary could answer, Adam began to lose patience and exclaimed, "Why does everything have to boil down to these old myths? I don't care about Adam and Eve or Arthur and Guinevere or flying fairies or man-eating giants or any of that hogwash, and especially not when my children are missing!"

"You, Adam," said Cedric, sternly, "should care because perhaps part of your mission in life is to learn patience, but you seem to be flunking that lesson."

Anne watched Adam's face turn to rage, and she quickly grabbed

her husband's arm before he could bolt across the room to lunge for
Cedric's throat.

"Mary," said Anne, feeling a bit desperate, "perhaps you could get
to your point a bit more quickly. We do want to know what this has to
do with the twins being kidnapped."

"Of course," said Mary. "I don't know that it is relevant to the
twins, but I fear it is. To boil it all down, yes, Adam and Eve were real
people; we are all descended from them, as incredible as that may seem
in our twentieth century scientific world, but we only have a distorted
fragment of their story in the Bible. As for Lilith, she was also real,
and perhaps not evil to begin with, but over time, she has developed
hatred in her soul. Life is not linear, as I said, but rather, we humans
continually evolve over the centuries, even as individuals, for, you see,
we reincarnate—no true loving God would give us but one chance to
get it right—instead we keep learning through many lifetimes. Think
of your life as being similar to a grade in school. Yes, it is pass or fail,
but if you pass, your life doesn't end. You go on to the next grade to
learn more. If you fail, you repeat that grade until you learn the lessons
needed before you can pass on to the next grade—up the ladder of
spiritual evolution, so to speak. Lilith has reincarnated several times,
but because she was one of God's first creations—well, we need not get
into the details right now of what happened in the Garden of Eden—"

"Thank God," Adam muttered.

"But," Mary continued, "because of her being one of the first
humans, she has had more experience at reincarnating than most.
She has had many lifetimes, and she has learned, through her time
on earth, Nature's greatest secrets. This knowledge has allowed her to
extend the length of each of her human lives. Besides being the biblical
Lilith, she has returned to earth as many other well-known women,

including Medusa—and no, she never had a head full of snakes—that was another myth—and then as Vashti, Queen of Persia, and later as Gwenhwyvach, also known as the False Guinevere."

"Oh! That's the connection!" exclaimed Adam.

"Yes," said Mary, "the Arthurian connection. I take it you dreamt of Gwenhwyvach, too?"

"Yes, I saw her and Constantine destroy Camelot in my dream," Adam confirmed.

"Exactly. She was the true enemy of King Arthur, and although she died as Gwenhwyvach, since that time she has continually reincarnated herself as one of her descendants. You see, she had a son with Constantine of Cornwall, and—"

"No, wait," said Adam. "In my dream, she told Constantine she had lied about his having a son by her and that he never did."

"Another of her lies," said Mary. "She not only had a son by Constantine, but that son was the ancestor to Ganelon and his sister Gudrun. Duke Ganelon married Roland's mother and tried to have Roland killed. And Gudrun was second wife to King Geoffrey of Denmark, who by his first wife, was father to Ogier the Dane; consequently, Gudrun plotted to bring about that great hero's death. And she has reincarnated several times since then, and each time, she has done her best to work evil in this world. The sad thing is that she incarnates each time with the intention to advance to a higher level and absolve her soul of her past misdeeds, but jealousy is at the heart of her nature. Jealousy that Adam chose Eve over her, for, at one time, they all three resided in the Garden of Eden together. Jealousy that Adam would choose another, though she had rejected him, and later, as Medusa, she likewise rejected Apollo; the stories say that the goddess Diana was jealous and cursed Medusa for being loved by Apollo, but the truth is that Apollo loved Diana, and Medusa's jealousy over their love turned her into a monster of a woman in her spirit, though not physically. Do not be surprised that those old Greek myths have some truth behind them for there have been many of us throughout history who have had the royal jellies and elixirs fed to us, making us, in a sense, super-mortals, yourselves included my dear children. I will explain later about the royal jelly, but—"

"We already know about it from the dream we had of Melusine," Anne interrupted.

Mary, Cedric, and Elizabeth all looked surprised by this comment, but Adam and Anne's attention to her made Mary continue without asking questions.

"Medusa decided she would not be a victim again. That life that was meant to help her to heal and evolve instead retarded her progress. By the time she returned as Herodias, she sought to wreak havoc, which is why she ordered her daughter Salome to ask for John the Baptist's head. Christ himself she would have killed had she had her way. She mocked him when he was on the way to Cavalry. He stopped and said to her, "Woman, Queen of Jerusalem, know you not you harm your soul by your words?" She only spit in his face and told him she would have immortality before him for she was jealous of his own immortality and the message he had brought to men to be freed from fear. She could not overcome her own fear, her own jealousy that stemmed from her deep sense of unworthiness. In all her many incarnations, she has often come close to saving her soul, even once in her incarnation as Gudrun, but each time, she has failed; sadly, each time, she has also increased her knowledge and power so that she is now the most dangerous force upon this earth."

"But what does any of this have to do with our finding out who kidnapped Lance and Tristan?" asked Adam.

"When Lilith last reincarnated," said Mary, "we were prepared for her, and while Merlin could not stop her from again entering this world, he did manage to trick her into entering a weaker body, one which we have held in a prison deep in the earth ever since."

"So you've been Lilith's jailor all this time?" Adam asked.

"Yes, I and others of our bloodline, though I am of the senior bloodline and, therefore, her primary keeper, and that is why I have kept my distance from you all these years; she is wise enough even to read thoughts, and so I did not want her to know where you were. It was only when your time to fulfill your own destiny was approaching that I returned home. As I said, I had not expected that time to be for another year or two, but your grandfather must have known better and purposely chosen that time to pass on and bring about these events."

Adam was stunned by these words, as his mother clearly saw.

"Don't be surprised, Adam," said his mother. "Your grandfather knew how special you were, and he always did what he felt was best for you. I regret deeply that I did not get to see you grow up, but I also had a task to do, and I had to stay far away from you because Lilith's descendants, besides continually seeking to free her and use her power, have also sought to destroy our line."

"Our line?" Adam repeated. "But I didn't know the Morgans were special until just now. I thought King Arthur's line was the special one."

"Yes, it is special," said Mary, "but there are many lines, and none more special than the line that has now culminated in you, Adam, and you also, Anne...."

Anne looked more surprised than Adam by this comment.

"I'm not descended from King Arthur," she said. "I'm Cedric and

Sarah's daughter, not Bram's."

"No, but your father and your late mother were also born of significant lines," said Mary. "Cedric, I think you should explain the rest."

Cedric looked troubled. He stared down at the floor for a moment, taking a deep breath. Adam felt himself growing tense, wondering what words his father-in-law would say. He was already annoyed that the man kept touching his mother's hand, and he sensed that Cedric had secrets he was not proud of, nor really wanted to share.

"Dad," said Anne gently, "tell me."

"Perhaps, Cedric," Elizabeth urged when he still hesitated, "you can do some redeeming of your past by coming clean now."

Adam, frustrated and losing his patience, got up from the sofa to pace in the back of the room while Cedric spoke.

"My role in this story is not glamorous," said Cedric, unable to look at anything but the coffee table as he spoke, "and it's honestly one of which I'm quite ashamed; Adam is annoyed with me, I know, and I cannot blame him, and I don't deserve the love and affection I have received over the years from this family, not from my best friend, Bram, or from Anne, who did not even know I was her father until a year ago.

"I have helped to make a mess of things, and I would be truly sorry for it, except that I've come to realize in this last year that all ultimately works for good. There's a passage in the Bible where Joseph is sold by his brothers into slavery in Egypt, only to rise to power and then reveal himself to his brothers when they come to him to beg for grain; they are astonished that he is alive, and they fear he will wreak his vengeance upon them, but instead, he tells them, 'You meant it for evil, but God meant it for good that He might save many people.' I think that can be said to summarize my own life—I have done things I meant for evil, but God has used them for good nevertheless.

"As you know, I tried to stop Bram and Mary from being together on the night when Adam was conceived. I acted as if I were just being prudish, but the truth is that I convinced Bram to visit America and pass through that town because I knew Mary was there. In fact, I reserved us rooms at the hotel Mary's parents owned in hopes I could then seduce her."

Cedric's sad expression caused Mary to carry on the story for him.

"But I recognized Bram as soon as I saw him," she said. "I had dreamt that he would be there, and I felt called upon to be with him. Although I didn't know what it had to do with my mission of guarding Lilith, a mission I already knew I was to begin soon after."

"And I knew you were to be Lilith's keeper," added Cedric, finally raising his head to look in Mary's eyes. "I learned such from my own father, who had the power of the sight, and who had told me of our family legacy not long before he died, although I only heard from him what I wanted to hear, interpreting my family's story to mean it was my task to take vengeance upon Arthur's descendants. You see," he added, turning to Adam and Anne, "I am a descendant of Constantine and Gwenhwyvach, and I have always believed they were the ones wronged and not Arthur, and therefore, I thought my family must stop Arthur's descendants from rising again. Such was my misguided motivation for wanting to mate with Mary—for my father had told me she was destined for Bram—but I was determined to thwart their destinies.

"I do not know how to explain all of this to you, Adam and Anne; it's almost like a knowing we of the bloodlines are born with—to know we must mate with one another, to fulfill a destiny. It's like a queen bee who by instinct knows when she emerges from her cell that she must kill the other queens before they are born so she can take her position."

"But I don't understand, Dad," said Anne, gently addressing him, "why you wanted to be with Mary, or why it was significant?"

"It has to do with the bloodlines," said Cedric. "There are ultimately four major bloodlines. You might think of them as the Big Four. From them have sprung thousands if not millions of descendants, most of whom know nothing about their pedigrees, but there are a select few of us chosen in each generation, as we've said, who know these stories. There is the bloodline of those descended from King Arthur, of whom Bram was a descendant. It includes Raimond, who married Melusine, and through them, it includes their grandson, Roland, and ultimately, it carries down to the Earls of Delaney. And then there's a bloodline of those descended from Constantine and Gwenhwyvach, and that line eventually mixed with the bloodline of Arthur for Ganelon the Traitor was of Constantine and Gwenhwyvach's line, and because his sister Gudrun later married into Melusine's line, that bloodline also is descended from Arthur; I am descended of that line, but the evil in its blood is stronger than the good."

"So you're telling me you are of the evil line?" Adam asked, stopping his pacing, almost ready to laugh at the absurdity of it all.

"If you wish to call it that," Cedric calmly admitted.

"Rather, the misguided line," said Elizabeth, reaching across Mary to pat Cedric's knee and dissuade Adam from anger.

"But then, what are the third and fourth lines?" asked Anne.

"The line of Morgana," said Mary. "The line my parents are from. Both of my parents are of that line; in fact, they were seventh cousins, and so their marriage was of significance, and consequently, I ended up being of greater significance in the bloodlines than most are."

"But wouldn't Morgana's line be the same as Arthur's?" asked Adam. "I mean, since Mordred was their son."

"Ah, but you see," said Mary, "Morgana had one other child, and Arthur was not that child's father."

"But I saw all the Tale of Camelot in my dream," said Adam, "and I saw no other children born to Morgana."

"No," agreed Mary, "but you also saw Melusine's tale, and you know that Morgan le Fay was part of that story, and you have even met her in person, so you know she still lives, so does it not stand to reason that in all the time since Arthur went to Avalon, nearly fifteen centuries ago, that Morgana, who has never aged, could have another child?"

"Oh," said Anne. "I feel another story coming on."

"Yes," said Mary. "There is far more to the story than what it sounds like Morgana and Merlin have already told you, but I'll save telling that for now, although the story of the Morgan line is fascinating in itself."

"But that's still only three bloodlines," said Adam. "What is the fourth?"

"The fourth is really a second offshoot of Morgana's line, and that is the line that Anne's mother, Sarah, belonged to."

"Your father, Adam," said Cedric, taking over, "was destined to marry one of Morgana's line. Naturally then, he mated with your mother, but because I got him to leave Mary before he knew of your existence, he then found himself attracted, as if by natural instinct, to his future wife, Sarah, who represented another branch of Morgana's line. However, I could not permit a wonder child to be born—one that would combine the Morgan and Arthur lines. At that time, I had no knowledge that Adam had already been born, that he was indeed the carrier of those wonder child qualities I sought in my own son."

"Adam *is* a wonder child, isn't he?" Anne laughed, standing up and walking over to her husband to draw him back to the sofa.

Adam smiled, feigning amusement, but as he sat down again, he said, "I'm hardly a wonder child."

"You are more so than you realize," Cedric replied, staring him in the eye. "In any case, I thought my own bloodline would be sufficient to create an equally or nearly equal child if I mated with Sarah, and so I did, and Anne was the result. It was too much powerful blood, however, for Sarah to bear, and consequently, she did not survive the childbirth; still, I cannot regret my seduction of her, for it has given me the privilege of having a daughter, whom I've watched grow into a beautiful young woman whose mother's goodness has outweighed her father's misguided behaviors. I tried as I watched you grow, Anne, to believe it would be enough for me to see you succeed to all of Bram's lands and title, but I had no idea Adam had even been born at that point, and my old anger rose up when you arrived on the scene, Adam, especially when I learned you had coupled with my daughter. I feared, and rightfully, that the evil in Anne's blood would be overcome with the good in yours so that your children, too, would be good, and not evil—although I did not think of it quite in that way then, for I did not think my mission was evil. After all, I had been raised to believe Eve, not Lilith, was the evil one, for Adam set aside Lilith, like a man who cheats on his wife and divorces her, to be with Eve. By that logic, Eve was the adulteress, while Lilith was the wronged woman—and her descendants have sought to avenge her ever since. Of course, all that was before I fell in love with my grandsons, which has dramatically changed my perceptions."

"This is all so crazy," said Adam, shaking his head. "You expect me to believe that, through countless centuries, all of this genetic engineering has been going on, and that despite all of your manipulative attempts, God or some such force has always meant for Anne and me to be together?"

"Yes, that's about it," Mary admitted, "although Merlin, not us, is the manipulator in your case."

"But for what purpose?" Adam demanded. "So Anne and I could have wonder children?"

"Yes, exactly," said Elizabeth, nodding her head.

"But...but then where are our children?" asked Anne. "I thought the whole point of this long explanation was that you would reveal to us where they are. I just want to know my children are safe."

"We needed you to understand about Lilith and her bloodline," Mary explained, "and to understand that while Cedric is of that line, he is not the only one. There could be others of her bloodline, perhaps distant cousins to your father whom we do not even know, who are out to hurt us and all of Eve's descendants—and especially those who are also King Arthur's descendants. While I trust Cedric is innocent of wanting to harm Tristan and Lance, since they are his own grandchildren, nevertheless, someone must wish them harm."

"I would never harm a hair of their precious heads," Cedric affirmed.

"So you really don't know who might have taken them?" Adam asked.

"No, Adam. If I knew that, I would have told you immediately," Mary explained. "I'm as heartbroken as you are about their being gone, but I had to tell you all this because I suspect that more than just a regular kidnapping has happened here."

"But who's to say it isn't just a regular kidnapper who wants money?" asked Anne.

"It could be," said Mary, "but then where is the ransom note? And do you think that possibility likely after all we've just told you?"

"But if kidnappers don't want a ransom," said Anne, "why take my boys? Why would they want to hurt our children?"

"If in some way Lilith or her descendants are involved," said Mary, "then she fears that your sons will grow up to be powerful men, and while it is unlikely their kidnappers would be able to harm them because of their sacred blood, Lilith could. She could use them in a sacrifice or some other horrible ritual equivalent to a Black Mass to bring about great evil. The worst thing that could ever happen is that she could escape and use them for her evil purposes to bring about domination of the world, and—"

"Domination of the world!" exclaimed Adam. "Oh, come on! This is sounding more and more like a bad science fiction movie."

"No, Adam, it's deadly serious," said his grandmother. "You do not know what evil Lilith contains within her now. Why, when I think of the evil she unleashed upon the world the last time she was free, and then only for a very short time...."

"What evil?" asked Anne.

"Evil you shall in time know about," said Elizabeth, "for it is very close to you especially, Anne, but it is not time yet for you to know."

"Then what can we do to stop Lilith?" asked Adam, seeing his wife shiver and putting his arm around her.

"We still don't know she's involved," said Mary. "To the best of my knowledge, she is still a prisoner in the secret compound in Seattle. But to answer your question, Adam, I don't think it's so much something you can *do*, but rather something you must *be*, something you must imagine yourself as being so you can overcome it."

"I just don't understand any of this!" exclaimed Adam. "You're starting to sound like Merlin in your convoluted speeches."

"Imagination," said Mary, struggling for words, "the thoughts we think...."

"Perhaps it's best that we leave it to Merlin to explain," said Elizabeth, jumping in as her daughter faltered, "for I have no doubt he is a guiding force behind all this."

"But where does Merlin even fit into all this? What does he have at stake?" Adam demanded. "It seems like he's manipulating everything and we're just his puppets."

"His or Lilith's," admitted Cedric. "We—your mother, and grandmother, and I, Adam—we don't understand it all either. We only know what our parents or grandparents told us. None of us has ever even met Merlin or Morgan le Fay, and only Mary has met Lilith."

"And I've avoided talking to her as much as possible," Mary added, "for she knows how to manipulate and control minds, so I cannot afford to risk discussing anything with her."

"I'm sure if Merlin has already been speaking to you," Elizabeth said, addressing Anne and Adam, "then you will be hearing from him again soon. All we can do is trust that he will have answers for you that we do not."

"Mother, since you are here," said Adam, "who is guarding Lilith now?"

"I am her primary keeper," replied Mary, "but only one of her many guardians. There are plenty of others at the compound to keep an eye on her while I am here visiting you."

"Adam, I have a headache," said Anne, tugging on his arm. "Come upstairs now. This is so much to take in. Let's go lie down for a little while before supper; I know you barely slept last night."

"I think we could all use a little nap," Cedric agreed.

"But this discussion hasn't solved anything," complained Adam as he stood up. "We still don't know where our children are or who took them."

"You're irritable," Anne told her husband, "and that will do no one good. Come upstairs with me and let's rest for a little while. We'll all think clearer then and can go back to trying to figure this out later when we eat."

Admitting to feeling exhausted, Adam went upstairs with his wife.

CHAPTER 4

ONCE ADAM AND Anne returned to their room, Anne collapsed on the bed. Adam went into the adjoining bathroom, and when he returned, he found Anne lying on her stomach, crying into her pillow.

Adam immediately went to the bed, cuddling up against Anne and putting his arm around her. But he could find no words of comfort; everything they were experiencing was just far too bizarre.

"Why us?" Anne finally asked, choking back her last sob as she turned to face him. He reached for the tissue box on the bedside table and handed it to her.

"I don't know," he replied.

"I mean," Anne said, wiping her eyes, "why did we have to be born into this family, and why are we being subjected to all this manipulating? It's not my fault that whatever happened in the Garden of Eden or at Camelot or to Melusine occurred. I had nothing to do with any of it."

"I know," said Adam. "It's not our fault, and it hasn't been our choice."

"Yes, it has!" said a voice from across the room.

Adam was so startled by these words that he quickly sat up, hitting his head against the bed's headboard.

Adam's first instinct was to reach for the gun in the bedside table in case it was their child's kidnapper—the gun he had considered buying several times in the last couple of days, but had not bought. Now he wished he had.

But then Adam saw the intruder. The man was suspended by all fours from the corner of the ceiling, upside down with his head hanging down and his beard parted on each side of his head so that he looked like an old woman. Who else could it be but Merlin?

"Oh, my God!" screeched Anne, not recognizing the great wizard, or madman, or whatever he might be, for he only became more of a conundrum with each passing day.

"Merlin!" exclaimed Adam, less from astonishment than to identify their visitor for Anne's sake.

"I told you I'd be back this afternoon," said the wizard before performing a somersault that landed him on the floor on all fours, from which he sprang up like an amphibian transforming into homo erectus. "Although I see you had your tea without me. Quite rude of you."

Adam simply glared at him.

"No matter. I had a mug of mead before I came. You English and your tea-drinking—not at all to my Celtic tastes actually."

"What do you want now?" Adam demanded.

"What...what did you mean that we chose this?" Anne asked, more gently, now that she realized he who was.

"Just what I said. You did choose all of this," said Merlin, stepping toward the bed.

Anne scooted up against Adam, who protectively wrapped an arm around her.

"Merlin, get out of our room," said Adam. "You have no business scaring—"

"But you did choose all this," Merlin repeated. "Think. Think deeply; not hard, but deeply. Are you not secretly enjoying this adventure?"

Suddenly, Adam felt Anne's body, pressed against him and tense, begin to relax.

"I don't know if I understand you," she said, sitting up and looking quizzically at the wizard.

Merlin sat down on the edge of the bed and patted her hand.

"My darling girl, we all make choices before we enter this world. It's all a great play, you know, and we all choose our parts. I'm a bit like the director or narrator, you might say, but we all have our roles to play."

"Merlin, whatever metaphors you want to use," Adam objected, "there's nothing playful about this business. We are terrified with worry over our children, and we want them back now."

"'Metaphors'! My, such a big word for you, Adam. And you're being so demanding. You need to learn some patience; even your father-in-law was just wise enough to have told you that. I know you're less willing to accept things than Anne—that's your male bravado getting in the way—but at least you understand I'm speaking in metaphors, so good for you. It is all a metaphor, you know—this life we lead—a stage play—and in this pseudo-Shakespearean tragi-comedy, we're well into the third of five acts now. But you do need to be patient so you don't flub up your part."

Adam was not listening to Merlin now so much as observing how

Anne had not shrunk back when Merlin touched her hand. Adam then removed his arm from around his wife and sat back against the headboard, inhaling deeply as he tried to remain calm.

"So," said Merlin after a moment, "I overheard your parents telling you how it all is—about your bloodlines and all that. In fact, Adam, your mother has given a superb performance in her role—really, she should get an award for best supporting actress in a drama. She's also kept good watch over Gwenhwyvach—such a prettier name than Lilith, I've always thought, though I've always been partial to Welsh names. Anyway, both your mother and your grandparents have been very faithful all these years to the family mission. Now Cedric—Cedric surprises me. He's sweet on your mother, Adam. I assume you're smart enough to have figured that out by now. It's a shame really because she's always been more focused on her mission than on romance, and I don't think she'll ever get over the love she felt for your father. But I expected Cedric to give us a lot of trouble. In fact, there was a point when I feared he might end up seeking to harm you and the children, but while he has a good dose of Gwenhwyvach's blood in him, sometimes people surprise you—after all, even Gwenhwyvach doesn't really want to be evil—she's just so consumed by her desire for revenge that she can't help herself. So I'm glad Cedric is siding with us; we wouldn't want your father to be the enemy now would we, Anne?"

Anne shook her head in agreement.

"You are exhausted, my dear," said Merlin, gently wiping a remaining tear from her cheek.

Adam, still fuming, replied, "What do you expect after what we've been through? Of course, she's exhausted." Too disgusted to remain on the bed, so close to the wizard, he strode to the window, but then he turned around and demanded, "Merlin, why do you have to interfere with our lives like this?"

"Don't you want my help?" asked Merlin, rising from the bed and going to sit in a chair.

"I do," said Anne, "if you can help us find our children. I'll do anything to get them back."

"Don't say that, Anne," Adam warned her. "We don't know if we can trust him."

"I haven't harmed you yet, have I?" asked Merlin, crossing his legs and arms as if he were highly offended by the thought.

"All right!" exclaimed Adam. "What do you want us to do then— bring you the broomstick of the Wicked Witch? Even if we did that, I have no doubt you'd end up just proving to us that you're a humbug. How do we know you can even get our children back, or that you or this Lilith woman have anything to do with their disappearance?"

Merlin began to giggle uncontrollably. Only after a couple of minutes, while Adam and Anne stared at him in disbelief, did he stop and say, "I've never had a magic broomstick; it might be a fun accessory. I think it would go nicely with my outfit."

Adam scowled, but Anne seemed to think it best to humor the eccentric old wizard.

"Wouldn't the Holy Grail be more appropriate?" she asked.

"Oh, don't get me started on that Holy Grail," Merlin replied. "The stories about it are so convoluted and ridiculous that they make my blood boil...." He stood up and began pacing the room. "The Holy Grail...leave it to the Christians to turn a Celtic relic into Jesus' cup filled with His blood. No, that story is the most confusing, mixed up bunch of nonsense around, and I've always resented how they've twisted my life story into it, as if I'd have a bunch of puny suffering

Fisher King descendants. Nope. No Holy Grail for you; no bloody Fisher King to save either, thank goodness. No blood, period. Good Lord, why would I want to carry around a bunch of blood all the way from Judea to Britain—I've always been kind of squeamish about blood—I sure wouldn't have stood there with a cup and waited for the blood to drip out of Jesus' side. That's rather grotesque, don't you think? But I did have descendants, of course, who ended up helping to populate Avalon, including yourselves, for as you must realize by now, the line of Avalon flows in your blood; you are the descendants of Arthur and Morgana, but they in turn are my descendants, so I have a vested interest in what happens to you, you see, and—it goes without saying—in what becomes of your children."

Adam had no idea what Merlin was babbling about now, and Anne looked at him as if she weren't following either, so Adam confessed, "You lost us. I don't know much about the Holy Grail, and what does Jesus' blood have to do with you?"

"Are you even listening, my boy?" snapped Merlin, scrunching up his eyebrows. "Merlin is the name you know me by, but my first name was Joseph—Joseph of Arimathea to be exact. Surely, you've heard the stories that I supposedly collected Jesus' blood as it dripped from his side at the crucifixion—collected it in the Holy Grail, and then I brought it to Britain and buried it at Glastonbury Abbey. Not that any of it's true, but I assure you, it's a very well-known story. You Americans and your cultural illiteracy! But, no matter; as I said, none of it's true."

"Let me get this straight," said Anne. "You're telling us that you're not Merlin, but Joseph of Arimathea?"

"I'm telling you that I'm Joseph of Arimathea, yes," said Merlin, "but I'm also Merlin. I've had a few other names over the centuries too—ever hear of the Wandering Jew, cursed to roam the earth until Christ's return?"

Anne looked like she might have heard of the Wandering Jew, but before she could reply, Adam said, "No," shaking his head and rolling his eyes.

"Well, Adam," said Merlin, "you obviously spent too much time playing football when you should have been learning history. Too bad your cousin Devin wasn't the chosen one—he's of the blood too, and from nearly as strong a strain as your own, though he doesn't know it yet, but I would not doubt that he still has more of a role to play in this drama before it ends."

"Leave Devin out of this mess," Adam snapped. "Just tell us what Joseph of Arimathea has to do with any of this. Wasn't he in the Bible?"

"Yes, I'm in the Bible," said Merlin. "I'm relieved that at least you know that much, though the gospel writers hardly did me justice. In truth, I was Jesus' uncle, the one who brought him to Britain as a child to learn from and teach the Druids, as you may recall from your dream of King Arthur. And when Jesus died, I had him buried in my own tomb in Jerusalem, although as you well know, he rose from the dead. And later, I returned and intermarried with Avallach's line, and—"

"Okay," Adam interrupted, "that's enough. I don't need to know more ancient history. I just want to focus on getting my children back."

"I'm hardly ancient history," said Merlin, winking at Anne, "not if I'm alive and well and sitting here with you."

Adam sighed in frustration.

"Merlin," said Anne, "we're just worried about our sons. Please, no more joking around. We love our boys dearly, and if you're here to help, then tell us how we can get them back."

"I'll get to that in time," said Merlin, waving his hand as if dismissing the topic, "but first—"

"But it's urgent!" Adam shouted.

"Oh, my boy," said Merlin, "you think so, but it's not really, you know. It's just—"

"Damn it, Merlin!" exclaimed Adam. "Help us find our children. Aren't you Merlin, the great wizard? What good are you if you can't stop a simple kidnapper, or at least help us to find out who the kidnapper is?"

"It's not that simple," said Merlin, calmly, "not when you consider that...I am the kidnapper."

"You!" said Adam, the blood rushing to his face until he saw red. Suddenly, overcome with rage, he shouted, "You goddamn madman!" and charged across the room, seeking the wizard's throat. But just as his fingers reached for Merlin's neck, he found his hand clasping only empty air.

Merlin had completely vanished.

Adam stood there, astonished, helpless, frustrated beyond words until he finally collapsed onto the bed and turned to face Anne.

"I don't understand," said Anne, beginning to cry again.

"I understand," said Adam. "That bastard gets his jollies by manipulating our lives as if he were some Greek god amusing himself with the fate of mere mortals. I'd sure like to get my hands on the asshole who died and made him God."

"I never said I was a god," said Merlin, his voice coming from above again, and over by the window.

Adam and Anne turned in the voice's direction, and then they saw Merlin floating up against the ceiling, perhaps to remain out of Adam's reach.

"I am not a god," Merlin repeated, "but I am old and wise, so you'll just have to believe that I know better than you. And, of course, I will help you."

"But why?" begged Anne. "Why would you kidnap our children?"

"My dear," said Merlin, now slowly spinning in circles as if he were Esther Williams doing underwater ballet in the air, "haven't the two of you learned anything yet? Didn't you read the stories of King Arthur as children? Don't you remember that when Arthur was just a baby, I took him away, hid him for his own safety until the time when he was meant to fulfill his destiny?"

"Are you saying that you've kidnapped our children to protect them?" Anne asked.

Merlin simply nodded affirmatively.

"Bullshit!" exclaimed Adam, jumping up from the bed and looking like he was ready to leap to the ceiling to tackle the wizard. "This isn't some damn silly play you're directing, Merlin. This is my family. I've kept my patience with you for far too long. I want my children back, or else—"

"What? Or else what?" Merlin hollered, for the first time losing his temper. "What are you going to do to me? Put me on the ground with one of those football tackles you used in high school? Do you think that will help?"

And then Merlin flew across the room, his hand extended before him, until it ran into Adam's chest; his fingers grabbed Adam's shirt collar and he lifted Adam up, flying across the room with him until Adam found himself pressed up against the door, three feet off the floor. Adam was astonished, and the sudden blow to his chest when Merlin grabbed him was so great that the bruise would remain for a week.

Next, Merlin let Adam fall to his feet, and then the wizard let loose a torrent of maniacal laughter as he flew in circles about the ceiling like a bat desperate to find a means of escape. After a dozen spirals in half as many seconds, he perched upon the windowsill, grasping his robe and stretching it out with his arms as if it were a cape. "I am like a vampire!" he exclaimed. "I am like an evil demon you puny mortals cannot even dream of fighting! I could break you, snap you like a twig! I could do cruel and murderous things to you of which no mortal has ever dreamt; such excruciating pain I could make you experience until.... Oops, I see fear in your eyes. You silly fools. Why do you give into fear so easily? Haven't you yet learned anything from this? Where is your trust and faith?" And then Merlin broke into giggling again, and hopped down to sit on the floor in a lotus position. "You don't need to be afraid, my children. I've got it all under control. Just be patient and listen to me for once without interruption and arguments. I just want to have a little fun, but I promise you that you have no need to fear me. Lilith is the only one you need fear. She's the enemy here, or to put it in your modern vulgar terminology, she's the bitch—not me."

And then Merlin closed his eyes and floated back up to the ceiling as if he were the Buddha ascending to Heaven.

Adam, still not recovered from the shock of being shoved against the door, sat down in the chair by the bed. Anne crawled up against the headboard, placing a pillow in front of her, as if for protection.

Merlin untangled his legs and descended once again to stand on the floor. As he did so, his long robe transformed into a pair of slacks and a grandfatherly sweater with a red and green plaid pattern. Now looking gentle and friendly, he stepped toward the bed. Anne, surprisingly, did not shrink from him when he sat down beside her, and a great calmness fell over her when he placed his hand on her shoulder.

"Dear, sweet, Anne," Merlin said. "I love you and Adam. I would never let anything happen to your children. I am protecting them. You can be angry with me if you choose. I understand such anger, and I forgive you for it, for I know this situation is more than the two of you can comprehend, at least at this moment; it is not your fault; you would have to have lived for two thousand years like me to understand it all, and even I don't fully understand it. But you see, it's all part of the fun. Perhaps you don't think it's fun right now, but if everything in life were perfect all the time, life would be awfully dull, wouldn't it? And we certainly wouldn't learn anything from it, now would we?"

After a moment, Anne said, "I really am trying to understand. For a moment, Merlin, you looked terrifying, but now you are so gentle, and I—I sense that gentleness is your natural state. I—but how can I believe, even though I've seen it with my own eyes, that you're able to fly around the room, or that you're two thousand years old?"

"Actually, I'm a little older than that," said Merlin. "After all, I was Jesus' great-uncle—Mary's uncle, in fact, so I was approaching middle age by the time Jesus was born, and I was definitely getting on in years by the time he died and rose from the dead, you know."

"Then you must be good," said Anne, "if you are Jesus' uncle."

"I am as good as a man is able to be," said Merlin. "As Jesus said, only our Father in Heaven is truly good. But I am certainly not bad nor evil, just a little flawed and still learning like the two of you are—I've just been in this school of life quite a bit longer so I've reached more advanced classes."

"But how could you have lived for over two thousand years?" asked Anne, her voice shaking, no longer out of fear but from excitement to have such a mystery explained to her. "Why has God allowed you to have such power beyond normal men?"

"As the poet Tennyson said, 'God fulfills Himself in many ways,'" replied Merlin. "No reason to think otherwise. With God, or more properly, the Goddess-God—but that term is a mouthful and does not even accurately define the mystery of the Supreme Being, who is above all human definitions of gender, race, species, or any other form of categorization—anyway, with God, all things are possible. The problem is that men are so egotistical in thinking they know better than God, or worse, thinking they are so much less than God, so unworthy, that they mess up everything and forget the power God gave them—the power of imagination, the power that lies in believing and acknowledging that all things are possible—instead, giving into their ridiculous and fear-based notions of human limitations."

"I think I understand that," said Anne, "but even if all things are possible, it's not natural for anyone to be so old. I've never even met anyone who's lived to be over one hundred, much less two thousand."

"With God, as I said, all things are possible," Merlin explained. "He asked me, in the form of His Son and my nephew, whether I would tarry after He was gone so I might help others come to Him. He knew some men would distort His message, trying to use it for their own power and control. He told me to keep sweetness and light in the world, to keep men's minds free of fear—that is why He came—to teach us to be free of fear, to conquer fear with love, to realize we were in this life to learn and to love. Not to focus on our misguided notions of sin and a need for salvation, but to believe in our own greatness. He entrusted me to carry out that message, and so I have spent all these centuries doing so, through my descendants, by aligning them with others who have also kept the faith—those who continue to believe and apply the Goddess-God's great message of love, freedom, and the power of the imagination to work miracles. I have made my mistakes certainly—but I have done what I could, through Arthur, through Morgana, through Melusine, through Avalon, and through many others, including you, my children." He took Anne's hand again before continuing.

"Over time, people twisted the stories about me. They decided I must be evil because I was able to live for so long. The truth is that Christ Himself had said we would live forever through Him. During the short time we both resided together at Avalon, it was He—my great-nephew—who taught me how to use herbs and honey and other nutrients from the earth to extend my life, and I have used them to pass on extended life to those few whom I have seen filled with talent and skill, faith and creative power, but most of all, those with benevolent hearts, such as Arthur and Morgana, and Roland, and even Ogier the Dane, whose story you will soon learn. But people who did not understand my mission spread silly stories that I was a shoemaker in Jerusalem, cursed for not letting Christ rest on his way to Calvary— they came up with the outlandish name of Ahasuerus for me—a name taken from a Babylonian biblical king with whom I certainly had nothing in common; in fact, I rather cringe at the name since that king's first wife was Vashti, one of Lilith's incarnations. You see, even those who claim to be Christians too often show themselves incapable of believing in the goodness of God and His love for them, so they seek to twist what is good into evil, including my own story, and sadly, my nephew Jesus' message."

"I—I remember," said Anne, "once when I was a girl, my father, Bram, took me to Glastonbury Abbey to see the ruins and I heard how King Arthur was supposedly buried there, and the story that Joseph of Arimathea came there with Jesus. So that story is true then; that's what you're saying?"

"Partly true, my dear," said Merlin. "The finding of Arthur's grave there by the monks was all a publicity stunt, but it is true that Jesus and I traveled to Britain. Just as I did with Arthur, I took Jesus away to keep Him safe until the hour came for Him to fulfill His destiny. He spent many years in Britain, in His late childhood, and again later, as a young man in His teens and twenties. We studied the religion of the Druids and He taught them much, and they Him, and He loved this land greatly. He visited Avalon, of course, and it was during that visit that He told me His wish that I marry into Avallach's family—you remember Avallach from your dream of Melusine—how Morgan le Fay told Melusine that Avallach and his brother, Albion, were giants who built the Tower of Babel and then later fled from humans to this land. Years later, when I returned to Britain, my daughter, Anna, married Avallach's son.

"In any case, it was a great happiness for me to have spent those years in Avalon with Jesus, and during that time, He prepared not only for His mission in Judea and how He would die, but He told me what my mission would be later, in returning to bring His message to the Britons—not His religion, mind you, for He did not set out to create a religion. Peter and Paul and the others, well-meaning and good men in their own rights, but perhaps not fully understanding Jesus, succeeded in doing that, you know. For the most part, they did well in following His message, and it really took a Roman emperor and a handful of popes to mess it all up, believing they were doing right, though it's never right to limit others' Free Will and force your beliefs on others. But anyway, yes, Jesus did live at Glastonbury with me for quite some time, and more specifically at Avalon."

Anne took all this in quietly. Adam remained seated in the chair; he had come upstairs with the intention to rest, forgetting Merlin had said he would come to them at tea time, and now he felt his lack of sleep seriously catching up with him. But Merlin's voice and his lessons about his nephew Jesus were spoken in such a soothing tone that soon Adam felt only sleepiness and was no longer filled with anger or even burning questions.

"There are all kinds of mixed up tales, as I said," Merlin continued. "Some about my coming to Avalon with a Holy Grail or a cruet of Christ's blood, and even a story about my planting my staff into the ground and it turning into the Holy Thorn, but the only items of any note that I possessed were the two golden rings Jesus gave me just before he returned to Judea to begin his ministry. Those two golden rings had been the ones originally belonging to Adam and Eve— their wedding rings. They were passed down through the centuries to Abraham and Sarah, Jacob and Rachel, David and Bathsheba, and ultimately, to Joseph and Mary. After Joseph died, Mary gave the rings to Jesus to give to his own wife, not understanding that His mission was not that of normal men and He would not marry. Instead, He passed them to me, for I was of the line of Abraham and David, a Levite like Mary of the royal priesthood through my father's line, but through my mother's line, also a descendant of King David. When my daughter wed into Avallach's family, I gave the rings to her to pass on to her descendants, and from her, all the lineage of Avalon has sprung. At that time when I first came to Avalon, Avallach was centuries old— millennia really. He told me he had been waiting to see the Christ child—and after I wed my daughter to his son, Bran the Blessed, he was prepared to depart this world. He was the last of the Nephilim of whom the Bible speaks, and so I have taken on, in his place, the role as patriarch of Avalon. His and my descendants have filled Avalon, as well as most of the earth by now, but only the most special of those descendants have remained at Avalon, some born there, others leaving, but their descendants feeling called upon to return there, as was the case with Ogier the Dane, whose tale, as I said, you will hear in full soon enough.

"As for the rings, you already know how they were passed down to Melusine's sons, but you do not know what became of those rings or the quest that Roland set out upon to reclaim the one that belonged to his great-uncle, Geoffrey Great-Tooth. That is the tale you have yet to hear."

"Merlin," said Anne, "I suspect these rings have something to do with our children? If you say our boys are safe, I trust you, but I badly want to see them. A mother does not want to be separated from her children, even if it's for their own good. Surely, you understand that."

"There, there, my girl," said Merlin, patting her hand. "Those rings are intended to be passed on to your twin boys, who have a great destiny awaiting them and will use the rings to achieve it, for the rings need not be used solely for marriage; they have many other powers, including the ability to bestow great wisdom on their bearers when used properly—wisdom beyond even my understanding."

"But I don't understand where Gwenhwyvach fits into all this," admitted Anne. "What does she want with the rings?"

"She is Lilith in her first incarnation, do not forget, and those rings first belonged to Adam and Eve. She thinks if she can control the rings, she can control mankind—the entire human race—for those rings represent the union of Adam and Eve, and the fruit of that union, their children. She refused such a union with Adam, and as a result, she has never felt complete, and she was jealous when Adam found such a union with Eve. Through all her incarnations, she has sought to obtain control of the rings, for only when she does will she have power to conquer and destroy the children of Eve."

"But isn't she a prisoner in her current incarnation, so why should we fear her?" asked Anne.

"Because," Merlin replied, "she is very powerful and cunning, having centuries of learning in her—her knowledge extends back to the beginning days of the creation, so it far exceeds my own. As her body ages in each incarnation, her mind develops more fully, and her power has now matured to the point where I believe she soon will be able to escape from her prison, and if she escapes, I fear none of us will be able to stop her from unleashing her full fury upon the human race."

Anne trembled, seeing that even Merlin's face looked ashen at the thought.

"She seeks nothing less than complete Armageddon for all of Adam and Eve's descendants," Merlin continued, "even those who are also of her bloodline, for revenge has completely consumed her. For that reason, I have hidden away your children to keep them safe, for she knows they are the most favored among her enemies, so I fear they will be her primary target. In the meantime, as we wait for her inevitable attack, I will do everything I can to prepare you to fight her evil."

"Merlin," said Adam, calmly, "I understand this Lilith is a powerful witch, but I assume she was not so powerful in the past as she is now, having had more centuries to obtain wisdom."

"That is true," Merlin agreed.

"What I don't understand then," said Adam, "is why you did not stop her before. I mean, when she existed as Gwenhwyvach, why didn't you try to destroy her then? Instead, you left Morgana in charge of Avalon, and then you disappeared for centuries."

"I did not disappear," Merlin replied. "I went to gather the Thirteen Treasures of Britain. I did so because I knew Gwenhwyvach would try to obtain them and use their power for her own evil ends, just as she has tried to get her hands on many other sacred relics over the centuries that I have successfully hidden away from her—such items as the Ark of the Covenant, the Spear of Longinus, Pandora's Box— though the box contains only Hope now, but we certainly don't want her to destroy Hope—and many more sacred objects whose names you would not even recognize. By doing so, I lessened the impact of her attack on Camelot and all mankind."

"That's all in the past anyway," said Anne. "What do we need to do now so we can be safely reunited with our children?"

"It is not what you need to do, my dear," Merlin replied, "but what you need to learn."

Starting to feel frustrated again, Adam asked, "And what do we need to learn?"

"For starters," said Merlin, "the story of your ancestor Ogier the Dane. Now if you'll just both lie quietly and go to sleep, I will arrange for you to dream that story."

"But," Anne objected, "we're expected down to dinner any minute."

"Yes," said Adam, "and the police said they'd update us on the investigation this evening—though, well, now that we know you're involved, Merlin, how are we going to explain all of this to the police?"

"Don't worry about the police," said Merlin, as if reading Adam's mind. "Their good intentions and incompetence have gotten in my way many times over the years. They will fumble about, but there's no way they can trace the kidnapping to me. I promise you both that all is well, but perhaps you should go down to dinner now. You are exhausted and have not eaten properly these last few days. Go eat, and you may tell your mother, grandmother, and Cedric what I have told you, provided you swear them to silence, which I know they will keep because Mary, at least, fears Gwenhwyvach's escape as much as I do. And they also deserve to be relieved of their worries. I have a few other things to do in the meantime, anyway, but do not fear that soon I will tell you Ogier's story so you can prepare for the future."

And then, after a kind, grandfatherly wink, Merlin again vanished into thin air.

Adam looked over to Anne, who smiled back at him.

"Yesterday was the worst day of my life," she said, "and today has been the craziest. But somehow, I think tomorrow will be better."

"I hope so," said Adam, not yet convinced, but when he stood and crossed to the bed, reaching out his hand to his wife and feeling her place her hand in his, it helped a little.

CHAPTER 5

"**L**ET'S GO DOWNSTAIRS**,**" Adam said.

Anne stood up, but when she stopped to take a deep breath, Adam could see how troubled she still felt.

"We didn't even think to ask Merlin where the children are," she said, looking him in the eyes. "Somehow, I feel he's been honest with us, that they're safe, but I still want to know where they are."

Adam wanted to believe in the best answer possible, despite the fear he still felt, so he replied, "Perhaps Merlin fears that if we know where the children are, it could endanger them. What if Gwenhwyvach got lose and somehow captured and tortured us to make us tell her where they are. You wouldn't want to hurt your children by revealing information that way, would you?"

"No, of course not, but I—I just want to see them," Anne replied. Adam put his arms around her and hugged her tightly.

"Come," he said after he released her, his hand again finding hers. "Let's go downstairs. Merlin said we could tell our parents and my grandmother everything. We don't want to prolong their worry any longer."

"It's funny," said Anne, trying to smile. "Who would have ever thought we would be telling our family that our children were kidnapped for their own safety by a legendary wizard, so he could protect them from some sort of biblical witch? It's all just so surreal."

"It is," Adam agreed. He took a step toward the door, but his legs hardly wanted to move. He felt like an old man, not a twenty-three year old who, just a couple of years ago, could have easily pushed aside all the opposing team to score the winning touchdown.

"Adam, are you okay?" Anne asked. "You're always so protective of me, but you need to take care of yourself, too."

"I'm just tired," said Adam, "but I think it's because I've been so angry. Merlin hit me really hard when he pressed me against the wall. It frightened me, you know. I think of myself as indestructible, but I never felt a blow like that—not even when I had two-hundred-fifty-pound linebackers charging at me. It made me realize there are powers in this world far beyond my ability to control."

"Adam, sweetheart," said Anne, kissing his cheek, "there have always been things we can't control. If Merlin has supernatural powers, or this Gwenhwyvach does for that matter, is that any different than a tornado or a hurricane that could destroy us? And yet, we go on living every day despite all the dangers that exist and are beyond our control. I think Merlin just needed to show you his power so you would understand that you can't bully him—that there are things bigger than you and me in this world, and as a result, we just have to trust him because there's really nothing else we can do."

"Trusting is what's so hard for me," said Adam. "I'm used to taking charge."

"Don't let trusting someone else scare you," Anne replied. "If anything, it should strengthen your faith in God and the good of the universe. Merlin is looking out for us, and considering that he's Jesus' uncle, I don't think we can ask for a better protector."

"But I've never been a churchgoing person," Adam said.

"Neither have I," Anne replied, "but my father—I mean your father—had a very deep faith in God; he wasn't all that religious, but he often told me that God would ensure that all things work out for the best. When I think of how your father raised me as his own daughter, all the while knowing his wife and best friend had betrayed him—well, that's kindness, but it's also faith—faith that in the end all wrongs will be righted, and we have to do the right thing, whatever life throws our way because God is ultimately watching out for us. And Adam, when you think about it, as difficult as it has been, it has all been working out for us; I feel like if we just hold on, the happy ending will still come."

Adam squeezed her hand and replied, "You're a wonderful woman, Anne, and I'm very fortunate that Merlin arranged for you to be in my life."

He kissed her on the cheek, and then hand-in-hand, they went downstairs to dinner.

When they reached the dining room, they were unexpectedly met by smiles, followed by Elizabeth's announcement, "Adam, Devin called while you were upstairs. He's boarding an overnight flight to London this afternoon. He'll be here early tomorrow morning. I told him you'd pick him up at the airport. His plane comes in at 8:30."

"Of course," said Adam, feeling exuberant at the thought of seeing his cousin. If anyone would know what to think about this mess, it would be Devin.

"He'll be landing at Gatwick," said Elizabeth. "I wrote down the flight number. I'll give it to you after dinner."

"Do you feel any better, Anne?" Cedric asked. "Did you get a little nap?"

"No, no nap," she replied, taking a seat at the table and nodding to Maggie, the serving girl, who stood by the kitchen door, waiting to carry in dinner. The girl curtsied and then disappeared into the kitchen. "But Adam and I had a good long talk with Merlin, and it has made us all feel better. I'll tell you about it as soon as dinner is served."

No one wanted the servants to hear the crazy truth about the family and its legendary connections, although they knew the servants grieved nearly as much as themselves over the children's disappearance.

Maggie returned along with Robert to serve the dinner, bringing in the soup and the main course. In Bram Delaney's day, there would have been several courses, and in Bram's father's day, footmen to serve, but Adam had felt uncomfortable with such behavior, and he also felt it unfair to keep the servants occupied throughout the evening when they could be home enjoying themselves or spending time with their families. One of the first things he'd done after inheriting the castle was to have a giant dishwasher installed. Cook insisted it couldn't get the dishes clean enough, but Maggie was grateful since she had usually stayed behind an hour after dinner to wash up. Adam had since told them to leave once dinner was served because he and Anne could fill the dishwasher themselves. Cook had threatened to quit over this lack of propriety, but Anne had convinced Mrs. Deneker to persuade her otherwise, and eventually, Cook did admit she would like to be home an hour earlier, so peace was restored. With such a large family party now, and the trouble over the children's disappearance, Maggie had offered to stay late each evening, but the entire family had refused, saying that the extra little work would help to keep their thoughts occupied.

And so, once the food was placed on the table, the serving girls said goodnight, and Cook came out to make sure all was well before she returned to the kitchen, still feeling a bit guilty for leaving early, although she had done so for several months now. And, finally, the family was left alone. Only Mrs. Deneker now resided in the main house. The rest of the servants had separate quarters in the former manor house where, in the last couple of centuries, guests or the occasional dowager countess had resided. Adam understood the servants could not all afford to live in apartments and travel from town every day, but he did not want them to feel they were living under someone else's roof, so he'd had the manor house converted into small but comfortable apartments for the servants, who, save for Cook, of course, had all been delighted by the change.

Adam and Anne now told the rest of the family all the details of their conversation with Merlin, keeping to the main points and thinking it best not to describe his often eccentric behavior from fear of offending him since they never knew when he might decide to make an appearance.

"It's all very strange," said Mary, when they had finished, "but it makes me feel better to know he's protecting the children."

"I still want to know where they are," replied Anne.

Cedric, seated beside her, put his arm around her and said, "I agree with Adam that it's probably for the best that you don't know. Hopefully, this situation can be resolved soon."

"But how will it be resolved?" asked Adam. "Merlin is apparently afraid that Lilith or Gwenhwyvach, or whatever her name is, will soon escape, so he wants to protect our children, but if it's likely she's going to escape, can't something be done about it? Do we just have to wait around until she does escape on the odd chance she might, and then once she does, what are we to do? If she's so powerful that we can't keep her prisoner, how can we fight or stop her?"

His voice was beginning to grow excited until his grandmother said, "Adam, drink some water. You'll make yourself sick the way your face is turning red."

"I don't blame you for being upset," Mary told him. "The points you make are all good and true ones, and I don't know what we can do if Gwenhwyvach escapes. My job is to make sure that will never happen."

"But Merlin thinks it a very likely possibility," Anne replied.

"Then we can only hope that Merlin and Morgan le Fay and the others at Avalon will know what to do to counter her efforts. I am not privy to secrets of such a high nature," Mary admitted.

"None of this information is very satisfactory," agreed Cedric. "But perhaps there is something we can do. Merlin told you that Gwenhwyvach wants control of the rings. You know, of course, that the rings are in our possession, so we can prevent her from acquiring them."

"I didn't know anything about the rings," said Anne.

Mary explained, "Bram had one of the rings and he gave it to me the night we were together. He didn't understand the ring's significance, but he said his mother had long ago given it to him and told him to give it to his one true love. I knew it was one of Adam and Eve's rings the minute he gave it to me, although I didn't tell him its history or significance. Still, I've kept it in my possession ever since."

"Do you have it with you now?" Adam asked.

"No, it's in a safe-deposit box—in a bank in Seattle," Mary replied.

"But where is the other ring?" asked Anne.

"I have it," Cedric replied. "I thought at one time of giving it to your mother, Sarah, but I feared Bram would take it. I could not risk him obtaining it because he was on the other side, you see. Until recently, I thought I was on Gwenhwyvach's side."

"'The other side,'" said Adam. "So you were never even truly my father's friend in any sense of the word, were you?"

Cedric looked like he wanted to reply, but after a minute, he hung his head.

Mary said, "Adam, let that go. It's all in the past now."

"But, Dad," said Anne, before Adam could reply, "how did you acquire the ring?"

"It's been passed down in my family. I must have one that Gwenhwyvach possessed at some point and passed to her descendants once she chose to leave her life and reincarnate into a new one. It was always my intent to get my hands on the second ring. That's partly why, besides just wishing to hurt Bram, I went after his wife, Sarah. I wanted to get the ring from her—you see, I assumed Bram would have given it to his wife. I had no idea he had given it to Mary. I was very disappointed never to catch sight of it all these years, for I dared not mention it to Sarah or Bram, though I've snooped about the house for it now and then whenever I was given the opportunity. As for the one I do have, I always meant to give it to you, Anne, when you were a little older. Or...well, that's not quite true. I hoped once Adam came into the picture that he would come across the ring somewhere—in Bram's safe or somewhere I had been unable to look, and then I could get possession of both of them and...well, I didn't know what then—I only knew from family stories that the rings brought great power. I didn't think I could dominate the world with them, but I thought perhaps they were like Aladdin's magic lamp and could bring me anything I wished. But it was not to be, and any dreams I had of possessing them I surrendered once I saw how happy Adam had made you and after my grandsons came into this world. If Gwenhwyvach is as evil as it appears, I never wanted to be on her side anyway. The family stories I'd heard said that she had been a queen robbed of her kingdom, and I grew up believing our family had been wronged and persecuted by Bram's family over the centuries, but now I am beginning to see that most of those stories were lies that only got distorted and elaborated upon even more as they were passed down from one generation to the next."

"Maybe," said Adam, "just maybe we need those rings to come together so we can defeat Gwenhwyvach."

"That could be," said Anne.

"The rings are very powerful," said Elizabeth. "Stories of them have circulated in my family too, and as Merlin told you, they were created for Adam and Eve. Doubtless, Gwenhwyvach is desperate to possess them, considering her hatred toward Adam and Eve. I know nothing of how to use those rings, but I suspect if anything has the power to stop Gwenhwyvach, the rings are the answer, provided that, in our amateur efforts to use them against her, she does not find it easy to take them from us."

"True," said Adam. "Our bringing the rings together may be precisely what she is wanting us to do. And it's also true that we don't even know how to use them."

"Sometimes, however," said Elizabeth, "we simply need to trust that all will work out. We need only take the next step that we see before us, believing that even if we can't see the top of the hill, each step will bring us closer to the summit."

"Dad," said Anne, turning to Cedric, "where is your ring?"

Just then the sound of an alarm went off, emanating directly from Mary's person.

"What's that?" asked Anne, jumping up in surprise.

"My pager," said Mary. "Excuse me." She stood up from the table and reached into her pocket. "I need to make a phone call."

Mary left the room for the hall where the nearest phone was.

"I didn't even know she had a pager," said Adam, looking at his grandmother. "Is it for her job at the—"

But Elizabeth shook her head, and then it dawned on Adam why his mother would need such an alert device.

They all grew quiet, trying to listen in on Mary's conversation since she had left the dining room door open. They could not make out most of the words, but none of them failed to hear her exclaim, "She's escaped! When? How?"

CHAPTER 6

NONE OF THE family could fully conceive what Gwenhwyvach's freedom might mean. Paralyzing fear made it impossible for them to listen with any attention to the remainder of Mary's short conversation. They all sat in dread, too shocked even to speak until a couple of minutes later when Mary, pale-faced, returned to the room. Their own drained faces told her they had heard the worst.

"What's going to happen now?" cried Anne as Mary stumbled to her chair at the table.

"We don't know how she did it," said Mary. "The camera monitors showed she was there all day, but then the screen went blank for several minutes, so they entered her cell to make sure she hadn't escaped, and she had vanished. It all just happened within the last hour. I—you can imagine they're all terrified.... I don't...."

Mary momentarily became speechless with shock.

"But how could she have gotten out?" asked Adam.

"I have no idea," said Mary. "Her cell is completely composed of lead and steel several feet thick, and it's in an underground cavern over a hundred feet beneath the earth. That place is like an impregnable safe. No human, no matter how clever, could have done it."

"But explain to us," said Cedric, "if she's spent her entire life in prison, as I think you said before, how she would even know how to escape or what lies in the outside world to give her the reason to want to."

"You're right—how would she know such things?" Adam agreed.

"It's a good question," admitted Mary. "Understand, we're not totally cruel. She has artificial daylight in her cell, although she's never seen natural daylight in this incarnation, and her room is really a house inside a large cavern the size of a football field so she has plenty of room to move about and exercise. And it's not like she is a wild child, unknowing of the world. We captured her mother, Lacey, when she was pregnant with Gwenhwyvach—we kidnapped her actually, but no one came looking for her. She was a heroin addict with all kinds of problems. Still, we kept her and Gwenhwyvach together until Gwenhwyvach was three years old. During those years, I think Lacey tried to love her, despite her own emotional issues and the unpleasantness of being our prisoner, but Gwenhwyvach just grew meaner and crueler. She used to pull her mother's hair, and one time while nursing, she nearly bit off her mother's nipple. At that point, Lacey begged us to free her; she showed us the scars and scratches on her body where Gwenhwyvach had attacked her, and she was convinced that Gwenhwyvach would kill her when she got older.

"We pitied Lacey, but we couldn't risk freeing her; she wasn't mentally stable or trustworthy, so we feared she would tell people about her prison, even though she had been brought there blindfolded. Whatever she said to anyone would probably have been dismissed as a madwoman's ravings, but we couldn't take the chance. We apologized to her that we could not free her, and we offered to hold her in a separate cell, but Lacey said she would rather be dead than caged. Finally, out of pity, we allowed her to take poison to put her out of her misery."

Mary paused momentarily, looking disturbed at the memory of Lacey's death. Only when Cedric reached over to squeeze her hand was she able to continue.

"After her mother's death, we began to see Gwenhwyvach's full fury because she no longer had anyone to torment. She aged quickly after that, spitting out vile words of how she hated us for killing her mother, calling us murderers. We tried to brainwash her by teaching her to read, and giving her only children's books with positive messages such as *The Wizard of Oz*, the Chronicles of Narnia, and *Pollyanna* to promote happiness and good behavior, but none of it made a difference. She was innately evil; when she played pretend, she would be a winged monkey or the White Witch Jadis, from the Narnia Chronicles, saying she wished she'd had a daughter just like her. Even those beautiful books' messages she perverted to her own ends. Nothing we did to try to change her evil nature made any difference."

"But then," asked Cedric, "how did she figure out how to escape from such a fortress if she was never taught anything about—I don't know, science, math, engineering?"

"No, we never taught her any of those things. Our goal was not to educate but to contain her and, hopefully, to make her less of a threat if we could alter her nature. Yet somehow the knowledge she acquired over centuries has remained in her cells, and so, she has grown wiser and more cunning with each passing year. At times, she has told us all her names from past incarnations and laughed at us and taunted us, warning us that she would escape to fulfill her mission, which from her warped perspective she believed was to stop the evil she claims the human race has for centuries inflicted upon the world.

"Understand, we did not let her taunt us. We did not speak to her. We did not even have physical or personal contact with her. Her meals were delivered to her through a tube, so she never even saw a human face in person after her mother's death, save occasionally, when we would project our images on a screen to remind her she was being watched, hoping to instill fear or good behavior in her, but she was too powerful to fear us, and I'm certain she knew we feared her, though we refused to show it. As I said, we never taught her anything of math, but once we caught her writing out math equations on the wall of her cell, using her own blood to do so. It was surreal and terrifying, and none of us knew what the equations meant. We even wrote them down and sent them to a renowned physicist, but he could not make any sense out of them. Her evil and cunning are definitely beyond human understanding."

"But what do you think she wants?" asked Anne.

"She wants to destroy us," said Elizabeth, "destroy all of King Arthur's descendants, all of Adam and Eve's descendants. We are her enemies for all eternity, or so she believes."

"We are her enemies," said Adam, "but only because she has made us so."

"But what can we do to protect ourselves?" Anne asked.

"I don't know," Elizabeth replied, shrugging her shoulders. "Keeping her a prisoner was the only solution. Now that her fury is unleashed, how can we protect the entire human race?"

"But shouldn't we notify someone?" asked Anne. "The Prime Minister, the United Nations, all the heads of state of every nation?"

"And tell them what?" asked Cedric, unable not to laugh. "That the demon Lilith has been unleashed to destroy humanity? Who would believe us?"

"She's not a demon," said Mary. "From my understanding, there are no such beings."

"She's close to it," Cedric replied. "She's evil and intent on conquering the world and murdering all of us."

"But what do you think she'll do first?" asked Anne. "Will she go after the twins?"

"No, they're safe. Merlin promised us that," said Adam. "He must have known it was almost time for her to escape; that's why he hid them away."

"You don't think—" began Anne.

"That Merlin is Lilith's accomplice?" asked Adam, practically reading her mind. "I have no idea what to think. If he is, what can we do about it? We don't even know where our children are."

"Mary, what do you suggest we do?" asked Elizabeth.

"We need to stay calm," Mary said, going to the buffet to pour herself a glass of brandy, the only alcohol any of them had ever seen her drink. She took a sip while they all waited for her to speak again. Finally, she returned to the table and said, "We can't overreact. Before I received the call, we were talking about the rings and how we need to bring them together. Gwenhwyvach's cell was built beneath the Seattle Space Needle, and the ring is in a safe-deposit box in Seattle. I'll fly to Seattle to get the ring and visit the prison compound to find out what else we might need to know about her escape. Since Cedric has the other ring, once I retrieve mine, we can quickly bring together their power."

"But we don't even know what to do with the rings," said Adam.

"I'm sure Merlin or Morgan le Fay will tell us," Anne replied.

"I'll go with you to Seattle," Cedric offered, turning to Mary. "It's too dangerous for you to go alone."

"Maybe," suggested Elizabeth, looking at Mary and Cedric, "the two of you can figure out what to do with the rings; Cedric can bring his with him so once you retrieve yours, no time is lost."

"No," said Mary. "I mean, I don't mind if Cedric accompanies me, but for some reason, I feel it's Adam and Anne who must use the rings, or perhaps the twins when they are older, which may be why Merlin is protecting them."

"I'll bring my ring anyway," said Cedric. "Perhaps Merlin will show up to teach us what to do with them."

"No," said a strange voice, suddenly coming from the buffet. "Leave your ring with Anne. You are not to use it."

They were all astonished and quickly turned to look at the buffet. Then Elizabeth shrieked. From the spout of the teapot, which had sat there empty since Cook had washed it after tea, steam was now circling and forming into the face of a wiry old man.

"Mary," said Merlin's voice, speaking from the steam-shaped face, "go to Seattle. Learn what you can, for you know I cannot physically interfere in mankind's actions. Cedric, leave your ring behind in Anne's care. You cannot risk Gwenhwyvach getting both of the rings at the same time."

Everyone sat in stunned silence for a moment as the steam subsided as quickly as it had appeared. Then Elizabeth said, "I take it that was Merlin?"

"Yes," said Adam. "He seems to enjoy dissolving into mist or, in this case, steam."

"I'm sure then," said Elizabeth, "that he knows best, so we should follow his instructions."

"But how can we be certain that was Merlin?" Cedric objected. "I've never seen him. And we didn't see him now really. Why didn't he just appear to us in human form like Adam and Anne say he has done before? For all we know, that image might have been created by Gwenhwyvach to trick us. Why would a great wizard choose to come out of a teapot?"

"Wouldn't it be just as ridiculous if an evil villain came out of a teapot?" asked Anne.

"Merlin has a strange sense of humor," said Adam, "which is why I'm certain it was him."

"This is no time for humor," Cedric replied.

He would have argued further, but Anne stopped him by saying, "I'll keep the ring safe while you're gone, Father. I promise. Where is it?"

"It's at my house," Cedric replied, "in a secret place. I'll bring it in the morning before Mary and I leave for the airport."

Adam looked at his mother, wondering whether she agreed with this plan, but before she could answer, Elizabeth spoke up.

"I think I understand why Merlin appeared that way," she laughed. "Cedric made a comment about Aladdin's lamp earlier, so Merlin was pretending to be the genie from the lamp. I think he does have a sense of humor. It was his way of letting us know he's been listening and watching over us, even when we can't see him."

Mary nodded, accepting Elizabeth's explanation as reasonable. Adam agreed, "That sounds just like something he'd do. You should have seen how he flew about the ceiling of our bedroom like a vampire this afternoon. I wouldn't put anything past him."

Regardless of these comments, Cedric smirked with distrust, then said, "We need to find out when the next flight to Seattle is. Hopefully, we can still get tickets."

"First class isn't usually full," said Mary, "though it's not cheap.

Adam, I hate to ask you to pay for my ticket, but—"

"Not a problem," said Adam. "And I have to go to the airport to pick up Devin anyway so I'll drive you both there."

Mary immediately went back to the phone and dialed the airport. She was on hold, listening to music, just long enough for Adam to run upstairs to get his credit card from his wallet. Soon they had reservations for two in first class for a 7 a.m. flight.

"I need to go home and pack," said Cedric. "I'll sleep at my house tonight and bring back the ring in the morning so Anne can keep it safe."

"All right," Adam agreed.

"I'll put it in the safe-deposit box here," said Anne.

No one said what they all were thinking—if Gwenhwyvach could escape her compound, she should easily be able to get into a safe-deposit box. But where else could they keep it safe?

"It's a plan then," said Mary, smiling at Cedric. "I'm glad I'll have company tomorrow."

"You better all get to bed," said Anne. "It's a two-hour drive just to get to Gatwick to catch your plane."

They all agreed to call it a night, and Cedric soon took his leave. Adam went upstairs and set his alarm clock for 3 a.m.

In the morning, Mary and Adam tried to leave without waking anyone, but Anne and Elizabeth could not sleep, so they came downstairs just a couple of minutes after them to see them off. Hugs and kisses were exchanged before it was even daylight as they waited for Cedric to arrive.

"I hope he didn't oversleep," Adam grumbled, feeling cranky at such an early hour.

"There's a car coming up the drive now," said Mary.

CHAPTER 7

"**I**T'S GONE!" EXCLAIMED Cedric, jumping out of his car and running into the house.

They didn't need to ask what he meant.

"Gone! Are you sure?" asked Mary.

"Yes, the ring was there when I checked a couple of weeks ago. I check on it every once in awhile to make sure it's safe," said Cedric, standing there helplessly.

Adam was all business as the others spoke. He went outside to open Cedric's car door and retrieved his suitcase to put in the trunk of his own car.

"We better get going," Adam said, going back into the house where everyone was discussing the missing ring.

"Are you sure you didn't misplace it?" asked Elizabeth.

"No, no, it's always in the same place," said Cedric.

"What should we do now?" asked Anne.

"We still have to retrieve the other ring," said Mary, "before Gwenhwyvach gets that one."

"Do you think she took Dad's ring?" Anne asked.

"Who else would have taken it?" Cedric asked.

"We have to go," said Adam. "We barely have time to get to the airport now."

Frazzled, they all quickly said goodbye. Then Mary, Cedric, and Adam climbed into the car. In a minute, they were starting down the driveway.

"Think, Cedric," said Mary, in the passenger seat, turning around to look at him in the back. "Maybe you forgot that you moved it, or maybe you just missed it somehow; maybe buried it under something else in the safe-deposit box."

"I didn't just miss it," Cedric snapped. "It's the only thing I have in that safe-deposit box, and no one else knows the combination, or even where it's hidden in the house. There's only one explanation."

"Quit yelling in my ear," growled Adam at his father-in-law as he turned the car onto the road.

"Adam," Mary reprimanded him.

"Sorry; I didn't get much sleep," he replied, "and this whole situation is starting to get on my nerves."

For just a second, Adam noticed a car with its lights off parked beside the turn into the driveway. He realized it must belong to an undercover police officer, who was watching the house. When its lights didn't turn on and the car didn't move to follow him, Adam figured the man had fallen asleep on his watch. He remembered how Detective Harris had told him not to leave the area, so he was relieved when he didn't see the car following him, though he would have explanations to make if they spotted him returning later.

"I'm sorry, too," said Cedric, sitting back in his seat. "I'm just frustrated."

"It's okay," said Mary. "You have reason to be. We're all nervous wrecks. Adam, don't drive so fast. Focus on your driving, not on our other problems, or you'll just make things worse."

Adam was in no mood to have his driving criticized, but since his mother was his critic, he kept his mouth shut.

"I just can't believe it," said Cedric. "She hasn't even been free for twelve hours. How could she have already gotten to my house and stolen the ring? And when? I was home for hours and never heard her. I didn't check on the ring until a few minutes ago, planning to keep it safe until I was ready to go, but even so, I doubt she could have broken in before I got home last night if she only just escaped not long before we got the call, and if I was home, why didn't I hear her?"

"I don't know," said Mary, "but then, neither do I know how she could have escaped."

"There's nothing we can do if it's gone," said Adam, and then he momentarily became distracted with his own thoughts before yelling, "Goddamnit!" in frustration and pounding his fist on the steering wheel so hard that he lost hold of it and almost sent them into the ditch.

"Adam, let me drive," said Mary.

"No, you're not used to driving on the wrong side of the road," Adam replied. "I'll be okay. I'll calm down. Maybe we just shouldn't talk about it for a little while."

They all agreed, and after a prolonged silence, they all began to feel better. They remained scared, but they had not yet given up hope. Adam spoke for all of them when he broke the silence by saying, "What I hate most about all this is how helpless I feel. What can we do if she's so powerful? What can we possibly do to defeat her?"

"We just have to wait and trust," Mary replied. "Merlin gave us counsel last night. I'm sure he'll help us again."

After that, they were mostly quiet. Both Mary and Cedric dozed off for a little while, and before long, Adam had reached Gatwick in record time just as the first streaks of daylight appeared in the sky.

Cedric and Mary woke up as Adam searched for a parking space.

"Are we here already?" asked Mary.

"Already?" said Cedric. "It'll be at least twelve hours before we get to Seattle. We've barely started."

"It's a long and boring flight," said Mary. "I'm glad I'll have you for company, Cedric."

"I wouldn't want you to go back there by yourself after what's happened," Cedric replied. "Not that I'm much of a protector."

"I appreciate not being alone, regardless," said Mary as Adam parked the car.

In a few more minutes, they had the luggage out of the vehicle and had walked into the airport. Adam waited while Cedric and Mary checked in at the ticket counter, and then he went with them through security to wait at the gate. Their conversation was limited since they could think of little other than their mission to collect the ring in Seattle and hope that Gwenhwyvach had not already taken it, although Mary assured them it was more heavily guarded in the bank there than Cedric's had been in his home. There was little more they could say since they did not want to risk strangers overhearing them.

"We'll call you once we find out more," Mary told Adam when it was time to board the plane. "If I explore Gwenhwyvach's cell, I might be able to find out more about what happened."

"Good luck," said Adam, kissing his mother on the cheek and then offering his hand to Cedric, who ignored it and instead hugged him.

"Just take care of my daughter," said Cedric, "and do whatever you can to protect my grandchildren, if you find them."

"I will," said Adam. "I promise."

Once Mary and Cedric passed through the gate, Adam found an airport restaurant and had breakfast while he waited another hour for Devin's flight to arrive. He ate an enormous breakfast of scrambled eggs and bangers, muffins, coffee, and juice; just because he was worried didn't mean he shouldn't keep up his strength, and he needed energy, considering he hadn't got much sleep. As he ate, he wondered how much he should tell Devin—Devin knew Adam and Anne's sons had been kidnapped, but it didn't sound like his mother or grandmother had told Devin anything else about their family's secrets; after all, they hadn't told Adam himself anything until the twins were kidnapped. Still, Devin had always had a proclivity for all things relating to history and legends. Adam knew Devin was certainly more knowledgeable than himself about King Arthur, and Melusine, and Charlemagne, and everything else relevant to this mysterious family of which they were members. Devin had also been known to have premonitions, so Adam wondered whether his interests in medieval legends were just natural proclivities for him, or whether he had known some of this information about the family's past but had kept it from Adam all these years. Adam didn't like to think Devin would ever keep anything from him.

Finally, after lounging at the table as long as possible while pondering over all these concerns, and eating all he could, Adam got up, utterly stuffed, and walked down the long airport hallways to burn off his excess energy and settle his stomach before he finally arrived at the baggage claim area for Devin's flight.

Once the flight's luggage began to arrive, but there was no sign of his cousin, Adam began to fear Devin had missed the flight, but after a few minutes, he appeared among the crowd. The minute Adam saw his cousin, who was more like a brother to him, he felt tears springing up in his eyes and a sense of relief. Devin was the smartest person he knew, and he had always been there for him. If anyone could help him figure out what to do, it would be Devin.

"I'm so glad to see you," said Adam, trying to hold it together as he hugged his cousin. For a second, Devin squeezed his cousin tighter than normal, and then they resumed their composure and watched for Devin's suitcase on the carousel. When Devin started to ask about the twins, Adam interrupted, "I'll tell you once we're out of the airport," so they would not be overheard.

"We need to get home," said Adam, as soon as the luggage was collected, "but we can stop somewhere quick if you're hungry."

"No, I can wait until we get to Delaney Castle, your lordship," said Devin, smirking as he followed Adam out of the airport and to the parking lot. "Last time I saw you, you were just a regular American guy."

"It has been almost a year, hasn't it?" said Adam. Devin had spent last summer with him in England, arriving just a few days before Bram's death, but he had returned to the States once school had begun.

"I'm sorry I haven't been here for you all this time," Devin said, "especially considering what's happened now. I haven't even gotten to see your kids yet."

"I know. I was looking forward to introducing the twins to their Uncle Devin," said Adam, "but I understand that you're busy with school, although I don't see why you couldn't go to school at Oxford or Cambridge or another school in Britain. You know money is no issue now. You can get as good or better a Ph.D. there as anywhere back in Michigan."

"Maybe when I finish my Master's, I'll transfer," said Devin. "With Grandma and your mom both visiting you here, the house back home has been awful lonely."

"I've missed you, too," Adam replied, "and you should be closer so you can see the twins grow up. Mom and Grandma are talking of moving to England anyway. There's nothing to keep them back in the States any longer—except you, of course."

They had reached the car by now, and as they climbed in, Devin for the first time turned to look closely at his cousin, instantly seeing the strain on his face.

"How are you holding up?" asked Devin, putting on his seatbelt. "Tell me what's going on."

"It's been crazy. I—I don't know even where to begin," said Adam, backing the car out of the parking lot.

"Do you know who kidnapped the children?" Devin asked. "That's the main thing."

"Ye-es," said Adam, "but to explain who it is—well, it's a long story. You'll have to be patient with me while I catch you up on everything."

"We have time; it's a long way to Delaney Castle," Devin replied.

"Okay," said Adam, pulling the car out of the parking lot. "There's just so many things that have happened since last summer, and...well, even when you were here, that I didn't tell you."

Devin looked irritated that Adam had kept anything from him, but after a moment, he said, "Go on."

"Well, I only didn't tell you because I was afraid you'd think I was crazy—I kind of thought I might be crazy myself. Anyway, it all started the first day I arrived in England when I met this man at the airport named Merle...."

As he continued to drive, Adam told Devin everything up to and including the dream of Camelot he'd had the day they had visited Cadbury Castle.

Devin's eyes kept growing wider and wider as Adam spoke, but not once did he say, "I don't believe it!" or "You've got to be kidding!" Instead, he surprised Adam by occasionally exclaiming, "Yes! Yes!" and pounding his fist into his hand while jiggling his leg in excitement.

"What do you mean by 'Yes!'?" asked Adam.

Devin replied, "Just keep talking. I'll tell you when you're finished."

When Adam did finish telling him about his dream of Camelot, he asked his cousin, "So, do you think I'm crazy?"

"No, not crazy at all," said Devin. "Deep in my heart, I've always felt there must be some truth to the legends of King Arthur. I didn't expect it to be the way you just told me, but I knew there had to be some historical basis to them. You don't know how exciting this is to me, Adam. I've loved the tales of King Arthur since I was a child, and I only wish that it had been me who...well, I just am so excited, but...but does all this have something to do with your children?"

"Yes," said Adam. "It does, and you wouldn't begin to believe—"

"And Melusine," Devin interrupted. "You were asking me about her on the phone the other night—does she figure into all this?"

"Yes," said Adam. "Melusine and Charlemagne and Roland and someone named Ogier the Dane, whose story Merlin tells me I have yet to hear, and I don't know all what else he hasn't told me, but it all figures in with the children's kidnapping. You see, Merlin, well... Devin, I'm scared. I'm scared that—"

"Of course, you're scared. That's understandable since your children are missing, but—"

"Actually, the children, oddly enough, are my least concern right now. Merlin assures me they're safe, but I don't know for how long."

Adam found it difficult to find the words to tell the rest of his tale.

"Just spill it all, Adam," said Devin. "Anything that you tell me is true, I'm going to believe. I know you don't lie or make up stories."

"Thanks," said Adam. "It's just that every day I have to keep asking myself whether I'm not going insane, but Anne says I'm not, and my mom and Grandma and Anne's dad don't think so either. In fact, they've known a lot about all this. Devin, we come from a really amazing family. I'll just go full steam ahead now and try to explain it all to you before we get home."

Adam spoke quickly, and Devin did not interrupt again as he heard all about the magic rings Melusine had left for her descendants that had been passed down for generations in the Morgan and Delaney families, and how those rings had initially belonged to Adam and Eve, and how Lilith—here Devin could not restrain from saying, "Lilith! Oh, my gosh!"—was after the rings, and finally, how she had escaped, and how Mary and Cedric had left that morning for Seattle to get the ring Bram had given Mary so long ago.

They were only a couple of miles from Delaney Castle when Adam finished his story. Then there was silence for several seconds before Adam said, "Say something."

"What's there to say?" asked Devin. "It's all incredible, and you're right. We do come from an amazing family. I can't believe Grandma never told me any of this, but I'm not surprised that Merlin says you're to play a key role in King Arthur's return. I—well, it's all crazy sounding and scary, but it's really awesome at the same time, and to be honest, I'm almost jealous that I'm not the Chosen One."

"I'm not *the Chosen One*," Adam objected.

"Yes, you clearly are," insisted Devin, "and it doesn't surprise me. I always knew you were incredible and were just not—well, not using your talents to their full potential."

"Don't be silly," said Adam. "We both know you're smarter than me. So why should it be me and not you, Devin, if we're both part of this family. Why do I have to be the special one, and—"

But he didn't finish his sentence as they pulled into the park of the castle. Police cars were all over the property again, so Adam said, "The cops are here all the time. I don't know what to do about them now. I mean, I can't tell them Merlin kidnapped my children. Don't say anything to them. Just let me do the talking."

Adam pulled the car up to the front of the house and rolled down the window since Detective Harris had spotted him and was clearly waiting to speak to him.

"Good morning, Detective," said Adam. "Back again, I see. Any new leads?"

"I was hoping to question your family some more," Detective Harris replied, peering into the car and past Adam to get a good look at Devin. "I also received a report from the officer I have surveilling the property that your vehicle was seen leaving this morning. Do you mind telling me why you would leave the property at four in the morning?"

"Oh, I'm sorry, Detective," said Adam, trying to sound sincere while hoping the officer who had seen him had only seen the car and not been able to see who was inside it; he would keep that a secret if he could so his mother and Cedric didn't get into more trouble. "I should have checked in with you, but I went to the airport to pick up my cousin, Devin. He's come to give moral support to all of us."

"I asked you not to leave the county without notifying me," Detective Harris replied.

"I'm sorry, Detective. I didn't think of it, and I was only gone a few hours."

Devin had by now gotten out of the vehicle. He walked around the car to offer his hand to the detective in hopes of smoothing over the situation. "Hello. Detective, is it?" he said as Detective Harris turned to look at him. "I'm Devin Purcell. Thank you for everything you've been doing to try to solve this case."

Detective Harris did not shake his hand, but simply said, "How exactly are you related to his lordship?"

"I'm his cousin. Our mothers are sisters. We grew up together back in Michigan."

"It's your grandmother as well then who is here?" asked Detective Harris.

"Yes, my Grandma Morgan," said Devin.

The detective had stepped away from the vehicle while talking to Devin, so Adam took the opportunity to get out of the car and collect Devin's luggage from the trunk.

"Please come in, Detective," he then said, opening the front door.

"I'd like to speak to your grandmother and mother again, your lordship, and her ladyship's father as well since they were all here the night of the kidnapping."

"Certainly," said Adam, trying quickly to think of excuses. "Although I think a strain of the summer flu has hit the house. My mother and Cedric haven't been feeling well, and my own stomach is queasy, too, though it could be nerves. If you'll wait in the library, I'll go see if they've come down for breakfast, or if they're too sick to leave their rooms."

Detective Harris did not reply, not revealing any sign of believing or doubting Adam's comments, nor protesting that he need not interview the family if they were ill. Adam had felt forced to lie, certain the detective would be furious to learn his mother and Cedric were gone; that would definitely seem suspicious when two children were missing. Nor did Adam think for a moment he could bring Detective Harris into their confidence; he appeared far too matter-of-fact to believe fairy tales might be true, and Merlin had given them no leave to share the family history with outsiders.

Once inside the house, Adam headed up the stairs, congratulating himself on saying he also felt ill, just to make the lie sound a little more real.

"I'll take you to the library, Detective," said Devin. "I know the way, and if there's anything I can do to help...."

In another minute, Adam had set Devin's luggage in a guest room and then gone to find his grandmother in her room. He quickly explained the situation to her and sent her downstairs, also prepared to lie about the stomach flu in the house, and how both Cedric and Mary had been vomiting just that morning at breakfast while Adam was away.

"We wouldn't want you to catch our germs," Elizabeth Morgan told Detective Harris not five minutes later in the library. "But I'll be happy to help you in any way I can, although I can't think of anything you haven't already been told."

Devin and Adam left their grandmother with the detective while they went to make Devin a late breakfast. The detective only stayed a few minutes, but he made certain to search out Adam before he left, saying, "I'll be back tomorrow. I hope your lordship's mother and your father-in-law will be able to talk to me then."

Adam heard the irritation in the man's voice and tried to placate him.

"Certainly, Detective," he said. "I know they are anxious to get answers. We so appreciate everything you're doing. Would you like some coffee before you go?"

"No, I'm too busy for coffee. I'll be back tomorrow," said Detective Harris, turning to leave.

"Have you had any luck with the case?" Devin called after him.

"Honestly," said Harris, pausing in his step, "I don't want you to lose hope, but I am completely perplexed. We've asked Scotland Yard to come in to help us, and we are even considering asking the American FBI to help."

"The FBI!" exclaimed Adam. "But the crime happened in England, so isn't that unusual?"

"It's an unusual case," said Detective Harris. "And remember, you and all your family are still suspects and you are, after all, American citizens. Please do not be offended when I say we need to investigate everyone and every possibility. The case has us completely baffled. We can't find one shred of evidence—not in the nursery, in the house, or on the grounds. Not a fiber of clothing caught on a bush, not a footprint or fingerprint anywhere, or even a clear means of entry. The kidnapper must have come through the nursery window, but there's no sign of marks on the side of the house, forced entry through the window, or soil from shoes on the carpet—all very strange considering the kidnapper would have had to walk through the garden if he were going to scale the outside wall. Such a lack of evidence of intrusion makes us think it had to be an inside job, you understand, which is why we're very concerned, and since your mother and grandmother are American citizens and now suspects, you can understand why we felt it proper to notify the authorities in the States."

"I'm as perplexed as you are," said Adam, "but I understand. I know you're doing the best you can, Detective, and none of us feel insulted by your exploring every avenue. Anne and I just want our children back and to know they're safe."

"I don't wish to alarm you," added Detective Harris, "but with each passing day, it becomes less likely we will find your children. I just want you to be prepared for that possibility...."

Adam sat down, feigning horror at the thought, and he did not have to feign too hard for while Merlin had assured him the children were safe, Gwenhwyvach was still lurking out there somewhere.

"We'll notify you as soon as we hear something," said Harris. "And let your mother and father-in-law know I'll be here tomorrow at nine o'clock to question them."

"I certainly will, Detective. Thank you," said Adam, walking him to the door.

A minute later, Adam returned to the dining room where he found his grandmother had joined Devin. "That was a close one," said Adam.

"We better call Mary to warn her to return on the first plane," said Elizabeth.

"She has a cell phone," said Adam in agreement. "I don't know if she'll have reception, but I'll try. She and Cedric must be well over the Atlantic by now."

CHAPTER 8

ADAM DIDN'T MANAGE to speak to Cedric or his mother by phone until late that night, and only then because Mary called him to say they had landed at the Seattle airport. After Adam told her about Detective Harris' inquiries, she assured him they would be on the next plane home. Unfortunately, they had arrived in Seattle after the bank had closed, so they had to wait for morning to get the ring out of the safe-deposit box before they could return. Tonight, they were going to the site of Gwenhwyvach's prison to investigate and talk to her other keepers. Adam would just have to figure out how to stall Detective Harris from becoming suspicious for a couple of more days since, by the time they flew back tomorrow afternoon and reached home, it would be a day later in England.

Adam did not know what he could do except repeat to the detective the same story of illness from the day before. Elizabeth suggested calling in a doctor and bribing him to tell the police that Mary and Cedric were deadly ill, but they all decided it was too risky to bring a doctor into their confidence; if the doctor decided to go to the police rather than help them, it would just make everything look more suspicious.

The next morning, Adam was so nervous about having to lie again to Detective Harris about his mother and Cedric's absence that he could hardly eat. Elizabeth was also clearly nervous since she barely said a word, but Devin and Anne tried to keep up a conversation about trivial matters.

When the doorbell rang, Adam almost bolted from his chair.

"Let Robert answer it," Elizabeth told him.

"No, I told him I would answer it this morning," Adam replied.

"All right," said Elizabeth, "but remember, while it's wrong to lie, if Gwenhwyvach is as powerful as Merlin says, the fate of the human race lies in our hands, so you have to be strong. Convince the detective that Mary and Cedric are sick, and ask if you can call him when they feel up to speaking, maybe this evening. They should be home by then."

"I'll go with you," said Anne, leaning over to give Adam a quick kiss as the doorbell impatiently sounded again.

"So will I," said Devin.

Seeing the rest of her family depart the dining room, Elizabeth had also followed them into the front hall by the time Adam opened the door to greet Detective Harris.

But none of them expected what happened next.

When Adam opened the door, before he could even say, "Good morning, Detective," two policemen burst through the entrance. In a second, Adam found himself shoved against a desk in the hall as the police grappled to get a firm hold on his wrists.

"Adam Delaney, you are under arrest," said Detective Harris.

"On what charges?" demanded Devin, about ready to jump in and help his cousin fight off the police, except that his grandmother held him back.

"You are charged with aiding and abetting in a criminal act and the possible kidnapping of your own children. You have the right to remain silent. Anything you say may be given as evidence in a court of law."

"But why?" Adam asked as the police handcuffed him. "What have I done? You said yesterday there was no evidence about the kidnapping."

"Come, your lordship," growled Detective Harris, getting right up into Adam's face. "Surely, you know your mother was killed yesterday in Seattle. It's been all over the television this morning."

"Killed? But—"

"Oh, my God!" shrieked Elizabeth.

"You know I warned you not to leave the county," continued Detective Harris, "yet you not only went to Gatwick to pick up your cousin, but I suspect you also drove your mother and father-in-law there, thus aiding and abetting two of the primary suspects in this case to flee the country. As soon as the police in Seattle knew your mother's identity, the FBI realized who she was and notified us, as well as that a man fitting your father-in-law's description had been seen traveling with her by plane. We don't know yet how she died, but your father-in-law is apparently nowhere to be found, which adds to our suspicions."

"Oh, no!" cried Anne, instantly fearing for her father. Elizabeth wrapped her arm around her. Devin, meanwhile, had been furious, but the news of his aunt's death made him feel like a dog who had been ready to fight, only to have a bucket of cold water thrown on him.

"What can I do, Adam?" Devin asked.

"You can help Anne post my bail, I guess," Adam replied as the police led him off to their car.

"Where are you taking him?" cried Anne.

"To the Bordenshire County Jail while he waits for a hearing and for the judge to set bail. Don't worry, your ladyship. If he's innocent, things will work out. I'll keep you posted if we learn anything further about the kidnappings or your father's whereabouts. I'll be back to question you all further about why your family members felt the need to flee the country in this manner."

And then the detective returned to his own car, following the police who were transporting Adam.

"Great! Just bloody great!" said Adam, after he had been fingerprinted, had his mug shot taken, been told to put on prison garb, and finally been shoved into a solitary jail cell. "Goddamn, Merlin! Now look at what he's gotten me into."

"You're being kind of selfish, aren't you?" asked a voice from the lower bunk bed in the corner. Adam was a bit taken aback, not having realized he had a roommate, but he wasn't in the mood to take any crap from anyone.

"Mind your own damn business!" he barked, whirling around to look at his fellow prisoner.

His cellmate now crawled out from the bunk while saying, "Don't be so rude. I know you're a bit stressed, but—"

"Merlin!" gasped Adam, recognizing the wizard, despite his being dressed in old-fashioned, black-and-white striped prison garb, which this particular jail had not used in nearly a century. Adam's own jail clothes were dark green. "Where the hell have you been?"

Merlin stepped right up to Adam, getting into his face, and said, "Boy, when are you going to learn to respect your elders? You young American whippersnappers don't have any manners anymore. It wasn't like that in my day—not even in your grandmother's day. The world is going to hell in a handbasket."

"My mother is dead and you're giving me a lecture on manners!" exclaimed Adam, turning around and pressing his face against the jail cell bars to try to stop the tears he felt welling up. "You're unbelievable!"

"You already knew I was unbelievable," Merlin replied, "or am I? You believe in me, don't you? I'm not likely to die like some Tinkerbell just because you don't believe in fairies. Come now, my boy," he said, putting his arms around Adam's shoulders. Adam tried to shirk him off, but Merlin did not let go. "You know I love you. I wouldn't—"

"This better not be some prison love scene," Adam snapped, spinning around.

"Now you're just being insulting," said Merlin, laughing. "Besides, if I wanted some man to be my prison bitch, I could do better than you."

"Shut up!" snapped Adam. "Just shut up and get me out of here."

"Now how do you propose that I do that?" Merlin asked.

"You're a great wizard. Break us out."

"Just think of the newspaper headlines if I did that," Merlin chuckled. "Why *The Sun* would have a field day with it. I can see it now: EARL AIDED IN PRISON BREAK BY LEGENDARY WIZARD! It would sell more papers than the Prince and Princess of Wales' separation or the Camillagate tapes."

"Merlin, please," sighed Adam, crossing to the lower bunk and sitting down, "please explain all this to me. How can my mother be dead? Did Gwenhwyvach kill her?"

"I can't answer that," said Merlin, finally sounding sober. "I can only tell you that there is great evil afoot, strong evil that is blocking my vision of events. As we speak, Morgana is doing her best to counteract it so we can learn more."

"Do you know where Cedric is?"

"No, I'm afraid not," Merlin admitted. "We don't even know where Gwenhwyvach is."

"I think she's in England," said Adam. "Cedric had one of the rings, you know, but yesterday morning, it was gone when he went to take it out of his safe."

"That may be," said Merlin, going over to sit on the toilet across from the bunk beds, "but as evil as Gwenhwyvach is, I think I would sense her if she were in England."

"For God's sake," said Adam, staring over at Merlin in despair, "tell me my children are still safe."

"They are safe," said Merlin, "although I still cannot tell you where they are, for your own good as well as theirs."

"Did my mother—did she suffer—did...."

"I don't know, my boy," said Merlin, sympathy now clearly in his voice. "The police found her dead and they're investigating the cause. And I hate to tell you this, but you'd find out on the television anyway, the reason it's getting so much international attention is that she fell, either dead or alive, from the Space Needle in Seattle. No one saw her being pushed or initially fall off the observatory deck, but several people on the streets below saw her land. It was quite the mess, I imagine, considering the structure's over five hundred feet tall. But don't think of it, my boy. I suspect she was already dead before her body was tossed off the observation deck; someone was likely just trying to make it look like a suicide or an accident. Hopefully, she didn't suffer much."

Adam was devastated to think of his mother dying in such a manner. He had only had a relationship with her for a little over a year, so he had still been looking forward to becoming closer to her. Never, if she had not told him, would he have imagined the secrets his mother had held, secrets that had kept her from being a mother to him all these years, and now, her secret had doubtless killed her.

"Adam, my boy," said Merlin. "You may not think this is the place or time, but there is more you need to know about the past and your family history. I told you that the tale of Ogier the Dane was vital to this story."

As Merlin spoke, he put his hand in front of his face, palm open, and blew some dust across the room in Adam's direction.

"Merlin, I don't think—" Adam began, but before he could finish, he found himself yawning.

"Aha! I knew you were sleepy," said Merlin. "Devin and Anne will have to wait hours before they'll be able to post your bail, so what better way to spend that time than with a story; oh, I know you might not think it the appropriate time, but I always do find a good story so very comforting, and I'm sure you do, too, when you allow yourself to escape into it, so let's have no more dilly-dallying and get right to it, shall we?"

"Whatever you say, Merlin," said Adam, suddenly much too sleepy to argue.

Merlin came over to the bed and gave Adam a little nudge to get him to lie down. Then he lifted Adam's feet up onto the bed and tucked a blanket around him.

"Now," said Merlin, once Adam had closed his eyes, "the tale of Ogier the Dane. Our story opens in Baghdad circa the year 803 A.D. Ogier the Dane has just been brought to the court of the great potentate,

Caliph Haroun al-Rashid, perhaps the most powerful man in the world and ruler of the Abbasid Caliphate, which at the time composed most of the Middle East and Northern Africa and superseded in power even that of Charlemagne's Holy Roman Empire or the slowly crumbling Byzantine Empire.

"Now, the caliph always loved a good story, just like me, so when he saw the strange appearance of the tall, blue-eyed, fair-haired hero Ogier the Dane in his kingdom, he was curious to know how such a man, one of the greatest and most renowned knights of Charlemagne's court, should come to arrive in his capital at the center of his kingdom—especially since Ogier had entered Baghdad on a magical flying carpet. Naturally, the caliph questioned Ogier on this matter, and Ogier agreed to satisfy his curiosity by telling his life story, and so, our story, as told in Ogier's own words, begins...."

PART II

THE TALE OF OGIER THE DANE

CHAPTER 1

IN THE GREATEST palace in Baghdad sat Caliph Haroun al-Rashid upon his magnificent throne. The caliph was regal and handsome in appearance, with dark hair and olive skin, and impeccable manners. He was entertaining a foreign guest, who sat in a smaller chair before him, and whose appearance was in stark contrast to his own. This guest was Ogier the Dane, a knight of renown from Charlemagne's court and a prince in his own right. Ogier was some years older than the caliph, who had attained his fortieth year, but he was in the full strength of his manhood; his once bright blonde hair had been bleached by the hot southern sun; his formerly fair skin was now ruddy red and spoke to his many years of traveling far from his northern home. Ogier had become the caliph's guest after his arrival in Baghdad, on a flying magical carpet, had caused the caliph's guards to arrest him and bring him to the palace. The caliph had found himself very curious about this exotic visitor, and so with little prodding, Ogier had agreed to tell Haroun al-Rashid the story of his life, beginning with his birth, as follows:

OGIER'S TALE

Great Caliph, as you have suspected, I am not of humble or poor origins, but rather, I was born a prince to the King and Queen of Denmark, and it is there I must begin my tale, for almost from the moment of my birth, strange and wonderful things have happened to me that I understand are not the lot of common men.

I was known in my own country as Prince Holger, but later when I went to Charlemagne's court—a tale I will tell in due time—I became known as Ogier le Danois, and so as Ogier the Dane I am best known today.

The first remarkable occurrence of my life took place when I was just days old, during my initial presentation to the court; it was not the day of my baptism or christening as the Christians would call it—for my parents and all of Denmark in those days were followers of the old Gods, Odin and Thor and all those who dwelled in the halls of Asgaard—but it was the day I was named and presented to the court as my father's son and heir.

Although it was a great day of celebration, considering that an heir had been born to the king, the presentation was not expected to be anything beyond the ordinary for such events. But it soon became an extraordinary day because of a visit from unexpected guests. I remember little of the early years of my life, but that day, as I lay in my mother's arms, facing the court, I witnessed such marvelous events that even a mere babe could not forget them.

My memory of that day begins just as my father presented me to the court, and the nobles and his other liegemen had formed a line to pay me homage and to swear to serve my father, the king, and his newborn heir. In the midst of this ceremony, first faintly, then growing ever louder, came the sweetest music that mortals ever heard. It seemed to originate from right outside the castle wall, but then it soared, as if carried on the wind, through the open window, and into the throne room. Nobody knew from whence such bewitching sounds could come, but many murmured how the music was so heavenly that they could only think we were to be visited by an angel.

But that misperception was soon corrected when through the window floated six female fairies. Each bore in her hands a garland of flowers and rich gifts of gold, gems, and other priceless valuables. I will never forget, from where I sat upon my mother's lap, the sight of these lovely creatures. They were so beautiful and so aglow with light that the courtiers later admitted to feeling great awe and fear at the sight of them, but I only laughed with glee to see their radiant beauty, and I felt a great happiness descend upon me.

My mother, however, seemed afraid of the fairies' presence, for I could feel her trembling once they had positioned themselves before the throne, the crowd having drawn back to provide a place for them to land, but instead, these six gracious beings hovered a few inches above the floor, their gossamer wings making a gentle, quiet, and cooling breeze.

Then the first fairy approached my mother and me, and said, "Fear not, good queen. We are here to bestow blessings upon your son."

The fairy took me in her arms, kissed me upon my forehead, and said, facing the court so all could hear, "Better than kingly crown, or lands, or rich heritage, fair babe, I give thee a brave, strong heart. Be fearless as the eagle, and bold as the lion; be the bravest knight among men."

I remember feeling such deep peace, and at the same time, such joy as she held me in her arms, and that peace and joy continued as I was passed into the arms of each of the fairies in turn.

When the second fairy took me into her arms, she sat down on my mother's throne for my mother had risen and later stepped aside when the first fairy approached, and though it would have been treason for anyone else to sit on my mother's throne, not a word was spoken when this fairy did so. For a moment, she dandled me fondly upon her knee, giggling with me, and then she looked me in the eye long and lovingly before she said, "What is a brave heart without the ability to do brave deeds? I give to thee many an opportunity for manly action."

The third fairy then approached while I was yet on the second fairy's knee, and kneeling before me, she took one of my hands in her own, and with her other hand, she stroked my hair, saying, "Strong-hearted boy, for whom so many noble deeds are waiting, I, too, will give thee a boon. My gift is skill and strength such as shall never fail thee in fight, nor allow thee to be beaten by a foe. Success to thee, fair Holger!"

The fourth fairy then took me from the second, who, with the third fairy, returned to her sisters, and this fairy then tenderly stroked my mouth and my brow before she said, "Be fair of speech, be noble in action, be courteous, be kind: these are the gifts I bring thee. For what will a strong heart, or a bold undertaking, or success in every endeavor, avail, unless one has the respect and love of one's fellow men?"

Then the fifth fairy came forward; she clasped me against her breast and held me tenderly for a long time without saying a word. Finally, she looked at all the court, and she then held me away from her so she could look into my eyes and said, "The gifts my sisters have given thee will scarcely bring thee happiness, for, while they add to thy honor, they may make thee dangerous to others. They may lead thee into the practice of selfishness and base acts of tyranny. That man is little to be envied who loves not his fellow men. The boon, therefore, that I bring thee is the power and the will to esteem others as frail mortals equally deserving with thyself."

And then the sixth fairy, the most beautiful of all, took me from the fifth; she lifted me high and danced about the room with me in rapturous joy, all the while singing sweetly a lullaby of fairyland and the island vale of Avalon, and then, although she never said her name, somehow I and all the court knew she was that fabled one, Morgan le Fay, sister to the great King Arthur and the Queen of Avalon.

When she had finished singing, Morgan le Fay placed a crown of laurel upon my head, and then a fairy torch appeared in her hand; when it lit by itself, it created a gasp of astonishment from all assembled. And then the Queen of Avalon said, "This torch is the measure of thy earthly days; and it shall not cease to burn until thou hast visited me in Avalon, and sat at table with King Arthur and the heroes who dwell there in that eternal summerland."

And then Morgan le Fay gently placed me back into my mother's arms, and with the torch still in her hand, she and the other fairies strewed the floor of the throne room with rich flowers and gems until all the air was filled with perfume and the angelic music resumed, and suddenly, a radiant sunbeam broke through the open windows until the room grew brighter and brighter and the light forced all to close their eyes, and at that moment, the music ended. After a second, when everyone opened his or her eyes, the fairies were nowhere to be seen, although the flowers and jewels remained.

And then I felt a great coldness come over me for the fairy's blessings and their prophecies of my future fortune and mighty deeds were all that a mother could ever desire for her child, and this overwhelming joy must have filled my mother's heart until it could not be contained and thereby burst. And in another second, my nurse ran to catch me as I tumbled from my mother's lifeless arms.

HAROUN AL-RASHID INTERRUPTS

"It is an astonishing and yet heartbreaking tale," said the caliph, his face bright with joy while his eyes sparkled with tears.

Ogier nodded his head in agreement and after taking a sip of his wine, he continued.

OGIER'S TALE CONTINUES

Yes, and that is but the beginning, Great Caliph. Let me tell you how I used the fairies' gifts and how the prophecies they made were fulfilled.

CHAPTER 2

ALTHOUGH I WAS to grow up motherless, I was lovingly cared for by my nurses. While these good women much petted me, my father made sure I was not spoiled or coddled too much so I learned to respect my elders and all people. To fulfill this goal, my father lured to his court the wisest men from the surrounding lands to be my tutors, and so I learned everything that could be known at that time in a kingdom on the edge of civilization where the Christ's religion had not yet spread; I did learn a little of the Christ from my tutors, but also much of Rome and Greece's heroes and Gods; still, I admit I much preferred the wondrous tales of my forefathers' Norse Gods. I was also taught history, and what little of mathematics my tutors understood so that I believe I had an education to be envied by most, although certainly not equal to those wise men of your own empire, Great Caliph, for I understand much of the West's knowledge was lost with the collapse of Rome, but it is still preserved here in the East. Despite whatever ignorance I may retain, I have always had the greatest respect for learning, even if my own inclinations have always been toward more manly pursuits.

While my father felt my scholarly endeavors were necessary, he only allowed a few hours a day for them, for a king is also a warrior, and so a prince must be trained in all exercises befitting a knight and future king. My instructors and all those whom I engaged in mock tournaments acknowledged that I was becoming a fine horseman, and they predicted that few would be so swift with a sword in the years to come. Needless to say, I grew to be tall and strong, and at least in the opinions of the ladies, handsome. But I took most pride in hearing a member of the court remark on my wisdom and common sense, and how one day I would have a great and glorious reign as king.

My father, perhaps determined to give me all I deserved, but also perhaps not ready to live in my shadow, now sought to extend his borders to create a mighty empire in the north. In those years, Charlemagne was himself just beginning to extend his own borders, and consequently, you can imagine the conflict that soon ensued between my father and that most Christian king.

But a greater conflict existed for me at home, for I had but barely begun to grow hair upon my chin when my father remarried. This marriage was to change my destiny, and it came about as a result of my father's conflict with Charlemagne. At that time, the King of the Franks dispatched an embassy of a hundred knights, led by one of his chief nobles, Ganelon, Duke of Mayence, to settle a border dispute between my father's kingdom of Denmark and his own growing empire.

Now my father had no desire to display anything but strength to Charlemagne's men, seeking to send them home in awe and fear of his power, but he was also terribly lonely, having lost my mother so many years before. Many of his nobles and the neighboring kings had sent their daughters to vie for my father's hand, but he had no desire to marry some foolish princess who would babble non-stop, as most women do, and be of little use to him in bearing the weight of a crown.

In those days, women were seldom sent as emissaries, but Duke Ganelon had been accompanied by his sister, the Lady Guntheuc, on his mission. This lady's courage in making such a journey, as well as her affectionate devotion to her brother, and most significantly, her stunning beauty—for she was of a darker complexion and looked quite exotic compared to the fair-skinned and blonde women of our northern lands—immediately won my father's heart. He soon so desperately desired her that he struggled to convince her brother to give him her hand in marriage.

I was astonished to see my father fall so in love, but having heard from his own lips how much he had loved my mother, and not really having known a mother myself, I could not help but wish him happiness; I even thought I might not mind having a new mother. Furthermore, I had heard of Charlemagne's great power and the fates of those who fought against him, their kingdoms vanquished, their lives lived out as exiles, if they even lived, and so I knew, despite my father's pride, that he could not hope to get the best of this great king. Now, let it be known that I am no coward, but while I did not wish to see my father bend the knee to Charlemagne, neither did I wish him to lose his own kingdom and make us all subject to the Franks. And so I decided it was in the best interests of myself, my father, and all of Denmark that I encourage him to make peace with Charlemagne and marry Lady Guntheuc. My father was quite pleased by my encouragement, and so within a couple of weeks of having first met her, he asked Lady Guntheuc to be his queen. But Ganelon was such a shrewd negotiator that he would not surrender his sister's hand without having his own desires met, and those desires were all to please his lord, Charlemagne. And so, thinking more of love than war, my father quickly conceded to all of Charlemagne's demands, including a yearly tribute, and he received a bride in return.

A wedding and feast ensued. Then the day after the marriage, at my father's insistence, his new wife traded her Frankish name for a Danish one to please her new subjects, and that same day, she was crowned as Queen Gudrun. A week of festivities followed, and then, with peace treaty in hand, Duke Ganelon and his knights returned to Charlemagne's court.

For a short time, all went well with my father and his new wife. Queen Gudrun proved to be fertile, quickly producing a second son for my father, my brother Guyon. But once she had a child of her own, she changed from a loving wife into a protective mother. While she feigned appropriate submission to my father's will, she was now sharp of tongue toward anyone who displeased her and unforgiving to any of my father's advisors who thwarted her will. Nor did it take long for her to decide, in her desire to promote her own son's interests, that I was her enemy.

Soon my stepmother had turned my father against me, making him jealous of how the people loved me, and even insinuating that I was plotting against him, although I was hardly more than a boy. Goaded on by her, my father gradually became cruel toward me; he often embarrassed me before the court, upbraiding me over the smallest of my faults, and he stationed a guard at my door, not for my protection, but I am sure, to spy on me and ensure I committed no treason. I was greatly hurt by this change in his affections, thinking he should know me better, but my stepmother's will was clearly stronger than his own. I could only hope that in time my unceasing love and loyalty toward him would convince him how groundless her accusations were. I also grew very attached to my little brother, thinking I must model good behavior for him since our father paid little attention to him and his mother was hardly a good role model. He was an affectionate boy toward me, and so, I was determined not to hold his parentage against him.

But my stepmother was relentless. Determined to be rid of me, she turned her ire toward my father, telling him he had been cowardly to concede so easily to Charlemagne's demands with no thought for his sons' inheritance; she claimed her own brother had falsely represented Charlemagne's power, and that my father had no reason to fear the King of the Franks. The result of this badgering was my father ceasing to pay the annual tribute money to Charlemagne.

This violation of the peace treaty caused Charlemagne again to send Duke Ganelon to our court, hoping the duke, as my father's brother-in-law, could yet reason with him and prevent war between their armies. But encouraged by my stepmother, my father held strong and even went so far as to belittle Charlemagne in front of Duke Ganelon. He said he had reason to believe all Charlemagne's claims to greatness were highly exaggerated, and then he showed the duke not only all the wealth of his treasure room, but he brought the duke and his men to his armory to see how many soldiers and weapons of war he had, and he showed him all of the castle's fortifications. "Tell Charlemagne," he told Duke Ganelon, "that I have a hundred such castles in Denmark, and not one of them has ever been surprised or taken by a foe." Then my father marched before the duke his army of ten thousand knights, clad in armor and mounted on powerful war steeds. "Inform Charlemagne," he added, "that I have ten times this many soldiers in my army and countless men throughout Denmark who will come at my summons, so if he wishes to learn which of us is the true master, I am ready to meet him."

Ganelon could not believe his ears. When he was finally able to speak, swallowing his astonishment, he begged his sister to speak reason to her husband. She, however, replied, "Denmark, not France, is my country now, and I will not see my people bend the knee to a Frankish tyrant." Then she made a shocking display of publicly spitting in her brother's face and telling him, "Go back to your king, little man, and tell him you have seen in the north a king like no other on this earth."

"I shall gladly, Sister," said Ganelon, wiping the spit from his nose. But while I expected anger to show on his face, instead, I saw a gleam in his eye so shocking that it made me turn to look at her to see how she received it. And I was even more surprised by the smirk on her face, as if they were enjoying a private joke between them. Then I grew suspicious; could this foreign brother and sister be plotting against my father? Might they even be plotting against my father and Charlemagne both? Was their behavior all a ruse to aggravate both rulers, and thereby, gain from what was left after these two great kings destroyed each other?

Needless to say, Charlemagne was enraged when Duke Ganelon delivered my father's boastful message. Immediately, he assembled an army of fifty thousand men and marched north with them to chastise my father. A terrible battle was fought on the border between their kingdoms. The ten thousand knights my father had paraded before Ganelon, saying they were but a small number of his resources, were, in truth, his entire army, and they were no match for Charlemagne's well-trained men. Within a couple of hours, the Danes were in retreat, but not before Charlemagne himself captured my father on the battlefield.

Our country had fallen to the Frankish king, and Charlemagne could have been far more vengeful than he was, but he thought less of his pride than the welfare of the Holy Church, so while he stripped my father of the title of king, he agreed to let my father continue to hold his lands as his vassal, the Duke of Denmark, in exchange that my father and all the Danes convert to Christianity.

Charlemagne also increased the yearly tribute he be paid to three times what it had previously been. Then, as a final show of his power, he ordered that the flower of Denmark's young men be sent to France to train as part of his army. Included among those young men was to be myself, no longer Prince Holger, but still the heir to a dukedom, should my father and I both remain obedient to our new overlord.

My stepmother, in tears—I suspect she could turn them on and off like a fountain—urged my father to concede to all of Charlemagne's terms. He hesitated, however, when it came to sending me as a hostage. Then in my very presence, my stepmother replied, "Holger has been nothing but bad luck for us. King Charles wishes us to be Christians, and Christians do not make alliances with pagan fairies, who are an abomination to the Holy Catholic Church and who seek to control Holger and you, for I have heard how at his birth they swore Holger would serve them. It can only be for the best that your son be sent away. Then perhaps the Christian God will have mercy upon us, for He is clearly greater than your own Gods of the North."

I was not surprised by my stepmother's words, or my father caving to her wishes. Honestly, I was thankful to leave them both. At least now I would serve a true king, one who was noble and strong, and not the puppet of a jealous woman. Nevertheless, I vowed I would one day return to Denmark to restore my father's throne and claim it for my own; how I would do that without rebelling against my lord Charlemagne, I did not know, but for the time being, I was content to let my fate be what it would.

My arrival at Charlemagne's court was difficult at first. I had no qualms with serving a king whom I admired for his power, but many of his knights and my fellow squires looked down upon me as a conquered enemy. I also initially resented when they refused to call me by my proper name, using their own Frankish version of it so that I became known as Ogier. Later upon reflection, I realized my name was more difficult for them to pronounce in their own tongue, but at first, I took umbrage at their decision of how I should be addressed.

Only the king's nephew, Roland, newly come to the court himself after having been raised in poverty and obscurity, befriended me. He and I were of the same age, and he was a squire in the household of Duke Namon of Bavaria. We became fast friends, and he quickly convinced the duke to make me one of his squires, for which I was grateful. Duke Namon was a wise and good man, and one of Charlemagne's most trusted counselors, and Roland was a true friend to me, one I saw as equally strong and skilled in arms, and so I was happy to be in their company. Together, at the duke's castle, Roland and I were educated, and we trained together daily, pledging always to be brothers in arms. And so for a short time, I was happy with my lot, while I waited for bigger and better things to come my way.

CHAPTER 3

B Y THE TIME I was eighteen, I excelled at all feats of arms and was greatly admired in the kingdom not only by my fellow squires but many of the king's best knights. Any old animosity felt toward me as the son of a conquered enemy had been forgotten, and believing myself truly among friends, I looked forward to the day I would be knighted and could lead an army for my father or Charlemagne, for my only distress was a feeling of my loyalty being divided between them.

That said, my father made no effort to recall me home or even to ensure my safety. After a few years, he again decided to try Charlemagne's patience by not paying the tribute. I have always suspected that Queen Gudrun was behind this decision and that she hoped to anger Charlemagne enough that he would put me to death, since despite my skill at arms and promise of being a valiant knight, I was still a hostage in a foreign land.

Finally, Charlemagne's patience with my father came to an end. He had waited months for the tribute to be paid, and he also was angered that my father had never come to his court to pay him homage. Frustrated, Charlemagne sent one last embassy to my father, demanding he come to him, with tribute in hand.

The embassy left for Denmark in the autumn, and when winter came early without any word being sent back, everyone assumed the roads were simply too treacherous for the men to return until spring. When the snows did begin melting and the time of Easter approached, Charlemagne decided to visit the town of St. Omer, where good Archbishop Turpin was preparing to celebrate the sacred feast with all due reverence and grandeur. The entire court gathered for the celebrations, including the king, queen, Princes Charlot and Louis, the princesses, and many nobles. Among the nobles was Duke Ganelon of Mayence along with his wife, the Princess Bertha, who was Charlemagne's sister and my friend Roland's mother; the princess had married the duke after her reconciliation with Charlemagne, following the death of her first husband, Roland's father, Sir Milon. And, of course, also in attendance that Easter were Duke Namon and many from his household, Roland and myself among them.

It was on the day before Easter, when all were looking forward to the celebrations, that the ambassadors whom Charlemagne had sent to my father's court returned. As they entered the king's presence, a great stir and muttering among all the court could be heard, and as they walked past me, I was shocked to see their bare faces.

"Sire," said the chief ambassador, "as you can see before you, we return, our beards shaved, our heads tonsured. Barely did we escape with our lives. We were locked up as prisoners throughout the winter, some of us tortured, and finally, we were released with this message from the Duke of Denmark: 'Tell your king that the King of Denmark'—my apologies, Sire, but he has taken to styling himself as such again—'the King of Denmark is no man's thrall and never will he do homage or pay a penny of tribute to any foreign tyrant.'"

All the court stood wide-eyed at these words, and silence descended as they watched Charlemagne's face turn red with wrath.

"The fool is insufferable!" Charlemagne exclaimed. "If he will treat my men in such a manner, then he can expect no goodwill from me toward his own at my court." Such words made me long to hide, for I knew they were directed toward me. But having been born a prince, even if my title had been taken from me, I would not act as a coward. I waited for Charlemagne's eye to fall upon me, and then, as expected, he said, "Guards, immediately place Prince Ogier and the other Danes in my court in prison. And prepare them for their deaths."

Everyone present gasped at this dreadful sentence, and I myself felt sick at the words, but I did not struggle or seek to flee when the guards bound me in chains. As I was led away, I heard Duke Namon pleading for my life, but the guards hustled me along regardless, and I soon found myself in the dungeon of St. Omer.

Later that same evening, Roland managed to visit me and told me the king had declared that once Easter week was past, I was to be hung before all the people. Meanwhile, Charlemagne was summoning all able-bodied men from all ends of his kingdom to march against my father.

I was certain there was no escaping my death, so I prepared myself to die honorably as a Prince of Denmark, refusing to see even a priest, for if I were to be Charlemagne's enemy, I would never partake of his religion, and so far, I had successfully avoided being baptized into a faith I did not believe. I admit to having been curious at first about Christianity, even going with the rest of Duke Namon's household to Mass for a time, but my curiosity did not last long, for most days it was all I could do to stay awake through the priest's long nasally chanting.

But, Great Caliph, in that moment, and believe it or not, by those of your own faith's actions, I was rescued from death. For just as Archbishop Turpin was finishing the Easter Mass, messengers arrived in great haste with letters from Pope Hadrian, and when those letters were read, all of Charlemagne's interest in fighting my father disappeared because a greater threat demanded his attention.

The Pope begged Charlemagne to come immediately to Rome's aid, for the Saracens had landed in Italy and taken Rome by assault. "I and the cardinals and other leaders of Rome have all fled to a place of safety," said the Pope's letter. "The churches have been torn down, the holy relics desecrated, and Christians put to the sword. I charge you, as a Christian king, to march at once to the succor of our Holy Mother Church."

As angry as Charlemagne was with my father, he was indeed the great Defender of the Christian Faith, and no other concern could equal for him that of protecting Rome and the Church. The king proclaimed that the army assembling to attack Denmark would instead set out tomorrow for Italy, the fight against my native country postponed for now.

"What shall we do with Ogier and the other Danish hostages?" Duke Namon reportedly asked the king, hoping for their release, but Charlemagne said, "They will all remain in prison except for Ogier; however, I fear you are too fond of him, Namon, so I will ask Duke Ganelon to take charge of him and bring him to Rome. Then after the Saracens are driven from the city, there will be time to hang him with the other pagans."

Roland told me of this conversation once I was released from prison. Although I was happy to retain my life, I did not relish the prolonging of my agony, yet I felt Fate or the Gods must have a plan for me if my death were to be delayed, even if it be the result of the Saracens' actions. Strange as it may sound, Great Caliph, I have felt a fondness toward the people of the Muslim faith ever since.

The following morning, I was released from prison in time to depart with the army. I was allowed to ride my own horse, but I rode among Duke Ganelon's men, his squires guarding me, and I the only one among the army not allowed to carry arms.

I need not detail for you the difficulties of long journeys, especially those over mountains. We spent many days traveling across France and over the Alps, and yet we made the greatest haste we could to rescue the people of Rome. As we marched, the army increased as more and more men joined us in each village and town where we stopped, in response to the king's earlier summons and the news that the Saracens had captured Rome. And when we reached the Alps, the Pope's messengers again met us, urging us to hasten.

Long and tedious was that journey, especially in knowing that every hour a Saracen could be slaying a Christian or burning a church, or so at least was the king and his army's concern, while I rode on, a prisoner, not even allowed to speak to my friend Roland or to kind Duke Namon, and granted only sufficient food to continue my journey. Each day, I looked for a way I might escape, but none presented itself, and each evening, I was chained and a guard was posted to keep watch over me in the camp.

Finally, the army descended from the Alps and into the beautiful land of Italy's Piedmont region, and that night, all were given the opportunity to rest from their travels, and much merriment and boasting filled the camp at the prospect of soon arriving in Rome to defeat the Saracens and send them scurrying back over the Mediterranean Sea.

I did not doubt the men had reason to celebrate, but to me, our arrival in Italy made no difference. I felt especially melancholic, for while we had been traveling, I had yet felt hopeful for my life, but now we would soon arrive at Rome, and while I had never seen a Saracen army, I also knew Charlemagne's soldiers had never been defeated, and so it would not be long before Rome was returned to Christian hands, and then my fate would be sealed.

And I could not help wondering how my father, even with my stepmother's influence, could care so little for my welfare that he would continue to anger Charlemagne, putting my life and the lives of all his people in jeopardy for his foolish pride.

My misery was soon distracted when a soldier entered my tent, accompanied by two of Ganelon's squires who had also been among my guards. "You have been summoned to appear before the king," said the messenger as one squire released me from my chains while the other watched me with his sword. I did not feel threatened by the squire, for I knew I could best him in swordplay, and I probably could have wrestled the sword from him before he could react, but I doubted I could escape from the camp with so many men in it. If the king now summoned me to my death, then so be it.

I marched with the soldier and squires, both now bearing their swords, to the king's tent. When I entered it, great trepidation filled my heart, but I refused to let it manifest upon my face.

I found the king surrounded by his peers, including Duke Namon, who nodded to me with a smile that told me to fear not. Then Roland stepped forward, and taking a harp from the court minstrel's hand, he passed it to me and said, "My uncle, the king, wishes you to entertain us as we celebrate our arrival in Italy by singing one of the songs of your country."

Now, I had heard the bards sing many times back in Denmark, and I had been trained in singing myself, but I had never performed before anyone. Nevertheless, bowing low before the king, I took the harp in my hands.

I knew I was among Christians, but I refused to sing one of their songs. I was a son of Denmark, where we worshipped Odin, and no songs were so great as the sagas of our Gods, and so both out of spite and my great love for those songs, I sang of the creation of the world, of the Norse Gods, of the great tree Yggdrasil upon which the world sits, and then I sang of Balder the Beautiful, son of Odin, whom none could harm until the mischief-making god Loki encouraged blind Hod to throw at him a bow of mistletoe, the only item that could harm him, and thereby caused his death. I sang of how from that event came the great Ragnarok, the battle of the Gods, and the final destruction of Asgaard, home of the Gods.

And as I sang, I saw that I had my listeners within my power, completely under my spell. I saw that they were helpless to move, to stop listening, to object to my story, even though it was a pagan tale and in conflict with their own belief in a time they called Armageddon, when the world would be destroyed and only those who believed in the Christ would be taken to Heaven, a place I was certain paled in comparison to Valhalla, resting place of the great Norse heroes.

I sang next of Thor and Odin and all the Gods battling against Loki and his children—Fenrir, the great wolf, and Jormungandr, the serpent, who was so large that he surrounded the earth and grasped his own tail, holding the world so tightly that if he should die, it would fall. I sang of how Fenrir's children swallowed the sun and the moon, and then the stars disappeared and the earth shook so that trees broke forth from it and the mountains toppled.

And I saw how my audience looked terrified, my every word making their hearts beat in fearful suspense.

I sang of how Jormungandr sprayed forth his venom throughout the air and into the sea until the sky split in two, and I sang of how the great tree Yggdrasil, upon which all the worlds existed, would shake, causing havoc for everyone.

I sang of Thor and Odin going to battle, of how Thor finally slew the serpent Jormungandr, but not before the serpent had poisoned him, leaving him to fall dead to the earth. I sang of how Fenrir swallowed Odin, only to be killed by his own son. I sang of the destruction of everything until Ragnarok was completed and all the world destroyed.

And then in the shocked silence that followed, I slowly began to sing of the new world that would arise. I sang of how the earth would reappear from out of the sea, and of how Lif and Lifthrasir, the only humans to survive, would come forth nourishing themselves on the morning dew, and of how their descendants would one day repopulate the world, and of how a beautiful daughter of the sun would rise to give the earth warmth again, and so the cycle of life would continue.

And I ended my song on a haughty note, saying, "Who is man to know the future, who is he to predict or even imagine what the Gods might do? And yet the myths of my people tell us that life will always continue, that all our fears are for naught, for even if the Gods themselves should be destroyed, we shall go on."

And when I had finished the song, a great murmur of pleasure rose throughout the tent, followed by cheering from the men. I had held them all spellbound, but I did not expect their praise for my song, nor did their opinions matter beside that of the king. As I sang, despite my boldness, I had never once looked at Charlemagne for fear his displeasure would cause me to end mid-song. But now as I looked at the king, I saw a tear upon his cheek.

And then he rose, and stepping toward me, he said, "Young prince, you sing remarkably well, and I would reward thee for the pleasure you have given us. Therefore, I give you reprieve of your life until we return to France."

I bowed to the king, as if in appreciation, yet I thought what a sorry prize he gave me, for the death sentence remained and was only delayed; still, I felt hope that I could yet escape death. But I did not plan to attempt flight, for that would leave me only an outcast among men. Rather I felt if the song of my Gods could move the hearts of the Franks, then surely, my Gods were with me, and somehow, they would deliver me from this situation.

"My lord," said Roland, kneeling then before his uncle, "I beg you, grant a full pardon to Ogier and you will not regret it, for he is the mightiest and most skilled in swordplay of all the squires; no doubt he will do great honor to your crown if you free him from this death sentence. I would pledge my own life that he will not betray you in any way."

And in seeing how my friend risked the king's wrath for me, I knew in my heart I would be loyal to Charlemagne if he did grant me full reprieve.

But Charlemagne inhaled through his nostrils and held his tongue for a minute before saying, "No, nephew, it cannot be unless his father should make good on his promises and bend the knee in homage to me as is his duty." Then he bid me be returned to my tent and kept under guard.

The next morning, Roland and one of Duke Namon's other squires entered my tent to tell me that, with the king's permission, I was to be returned to Duke Namon's care. This turn of events was no lessening of my sentence, however, for the Duke's nephew, who had accompanied us on the campaign, had fallen ill, so I had been chosen to be his nursemaid. Nevertheless, I was greatly pleased for Duke Ganelon's men had been rude and rough with me, forcing me to tolerate their occasional blows and frequent harsh words, but now I would be among friends again. So even if my days remained numbered, my spirits began to lift, and I knew Fate might yet intervene in mysterious ways once we reached Rome to face the Saracens.

CHAPTER 4

T HE NEXT MORNING, before Charlemagne's army could even begin to march, more messengers came from the Pope, praying for Charlemagne to move quickly. "The heathen are triumphing!" they cried. "The Holy Father begs you to hurry. They are putting all the Christians to the sword."

Enraged, Charlemagne ordered his army to move forward, and soon I found myself back in the saddle with my old friend Roland by my side. No longer feeling like a hostage, despite my impending death upon our return to France, I was eager to fight. Roland and I both lamented that because we were not yet knights, we would have to stand back, not taking any active part in the battle while letting the knights we served receive all the glory.

In truth, Roland was madly eager for a fight, boasting what he would do to the pagan enemy if he only had the chance. I did not feel such loyalty or religious fervor, but fame was my whole desire, as I admitted to him, saying, "What makes me unhappiest is that soon my life will have ended, and yet I have not in any way distinguished myself in arms. What more is there to live for than to make a famous name for myself since my father has forsaken me and I am a hostage in a strange land? And what could be more glorious and honorable than to have my name remembered after me? For nothing but fame lasts in this world."

"You will not die without having proven yourself, Ogier," Roland assured me. "I will continue to intercede with my uncle to spare your life; let us wait until he defeats the pagans and is in a good mood and willing to grant me a boon. Then I will persuade him to knight you so that you have nothing but a long life and great deeds to look forward to."

I again thanked my friend, but I remained skeptical, and I doubted whether the king, who claimed to be the bastion of Christianity, would follow the example of forgiveness that his religion's progenitor had modeled.

Soon the army arrived at Sutri. Roland now became full of chatter, pointing out to me all the places he had known in his boyhood there, beginning with the rocky hilltop where he said he had first watched Charlemagne's approach with his childhood friend Oliver, who was also a squire in Duke Ganelon's household and traveling with us to Rome. Then he pointed out the castle of Count Rainier, Oliver's father, where Roland had gone and declared to Charlemagne that he was his nephew. That courageous act had led to the king forgiving Roland's mother for their old feud over her marriage to Roland's father, although Roland did not explain to me what Charlemagne's objection had been.

It was enough for me to know that Charlemagne had forgiven Roland's mother, so perhaps he was capable of forgiveness, although forgiving one's sister was far different from forgiving one's enemy's son.

After passing through Sutri, our army was nearly halfway to Rome when the Saracen host came riding toward us, ready to engage us in battle. Charlemagne decided to attack them at once and charged Duke Namon with leading the army. While Roland, Oliver, and I were of the duke's company, because we were only squires, we were left in the rear to watch the battle without partaking in it, so you can imagine our disappointment.

Among the men with the army was an Italian named Alory. Because we were in his native land, he had been given the honor of bearing Charlemagne's standard, the sacred Oriflamme. As the battle began, we watched the standard progress across the field, with Duke Namon and the bravest of the Franks following behind it. Upon our army's first assault, the Saracens fell back in confusion and the Franks marched forward, prepared to take the day, but after a short while, the Saracens held their ground. Then fear struck Alory's heart, and showing his true colors, he and his Lombard companions turned and fled the battlefield, carrying the Oriflamme with them. When the Saracens saw the Oriflamme moving away from them, they were convinced the enemy was in retreat, and the Franks became confused to see the Oriflamme departing in the distance when they had not heard the call for retreat.

Roland and I stood, astonished by what we saw. Because of Alory's fear, Duke Namon was soon surrounded by the Saracens and taken prisoner, and then we saw Charlemagne himself nearly knocked from his horse. At that point, I burst with rage and lost all self-control.

"Roland, we must go to their aid!" I exclaimed, and then I raced across the field, Roland but one step behind me, and our fellow squires gladly running to assist us. We ran straight toward Alory and the Lombards, who were fleeing in our direction with the Oriflamme.

As these cowards came up the hill on horseback, Roland and I charged toward them, shouting, "Turn back, cowards! Go back and fight!"

"We are bested!" exclaimed Alory, panic written across his face. "Death awaits us if we go back."

"Better to die with honor," declared Roland, "than flee as cowards!"

"By Thor," I shouted, "you will die, Alory, if you do not go back, for I will slay you myself!"

Alory's look of fear now turned to one of disgust as he responded, "You are but a squire, a boy. You have no business speaking to a knight like myself in such a manner. Now step aside or I will run you down," and setting spurs to his horse, he sought to ride past me.

But I ran forward and grabbed his horse's bridle, forcing his steed to a halt, and then I reached up and yanked Alory from his saddle. The man toppled to the ground, but his wounded pride quickly set him on his feet, and he drew forth his sword as I was about to mount his horse to join the battle. When from the corner of my eye I saw the flash of his sword, I turned, and having no weapon of my own, I ran forward, ducked under his sword, and struck his jaw with my fist, landing him on the ground so violently that he was too weak to regain his feet for several minutes. I now grabbed his sword and the Oriflamme, which lay on the ground, and mounted his horse.

"Come, fellow squires!" exclaimed Roland. "We will fight for Charlemagne, France, and the Holy Church!" Then ripping a sword from a mounted Lombard, Roland demanded that the soldier surrender his horse and armor. In a matter of moments, the other squires and I had stripped the Lombards of their armor, their weapons, and their horses. Then charging across the battlefield, Roland and I led our unlikely band to the king's aid while the cowardly Lombards ran into the hills, seeking caves to hide in since they had no armor or weapons with which to defend themselves.

By this time, over half of Charlemagne's army had fled or been killed because of the confusion. The Saracens were beginning to congratulate themselves on an easy victory, and doubtless, they were envisioning how they would soon rule Rome and feed all the Christians to the lions in the Coliseum, or so I thought at the time. I must pause here, Great Caliph, to apologize for any misguided words I may say toward your Muslim brothers at this time, for I did not yet know them well, nor that they were in truth more tolerant of other religions than were the Christians; not that I ever considered the Christians very tolerant after their missionaries and then Charlemagne, great king though he was, tried without ceasing to force their beliefs upon my own people of Denmark.

Nevertheless, my first concern at that moment was to prove myself a worthy knight, so Roland, the other squires, and I charged into the melee. Soon we were at Charlemagne's side, he having regained his horse. Within minutes, the Saracen host thought itself trapped as the reinforcement of squires began to circle them. Quickly turning around, the Saracens fled back toward Rome with us in hot pursuit.

Charlemagne then went after Corsuble, the Saracen king, determined, as he later told me, to have that man's head, but seeing their king in danger, two of the Saracens swooped in to his aid and charged Charlemagne. With their lances, the Saracens thrust at the king's horse until it collapsed beneath him. Charlemagne had barely regained his feet before they had circled back, intent on finishing their murderous deed, but I had seen the king fall, so I quickly set spur to my horse to rescue him.

I still held the Oriflamme from leading the charge, half-forgetting it was not a sword until I was upon the enemy. I charged until one

Saracen lost his wits, fear causing him to turn around his horse so quickly that it tripped and the man fell, to be trampled to death by his own steed. The other Saracen soon felt me whack the Oriflamme against his skull, knocking him senseless to the ground. Next, I dismounted, quickly helping Charlemagne up onto my own horse, while I grabbed the steed of one of the fallen Saracens.

"Brave, Alory!" shouted Charlemagne, thinking me that great coward because I bore the Oriflamme. "I thought I saw you fleeing, but now you have proven yourself steadfast. I shall soon reward your bravery."

I heard the king's words, but there was no time to correct him, and how does one correct a king? Instead, I set spurs to my steed, and onward I rode in pursuit of the Saracen host, though it was hardly a host any longer, its numbers quickly declining in the wake of the brave squires' advance. Within just minutes, it was clear the Saracens had been defeated. Only a remnant of them would make it back to Rome, leaving the Franks as masters of the field.

Now Charlemagne blew his bugle, calling to him all his knights and peers who had survived the battle. Then Archbishop Turpin set aside his helmet and sword, and placing his bishop's mitre on his head and taking his crosier in his hand, he sang the solemn "Te Deum Laudamus," then led us all in thanking God for giving us the victory. I will admit I did not join in, for I thought the victory more my own doing than that of God. Yet, while I did not share my comrades' Christian faith, I was relieved to see the look of peace and joy on the king's face.

When the song had ended, I stepped forward and laid the Oriflamme, now torn and stained with dirt, at Charlemagne's feet. But when I sought to step back, the king came forward, and placing his hand on my shoulder, he called me "Alory" again and thanked me. I knelt down before him, unable to utter a word from fear that if I corrected him, I would experience his wrath.

Roland now spoke up, saying, "Sire, this man is not whom you think," and turning, he withdrew his own helmet, for the king thought him one of his knights and not his nephew the squire, and while Charlemagne stared at his nephew in astonishment, Roland reached down and removed my own helmet.

The king was so taken aback at my true identity that he took a step backward, momentarily speechless. Then Archbishop Turpin declared, "How great is our God when He turns the humble into the mighty and shows His greatness by saving our king and army with the least of our men."

And suddenly, Charlemagne came forward and placed his hands on my arms, lifting me to my feet. Then he unexpectedly embraced me and said, "I forgive you, Ogier. What other man would save my life, returning such good to me when I have vowed to hang him?"

And then Duke Namon also came forward, and putting an arm around both Roland and me, he addressed the king. "My lord, why not knight these young men here? They have done more this day than any of our host."

"They have richly earned it," Charlemagne agreed. "We will indeed knight them tomorrow morning, after they spend the evening in prayer and fasting, and never have I been so proud to knight any men, for I can think of none who are more deserving."

A cheer went up among the Frankish army at these words, and for the first time in my life, I felt I was truly loved and appreciated for my abilities—never had I felt so good in my life, save perhaps for that magical moment when I had been held in the fairies' arms, and now that I was to be made a knight, I felt their blessings upon me might not have been for naught.

Even then, however, I sensed the hatred, perhaps the jealousy against me, from Ganelon, Duke of Mayence and brother to my stepmother, Queen Gudrun. I also sensed the disdain that Charlemagne's son, Charlot, held toward me, for when Roland and I acknowledged the army's cheers with smiles and by shaking our fists in triumph, Ganelon and Charlot stood silent and frowning. But I would not let them ruin my day of triumph.

When we returned to the camp that evening, Roland and I fasted overnight and kept our watch together over our arms, alone in our tent. Roland said we were to kneel and pray throughout the night so we would be worthy to be knighted on the morrow. I thought I had already proven myself worthy, but Roland was too good a friend to argue with, so I knelt beside him, thinking if the Christ were truly a god, it could do no harm, and so I asked for his blessings upon me, as well as silently asking for the blessings of Thor and Odin, and I will not deny that during the night, I felt a stirring in my soul that I could not understand, a desire to do right by my fellow men, to aid those in need and bring about justice. I did so crave to be acknowledged for my greatness, but I felt no desire for land or wealth or to wear a crown as a result of my deeds; I simply wished to be acclaimed as a great and good man, one who had done his best and excelled all his life. I did not understand this sudden deep desire, but for the first time, I felt I could decide my own destiny and also succeed at whatever task I chose. And I also felt a presence—I know not if it be the same thing as the Holy Spirit, or the spirits of my ancestors, or perhaps it was the very presence of the fairies and Morgan le Fay herself—but it made me feel confident that I would be aided in all my endeavors by a force greater than myself.

That next morning, Roland and I and the other squires, who had aided us in the attack against the Saracen host, knelt before Charlemagne. Archbishop Turpin performed a solemn service, speaking of the great duty that knights had and warning us to be strong against temptation. Then taking the swords the king himself had chosen for us, the archbishop blessed them and placed them upon the camp's makeshift altar.

Now Charlemagne stepped forward, his sword in hand. He stopped before each one of us, smiting us upon the shoulder with his sword three times and saying, "In the name of God and St. Michael, I dub thee knight: be valiant, loyal, and true!" But when he came to me, he said my name, "Sir Ogier," in such a way that I dared to lift my bowed head to see him smiling upon me.

Then Duke Namon came forward to lace my and Roland's golden spurs about our ankles, to invest each of us with a coat of mail, and to buckle on our breastplates. And Archbishop Turpin presented us with our arms and gauntlets, and finally, Charlemagne handed us our swords from the altar.

The sword I received was a plain steel blade that bore the inscription:

WEAR ME UNTIL YOU FIND A BETTER.

But Roland, being the king's nephew, was given a wondrous sword with a jeweled hilt, and an edge so sharp that it glared in the morning sun. Later, when Roland allowed me to hold and admire it, I read engraved upon it:

I AM DURANDAL, WHICH TROJAN HECTOR WORE.

At that time, neither Roland nor I knew it, but not only did he bear the sword of a great hero, but one who was his ancestral cousin, for Roland was himself descended from Aeneas, last of the Trojans, who had been cousin to Prince Hector, and whose great-grandson Brutus came to Britain. It was from Brutus that King Arthur was descended, and from King Arthur that Roland was descended on his father's side, though it would be years before he would have this ancestry revealed to him.

After receiving our swords, my fellow newly-made knights and I all took the oath of chivalry, swearing to be faithful to God and loyal to the king. We promised to revere and protect all women, to be mindful of the poor and helpless, never to engage in an unrighteous war, never to seek our own exaltation when it would injure another, and always to speak the truth, to love mercy, and to be just toward all men.

Then Charlemagne blessed us and promised to love us as his own sons, and we in turn promised to love and honor him as our father in knighthood. I found this moment perhaps the most moving of all, for my father had not been loving toward me, and until this moment, neither had Charlemagne, but now for the first time, I felt I had found my place, my home in this world. My heart sang with hope as I stood, donned my helmet, and then mounted my steed to join the other newly knighted in parading around the army camp. It was a day I shall never forget, not only because it was the day I was made a knight, but because that day I think I learned I had a soul and was a person of value with a mission in this world, although I could little foresee the strange turns that mission would one day take, ultimately leading me here to you, Great Caliph.

Later that day, while Roland and I were resting in our tent before embarking on the next day's march to Rome, we heard a great commotion in the camp. When we stepped outside, we learned from a fellow knight that Charlemagne had ordered Alory to be brought to him to be punished for his cowardice.

Roland and I quickly joined the other men rushing toward the king's tent. Once there, we found Alory on his knees before the king, being ordered to give his excuse for fleeing the battlefield. The poor coward was speechless. When it was clear the disgraced knight could not find his tongue, the king asked his peers how they thought Alory should be punished. Duke Ganelon answered, "Let him be disinherited from his lands. Let him never be allowed to show his face at court again. And let him be stripped of the honor of knighthood."

But I found that my heart went out to Alory, and stepping forward, I knelt before Charlemagne, saying, "My lord, as a newly-made knight, I feel strongly that I must speak for justice toward my fellow man. It is true that Alory has acted cowardly, but if you were to disinherit and make outcast everyone who flees from your ranks, you quickly would lose half your army. Fear is the natural state of mankind, and we cannot blame him for surrendering to it. I pray you to forgive him and leave his inheritance intact; it is more than sufficient punishment that he not be allowed to carry the Oriflamme or participate in battle ever again since such duties have proven too great for him."

I know not where I found the courage to speak such words to the king, but I felt I had been disinherited myself, and I regretted the anger I had shown in striking a blow to Alory the previous day; furthermore, if he had not acted as he had, I would not have achieved knighthood or the king's favor, but still be under threat of hanging when we returned to France.

The king looked at me, surprised by my words and uncertain how to respond. As we all awaited his judgment, I felt a hand on my shoulder. Looking up, I saw Roland standing beside me. "My lord and king," said my friend, "Sir Ogier speaks rightly and I crave you to pardon his boldness because his words are those of mercy, as is only right for a goodly knight to speak."

I felt my heart leap with joy as I heard myself again referred to as "Sir Ogier" and my bosom friend calling me a "goodly knight." And I saw a smile spread across Charlemagne's face. And then the king said, "On this day, I cannot deny anything to my two bravest new knights. So be it. Alory, you are banished from our presence, and I trust that shall be sufficient punishment that you will not repeat your cowardice."

Then Alory stood and two knights stepped forward to lead him away, but not before I saw him look in my direction, his eyes overflowing with gratitude.

And again all the army cheered me, save Ganelon, who looked disgusted that I had dared to interfere and overturn his sentence against a traitor—ironic, considering the day would come when he would prove a traitor himself.

HAROUN AL-RASHID INTERRUPTS

"That is quite a tale of bravery," said the caliph, "but it is not unlike those of many great warriors who have earned their spurs through valor, so I find it not so marvelous as you promised. What of the fairies who appeared at your christening, and what of your father and evil stepmother? I am more anxious to hear of them."

"Fear not, my lord," Ogier replied. "They will reappear and play major roles in this affair, but I merely wished you to know how I found a place of honor among Charlemagne's men, for I know your court and his have been on friendly terms, and I beg your hospitality based upon that friendship between your two kingdoms."

"Hospitality shall be granted to you," said the caliph, yawning, "and you will partake of it this evening. You may finish your tale in the morning."

"As you wish, Great Caliph," Ogier replied, bowing to the ground as Haroun al-Rashid clapped his hands and then ordered his men to take Ogier to a private chamber. Soon the Dane found himself led through a maze of rooms to a pool where beautiful maidens bathed him, and then they led him to the softest bed he had ever known. There he slept the sleep of an angel, to wake thoroughly refreshed for the first time in many years.

Ogier spent the next day wandering about the gardens of the caliph's palace until evening when Haroun al-Rashid summoned him to dine privately with him and resume his tale.

"I wish to know about the fairies," the caliph repeated. "Are they like the genii who dwell here in the Middle East?"

"That I do not know," replied Ogier, "but I shall tell you of my future experiences with them, I promise, Great Caliph. However, first I must explain to you how I became a friend of the Muslim people for, you see, I had been fighting the Saracens with Charlemagne and thought, therefore, that all Muslims were my enemies. I know not why I thought so just because they were the Christians' enemies while those of my own religion had no quarrel with them. I trust you will find it agreeable to hear how I came to be tolerant toward your people as I continue my tale, and then, I will reveal how Morgan le Fay and her fellow fairies again entered my life."

"Proceed," said the caliph, nodding his head.

CHAPTER 5
OGIER'S TALE CONTINUES

T HE DAY AFTER I received my knighthood, Great Caliph, the
army marched on Rome and encamped on the banks of the Tiber
River, just outside the city. We waited there for the Saracens to ride out
and attack us, and should that not happen, Charlemagne planned to
lay siege to the city, although he did not wish to starve or in any way
harm the innocent Christians inside its walls.

But just because the king considered the Saracens to be pagans
did not mean they were foolish enough to sally forth and attack our
far mightier force. We had taken so long in traveling to Italy that they
had known we were coming and had prepared themselves by ravaging
all the land, harvesting the crops, cutting down the vineyards and
orchards, and bringing all the cattle inside Rome's walls to prepare
themselves for a long siege, while leaving us without food in the area
when our own supplies should run out.

As the weeks went by, without us having any success in our
attempts to draw forth the enemy or to make a break in the city wall,
the Franks began to complain that they had been too long away from

home. Ganelon soon manipulated some of the weaker-minded knights into believing, without his directly saying anything treasonous, that Charlemagne was an ineffectual leader and that they would do better to follow young Prince Charlot; Ganelon even flattered the prince into believing himself a better warrior than his father the king.

While Ganelon feigned great affection and friendship for Charlot, it was obvious to Roland and me that he wished nothing more than to see all Charlemagne's progeny fail, in hopes that he might someday see his own son, Charlemagne's nephew, crowned king. And Charlot was fool enough to listen to Ganelon's counsel, for he was desperate to win the praise of the people by proving himself a hero. He figured then he would have a better chance to be chosen as his father's successor since the Franks did not always pass their crowns to their firstborn.

Desperate for his father's attention and approval, Charlot fell prey to Ganelon's urgings, and in the sixth week of the siege, he, with two thousand young men as hot-headed and hare-brained as himself, secretly left the camp at nightfall to ride toward the city, intending, by a bold dash upon the enemy, to bring relief to the Christian garrison held up inside the Capitoline Fortress.

But the Saracens knew well that in time the Christians would try to aid their own. Chief Karaheut, the Saracens' bravest leader, lay in ambush with five thousand soldiers, waiting for such a foolish attempt. So as soon as the Christian army drew near, the Saracens rode forth from their hiding place and attacked Charlot's unsuspecting band. The battle's clamor was so loud that it was heard as far away as our camp, and Charlemagne, who was up late with his advisors, quickly called his men to arms to save his foolish son and companions.

Roland and I heard the call and immediately responded, mounting our steeds and rushing into battle with the rest of the army close behind us. When the Saracen force saw us coming, Chief Karaheut ordered his men to retreat, and they fled back through the gates of Rome. Charlot then ordered his men to follow, but the Saracens were too fast for them and were quickly behind the city walls.

Charlemagne now rode up to his son and shouted at him before all the men. "You fool! What kind of a prince are you to defy your king?" As he spoke, the king raised his mace in the air and shook it at his son until we were certain he would strike Charlot, but Roland, ever fair of speech, rode up to his uncle, the king, and begged him to forgive his own son.

"Sire, we must not let the Saracens see us fighting amongst ourselves," he wisely counseled. "And it cannot hurt to let the Saracens think they have won a victory, for that will make them confident and foolishly daring next time they meet us, not realizing they only defeated a small number and not our full Christian force."

The king, seeing the truth of Roland's words, allowed his anger to cool.

"You are wise, Roland," he said. "I would that you were my son instead of this hotheaded fool."

He rode then back to camp, Charlot following behind, his head bowed in shame to have received a tongue-lashing from his father before all the Christian host, and no doubt, his heart filled with hate for his cousin, who had his father's favor.

The next day, Roland and I were called to Charlemagne's tent to give the king our advice as he spoke with his peers about the best strategy for attacking the city and pulling down its walls. Charlot was present, but whenever he tried to speak, his father coolly ignored him until he stepped back to sulk in a corner; indeed, I am certain it was only Roland's presence that kept the king from turning and smiting Charlot with his fist for his childish behavior.

Then at the noon hour, Chief Karaheut unexpectedly arrived as messenger from Corsuble, King of the Saracens. He came to Charlemagne's camp, riding on a donkey, and accompanied only by two squires. He was unarmed, and very richly dressed, even wearing a turban of red satin embroidered with gold. Charlemagne went out to greet him a few dozen yards from the camp's edge, followed by those he had asked to join him in council.

When Karaheut was within twenty feet of Charlemagne, he royally saluted him, saying, "In the name of the one true God, whose name is held sacred by Christian and Muslim alike, I, Karaheut, Chief of King Corsuble's forces, do greet thee, the mighty Charlemagne, King of the Franks, and all your barons and noble knights, but most of all, I greet the brave Ogier, Prince of the Danes."

Upon these words, a murmur of astonishment arose, for I had been a squire but a few days before. I did not know that anyone amongst our foes would have had reason yet to know my name, and if it were known as the result of the recent skirmish we had fought, then Roland's name should equally have been mentioned.

"What is your errand, Sir Karaheut?" Charlemagne asked, and I think even he was a bit riled that I should receive preference over him in the emissary's greeting. As for Prince Charlot, I need not mention how he scowled at me.

"I am the bearer of a message from the great Corsuble, King of the Faithful. He bids you leave him in peaceful possession of this city of Rome which he has taken in honorable war, and which is, therefore, his more than yours. He grants you ten days to leave Italy with all your army. If you go not, he will meet and defeat you in battle and not have mercy upon any who calls himself a Christian."

I looked at Charlemagne as these words were spoken, and I saw his face redden almost to the same degree as it had the day before when he had shouted at Charlot. Wisely, however, he took a moment to gather his words before saying, "Never have I allowed an infidel to stop me from doing my Christian duty. I will fight your master, and God, whom you claim to revere as much as we, will decide who is in the right, for we did not come to rape and slaughter and take what is not ours, but to help those who have been plundered and unjustly put to the sword by your people."

"Let God then be the judge," Karaheut replied, "for He knows full well that while we conquer, we do it in His name to turn people to His worship and to follow the path laid out by His prophet Mohammed, peace be upon him. Yet, King Corsuble, to show his great wisdom and mercy, has ordered me to tell you that if you will not withdraw peaceably, he does not wish to cause the death of so many lives. Therefore, let the bravest man among you meet me in single combat, and let the issue of that fight decide who shall be the master of Italy. If I conquer, Rome shall be ours, and you shall return at once across the Alps. If I am beaten, the Hosts of the Commander of the Faithful will at once sail back over the sea, leaving Rome in your hands."

I was amazed by this turn of events for, despite King Corsuble's bragging that he would put all Christians to the sword, he clearly feared Charlemagne's army, as well he should.

"Let it then be so," said Charlemagne. "I agree to one-on-one combat. Duke Ganelon shall accept your challenge."

Ganelon now stepped forward, looking proud to have been chosen as the king's bravest man, but Karaheut only looked at him disdainfully for a moment and then replied, "I will do battle solely with Ogier the Dane."

"Surely not!" exclaimed Prince Charlot before anyone else could reply. "Ogier is but a boy, worthy only to be at his mother's knee, or in a dairy making cheese back in Denmark. We have far braver men than him."

"Nevertheless, it is he I will fight," said Karaheut, "for I know him truly to be the bravest and greatest among you. To defeat anyone else will not bring me the glory I desire and deserve."

"Why do you choose Ogier?" Charlemagne asked. "As my rude son, who speaks out of turn, has said, Ogier has only just been made a knight and is inexperienced. It is unfair to us to send an untried knight into battle against an acknowledged champion such as yourself."

"My master, King Corsuble," replied Karaheut, "had a dream last night in which a beautiful maiden, a genie he believes, whispered into his ear that Ogier the Dane was the greatest warrior in both our armies and our fate rests in his hands. Therefore, I am here to challenge him, to dispel my lord's fears and prove that no true Muslim need fear any Christian."

I thought then how Karaheut did not know that I was not a Christian, but it seemed a small matter not worth mentioning, especially when Charlemagne now turned to me and asked, "What say you, Sir Ogier? Will you fight this man and let the fate of all Christendom lie in your hands?"

Before I could accept, Prince Charlot turned to Karaheut and said, "Saracen dog, do you think we will give up Rome because you defeat a boy in battle? What trickery is this? No, I, Charlot, son of Charlemagne, will meet you in battle and send you back to your king with your tail between your legs like the dog you are, having left you with scarcely a drop of your life's blood."

Karaheut's lips then pursed up as if to contain his tongue, but after a moment, he spoke to Charlemagne. "Great Christian king, it seems to me your boy steps out of line. We do not allow our children to speak for our warriors. I beg you to curb his tongue and let me fight the man I have named previously. If I were you, I would not allow this princeling to insult kings or their representatives, much less the finest knight in his enemy's army."

"The great chief speaks wisely," said Duke Namon, stepping in before either Charlemagne or Charlot's anger could get the best of him. "Sir Ogier has proven himself brave and capable in battle, and he does not deserve such insult, even from a prince, for he is a prince in his own right and, therefore, Prince Charlot's equal, nor would any of these many knights and barons gathered here wish to be spoken to in such a manner."

Charlemagne did not wish to look weak before the Saracens, nor was he pleased with his son. "Charlot, return to your tent and await my displeasure there," he said, "after you make your apologies to Sir Ogier and Sir Karaheut."

Charlot appeared astonished by these words, and I was too embarrassed by his shame even to look at him. Instead, I turned toward Karaheut, who simply winked at me, as if he greatly enjoyed watching the prince squirm. Finally, after what seemed like an hour, Charlot muttered, "Sir Ogier, I am sorry if I have offended you," and then he turned on his heel with a scowl and disappeared from our ranks.

Charlemagne let him go and said to Sir Karaheut, "I apologize for my son. You need not fear that he will not be duly punished." Then he turned and beckoned me to approach, saying, "Sir Ogier, I apologize to you as well for my son's behavior," and by now I had stepped close enough that he placed his hand on my shoulder and added, "and I vow to you that he shall not insult you again. Now, are you willing to meet this Saracen chief in battle?"

"Aye, my lord," I replied. "I fear not man, for I know God is on my side."

I knew not where I found the words I had just spoken, nor even truly who was God, be it Him of whom I had heard the Christians speak, or Allah, or Odin. I only knew that God must be mighty, and if He were the all powerful Creator, then He had overseen my being favored at my birth, for why else would the fairies have come the day I was presented to the court as my father's son and heir?

"It is good," said Karaheut, hearing my words. "We need not put on a show for anyone. Tomorrow at noon, I will meet you alone at the meadow along the Tiber, and there we shall fight on foot with swords."

Although I heard some men murmuring that I could not go alone, for I might be ambushed, I simply bowed in agreement, and then Karaheut turned and rode back toward Rome, the gold of his garments blinding us when the sunlight hit them as his horse galloped away. Once the Saracen chief had disappeared from view, I returned to my tent, wondering whether on the morrow I should meet my death, for perhaps I had called upon a God who would not aid me because I was not truly His follower.

At sunrise the next morning, I mounted my steed and rode toward the Tiber. I felt surprisingly calm. During the night when sleep had not readily found me, I had decided that whether or not

God would aid me, there was little I could do about it; instead, being the best in combat among all those with whom I had trained, and even notably braver than many of the seasoned knights in Charlemagne's army, it was up to me whether I should succeed against my enemy. I would not be one to sit and pray and wait for some unseen God to save me. Instead, I would hold strong to my courage and fight my own battles.

When I reached the meadow, I could not help notice the fabulous armor of Chief Karaheut, finely made and sparkling in the sun. His shield of steel was inlaid with gold and engraved with words of mystic meaning, perhaps to intimidate his opponents with the thought of a curse or enchantment. Karaheut's helmet contained five gems that in the bright morning sun shot forth beams of light. And as I would later learn, his sword had been made by the giant smith Brumadant centuries ago, and after Roland's Durandal, Charlemagne's Joyeuse, and King Arthur's Excalibur, it must have been the greatest sword in the world. It was said that Brumadant had tempered the sword in dragon's blood, and when he had finished it, he had tried it by rendering it against a piece of marble and slicing it through the stone, although a palm's length of the tip had broken, making it always called "Short." Despite that, it was a sword that had never known defeat in battle, and Karaheut prized it dearly, for just the sight of it brought terror to his foes.

When Karaheut saw me approaching, he rode forward to greet me and chatted pleasantly about the best place for the battle until we settled on a grassy knoll. We dismounted and prepared for our duel while our horses munched the grass. I had just drawn my sword and was about to engage in combat with my noble enemy when I heard footsteps behind me, and then Karaheut shouted, "Foul!"

Turning, I saw thirty Saracen horsemen thundering toward us, bearing down upon me, intent to kill me! Apparently, King Corsuble had insufficient faith in Karaheut and his mighty sword, so he had set up this ambush. The honorable Karaheut was so disgusted by this breach of conduct that he swung his sword at the intruders, jumping in front of me, as if for my protection, and smiting from his horse the first foe who approached. I quickly readied my sword and struck the next attacker, but the enemy far outnumbered us. We were swiftly surrounded, our assailants' swords pointed at both of us.

Then one man moved his steed forward and spoke in the Saracen tongue. After a moment, Karaheut translated for me.

"He says, 'You are our prisoner now, Ogier the Dane, and will come with us.'" Meanwhile, three of my enemies had dismounted, and they now came forward to take my sword and put me in chains. I saw no point in struggling for they had me surrounded, and there were too many to fight, so I simply submitted, trusting they meant to hold me for ransom and that Charlemagne and his men would soon come to my rescue.

Karaheut, however, was not so placid. He responded to his countrymen in anger, and although I did not understand his language, I knew he was protesting such treatment of me. My principal captor responded with equal ferocity, while he tied me by a long rope to a saddle so I might follow the horse on foot with my hands chained together. Karaheut was soon by my side, apologizing to me and begging me to understand that he had not been involved in this lack of respect for me or this defiance of the rules of fair combat. I, in turn, let him know I did not hold him responsible.

"I will speak to my king on your behalf," Karaheut told me as we made our way to Rome. But I had no hope in the success of his goodwill, for his king was clearly no man of honor.

When we reached Rome, I was paraded through the streets, but I paid no attention to the Saracens jeering at me; rather, I looked up at everything I saw, marveling at the beauty and glory of the eternal city. After a short while, we arrived at a beautiful villa, and I was led into its lush garden where under an olive tree sat Corsuble, King of the Saracens, surrounded by his court.

Instantly, the courtiers crowded around me, all eager to catch a glimpse of this fair-skinned, blonde-haired warrior so unlike themselves. They made many gestures and exclamations in their tongue to each other, none of which I understood. I saw great fear of me in some of their eyes—and plenty of hatred in others. Then Karaheut stepped forward, and without so much as bowing or kneeling to his king, he spoke in angry tones, doubtless protesting such treatment toward me.

The king replied in a vehement tone, refusing to hear Karaheut's appeal, and when the Saracen chief persisted, the king ordered Karaheut from his presence. All this was obvious to me through their actions, although the words themselves I did not understand. Karaheut finally departed, his face filled with rage, but never will I forget how noble and brave he was to argue with his king for a stranger's life. I vowed then that should I live, I would be his sworn friend and never dishonor a man simply because he was a Muslim.

The king must now have ordered me to be brought forward, for I was pushed toward him by his men. He spoke to me in his tongue, but I understood not a word. He turned and spoke to his counselors, but I knew not what they said either, and I began to regret that Karaheut had left, for I knew he could at least speak Frankish and translate for us, and I seriously doubted anyone present spoke the musical tongue of my native Denmark.

At that moment, a graceful young woman entered the garden. When all the court bowed as she passed through the crowd, I realized she must be Corsuble's daughter. She stopped before the king, just a few feet from me, and after speaking a few words to her father, she turned to address me.

Surprising me by speaking in the Frankish tongue, she said, "I am Glorianda." And well her name suited her, for she was glorious to look upon, clad in costly purple silk embroidered with gold and wearing dainty slippers. Her olive skin was flawless, her eyes dark and piercing. I thought I could never grow tired of gazing upon her, such was her beauty. "Fear not," she told me. "My father wishes to kill you, but he will deny me nothing. You are handsome, and tall and strong, and noble of countenance, and so unlike any man at my father's court that I would have you for my husband."

My mind reeled at these words. No Frankish or Danish princess would have been so forward with a man, and certainly not with a knight, much less a prince as I was truly. Yet she had won my heart the instant I saw her. What exotic delight would I know to be with one such as she—one who was like the beautiful houris I had heard existed in the Muslim version of Heaven—one who would have made jealous all the Valkyries in Valhalla, where I hoped to spend my last days, although Morgan le Fay had already told me I would go one day to Avalon.

I listened as Glorianda argued with her father in the Saracen tongue; both were quite stubborn from what I could tell. I did not understand how he could even argue with a daughter as beautiful as she, yet after a few minutes, it became clear that she would not get her way this time.

Then King Corsuble rose from his throne, and pointing his finger at me, he shouted something I did not understand, but the next minute, armed guards had grasped my wrists and were dragging me away, and I prepared to die while Glorianda looked on with sorrowful eyes but spoke not a word to me.

Rather than be taken to a gallows or be forced to kneel while my head was severed from my body, I found myself thrust into a cold, dark upper cell in a tower, to await whatever would be my fate.

I lay there in the cell, without food or water, all that evening and through the night. After a few minutes of searching, I gave up all hope of escape; the prison was impregnable—the door of oak was too strong to break, and the only window, grated over with bars, was scarcely large enough for my head to fit through, much less my body, and I had climbed up several flights of stairs, so even if I could escape through the window, I would doubtless meet my death if I tried to leap from the tower.

I had no choice but to wait for my death. I spent the hours thinking of the beautiful Glorianda—would she continue to plead with her father for my release, or arrange to help me escape? And I thought of Morgan le Fay, who had promised I would visit Avalon, but whom I had never seen since my infancy; I only knew that heroes went to Avalon or Valhalla so they would not die, but if I were killed, I knew not what fate I could expect in the next life, if there were one.

All the next day, I waited, every moment expecting to be dragged from my cell and put to death. By the time the sun set on my second day of imprisonment, I started to think the king and even the guards had forgotten me. I could see through a small window out onto the street, but there was nothing to see except the people going about their everyday tasks. Then, just as I prepared to sleep, I heard a great tumult in the streets, and I jumped up to look out at the scene below. At the same moment, the door of my cell opened, and a man, accompanied by two guards, stepped in to give me a meal.

I was ravenous, but the tumult in the street held my attention. I saw a great company of soldiers and courtiers coming through the streets, headed toward the king's palace and dressed in clothes unlike those of the Saracens, but they were nevertheless dark-skinned men and more likely to be pagans than Christians.

"Who are these men?" I asked my jailer in astonishment, pointing excitedly to the window.

My jailer did not understand my words, but he must have understood my meaning. "It is Brunamont, King of the Moors of Maiolgre," he told me. At least, that is what I took his words to mean, though both the name of the king and his country were strange to me. This king was a great, tall, dark man. He rode upon a powerful Arabian stallion like none I had ever seen, and as beautiful as the Princess Glorianda was, I thought she was no more beautiful than that horse, which was exactly the kind of steed I longed to ride.

My jailer then left me with my meal, which I ate slowly, for I dreamt of what it must be like to own such a horse, and what adventures I might experience upon it should I go to foreign lands, such as Maiolgre, wherever that might be. That I, a prince of faraway Denmark, should travel so far as to see the eternal city of Rome, though I had seen very little of it yet, seemed marvelous to me, and now I longed to live and know many more adventures and visit great and glorious lands, and to meet more people, for if Glorianda and Karaheut were any example to me, I had learned that not every Saracen was a devil in his heart.

That night, I dreamt of sailing on a ship over the Mediterranean to ancient places I had only heard about—to Greece and Egypt—and then perhaps travel overland to India, and even to faraway Cathay. I had many fine and wonderful adventures in that dream, although when I woke, I found that I quickly forgot them, save for the sensation that a great future lay before me. I took the dream as a good omen that somehow I would survive my imprisonment.

The next day, I hoped again the jailer would come to me with food, but I waited all the morning. I again watched the people milling about in the streets, but no sign of the great king of Maiolgre and his people appeared.

And then when the sun was at its highest peak in the sky, the door opened, and this time, a well-dressed soldier stepped forward, accompanied by several men. They chained me again and hauled me forth from the chamber, although far more gently than before. I now thought perhaps my dream had been only a dream and not an omen at all, for I did not doubt they were bringing me to my death, while their gentleness merely reflected the respect due to a condemned man.

I was surprised, however, when I found myself not going to a place of execution but being returned to the palace. In another minute, I was in a throne room where Corsuble was holding his court. The second after I saw the king, I saw the great giant Moor, King Brunamont, seated beside him, and on his other side was the beautiful Glorianda.

The princess rose from her chair and stepped toward me, saying, again in the Frankish tongue, which none but the two of us could understand, "Ogier, Prince of Denmark, my father wishes to marry me to King Brunamont."

I was surprised by this turn of events, but I wondered why I was summoned to hear such tidings. Then I read in the princess' eyes what she hesitated to say.

"Do you not wish to marry him, Princess?" I asked.

Her nostrils flared in a most charming way as she remarked, "He is terribly ugly, is he not?"

I could not help but smile; certainly, Glorianda deserved a better husband than Brunamont; even his handsome horse deserved a better master. But the situation's seriousness kept me from saying more, save to ask, "Why have I been summoned here, Princess?"

"I begged my father to let me have a champion. Karaheut has been my champion until now, but he has disappeared from the city. Indeed, some say he has gone to your King Charlemagne to offer himself as a prisoner because of the way my father has betrayed you. Still, I do not wish to marry King Brunamont, so I have asked that a combat be held to decide the matter, and my father has agreed, knowing full well that none but Karaheut could defeat Brunamont. For that reason, I am asking whether you will be my champion."

"And if I should agree," I replied, "what shall be my prize?"

She seemed surprised by my question, then slowly replied, "The pride in knowing that you have righted a wrong."

"In any other case," I said, "that would be sufficient prize, but in this case, I shall ask myself then for your hand."

I saw the blood rush to her cheeks, but then she cast her eyes down and replied, "Great knight, you must know that while we both desire it, even though I have asked my father already, he will never allow me to marry a Christian."

I dared then to place my hand under her chin and lift her eyes to mine.

"I am no Christian," I stated.

"Perhaps not, but you are not a Muslim either," she said.

"Perhaps I could convert," I suggested. "What does it matter what god I follow when I cannot see Him, but I can see the beauty before me that I long to hold in my arms?"

She stepped back, and for a moment, I thought I had insulted her, but I saw only sadness in her face, and then she said, "It can never be, fair knight. I will not deny that I think you would make a fine husband, but my father would never consent. So I ask that you fight this battle for me solely as a favor for the love I bear you."

Here the king let out a flood of angry words at the delay, and when he had finished, seeing I would get nowhere now, but hoping that I might make better progress after the combat, I said, "Fair princess, I will do as you bid, and it will be my great honor to serve you."

Clapping her hands together in joy and relief, she now turned to her father and must have told him I would fight Brunamont.

Less than a minute after she finished speaking, I was led back to my cell, uncertain whether the king had agreed that I should be his daughter's champion. But soon after, I was brought several plates of food, presumably so I could keep up my strength for the battle, which I assumed would be the next day, for no one had informed me otherwise.

I had barely finished my meal when my cell door opened and in stepped Karaheut. I was overjoyed to see him. He quickly informed me that he had indeed returned to the Frankish camp and offered himself as a prisoner, but when word reached the camp that I was to fight Brunamont, he had begged Charlemagne's permission to return to Rome and aid me. He had brought with him his own armor, and he gave to me his noble sword, which I both coveted and feared more than anything on earth, so at first I was resistant to use it.

"Take it," he insisted, "and if you should conquer with it in battle, not only shall you be freed, but you shall have it as your reward, as recompense for all the evil that has been wrought against you."

Then I took the jeweled hilt in my hand and looked at the inscription on the blade. It was written in a tongue I did not know, but Karaheut translated it for me as:

I AM CORTANA THE SHORT.
HE WHO HAS ON HIS SIDE RIGHT,
NEED NOT FEAR THE WRONGDOER'S MIGHT.

Considering the great, ugly warrior I would face on the morrow, I hoped the sword's words were true.

The next morning, Karaheut and I rode together to the place of battle, a treeless island in the middle of the River Tiber, and when we arrived, a barge carried us across to the island where we awaited my opponent. I was surprised, upon reaching the island, to look across the river and find many of my comrades from Charlemagne's army, including Roland, Oliver, and the king himself, on the other shore, come to watch the combat.

And then the cowardly Charlot called out, "Ogier, save yourself! Swim across the river now, for you can never defeat Brunamont, who is said to be the strongest man in India and Africa combined, and his sword more deadly than a cobra's bite!"

"I am no coward!" I shouted in reply, and then I turned my back to my friends so their pleas for me to save myself could not tempt me.

A few minutes later, the royal chariot approached the shore, bearing King Corsuble and the Princess Glorianda, and behind them rode Brunamont upon his famed steed, Broiefort. He was a monster of a man upon a giant of a horse, but I did not fear, for I held Cortana, and I knew I had right on my side; after all, I had been taken a prisoner through foul play, and I was champion to a princess being forced to wed against her will. And as I waited for the combat to begin, I felt the sword gently move in my hand as if to assure me I had nothing to fear. Then I looked up to Heaven and said, "Great Father Odin or Allah or Christ, or whatever name you prefer, I pray you give me victory today, not for my glory, but for the good of the Princess Glorianda, and so that the Saracens will see that a true knight, whether he be Christian, Saracen, or Norse, is not one to be trifled with, for right is on his side."

By now, Brunamont was being ferried across to the island, still arrogantly seated upon Broiefort, no doubt to intimidate me by enhancing his great height. Upon the ferry's landing, he dismounted, and then with great long strides, he advanced toward me, laughing as he brandished his sword above his head. He mocked my comparable puniness, taunting me with words I did not know, but whose meaning I could well imagine, and none of them true, for nothing was questionable about my manhood.

I had barely drawn my sword to meet Brunamont when I felt it pull me forward, and my arm flying upward, my sword met my opponent's in mid-air, making a great ringing sound that echoed again and again. After a moment, we each pulled back our swords, and then the fight was on, with constant thrusts and clanging of metal. At times, I drove Brunamont toward the water; at times, he rallied and drove me back. Many a lunge I made toward him, but my sword being a fragment shorter than his, I could not get close enough to wound him. Once he struck so close that he scratched my shoulder. Once I struck so hard that I knocked the sword from his hand, but he was fast on his feet and quickly grabbed it up again. Another time, I stumbled and fell and his sword came down, but I rolled out of the way quickly and managed to give his leg a whack with my sword as I rose; this move sent him howling and hopping backward several paces. Then I chased him back toward the water, and as I did so, I heard a roar of disdain from the Saracens, quickly drowned out by the cheers of the Franks. But Brunamont rallied and stood his ground. Our swords continued to swing back and forth, meeting, clanging, parting, and then meeting again until I felt the strength from my body begin to leave me, and I saw the sun in the sky begin to decline. I could see that my opponent, however, was becoming winded as well, and recalling the inscription on Cortana that the wrongdoer need not be feared, I raised my sword once more and ran toward Brunamont. He saw me coming, but he raised his sword a second too late, such that the full strength of my blow came down on the tip of his weapon, shattering it.

For a second, we stood there, realizing he was now weaponless. Then he tossed the remaining handle from him, and as I raised my sword to strike the final blow, the coward ran from me and jumped into the river, submerging himself and not rising again, so that we knew not whether he had drowned from the weight of his heavy armor or simply escaped. It mattered not. I was the champion.

"Go now, Prince Ogier," said Karaheut, approaching me. "Take his horse, Broiefort, for it is yours by the rules of combat, and take with you my sword as your reward, and return to your friends before the treacherous Corsuble has his army cross over to the island to kill you."

But in my triumph, I was stubborn and said instead, shouting so all might hear, "I have won by fair contest the hand of the Princess Glorianda and now I claim it."

And I looked across the water where Glorianda waved her scarf at me with exuberant joy. I was almost ready to jump into the river and swim across to her, but Karaheut held me back.

"It cannot be, Prince Ogier," he protested.

"Let me go!" I demanded, and before I knew it, we were in a wrestling match.

"I seek only to protect you from further treachery," said Karaheut.

And then I heard Glorianda's cries come across the river, and separating myself from my assailant and would-be friend, I saw Corsuble dragging his daughter away and his guard closing around her. Then Karaheut told me, "See, Corsuble is no honorable man. He will never let you wed his daughter, and if you pursue her now, his men will kill you."

"Ogier, I love you!" I heard Glorianda cry, but Karaheut held me fast, and I knew if I were to pursue her, it would mean my death.

By this time, Charlemagne, Roland, and Oliver had crossed over to the island, and they begged me to rejoin them, but for many minutes, I was too heartbroken to speak. "I will have her!" I declared. "I will find a way to have her!" And again, I tried to go after her, but now Roland tackled me to the ground, and Karaheut and Oliver each pinned down one of my arms while Charlemagne stood before me, saying, "Good Sir Ogier. No one doubts your heart and love. Still, I cannot understand how you could love a Saracen maiden. She must be one far above most of her kind for you to care so, and yet, it can only spell disaster should you pursue her."

"It would be an alliance," I replied. "It could be a means of peace."

"There can be no peace," said Charlemagne, "when they do not respect our religion."

"Your Christianity is not my religion," I growled, "and what respect have you shown to theirs?"

"Your words are wise, prince," said Karaheut, although he still held down my arm, "and if it were up to men like you and me, peace would be achieved, but there is a stubbornness in most men's hearts, be they Christian or Muslim, a desire to prove their religion is right so they can claim themselves superior and thus degrade the very men who should be their brothers. Such it has been for centuries and it is unlikely ever to change."

Then all four of them spoke words of kindness to me, of consolation; they even suggested I would someday forget Glorianda and find another princess to love and wed. In time, I was let loose after I had promised not to run. Instead, I sat on the ground, finding myself defeated, not by one physically stronger than me, but by mere prejudice.

Finally, darkness fell. Karaheut now told us he must take his leave and return to his king. Charlemagne offered to make him a general of his own army if he would remain with us, but he replied, "Great king, with all respect, your northern lands are too cold for my blood, and I would not be myself were I not among my own people, and so I bid you farewell with the greatest of respect, for I wish my own king were one like you."

Then that great chief departed from us, and soon after, my friends raised me from the ground. I remained too heartbroken to do anything more than let them lead me back to the Frankish camp.

That evening, a messenger came to Charlemagne from King Corsuble, informing him that the Saracens would withdraw from Rome and leave Italy completely. No doubt, the way I had defeated Brunamont had put fear into their hearts, making them think all the Franks equally as mighty—for they understood not that I was a Dane. Three days later, I rode beside Charlemagne as we triumphantly entered Rome. The Pope himself greeted us at the holy church of St. John Lateran, and there he gave us his blessing and expressed his gratitude to us for driving the Saracens away. After several days of rest and seeing the sights of Rome, we then returned to France, I having proven myself a hero and won my sword and horse.

But I did not forget Princess Glorianda. Many a night to come, I would dream of her, and many a time I would catch myself daydreaming about how she might yet be mine. And I also began to feel within me the first stirring desire to travel to faraway lands, for I realized a whole world lay beyond Christendom's borders of which I had been given but a small glimpse. Little did I know then that my next journey would not be to the Far East, but back to Denmark.

CHAPTER 6

OF COURSE, I had many more adventures at Charlemagne's court, from jousting tournaments to witnessing the occasional marvel that would occur, but I will pass over all those events, for they are not of concern to my primary tale, and I do not wish my story to be too long. It is sufficient to say that I was quite content as a member of the Frankish court, perhaps largely because I was greatly admired, and despite our earlier differences, I felt a loyalty growing inside of me toward Charlemagne. He truly was the greatest of kings, so I was ready to fight for him whenever trouble arose, and border skirmishes with the Moors of Spain, or Saxon rebellions, or various other internal problems kept us constantly occupied.

I could almost say I was happy during this time—at least, I tried to convince myself I was—for I had good friends and plenty to eat, and I could joust and prove my valor in many a tourney. Yet, at times, I felt like I was stuffed in a prison, Charlemagne's empire being that prison, and I fighting to preserve its borders, although I longed to travel beyond them, for I could not forget that as treacherous as the Saracen king had been and as ugly as Brunamont was, they came from what to me seemed to be fabulously exotic places, and I also imagined there were some other great warriors like Karaheut in those lands that I would welcome as comrades. But most of all, I could not forget the memory of Princess Glorianda's beautiful eyes. I knew that while I remained at court, being one of Charlemagne's Paladins was the highest glory I could aspire to, but now I found that I aspired to something more, something I could not quite name, but that I knew did not exist within the Frankish domains.

I had by now ceased almost completely to think about my father and his kingdom, or to consider how I might someday be a king, and when that possibility did register in my thoughts, I would quickly dismiss it, not wishing for my father's death, despite feeling he had abandoned me to my enemies—who had since become my best friends. Furthermore, my father's title now was officially that of Duke of Denmark, with Charlemagne as his overlord, so while many still referred to me as a prince, I knew that being a king was beyond my reach. Nor did I wish for a king's duties for I felt they would only leave me trapped in a castle and a kingdom far smaller than Charlemagne's own, which I already felt too narrow.

Then one spring day, I was surprised to see a group of Danish knights arrive at the Frankish court. They brought with them several chests full of gifts for Charlemagne as well as a great deal of treasure in gold coin and valuable trinkets that more than made up for the years of tribute Charlemagne had been demanding but had failed to receive.

As soon as I spied the Danes in the courtyard, I rushed to the throne room, arriving just in time to hear their spokesman address Charlemagne.

"Sire," said the Dane, "our lord, Godfrey, Duke of Denmark, humbly begs your pardon for his past offenses and asks that you receive this tribute as a sign that he prostrates himself before you as your loyal and faithful vassal. He wishes to make you amends for all his past misconduct, and he begs that you come to his aid. The shores of his kingdom are being ravaged by pirates and strange sea-kings from Thule who are burning and pillaging villages, raping women, and putting able-bodied men to the sword. No one but you, great king, is capable of ending their fury and saving his people."

Charlemagne looked so surprised by these words that he was rendered almost speechless. Taking his silence as an opportunity, I was about to go down on bended knee to beg him to fulfill my father's request, not out of affection for my father, but for the love I bore the people of my native land who did not deserve such misery. But just as I was about to step forward, Charlemagne made his response.

"Worthy knight, we acknowledge the good behavior of your lord Godfrey in sending the overdue tribute, and we would not wish to see his people needlessly slaughtered. Rest here this evening, you and your men; eat and sleep with us, and on the morrow, return to Duke Godfrey and tell him that we will send an army to his aid."

The knight knelt down before Charlemagne, thanking him for his kindness with a great look of relief upon his face, for no doubt, he had feared Charlemagne might not take kindly to his mission after so many years of strife between their countries.

Then Charlemagne beckoned me to step forward, and with my father's knights still present, he said, "Sir Ogier, your father, the Duke of Denmark, is sorely pressed by his enemies and in need of our help. No one knows better than yourself how he has neglected and cast you off among strangers. And yet it is our wish that you lead a company of warriors to his aid; none of my men know the land of Denmark and its people as well as you. If you go to fight under my banner, you will do a great deed in bringing succor to your people and peace to their land, as well as strengthening the ties between Denmark and France. Will you take upon yourself this mission for the sake of your people, if not for your father?"

"My lord," I said, kneeling before him, "never let it be said that anything but death stopped this son from helping his father, regardless of his past wrongs, for I have learned at this Christian court what it is to forgive."

And in truth, the Christian concept of forgiveness had moved me greatly; I had seen how it could release anger and be replaced with friendship, such as Charlemagne and I now had for one another. And while I still had not embraced the Christian faith, I had come to appreciate many of its tenets.

"It is well," said Charlemagne, "and nobly spoken. Tomorrow, take with you a thousand of my finest knights and show your father that neither his son nor a Christian king holds a grudge for past wrongs when others are in need."

I bowed to the king and then immediately set about preparing for my campaign to rescue my homeland from the strange and violent sea-kings.

In the morning, Roland came to me to say he had gained permission from his uncle, the king, to accompany me to Denmark for, like myself, he grew weary of a life at court and longed for adventure so he could prove himself with great deeds. His presence quickly invigorated the men with great enthusiasm and added to their courage as we began our journey.

Our march was rapid, and within just a few weeks, we were crossing the border into Denmark. But we did not arrive in time to do battle with my father's foes, for the sea-kings, as soon as they heard Charlemagne was sending an army to my father's aid, had fled on their great ships back to their northern lands, doubtless aware that they were not strong or organized enough to fight his great army; rather, they were simple cowards who sought to plunder and attack unsuspecting people who made easy victims. Nevertheless, we marched on to my father's castle, lending aid along the way to those who had been attacked and striving to make sure all else was well in the kingdom.

When we were yet a couple of miles from my father's castle, we caught sight of it in the distance, and then as we approached it, a great dread settled over my soul, for I saw the towers were draped in black cloth, and soon after, we heard the bells tolling out a solemn knell. I admit for a moment that I hoped they were a sign that my stepmother had died, but then I saw the black banner above the gate with my father's coat of arms painted upon it. When we were but a mile away, a company of knights rode forward to greet me, leaving me in no doubt for whom they mourned.

"Greetings, Prince Ogier," said the chief knight as he stopped and saluted me.

"What are all these signs of mourning for?" I asked, fearing the worst. "We expected to be greeted with cheers of triumph for our driving the sea-kings from my father's shores. What has happened?"

"My noble prince," said the knight, "I am most sorrowful to inform you that your father, our late good King Godfrey of Denmark, has died this morning. He tried to hold on until your arrival, but alas, his strength was not great enough."

I was surprised by the man's use of "good" and "king," but realized those words were said out of politeness, not accuracy. Once his other words had sunk in, I replied, "I am truly sorry to hear of my father's loss. I will go then to comfort my brother and stepmother."

"As you wish, my lord," said the knight, turning around to lead us back into the castle, where all was silent because of death's recent visit. As I entered the courtyard on my horse, I suddenly felt myself overcome with grief that I had never been reconciled with my father, nor told him that I loved him and had forgiven him for how he had wronged me. Unable to stop myself, I now wept openly. Roland dismounted to help me down from my own horse, placing his hand upon my shoulder once my feet were on the ground. After a moment, I felt composed enough to venture into the chamber where I was told my father rested upon his bier. I went forward, trying to be strong, but at the sight of my father's pale, wan face and the wrinkles creasing his brow, I wept again, feeling how short life is and how little time we have to love our fellow man, yet we waste it in feuding over small matters.

I knelt down then before my father's remains to pray that Odin grant him life in Valhalla or God give him life in Heaven, despite his failure to convert to Christianity. Finally, Roland pulled me to my feet, telling me to come and eat and then bathe myself so I would be refreshed for the funeral the next morning.

We followed a servant who took us to a chamber where we could wash ourselves and be made presentable. After a couple of hours, we then made our way into the banquet hall where I was greeted by my father's oldest counselor, who placed his hand on my shoulder and said, "My lord, let me be the first to greet you as King of Denmark. Your father's final words were, 'Let Ogier be king.'"

At that moment, my stepmother and young brother entered the room. I had no doubt she had heard the words the counselor had spoken, so I replied to him, "Speak not further of this now. My father was not a king but died as Duke of Denmark, and the choice of his successor depends upon the good grace of my lord, King Charlemagne."

"If you will bow your knee to another, Ogier," stated my stepmother, stepping toward me, "you are not worthy to succeed your father, regardless of what his choice may have been."

"Forgive me, your majesty," said the counselor, addressing the queen, "but you cannot take from Prince Ogier his right as his father's heir."

I looked at the counselor, then back to my stepmother, and then to my friend Roland to see what he thought. Before another word was spoken, however, I heard weeping, and looking at my little brother, Guyon, I saw his tears.

"Do not cry, Brother," I said bending down to hug him. "Father is in Valhalla now with the heroes."

"I am not crying for myself or our father," said my little brother, "but for you, Ogier, for I still have my mother, but now you are completely an orphan."

My heart filled with great love for my brother at these words. And while I had always disliked my stepmother, I could hear in Guyon's words his love for that woman; therefore, I felt my forgiveness of my father must extend to her as well. And while, by all rights, the dukedom should be mine, I knew I wanted it not. Still, should I refuse it so it passed to my brother, would not his mother try to influence him for her own purposes, thus bringing further calamity upon my father's land and my people, just as, for years, she had already done by goading my father to defy Charlemagne?

I returned to my feet, my brother's hand clasped in my own, and I stood and considered for a moment while everyone looked at me, awaiting my response. What action should I take? Where did my true duty lie?

And then the answer came to me in the most unexpected manner.

Breaking forth, through the window of the banquet hall, came a great light that flowed into the room and circled above our heads, and then I heard a voice like that of an angel.

"Ogier, take not the crown," it gently said. "Leave it to thy younger brother, Guyon. It is enough that you be known as Ogier the Dane for great fame awaits you, and a greater kingdom than Denmark shall one day be yours."

I truly did think it an angel from Heaven who spoke, so I crossed myself, believing perhaps the Christian God was now favoring me because I had shown true Christian forgiveness.

Then, turning to my stepmother, I said, "Milady, all that you have long desired has now come to pass. Your son shall be Duke of Denmark."

And I went down on my knee to embrace my brother, saying, "My brother, Guyon, your father and mine will not be returning to us, so you must be very good and kind and show love and justice to your people as our father would have wished. Do you think you can be a wise and just lord to the Danes?"

My little brother, who was but the age now to serve as a page, nodded his head and said, "I was born to be a king, you know. Father never let me into the throne room, but my nurse has told me all the stories of King Arthur and King Charlemagne, and I want to be a king just like them."

"For now," I told him, solemnly, "you are but a duke, but if you stay true to that desire to be good and great, perhaps someday your crown shall be restored to you, and more importantly, your people shall hold you dearly in memory long after your last days have passed."

And then I embraced my brother, kissed his cheek, and added, "My dear brother, I acknowledge you as Duke of the Danes, although you must also accept Charlemagne as your liege lord. If you agree to this condition, I and the king's army will leave this kingdom in peace, wishing you all goodwill, and we will only return should you need our service. Do you and your mother agree to these conditions?"

"It is not for you to impose conditions on a king," my stepmother objected, but my brother, with a regal wave of his hand, silenced her, and then said, "Good Prince Ogier, beloved brother, I will not forget your kindness. I agree to all. When you return, pay our respects to your king. We wish you did not have to leave our court, but we know a greater duty must lie before you, as the good fairy has said."

I was surprised by this speech, both for the maturity of it, and that he would refer to what I had thought to be an angel instead to be a fairy. His words made me think that perhaps Morgan le Fay had not forgotten me, and the words I had heard that I should someday have a kingdom of my own remained in my thoughts long after I left Denmark and returned to France.

Upon my arrival back at the Frankish court, Charlemagne graciously accepted that my brother would succeed my father, and to show his goodwill, he did restore to my brother the title of King of Denmark, asking only that the tribute continue to be paid. I was grateful for this kindness to Guyon, and so I swore in my heart that now I would ever be friends with Charlemagne.

CHAPTER 7

I FEAR, GREAT Caliph, that I am boring you by going on too long with my tale just to answer your question of what I am doing in your domains, but I am almost ready now to explain how all these events I've described have led to my arriving in Baghdad. You see, if I had taken the crown of Denmark, I would still be in my far northern homeland rather than your warm country, but instead, I remained in France as one of Charlemagne's knights for several more years. There always were adventures to be had and skirmishes and battles to be fought, although from listening to the bards' songs, I know that each year they exaggerate those stories more and more until no trace of the truth exists. Yet while I have shook my head in doubt when I have heard them sing of princesses from foreign lands with magical rings and flying horses, I have since come to marvel that what they invented was, ultimately, not so far from the truth, for a magical ring and a flying horse will still figure in this tale, to your great amazement, I suspect, as they were to mine.

I will pass over the rest of my time at Charlemagne's court until that saddest day of my life, which, ultimately, led me to be here in Baghdad.

At that time, the Moors had been threatening the borders of France, coming over the Pyrenees to ravage and pillage the land. In the past, Charlemagne had led armies to drive them back over the mountains, but Marsilius, King of the Moors, would always have his men sally forth over the mountains again as soon as Charlemagne had left, so this time, Charlemagne decided he would teach Marsilius a lesson. The king rallied a great army and marched south, over the Pyrenees and into Spain, destroying villages and sending fear into Moorish hearts. The enemy quickly fled south, leaving only the Christians behind, and, of course, the Christians threw open their city gates to welcome a Christian king.

The Frankish army marched right through the middle of Spain, dividing it in half, as well as separating Marsilius' army until Charlemagne and his knights reached the southern capital of Cordova. Once there, Charlemagne turned Marsilius' former palace into his headquarters. Meanwhile, the Moorish king had fled as far as the seashore, from where he sent emissaries, begging to make peace with Charlemagne. Roland, Oliver, and I were with Charlemagne when the emissaries arrived; these Moors foolishly came with haughty boasts of how their army would soon be joined by their Saracen brothers, hoping to frighten Charlemagne into retreat, but Charlemagne merely laughed and reminded them of how he had defeated the Saracens, driving them from Rome. After many such false threats, finally the emissaries gave way to despair and begged Charlemagne, "Sire, tell us what our master must do in order for you to leave his country and people alone."

Rather than reply, Charlemagne asked, "What has your master authorized you to offer as peace terms?"

Then the men said, "If you will go back to your own country and cease this unhappy war, Marsilius promises that he will go to Aix at Michaelmas and be baptized as a Christian; he will do homage to you then for Spain, and he will faithfully hold it in fief from you; he will give you a great store of treasures—four hundred mules loaded with gold, and fifty cartloads of silver, besides numerous bears, lions, and tame greyhounds, seven hundred camels, and a thousand falcons. Too long has this cruel war been waging. Marsilius would have peace."

Charlemagne listened and then sat silently for a minute or two, though I did not know whether his silence was from considering the offer, or merely to hold the emissaries in suspense. Finally, he turned to all his peers, who stood beside him, and said, "What think you of Marsilius' peace terms?"

Roland, whom I am sorry to say was more hot-tempered than I, exclaimed, "Put no trust in Marsilius! He is the most faithless of pagans and speaks only lies. Carry on the war as you have begun, and talk not of peace until we conquer all the way to Granada so the entirety of Spain is ours. This land previously belonged solely to Christians, so it is our duty to Mother Church to make it so again."

I always quivered inside when my friends used religion as their justification to wage war, and that the Moorish king should submit to Christian baptism made me think how little his Muslim religion must truly mean to him, nor did I forget how Charlemagne had first tried to enforce Christianity upon my own Danes. Not for the first time did I feel both Christians and Muslims saw their religions as worth following only when it suited their convenience. I fear, Great Caliph, I offend you by such words, for I am sure there are many Christians and Muslims who are very devout and true to their faiths, but yet, I have not seen many such believers in positions of power, although I trust you, yourself, are the exception. I thank you, Great Caliph, for not showing your anger at my words, for I do not speak them with ill will, but solely as one who has been a longtime observer, but ever an outsider, to both religions.

Charlemagne remained silent when Roland finished speaking. He frowned, not from displeasure over what his nephew said, but from deeply considering its merit.

But then Duke Ganelon stepped forward, and with a curling lip, he asked, "If Marsilius offers to do fealty for Spain, why should we refuse? Why march on to Granada, laying waste to the land and towns all the way, only to win through battle and loss of life what we are offered now? Anyone who advises you otherwise, my king, holds our lives to be of little value."

Although Ganelon obviously spoke to degrade Roland, I was surprised when Duke Namon agreed with him, adding, "If Marsilius admits he has been beaten and asks for mercy, it is not knightly, nor Christian, for us not to show it. I agree we should accept his terms and have peace."

Now all the other peers, except Roland and Oliver, began speaking in agreement, saying such words as, "The duke has spoken wisely. Let us have peace!"

"It is well," answered Charlemagne, "and so it shall be. But whom shall we send to Granada to sign the treaty with Marsilius and receive the gifts he pledges?"

Then all the peers began arguing about who should go, each suggesting someone other than himself for all feared that Marsilius would show his wrath to the messenger, despite his claim that he sought peace.

Finally, Roland stepped forward and said, "Sire, I will go."

"No, nephew," Charlemagne replied, shaking his head. "You are too quick to anger, and you do not favor this peace. I fear you will lose your temper before Marsilius."

"Then," said Roland, "send Duke Ganelon since he wishes for a treaty with our enemy."

Immediately, Ganelon poked his nose in Roland's face and spat out his words, saying, "Fool, would you send me on such an errand? I know full well you wish my death for having married your mother. Fine, I shall go, but when I return, I will teach you a lesson you shall not forget."

"Speak softly, Stepfather," Roland replied. "If you are afraid to go, I am certain the king can find someone else."

Ganelon's face now turned red with rage, yet holding his tongue, he turned to the king.

"Sire," he said, "if it be your wish that I go to Marsilius, I shall do so, but I know full well how false-hearted these Moors are, so do not expect my return. I ask that once you hear of my death, you care for my young son, Baldwin, to whom I leave my lands and all my wealth. Keep him well and do not let others make false claims on what is rightfully his." Here, Ganelon sent a meaningful look toward Roland, as if to suggest that noble knight would rob from his own brother.

"Ganelon, you are too fearful, and too tender of heart," Charlemagne replied. "No one shall harm young Baldwin, you have my word." Then the king handed Ganelon the staff and glove that messengers carry as a sign of their office and added, "Go now on your errand and you will soon learn there is nothing to fear."

Ganelon took the staff with his right hand, but his left hand trembled so much with fear that when he reached for the glove, he dropped it.

The peers whispered, "That is an evil omen. No good will come of this peace treaty."

But Ganelon ignored their words. Roland retrieved the glove and gave it to his stepfather, and then without a word of thanks, Ganelon called for his horse and quickly departed, taking a host of knights with him.

Three days later, after we all waited with much anxiety, Ganelon returned, bearing with him rich gifts from Marsilius for Charlemagne. It would not be until later that we also realized he returned with a heart filled to the brink with treachery, for he had made a deal with Marsilius to convince Charlemagne to return to France, believing all was well, only to have Roland and Oliver's legion, which always brought up the end of the king's army, be ambushed in the mountains and slaughtered by the Moors.

HAROUN AL-RASHID INTERRUPTS

"Prince Ogier," interrupted Haroun-al-Rashid, "your story continues on and on, and while it is not uninteresting, we have heard, even here in Baghdad, the songs the bards sing of Roland's last battle and death and how it was caused by Ganelon's treachery. It is a beautiful song, but a long one, so if you please, it is sufficient to say that Roland and Oliver died because of the betrayal of Ganelon, so please skip over that part of the tale for I am growing sleepy and would like to go to bed."

"I apologize, Great Caliph," Ogier replied, "for taking up so much of your time, but I fear I cannot easily finish my tale this evening, so as you say, it is sufficient that you know Roland and Oliver were overcome by the Moors and believed dead, but therein is the magical part of the tale that you do not know, for while Oliver's body was found, we did not find Roland's. We assumed he was among the dead, but many of the men were so wounded, bloodied, and stripped of their armor by scavengers that we could not identify them. Charlemagne, not wanting to upset his people, and especially Roland's mother, pretended that Roland's body was found, and he had an unknown soldier buried in great state in the Basilica at Blaye in a tomb with Roland's name upon it, and beside him were buried Oliver and Archbishop Turpin, who also was killed in the attack. Although I was one of the few who knew a false body was buried as Roland's, still I could not help but doubt that my friend had been killed, for the Moors were not ones to take prisoners, so there could have been no other outcome for him.

"I will finish this part of my tale now, quickly, Great Caliph, by simply saying that Ganelon's treachery was eventually known, for Charlemagne returned into Spain and punished Marsilius, capturing and interrogating him to find out how he knew Roland's legion would make up the rear, and then Marsilius, under threat of torture, revealed Ganelon's treachery.

"Once Charlemagne knew there was a serpent in his court, he had Ganelon bound and carried back to France in disgrace, dressed in a felon's clothes. Then at his court at Aix-la-Chapelle, Charlemagne held a council of his peers to try the traitor. 'Here is Ganelon, whom I pray you will judge as you think best,' said the king. 'He has traitorously caused the death of two hundred of my men, including good Archbishop Turpin, the brave Sir Oliver, and my own dear nephew, Sir Roland. He betrayed us for gold and because of the ill will he held toward Roland, his own stepson, who never did anything in truth to harm him. What shall be his fate?'

"It took all the peers only minutes to come to an agreement, and then, Duke Namon stepped forward as spokesman for them—that he with his gentle heart should feel such a sentence appropriate spoke truly to Ganelon's evil nature. 'Let Ganelon the Traitor,' said Duke Namon, 'be torn limb from limb by horses, and once he is dead, let him lie in an unmarked grave like a poor peasant.'

"Charlemagne agreed to this sentence and had it carried out that very hour, but afterwards, I heard him say, 'Such revenge or justice, call it what you will, cannot bring back my dear nephew.'

"Now, Great Caliph, I will end my tale for this evening for to tell you how I came to your land still requires many hours, but you now know all of the beginning."

"You speak," said the caliph, "as if Roland perhaps did not die. Is that true?"

"How I came to know it as truth is a story I will reserve for another evening, my lord," said Ogier, "but I will not deny that you have guessed correctly."

And then Ogier stood and bowed to the caliph, who, with a wave of his hand, dismissed his guest. The Dane then returned to his bedchamber until the great Haroun-al-Rashid should summon him again to hear the remainder of his tale.

CHAPTER 8

THE NEXT EVENING, the caliph requested that Ogier the Dane dine with him, and once Ogier was in his presence, Haroun al-Rashid dismissed everyone else and said, "I have many pressing affairs of state, but I am eager to hear the rest of your tale, and I hope you can finish it this evening."

"That I cannot promise," Ogier replied, "for there is much yet to tell, but I will do my best to tell it quickly."

"Very well," replied the caliph. "Despite my complaints about its length, I find myself completely caught up in it, and such a tale should not be rushed or it will lose its flavor and suspense. I simply find myself anxious to know how it will all turn out."

"I will continue then to tell you of my adventures," Ogier said, "but how it will turn out has yet to be determined, for neither my life nor my quest are over, and you yourself, Great Caliph, may have some say in the direction it will yet take, as I will in time explain. But for now, I will relate to you everything from where I left off last night until the time I arrived in your great city."

"Fair enough, Prince Ogier. Proceed," said the caliph, pouring wine for both of them as Ogier began.

OGIER'S TALE CONTINUES

Many tales have been told of me, of the women who have loved me, for many a woman wants to love a great knight and many noble women have been named by the troubadours as my wife, but the truth is that I never married while I lived at Charlemagne's court because I was so haunted by the memory of Princess Glorianda's lovely doe-like eyes and her olive skin that I could only think inferior the beauty of those fair-skinned, blue-eyed girls of the northern realms. Many times, my friends, and even Charlemagne himself, tried to press me to take a wife, but each time, I refused, and after the death of my closest friends, Oliver and Roland, my heart became less willing to give itself to another, for I realized how temporary life is.

Much speculation, I understand, has also been made about how I came to leave Charlemagne's court—I have heard the rumors that a dispute arose between us, or between his son, Charlot, and me, and even that I killed Charlot in anger, but none of those stories are true. I had always longed to wander in foreign lands, and now that my closest friends were gone, and I had no kingdom to rule, and Charlemagne's crushing blow to the Moors had resulted in a long and stable peace, I grew bored at court and felt I had no reason to remain.

And so, finally, I went to Charlemagne and informed him of my decision to seek adventure in other countries, hoping that a change of scenery would bring some new life to my spirit, which had grown somber since my friends' deaths.

Charlemagne, however, did not wish me to leave without some purpose. "Lead a crusade to Jerusalem," he suggested. "Free our

Christian brethren from the Muslims who persecute them."

But this I refused, for I had no interest in fighting religious wars when neither Christianity nor Islam appealed to me. Neither did the many Gods of my native religion appeal to me any longer; I have never been able to find comfort or logic in the tenets of religion, I fear. They are fine for other men who need rules to live by, but I have always thought myself wise enough to know good from evil without some bishop constantly seeking to manipulate my conscience.

Still, Jerusalem seemed as good a place as any to find a change of scenery and seek adventure, and so I decided it would be my goal.

Several weeks had now passed since our return from Spain and the deaths of Roland and Oliver. As I prepared to make my journey, I came across a letter I had set aside when I first returned home, too full of grief to have felt any inclination to read it. Charlemagne was a great advocate of learning, so Duke Namon had made certain Roland and I and all his household should be taught to read, but while I could make out my letters, I was always more a man of action than words, and so I never bothered to read anything I did not have to. But now, knowing the letter had come from my brother, King Guyon of Denmark, I thought I should at least read it and even write to tell him I would be departing Charlemagne's court. After all, I was heir to the Danish throne, though my brother was not more than ten years away from when he might wed and sire a child, which would relieve me from any future troubles of statehood.

And so I read my brother's letter, expecting to hear of the troubles in his kingdom, but instead of weaving a tale of the usual famines, peasant uprisings, sea-wolf attacks, or matters of state, my brother begged me to come visit him because he was lonely since his mother had left him for reasons he could not fully understand. "Mother," he wrote, "some months ago, married Geoffrey, Count of Lusignan, a man whom I understand is many years her senior. I do not know how she arranged it, only that she must have been corresponding with him because one day an emissary came from him with a proposal of marriage, which she accepted, and she departed the very next day. I begged her not to leave, telling her how I needed her counsel, but she told me I was now grown old enough to rule on my own, and that I must not be selfish but let her seek her own happiness."

I was greatly shocked by this news, having thought my stepmother would have enjoyed manipulating my brother so that, through him, she might rule Denmark, but I must admit I was relieved to know he was freed from her influence. That said, I was no replacement for his mother, and I thought it best not to mollycoddle him. If he were to be king, he must learn that a king can have no friends. I wrote and told him I was as surprised as he was by his mother's marriage and that I wished him well, adding that I regretted my inability to visit him because I was going on crusade to the Holy Land—that was not exactly true, but it sounded like an excuse he would understand, especially since he had recently embraced Christianity to please Charlemagne.

Once I sent off the letter, I continued to make preparations for my journey, but the marriage of my stepmother nagged at my thoughts until I recalled that she was the sister of Ganelon the Traitor, giving me all the less reason to trust her. Perhaps it was a farfetched thought, but I could not help wondering whether her sudden decision to marry might be in some way tied to her brother's recent treachery. I had no doubt the two of them had tried to manipulate both my father and Charlemagne, so it would not surprise me if she now had designs on the aging Count of Lusignan. Because the count was one of Charlemagne's vassals and word of the marriage had oddly not reached his court, I decided, after giving it much thought, that the king should be informed that his old enemy now resided within his domains. That said, I did not want to overstate the marriage's significance, so I saved it for dinner conversation that evening.

"My stepmother," I said to Charlemagne when I was seated near him at supper, "has apparently left Denmark and remarried."

"That is good news indeed," he replied, "for like you, I have never trusted her. It is a relief to know she will no longer be near your brother."

"True," I agreed, "but I do not understand why she would marry now, or why she chose the man she did."

"And who is the unfortunate man?" the king laughed, reaching for his wine.

"One of your vassals," I replied, "Geoffrey, Count of Lusignan."

"Geoffrey of Lusignan!" exclaimed Charlemagne. "Why he is practically ancient—old enough to be my father, I should think. He is extremely rich, though. Is she after his wealth, do you think? I imagine that must be her reason for he must be at least twenty years her senior."

"He is an odd choice," agreed Duke Namon, who was seated with us. "He has never been married, and it has often been rumored that no woman would have him because of his mother."

"His mother?" I said. "Why? What was wrong with her?"

"His mother," replied the duke, "was Melusine, the serpent princess—a terrible fairy whose children were all deformed and monstrous and—"

"That's enough," said Charlemagne. "The good duke forgets that my sister married one of those children."

"She did?" I said in surprise. "Which sister?"

"Princess Bertha," he replied, "and although I opposed the marriage at the time, I wish for her sake her husband had never died. I had first wanted her to marry Ganelon, whom she did marry later, but initially, she opposed it to elope with Sir Milon. I was furious at the time, but considering how Ganelon turned out, I imagine she was wiser than I in making her choice."

"Then," I said, trying to wrap my head around all this, "my stepmother has married...Roland's uncle?"

"Yes," said Charlemagne, a bit surprised himself by the thought. "Count Geoffrey is as much Roland's uncle as I am."

"Is it not strange then," I said, "that she would marry Roland's uncle when it is her brother who brought about Roland's death?"

"It is strange," Duke Namon agreed.

"And it is also without my permission," Charlemagne now fumed, "for my vassals know they cannot marry without my approval."

"Surely, it can hardly matter," said Duke Namon. "She must be past childbearing years now, and Count Geoffrey is unlikely at his age to father a child."

"If Count Geoffrey has no children, since Roland also died without any heirs, who will be Count of Lusignan upon his death?" I asked.

"The title and lands will revert to the crown," Charlemagne replied, "for there are no others of the family left alive."

"When do you propose to depart from us, Sir Ogier?" asked Duke Namon, changing the subject.

"Early in the morning," I replied.

"We wish you would not go," said Charlemagne, "but nor do we enjoy seeing your sad face at court. Go and return to us happy and ready to be a great knight of this court once more."

That evening, I did not return to the subject of my stepmother and Count Geoffrey's marriage, but I could not stop thinking of it, so I did not hear much more of the conversation.

I excused myself early that evening, promising to bid goodbye to everyone in the morning prior to my departure. For now, I wanted to be alone with my thoughts, and before I fell asleep that night, I decided to change my plans. Perhaps I would still go on to Jerusalem, but first I would stop in Lusignan under the pretense of visiting Count Geoffrey to inform him of his nephew's death, just in case word had not yet reached him, and to congratulate my stepmother on her marriage—she would not be pleased to see me, of course, but for whatever reason, I felt I had to make the visit. It just seemed too strange to me that the sister of the man who had caused Roland's death should now marry Roland's uncle. What possible plot could she now be concocting in her evil brain? I hated to think that way of her, but the marriage was otherwise inexplicable to me.

CHAPTER 9

G REAT CALIPH, I will skip over my journey to Lusignan for it was only a few days' travel by horse from Charlemagne's court, and I found my way there without incident or trouble, although I had never visited that region before.

When I was still a good ten miles away from the town and castle, I stayed at a roadside inn, and without revealing my identity, I asked questions of the owner and his wife about Count Geoffrey. All they could tell me was that he had recently wed a stern-looking but noble lady who was said to have been a queen prior to their marriage, and so the common people were quite proud their lord had married so highly. They seemed ignorant of her family—they did not even know what country she came from, for they were simple peasant folk and more inclined to repeating stories than keeping track of the politics and genealogies of various royal dynasties. When I asked them whether they had ever heard that the great hero Roland was related to the House of Lusignan, they told me they had no knowledge of such a connection, but they did tell me many of the marvelous tales they had heard of his adventures, including riding on a flying horse to strange lands, traveling to Cathay to see a princess, and other such nonsense. It was all I could do not to ask them what exaggerated tales they had heard of Ogier the Dane.

And they had many marvelous tales to tell as well of Melusine, the mother of Count Geoffrey and Roland's grandmother. I had heard nothing of Melusine prior to this, perhaps because, out of respect for Roland, she was considered a taboo subject at Charlemagne's court, but here in her old haunts, she was a topic of great discussion and speculation. Some of the local peasants seemed quite frightened to go near the castle, for they said Melusine could be seen flying about it at night, breathing fire on any who ventured to approach. Others claimed they had seen her swimming with her mermaid tail in the surrounding brooks, and they attributed her presence as being the reason why there was bad fishing that spring.

I could not help but silently chuckle over these stories, yet I also wondered what, if any, truth there was behind them; after all, Roland had been, after myself, the finest specimen of manhood at Charlemagne's court, so how could he have a grandmother who was part-serpent or part-fish, or even have the deformed uncles whom the stories claimed were Melusine's children? Nor had he ever mentioned Melusine to me in all the years we had been friends. Did he know she was his grandmother, or had he simply been too ashamed by the stories to mention her? But it did not matter. I had more important matters to consider than unraveling the origins of such fantastic tales.

I went to bed that night pondering how I should make myself known at the Castle of Lusignan. Would I even be allowed entrance, and what kind of man was Count Geoffrey to marry a woman so much younger than himself, a woman he had never even met until after he had proposed to her through his emissary? And how would my stepmother react when she saw me? Would she unleash her wrath upon me in ways she felt she could not do previously because of my father and brother? Why did my curiosity drive me on to this meeting?

My concerns, however, seemed to amount to nothing in the morning. When I went down to have breakfast in the inn's great room, it was filled with people all talking loudly.

Surprised by such a commotion so early, I asked the innkeeper the reason for it. He replied, "Count Geoffrey has been murdered, and by his wife no less."

"Murdered!" I exclaimed, and before I could give it further thought, I ran to my horse, quickly saddled and mounted him, and rode to the great Castle of Lusignan.

I never could have prepared myself for the sight of such a castle, for it was far larger even than anything owned by Charlemagne, much less my father—it must have been the grandest castle in all Christendom. And upon seeing it, I could well believe what the innkeeper had told me—that the fairy Melusine had used her magical arts to build it—for it was an architectural wonder indeed. But I had no time to marvel over it now. I rode up to the castle gate and demanded entrance.

"What is your business here?" asked the guard through the portcullis, his voice sounding both annoyed and high-strung.

"I am Ogier the Dane, one of King Charlemagne's Paladins, and I come with a message from the king for Count Geoffrey."

"Then you have not heard," the guard replied, his tone a bit more respectful now that he knew my identity. "Count Geoffrey is dead, murdered in his bed."

"I have heard," I replied, "and I wish to see his lady, in the king's name."

"His lady did the murdering as far as any can tell, considering that she fled during the night before the deed was discovered," replied the guard, "though I don't expect she'll get far, being pregnant with child—her belly's as big as a sow's."

"Which way did she go?" I demanded.

"Are you daft?" the man replied. "I said she left in the night before anyone knew it. No one knows how she did it, but Count Geoffrey was found dead in his bed early this morning, and I'd say since she has fled that she's obviously guilty. The doctor thinks she poisoned the count, but if you ask me, that one was a she-devil, so I wouldn't be surprised if it were witchcraft."

"Thank you," I replied, not caring to hear more, and I turned my horse away from the castle, uncertain now what to do. It was too late to save the count. Should I go on to Jerusalem as I had originally planned? But hold—a murder had been committed. As the king's man, was it not my duty to bring her to justice? The guard said he did not know where she had gone, but I could search for her—perhaps someone in the village saw her pass through.

My brain reeled with the thought that Roland's uncle was dead, and I could not doubt for a minute his death had been planned all along by my wicked stepmother; she was obviously up to no good, but what had she to gain by killing Count Geoffrey? I had suspected she desired power and wealth, and when I saw the great size of Lusignan, I did not doubt Count Geoffrey had been wealthier than my own father, and perhaps even Charlemagne himself, but what was to be gained by killing him and then fleeing?

And what did it mean that she was now pregnant? Why kill her husband if she were pregnant with his child? And the man had said her belly was big as a sow's, yet she could not have been married to Count Geoffrey more than a few months—certainly not long enough for her expected child to show already. Had she married him to hide an indiscretion committed with a man back in Denmark? None of it made sense to me. Of course, Melusine's children were said to have been monsters—I had thought those just exaggerated stories considering Roland was perfectly normal, but perhaps there had been some abnormal trait that Count Geoffrey had passed on to his child so that it did grow rapidly—but that was too scary to think of, nor would I ever know unless I caught her.

Not knowing what else to do, I rode at a furious pace to the next village, a few miles down the road, thinking I would begin to make inquiries there to learn whether anyone had seen her.

"I think I saw her just before dawn," the village priest told me. "I had just gone to ring the bell to call the worshipers to prayer when I saw a great fat woman come riding through town on a horse. Never would I have thought it was the countess."

I asked which way she had gone, thanked him with a gold coin, and then headed immediately in the same direction. She must have had a good three hours on me, but now I felt determined to find her, and while she might conceal herself somewhere, she could not easily outdistance me for long, given her condition.

But what would I do when I caught her? Despite her being a lady, I felt I wanted to wring her neck as payment for her evil deeds, but then I remembered she was my brother's mother, and so I could not bring such heartache to him. Nor should I kill a woman who was with child, a child who would be my late friend Roland's cousin and my half-brother's own half-brother or half-sister.

No, if at all possible, I would capture her and carry her back to Charlemagne's court so she could be brought to justice. To think that such a mighty giant-killer should die at the hands of such a fiendish woman—how disturbing that a woman should behave in such an unfeminine manner.

Throughout all that day, I rode without stopping, save to question people along the road, and each time I stopped to question them, I learned that yes, a strange woman with child had ridden through the town or passed their farm at a furious pace such that they did not know how she could not have feared for the child she carried. First, I had estimated she was three hours ahead of me, but by afternoon, it was clear she was not more than two, and by evening, only one. But as nightfall approached, I knew it unlikely I should catch up with her. My horse and I were both exhausted, so finally, I had to give in to my body's demands for rest. After I stopped beside a brook for water, I saw a small farmhouse in the distance and made my way there, seeking refreshment and perhaps a bed for the night.

The farmer and his wife looked frightened to find a knight at their door, but I made it clear to them they had nothing to fear, and I paid them well for the bread and cheese they gave me. They had not seen any woman ride by or heard anything about the events at Lusignan, for I was now a good seventy or eighty leagues from the castle and they were isolated folk who often went all day without intercourse with other people. Not wishing to frighten them further, I thanked them for their kindness and then slept under the stars for a few hours.

Waking just before dawn, I saddled my horse, grateful to have won him from Brunamont, for never was there a steed with such speed and stamina, and I needed all he had in him for this long journey. Long before dawn, I set out again, determined to get a head start on my quarry, as I had begun to think of her, for, in truth, she was the hunted.

I had no doubt that I could restrain Gudrun if I caught her, but

I had nothing on me to serve that purpose; therefore, shortly after daybreak, when I came to a small village, I purchased a sturdy rope from a still sleepy merchant so I could bind her once she was in my power; I then planned, if need be, to throw her, bound, over my horse until I could find the local sheriff to aid me in arranging for her return to Charlemagne's court.

When I asked the merchant who sold me the rope whether he had seen the lady, he told me a wealthy-looking woman who was with child had arrived and stayed at the inn the night before. Hopeful that she might not have left yet, I quickly went to the inn, demanding of the innkeeper to see the woman.

"Are you the father of her child?" he laughed. "Did you have a lover's spat?"

A blow to his chin soon taught him not to disrespect his betters; I was not usually one to lose my temper, but the more I thought of the matter, and the more lack of sleep made me irritable, the more I felt it a matter of life or death that I capture Countess Gudrun, the murderess.

Rubbing his chin, the innkeeper told me she had left just a quarter of an hour before, alone on horse, despite his protests that it was not safe for a woman in her condition to travel alone, and then he pointed me down the road she had taken.

I gave him a silver coin as compensation for his information and the blow from my fist, and then I set off again.

But when half an hour had passed and I had still not caught up with Gudrun, I was surprised and wondered whether the innkeeper had tricked me. I even stopped to check for fresh hoofprints upon the road to make sure I was headed in the right direction; there was only one pair of prints at that early an hour, and they were fresh indeed, a sign she could not be but minutes ahead of me, yet it amazed me that a woman nearly twice my age and with child could maintain such a speed.

I will not weary you, Great Caliph, with every detail of my journey for it is sufficient to say that I did not catch her upon that road. Somehow, inexplicably, she managed always to stay ahead of me, and after another couple of days' pursuit, constantly assuring myself by questioning people along the way that I was on the right path, I arrived in Marseilles, only to be told she had taken passage on a ship whose sails I could just dimly spy on the sea's horizon.

"Where is it bound?" I demanded of my informant as I stood gazing in anguish at it fading into the horizon.

"It will call at many ports," he replied, "but its final destination is the Holy Land."

The Holy Land! Could she be traveling to Jerusalem? How ironic, considering I had previously thought to go there. But why would she choose to make such a journey? Surely, she was no devout Christian going on pilgrimage. Was she seeking forgiveness there for her husband's murder? Was it possible that through her witchcraft, she knew I pursued her, so she thought crossing the sea would be her surest means of escape?

My informant did say that the ship would make many stops, including at Messina, and then Acre, the port to the Holy Land. One had to travel by land from Acre, he told me, to reach Jerusalem.

It would be a long journey, but I felt compelled to follow her. Within the hour, I was myself aboard a ship to Messina, hoping to catch her there before she could journey farther.

CHAPTER 10

ONCE I WAS aboard the ship, I felt I had a much better chance of catching Gudrun. I had managed to stay on her trail for hundreds of miles across land when she could have turned in any direction and I might have lost her, so now it was unlikely she could easily escape me while on a ship, even if I were on one a few hours behind her. A pregnant woman was bound to be very noticeable, even scandalous, since she was traveling alone, so many would notice her and be able to tell me where she went, even if she should manage to journey on from Messina before I reached there. I could not rationally explain why I felt such a need to pursue her, but I had a lingering suspicion she was bent on causing evil, so until I had her in my grasp and heard her confession, I would not let up, for evil could not be allowed to run amuck.

But the ship I found passage on had hardly left shore before the wind changed and the sky darkened. The captain quickly ordered all the passengers below deck, but I stayed to offer my help, for I was strong and I could see that every able-bodied man was needed. My insistence soon proved to be my salvation, for the storm worsened until the ship was smashed up against some rocks on a strange island the captain did not recognize. But before we could seek land, the wind sent the ship surging back out into the sea, the waves crashing over us, then pulling us back so that the bow again hit the rocks and the hull scraped against them, causing a hole to open and the ship to fill with water. Over the nearly deafening wind and the great sea's roar, I could hear the passengers' screams. One or two managed to make it up on deck, but already we were sinking. The sailors struggled to get into a rowboat, and I think one or two did, but the waves were like mountains, rising before us, lifting us high, then dashing us down, so even if any of my fellow passengers did make it into the rowboat, I have no doubt they met a watery grave.

Meanwhile, on the ship's deck, we found ourselves swept about by one shower of water after another, while the waves lifted us so that we felt like we were sailing through the air; then the sea let us fall until it was a marvel the ship did not topple sideways. Within minutes, I am sorry to say, I found myself alone on deck, all my companions swept overboard, and I had remained only because I had tied a rope about my waist and to the mast, thinking it the sturdiest piece of the ship, so likely to be the last one to sink.

When I heard a great ripping sound, I felt terror like I had never known, and then before my eyes, I saw the ship split in half, the break happening just feet from where I stood. The half I remained upon was again lifted onto a wave, and I was sent soaring up into the air, still tied to the ship's mast. And then as the wave retreated, my piece of the ship went flying forward, spit forth by the sea, and I saw myself plummeting toward the rocks of the shore. The tip of the mast hit the shore first, and suddenly, I was somersaulting through the air, then felt myself falling as the ship slid down the rock and into the sea.

Once all movement had come to a halt, I found myself hanging upside down—and underwater. I struggled to untie myself from the mast, the top of which had ground itself into the sandy sea bottom. I could see a great reef perhaps twenty feet from me—though distance was deceptive underwater. I knew I could swim to shore and to safety if only I could get myself untied. Somehow, my sword had managed to stay attached to my person, so I drew it forth to aid me, but the rope was so tight that I could not slide the sword between my leg and the rope to stretch or loosen it.

Carefully, I attempted to hack sideways with my sword at the rope against the mast, as if my sword were an ax, but after being pummeled so much by the waves and now running out of air, I could feel my strength and dexterity quickly leaving me. Worse, when I loosened my fingers just a bit to get a better grip on my sword, the current was so strong that it pulled the sword from my hand. In near despair, I watched my only means for escape float away and vanish into the deep sea's darkness. Tempted now to panic, or just to open my mouth to let the water fill my lungs and bring about my death more quickly, I fiercely struggled against the rope to free myself.

My lungs now bursting, I thought I was beginning to hallucinate when I saw a knife near my midsection, held by a hand that was trying to slice the rope and free me. When I looked beyond the hand, I saw hair and what looked like a fish's tail, but the water was dark and murky, and I was slipping into unconsciousness. The last thing I remember was the feeling of an arm encircling my chest and pulling me upward.

When I woke, I was lying on the shore, not in the sand, however, but on a beautiful Oriental carpet—and surrounded by five olive-eyed maidens.

"Where am I?" I muttered to myself, more in wonder and awe than expectation of anyone answering me, for I doubted these beautiful houris spoke Frankish or my native Norse tongue. I call them houris because they were so beautiful that I could only think I had actually drowned before I reached the shore, and by some strange circumstance, I now found myself within the Muslim paradise, surrounded by beautiful virgins, as I had heard was the reward for Muslim defenders of the Faith when they had fallen in battle. Did the Christian God not think me worthy of Heaven, or did my own Gods deny me the promise of Valhalla? But how could I complain when surrounded by such beautiful women—each one comparable to the Princess Glorianda, whom I had long loved, and each also, I would quickly discover, eager to serve my every need.

They did not reply to my question of where I was, save to laugh, and then they all sat down around me, two on each side, and one behind me, who took my head into her lap, while the others plied me with grapes and wine—I had always thought the Muslims abhorred alcohol, but it appeared to be allowed in their paradise.

I found that I was famished and dehydrated from all the salt water I had been exposed to, and so I gladly partook of the nourishment the maidens gave me as they talked among themselves in a tongue I could not comprehend. Once my strength began to be restored, I wondered how it was that I would feel hunger and thirst—bodily conditions—when I was in Heaven. Then I felt the need to relieve myself, although I held off doing so for as long as I could from fear the maidens would then leave me. Obviously, I was not dead but still quite human. I touched my forearm and ran my fingers along an old scar won in a swordfight that was still there. When I finally struggled to my feet to relieve myself, my back ached from where it had been banged numerous times against the ship's mast. The pain made it clear my life was not over, and that I was not in Heaven but, rather, some strange exotic land.

My mortality did not seem to bother my five voluptuous, dark maidens, who quickly ran to me when I returned from watering a tree. They now grabbed my hands and pulled me away from the beach and into the nearby forest. I did not know where they were taking me, but I would have willingly followed them anywhere; nevertheless, I feared that if they were sisters who were now bringing me home, their father might quickly have other plans for me than to let me compromise his daughters. Nor was I armed or able to defend myself. All I appeared to possess were the rags on my back that had once resembled clothes. And for a fleeting moment—as I proceeded onto a path through a forest of palm trees and exotic plants with a virgin on each arm, two behind and one in front leading the way, all talking and laughing in a musical foreign tongue—I realized that if I were alive, unless I had managed to land on the island of Sicily, which included the seaport of Messina, I was unlikely now ever to catch Gudrun. And even if I were in Sicily, by the time I made it to Messina, she could be on another ship embarked to I knew not where.

But my thoughts of Messina and Gudrun were quickly replaced by wonder at the sight of the great palace that rose before me when we came out of the forest. It was not a towering castle, but rather a much lower and broader Moorish-style palace with great courtyards like those I had seen in Cordova. It was astonishingly beautiful, with porticoes and porches, lush gardens, and a flowing fountain in its courtyard. Planted along its walls were orange trees like I had seen in Spain. This palace seemed the very embodiment of ease and beauty, sensuousness and peace, all at the same time.

The dark-eyed maidens quickly led me through the courtyard and into the palace, and although I feared they might be bringing me to their father, instead, I found myself beside a great indoor pool where they began to undress me. I admit I grew quite aroused by this process, but they only giggled at the sight of my natural sword becoming erect, and then they urged me, with gentle but adamant pushes, to get into the pool. Soon, a couple of them, though still lightly clothed, joined me in the pool and began to massage my shoulders with oil. I admit I made an attempt to reach for one of the women with desire, but my hand was quickly pushed aside and I was given a disapproving look. So I decided instead to abandon myself to whatever treatment they were willing to give me since they now knew I was receptive to their beauty. But while they were very attentive to me—washing my hair, scrubbing my back, and kneading my sore forearms—they in no way acted in an improper manner. Did I dare to hope they simply wanted me to be both fragrant and well-rested for a night filled with pleasures yet to come? Since I was by no means a prudish Christian, should the opportunity arise, I would avail myself of it. God or the Gods had given me natural manly instincts, and now Fate had placed five beautiful maidens in my path, so I felt it would be a crime against the Gods not to take full advantage of the situation.

When these beautiful creatures had finished bathing me, they anointed my head with oils and perfumes that, I admit, made me feel quite sleepy. Then, to my disappointment, they dressed me in a great flowing robe they firmly tied shut, and they led me to a bedchamber where two of them joined me, one on each side, as I reclined upon the bed. But I barely had felt one of them soothingly give my chest a stroke before I reluctantly drifted off to sleep.

When I awoke, the morning sun was shining. I lay there a few minutes, recalling my pleasant experience of the evening before and anticipating the pleasures I still hoped for, yet wondering whether I had dreamt it all. But looking around me, I was clearly in the same golden chamber as the previous night, lying upon the same bed with the same satin sheets, and with the same scent of perfumed flowers wafting in through open arched windows. A deep sense of complete contentment consumed me once I realized I had not dreamt the memorable experiences of the day before.

I climbed out of bed, wrapping my robe about me, although it scarcely hid my excitement at the thought of the maidens. Before I could finish crossing the room, the door opened and in stepped three of the ladies, one to open the door, one bearing a great tray of food, and another bearing a large decanter of wine and a chalice.

I bowed and thanked them in Frankish. When they did not understand my words, I thanked them in Catalan, having picked up some of that tongue during my journeys with Charlemagne through Spain. I even tried the few Latin words I knew, but the girls simply smiled and giggled as they set the food and drink on a small table for me. Then they gestured that I should sit and eat. I did as I was instructed. She who had the decanter refilled my cup with every sip I took while she bearing the tray of food fed me fruit and bread with her own fingers. The third maiden stood behind me, gently stroking my hair and massaging my shoulders as I dined.

After a very pleasant ten minutes or so of this playful meal, the remaining two maidens I had seen the day before entered into the chamber and proceeded to dance for my entertainment. They were dressed in rich silk gowns, their tiny tight bellies undulating with the music. I did not know the music's source, but it filled the chamber, and the dancers, in time with the music, shook the little bells they held in their fingers, as well as their supple bodies, while they gazed at me from above their veils. I do not know why they wore veils, for the other maidens had not up until now—I suspect it was only to add to the experience's exotic mystique and make it more pleasant for me.

Indeed, they seemed to want nothing but to serve and pamper me, which no doubt gave them great pleasure. When I tried to ask them a question or make gestures with my hands, they simply shrugged or turned away their eyes, and then they would stuff more food in my mouth or stroke my arms as their eyes grew wide in wonderment over the size of my bulging muscles; they kept trying to wrap their small hands around my arms and would laugh at their failed attempts. Now and then, one would tease me by sitting upon my knee, but whenever I thought it might be the moment when I could steal a kiss or stroke one of her perfectly round and luscious breasts, she would quickly leap away from me, giggling and making me feel a tad ridiculous. I did not doubt they all felt very fond toward me, and to say I liked them very much would hardly describe my pleasure, happiness, and great enjoyment to be in their presence. Yet it was frustratingly clear to me that they would not allow me fully to prove my manhood with any of them.

When finally the dancing, eating, and flirting came to an end, they led me out to the gardens. I tried to walk in pace with them, but they were constantly leaping about, circling me, and showing such exuberance that I found it almost difficult to walk at all. They amused themselves and each other by pretending to fight over me, making comical faces, batting their eyes at me, feigning to swoon, and then bursting into fits of laughter until I could not make any sense of their intentions.

"Where am I? Whose palace is this? What country is this?" I repeatedly tried to ask in various languages, but if they understood me at all, they would not provide answers to any of my questions.

We spent the morning in the gardens, then had lunch by the fountain in the courtyard. We spent the afternoon on the beach; I chased them about in the surf, and then I pretended to swim away from them until they came and pulled me back to shore. We rolled about in the sand and mock-wrestled, but again, whenever I got too close or hinted at a desire for intimacy, they pulled away from me.

When evening approached, they brought me back to the palace and bathed me again, only this time, when we had finished, they did not lead me back to bed, but rather, they took me down a long hallway I had not yet explored. The passage led to two large golden doors carved with reliefs that told stories of heroes or Gods I did not recognize. Two of the maidens, one on each side, opened the doors, while the others bade me follow them into the chamber. As I stepped in, and before I could adjust my eyes to the room's darkness, a beam of light shot through the room, illuminating it as one of the maidens nudged me forward. I laughed with delight as I watched the other two skipping in front of me, tossing about rose petals—I know not where they got them—and singing in a tongue I still did not understand.

We must have proceeded in this fashion for several dozen yards before I was able to see past the glowing light at the end of the room to spy a beautiful woman with raven hair. Unlike the other maidens, this woman had skin of ivory, declaring her of the northern rather than southern climes. She sat upon a gold and bejeweled throne, but when I was perhaps twenty feet from her, she rose and beckoned to me with her hand.

"Approach, Prince Ogier of the Danes," she said in a voice both regal and gentle. "You have nothing to fear here."

I did as she bid me while the maidens ceased their dancing and singing and went to sit on cushions scattered about her throne's dais. I stopped before the short flight of steps in complete wonderment.

"You look much better, Sir Ogier," said the beautiful woman. "Far more ruddy and handsome than when we fished you from the sea. I believe being petted and pampered by the gentler sex has done you a wonder of good."

"Indeed it has, milady," I replied. "I wish never to leave here; I have been treated so well, and I seek only in some way to repay you."

She laughed a long and truly jolly laugh before she finally replied, "I doubt that not, Sir Ogier, and I suspect I know how you would like to repay us, but you know in your heart that such a desire cannot be. You came to us shipwrecked and in the midst of a desperate mission, a mission you must continue."

I felt my entire face frown, not liking this reminder. Why should I be the one to bring Gudrun to justice when I would prefer to spend the rest of my days in this veritable paradise?

"Ah, but you see," said this beautiful creature, as if reading my mind, "this is not a heaven of any sort, but rather very much a part of your world, and yet not a part of it for not everything here is as it seems. We do have a few Muslim heroes who have come here to reside with us, it is true, but the Happy Isle of Avalon also has its share of Trojans and Greeks, Romans and Britons, and numerous others, and we have even made room now for the Franks and Danes yet to come."

"I do not understand, milady," I admitted.

"I think you do, Ogier. Was not all this revealed to you shortly after your birth?"

Feeling confused, I knew not what to say. And then I heard more giggling from the maidens, but higher-pitched and more raucous than before, and when I turned to look at them, I saw that their dark eyes, raven hair, and olive skin had somehow been replaced by blue and green eyes, red tresses, and snow white complexions. But most surprising of all were the little gossamer wings springing up from their backs, and they had shrunk from being nearly as tall as a man to only three or four feet in height, yet their heads were as high as my own, for they were fluttering their wings a couple of feet above the floor.

And then I knew.

"You are the fairies who granted me blessings on the day I was first presented to my father's court."

The woman who had spoken to me nodded and said, encouraging me to continue, "And...?"

"And," I said, amazed by the very words I was speaking, "I believe you must be the great Morgan le Fay, Queen of Avalon."

She bowed her head in confirmation.

"Milady," I said, my heart leaping up joyfully within me to find they had never abandoned me as I had occasionally feared, "I have understood that at the end of my life, I am to come to Avalon to meet you and King Arthur. Does this then mean that my life on earth has truly ended?"

"Do you wish it so?" asked Morgan le Fay. "You have enjoyed your time with my dark-eyed Saracen maidens, which makes me suspect you would enjoy returning to the world to find your beloved Glorianda."

I hesitated, not knowing how to reply, thinking the Queen of Avalon might be offering me a choice. But if so, I did not know what choice to make or what words to use in making it, nor did I dare to speak the words I suddenly and so strongly felt.

"Be honest with me, Ogier," she persisted. "You will do disservice to us both if you are not."

"Milady, the Princess Glorianda is indeed beautiful, and until this moment, I would have moved heaven and earth to call her my wife, but...."

"But?" she urged.

"But it is unlikely I could ever wed her because of our separate faiths and cultures, and while I am certain we could overcome those obstacles, her father would never consent to such a marriage between us. It would only result in war and strife and misery for countless people, and...."

"Go on," she urged me.

"And, I must confess, now that I have looked upon your beautiful face, milady, I know that of Glorianda can never compare to it. I mean you no disrespect, but no matter what earthly woman I find myself with, for the rest of my life, your face is the one that shall always be before me."

"You give me no disrespect, Sir Ogier. You speak truthfully, though you fear your words. But you have no reason to feel such fear."

She stepped down from her throne and put forth her hand. I raised mine and allowed her to clasp it. Then, leaving behind her companions, she led me through the hall and all the palace and out into a garden. There she sat down upon a pillow in a small clearing surrounded by trees that granted us privacy. Next, to my great surprise, she requested, "Lie down, Ogier."

I hesitated, but then I dropped to my knees. As I stretched out my legs, she gently placed her hand on my shoulder, encouraging me to lie down until my head rested in her lap.

Stroking my hair, she said, "Surely, you are the most handsome man who has ever lived. Your hair is as golden as corn, you are as fair as King Arthur, and yet as ruddy as King David. You are built like a veritable Hercules, yet you are as slender and swift as Hermes. You are perfection, Ogier. Do you know that?"

What could I say to such praise? Why did she flatter me so? I was a great champion, it was true, but even I was not deserving of such adulations.

"Ah, you do not know any of those men to whom I have compared you, do you, Ogier," she continued when she found me speechless. "They are before your time, and my own, save my brother Arthur, yet some of them reside here in Avalon so I have had every opportunity to admire their masculine beauty and learn their inner natures, and therefore, I can tell you with all honesty that none is so handsome and perfect, so noble, so good, so pure of heart as yourself. You have not set yourself up to be a saint, it is true, but neither do you bow the knee to a religion you disbelieve or serve a king blindly, for Charlemagne, despite his faults and temper, is a good and noble king, the best since my brother, and you do well to serve him, but there are other matters of greater importance than kings in this world. There are true and noble lovers, and men so strong, so handsome, and so brave that their seed must not be allowed to disappear from the human race. Dear Ogier, even I do not have the right to take you against your will, but I would make love to you and bear you a child. Would you like that, my strong, handsome prince?"

What could I possibly say to such words? I was greatly surprised, and yet my heart also burned with pride to hear she found me so desirable. "Milady, I am deeply honored," I replied, intoxicated by the very smell of her perfumed skin. Her enchanting eyes peered into mine as she spoke, and her fingers ran through my hair. And yet I was uncertain what she truly wanted from me, so I added, "But am I then to remain in Avalon forever?"

"Would it grieve you to do so?" she asked.

"Indeed, it would not, milady," I admitted, "but I...I believe I have a purpose on this earth that I have not yet fulfilled. You see, I was shipwrecked while pursuing a woman who—"

"Shh. Did I not already make clear that I know all that?" she asked, placing her finger over my lips. I wanted to open my mouth and swallow her delicious finger, but as my lips tried to curl about it, she laughed and pushed my head from her lap. Then she sprang up, leaving me sprawling at her feet.

"You have conquered me, milady," I said, rising enough to kneel before her. "I will do anything you wish."

"I wish to bear your child, Ogier, but first I will tell you why," she said, gesturing for me to rise. "Your mission is not completed yet. You must continue your pursuit of Gudrun, for I have a great interest in your quest as I will explain tomorrow, but for now, it is sufficient to say that Gudrun is an evil woman, full of spite, and not above murder, and while a knight as great as yourself doubtless fears very little, nevertheless, there is no guarantee that she will not harm you with her witchcraft—for she is quite adept in the dark arts. It would rend my heart to have harm come to you, yet what you must do is necessary. Still, should you fail, another must be ready to complete your quest— and no one but your son could be your equal, so I desire to bear your child, plus it would comfort me greatly to have your son should I lose you. Do you understand, Ogier? I have loved you since the day you were born. Of course, all women in this world who see you love you, but only I am to have you. We cannot let love interfere with our duties, but in this case, your returning my love would aid us in fighting this evil."

I admit I did not fully understand her reasoning behind her request, but she was Morgan le Fay, so who was I to refuse her?

"Milady," I replied, "if, as you say, I am the most handsome man in this world, then it is only right that I be at the service of the most beautiful woman who has ever lived. I will do whatever is your will."

Then she smiled and drew me into her arms, pulling me close, and giving me a long and stimulating kiss until I could resist no longer. I reached down and swept her up into my arms, asking, "Which way?" and carried her inside the palace. In the hall, we passed her maidens, who smiled mischievously at me but did not impede us. Following Morgan le Fay's directions, I bore her to her chamber. There I lay her upon the bed, and then I spent with her the happiest night of my life.

Great Caliph, I cannot even begin to tell you how it is that I managed to rise from that bed the next morning after so many hours of pleasure and so little sleep. I would not have risen at all save that when I woke, my beloved was nowhere to be seen. So I quickly bathed and dressed, surprised and alarmed by the silence in the palace, half-expecting every moment that the fairies would come to bring me food or lead me to Morgan le Fay, but when none had yet come once I was dressed, I ventured forth to find the palace deserted. Finally, I went into the courtyard, and there by the fountain, I found Morgan le Fay waiting for me with a tray filled with bread, fruit, and drink for our breakfast.

"Come, gentle lover," she said, inviting me to sit beside her. "Eat your fill while I explain a few things to you."

I thought it only polite to ask her how she had slept, but as I started to form the words, she dismissed them with a wave of her hand. "Our goal has been accomplished," she replied. "That is what matters. We had a splendid time together, and the child is already growing in my womb."

"I feel so honored that you wish to bear my child, milady. I hope he will be a comfort to you should I perish in my quest, considering that you say Gudrun is a sorceress."

"Ogier, I do not want your child for myself, but for your sake, and the sake of all mortals. I wish to make the world a better place, and this child shall help in my purposes, but now, let us speak of your purpose. Eat while I tell you what you do not know about your stepmother, Queen Gudrun."

And then she began to weave most amazing and horrifying tales about Gudrun, not only about my stepmother's purpose in previously wanting to kill me at my father's court, but how she was more than human—truly an almost supernatural being, an evil woman named Lilith, who since ancient times has been intent on destroying all the human race. This evil woman's dearest wish is to obtain the golden wedding rings that originally belonged to Adam and Eve, the progenitors of the human race—of whom I had heard from my Christian friends, although I had always thought the story all make-believe and nonsense. My religion had taught me that the first man and woman had been made from a tree by Odin, but it mattered not to me, and clearly, the Queen of Avalon was wiser and more knowledgeable than I.

Morgan le Fay concluded her story by saying, "One of those rings that Gudrun wishes to obtain is in the possession of your friend Roland, and the other was in his Uncle Geoffrey's possession. I suspect Gudrun's reason for killing Count Geoffrey was to obtain that ring. However, she does not know what became of the other ring—most likely she believes, as do you, that Roland is dead. She expected Ganelon to find it and give it to her, but as you know, Roland's body was not found. She now believes that ring lost, but the truth is that Roland yet lives and continues to wear it. Regardless, she now thinks if she can return to Jerusalem, built where once the Garden of Eden existed, with the ring she now has, she will be able in that Holy Place to access certain powers hidden in the earth to determine the other ring's location. Should she find the other ring, she will have powers like none who has ever resided upon this earth before, and then the horror and destruction she will wreak upon the human race will be indescribable. She is even now well on her way over the sea, and once she lands in the East, she will make her way to Jerusalem. You must stop her before she can reach the Holy Land to prevent her from using the ring she has or trying to obtain the other one. Do you understand why it is so important that you stop her?"

"I think so, milady, but please, is it true what you say—that Roland is not dead?"

"No, he is most assuredly alive. He was rescued from the battlefield and healed by one of my great friends. He is now in Jerusalem, waiting for Gudrun to arrive so he may stop her. There is not time for me to explain more to you—Roland can tell you his own story when you see him. Are you ready to take on this mission?"

"If my stepmother is really this evil creature, as you say," I replied, "and she is intent on destroying the human race, then it is my duty, milady, to stop her, besides which I would do anything for my friend Roland, and it goes without saying, milady, for yourself."

"Well said, noble Ogier. I trust that you will succeed, but should you not, do not despair, for now a future hero lies in my womb who will continue to fight against this evil woman if you do not succeed."

"I shall not fail you, milady," I promised.

"Very good," she replied. "Have you now eaten sufficiently?"

"Yes, and I am ready to begin this quest," I said, setting down an apple core beside the orange peels and breadcrumbs that were the remnants of my breakfast.

"So be it," she said and clapped her hands together.

Suddenly, I heard a loud whooshing sound, and looking up, I saw a great winged horse come through the sky, his wings first gracefully beating and then allowing him to soar downward and land in the courtyard.

"This is my steed, Papillon," said Morgan le Fay. "We of Avalon are allowed only rarely to assist and interfere in mankind's story, and even then, we can render you only limited help. Papillon will fly you to Messina, but from there, you must journey on your own. Remember, Gudrun has a good couple of days' start on you, so you must make haste. You will find attached to Papillon's saddle a bag of food provisions and your sword attached, as well as some coins to buy yourself new armor. My maidens were able to rescue your sword from the sea's depths, but I am afraid your old armor was badly ruined in the shipwreck."

"Thank you, milady," I said, standing and bowing.

Morgan le Fay now stood herself and planted a most memorable kiss upon my lips. I was then tempted to sweep her up into my arms again for another night of pleasure, but she quickly broke off her kiss, urging, "Make haste, my great and true love."

And in a daze of love, I turned to Papillon and lifted myself up into his saddle. The moment I was upon his back, and before I could so much as say, "Goodbye" to Morgan, he flew into the air; I quickly grabbed tight hold of his reins, and soon I was high above the palace, parted from the most amazing and beautiful woman I will ever know.

HAROUN AL-RASHID INTERRUPTS

"I can hear no more tonight," said Haroun al-Rashid. "I wish to go to bed and dream of the beautiful Morgan le Fay before I learn how you came to my domains, for Jerusalem is part of my caliphate. But your further stories will keep for another day."

"As you wish, Great Caliph," Ogier said, feeling not an ounce of jealousy that the caliph should wish to dream of the woman he loved, for just as Morgan le Fay had told him that all women desired him as the world's most handsome man, so it would be only natural, Ogier knew, that all men should likewise desire her immortal beauty.

And Ogier himself retired to his room and had a dream very similar to that of Haroun al-Rashid that night.

CHAPTER 11

WHEN HAROUN AL-RASHID next called Ogier to him, it was early afternoon, but the caliph said all his other work would have to wait while the Dane finished his tale, for he could not concentrate on anything from wanting to know so badly whether Ogier ever did capture Gudrun and how the knight had eventually ended up in his own capital of Baghdad.

"Please continue your story but make a quick end to it," the caliph requested, and so Ogier, nodding his head in assent, began to speak again.

OGIER'S TALE CONTINUES

I do not know if I can finish my tale quickly enough to please you this evening, Great Caliph, but I will skip over any unnecessary details, including my Mediterranean journey, and simply say that Morgan le Fay's great flying horse, Papillon, landed me in an obscure location about a mile from Messina, where it would not be seen, and from where I could easily walk to the harbor. I soon took passage on a ship and crossed the sea without incident; we made a couple of stops in Greece and then Cyprus, and then we arrived at Acre. From there, I found another ship to take me south until I approached near to Jerusalem, and then I found a guide to lead me overland to the holy city.

By that time, I realized that to enter your empire as a knight, Great Caliph, would raise eyebrows, and I might be perceived as a threat, so over my armor I donned a pilgrim's robe, and despite the extreme heat, I made my way to Jerusalem so dressed, wondering why Gudrun wished to be there. Morgan le Fay had told me the Garden of Eden had once existed where Jerusalem now stood, but that I could not believe, for everything was almost a desert, dry and dusty with just little, scraggly trees and plants that made me long for the deep, dark green forests of France and Denmark.

I need not describe for you, Great Caliph, the ancient City of Jerusalem since it lies within your domains, but perhaps it would interest you to know my first impressions of it. Because I know how the city is revered as one of the holiest places on earth by you Mohammedans as well as the Christians and Jews, I was not prepared at all to think of it as anything other than a great shining city of light with gold-crowned domes, but instead, I found it old and foul, the streets full of horses, donkeys, and stinking camels, and the great sand and dust of the road covered everything, making people soiled and parched. Personally, I find it far inferior to your own magnificent capital of Baghdad, Great Caliph, and save for it being the site of significant moments in the lives of Christ Jesus and the Prophet Mohammed, it has little to recommend it.

I beg your forgiveness, my lord, for I do not wish to speak ill of a holy place, but not being of your faith, I was not as impressed or moved by the city as I had expected to be. It did not help that I had difficulty speaking with the inhabitants. As cosmopolitan a city as it is, it took me nearly a day before I found a pilgrim who spoke Frankish, and I knew better than to think I'd find anyone who could speak Norse. This pilgrim, thankfully, was able to lead me to a small Christian church where I met a priest who could speak many languages, including Frankish, Aramaic, and Arabic, and who was himself from Italy.

I decided to ask this priest for help in my search, though I knew not how to explain my strange quest. I felt it best to make subtle inquiries, claiming that I was searching for my mother, whom I said was a great lady from the North who had recently come to Jerusalem. We had, unfortunately, been separated, I continued, she sailing to Palestine before me, and now I was hoping to find her.

The priest kindly agreed to make inquiries for me. Meanwhile, he found me lodging at a nearby monastery; the monks there were used to offering shelter to pilgrims, and I daresay the pilgrims' generosity in return is what fed the monks.

The next morning, although I wanted to wait for news or go out searching for Gudrun, I politely allowed the monks to subject me to attending Mass, followed by joining a group of pilgrims who were to visit the city's various holy sites, including the Dome of the Rock and the Place of the Skull where the Christ had been crucified. I held no reverence for these places, never having become a Christian, and yet, now that I was in Jerusalem, I felt a certain curiosity to see them since they were held sacred by most of my friends; if there were any truth to the Christian religion, perhaps here I should be able to verify it.

But while the pilgrims prayed and sang as we climbed the Place of the Skull, I felt only exhaustion from my long journey, plus irritation from the hot sun that caused me to sweat profusely, and frustration that my horrid stepmother had managed to escape me. In fact, all I wanted was to return to the monastery and lie under the shade of a palm tree with a cold glass of water, but despite the marvelous colored-glass drinking vessels I had seen among the street vendors, which were like nothing I had ever seen in Christendom, I didn't think any cold water to fill them existed in this desert land.

As the pilgrims swarmed about me, their chanting making me dizzy until I thought I might begin to hallucinate, a tall, well-built man in pilgrim garb approached me. He looked straight at me, and for a moment, I thought how he had a warrior's build and stance, and I suspected he might be going to attack me. Tensing up and realizing I had left my sword at the monastery, I prepared myself for a fight. But then I had the shock of my life when he pulled back his hood—there before me stood the truest friend I have ever known.

"Roland!"

His name had barely escaped my lips before he had his hands on my shoulders and was saying, "Well met, old friend. I knew you would soon show your face."

"How? How know it? How...how are you even...? We thought you...." Yes, I know Morgan le Fay had told me I would see him again, but until this moment, I had been afraid of believing it from fear I would only end up disappointed.

"I am alive and well, good Ogier," he assured me, "and I believe you and I are meant to complete this quest of ours together."

"Then you know why I am here in Jerusalem?" I asked.

"I do not, save that I have been told you are to help me, and perhaps I am to help you also, or so Merlin explained to me."

"Merlin!" I exclaimed. "Surely, you don't mean...?" But I knew he did. For had I not been under the lifelong care of Morgan le Fay, the great wizard Merlin's pupil in magic? Then why should it seem wondrous that Roland had spoken to that very great sorcerer? And yet, could anything seem more wondrous?

"Come back to my lodgings with me, my friend," said Roland, "and I will tell you all about it. You will find I am not quite the Roland you knew, for I have had many adventures in the time since last we met, and I imagine you have had your own to tell me of as well."

I accompanied Roland most willingly, although I expected an inn and found us instead at what seemed far more like a palace. He brought me inside and to a great bath where we stripped off our dirty clothes and bathed our sweaty bodies, giving them relief from the incessant heat and dust, and then freshly clothed ourselves, although I was disappointed not to find any beautiful women present to massage or perfume us during this process—clearly, I had been far too spoiled during the time I was in Avalon.

Then Roland led me to a quiet chamber where he called for a meal to be brought, and as we dined, we shared our stories.

To tell you Roland's story would take as long as it does to tell my own, so I will simply say that he related to me how he had been wounded at the Battle of Roncesvaux, but Merlin had found him and restored him to health, then taken him to see his grandfather, Count Raimond of Lusignan. Roland did not even know that his grandfather, whom he had never met before, was still alive. Count Raimond resided in the monastery of Montserrat, and upon their meeting, the old man told Roland a long and convoluted story of his family history, which I would have found quite unbelievable had I not had my own dealings recently with fairies. As I have already explained, Roland's grandmother, Count Raimond's wife, was the great fairy Melusine; she was mother to several children, including Roland's father and his uncle, the late Count Geoffrey of Lusignan, whom my stepmother had wed and then murdered, stealing the golden ring I was now seeking to regain.

When Roland had finished his story, I told him how I was seeking to find my stepmother who had married and then murdered his uncle, and how Morgan le Fay had told me she was an evil being from ancient times. Roland and I agreed we had been destined to meet here in Jerusalem to bring Gudrun to justice as well as to reacquire the ring, even though we knew not what power the ring held, or how it could be used in conjunction with the one Roland always wore upon his finger, although until now I had never thought to question him about why he wore it.

Once we had finished our stories, Roland accompanied me back to the monastery to collect my belongings so I could stay with him. He had reached Jerusalem several weeks before me, so I was relieved to see he had no trouble leading me through the labyrinth of crowded streets back to the monastery.

As soon as I entered the building, I was delighted to find the priest I had previously befriended waiting for me.

"I have news of the woman you seek," he said. "She was seen leaving Jerusalem just an hour ago. There can be no mistake about it because she was with child and looked ready to burst forth. The sight of her caused a great stir in the street, for women do not so flaunt themselves when they are in that condition. Her behavior is disgraceful, but she found some poor Muslim in need of money to assist her. She was last seen being led by him and riding on a donkey. In such a condition, I suspect she will end up delivering her child on the road and that—"

"Which direction did she go?" I interrupted.

"North. Someone said he thought he heard her say something about heading toward Bethlehem, which is just a poor town, a—"

"Bethlehem!" exclaimed Roland, his eyes growing wide with horror as he looked at me.

"We must hurry," I replied and went into my solitary chamber to collect my belongings so we could depart, but Roland followed me, and once we were alone, he exclaimed, "Ogier, do you not understand? She is going to Bethlehem. She—"

"Yes, we must be after her," I agreed.

"But Bethlehem—and she is pregnant with child—and being led on a donkey. She is—why, she is planning to...." Clearly, Roland was so terrified by whatever he imagined that he could scarcely find words. "I can't believe it, at least I don't want to, but considering the power you said she has according to Morgan le Fay, then Bethlehem, well, it...."

And then I understood what Roland feared to say—and feared even more to believe.

I had little belief in the Christian God, so it took me a bit longer to draw conclusions, but Bethlehem was where the Christ child had been born, and his mother, the Virgin Mary, had traveled there on a donkey, or so I believed the story went, so if Gudrun were riding there on a donkey, when she doubtless could have afforded a horse or camel, then—then she was making a mockery of Christ's nativity. Could it be...that she intended to replicate it, and....

"She seeks to bring the Antichrist into the world!" exclaimed Roland.

It was unthinkable, unbelievable, and yet, why else would an evil pregnant woman, truly an ancient spirit who had hated Adam and Eve and all the human race for centuries, seek to give birth in Bethlehem?

Quickly, I buckled on my sword. Then I went to find the priest and ask where we could obtain horses to take us to Bethlehem; soon, we were at the stable, tossing coins at the horses' owners and demanding to know in which direction lay Bethlehem.

In another five minutes, we were galloping through the streets and out Jerusalem's gate, stirring fear in people's hearts as we nearly ran them down, but they would soon know far worse fear if we did not stop the evil Gudrun.

"She could not have gotten far on a donkey!" exclaimed Roland as we raced over the rocky road. Bethlehem, the stable owner had told us, was only about five or six miles south of Jerusalem. Surely, riding on a donkey, she couldn't have traveled that far in an hour, and even if she had, perhaps she had not yet given birth to her child.

As we rode at a furious pace, kicking up sand and dust in our wake, my thoughts were racing. What would we do when we caught her? How could we hold her? We were not the law in this country. We should put her to the sword, or at the very least hang her—it would serve her right—but such a crime would only bring upon us the wrath of the local community, and I had heard these Muslims were fierce in their justice, believing in an eye for an eye and a tooth for a tooth to a far greater extent than the Christians, so should we kill her, were we not likely to suffer the same punishment? And could we murder the mother of an unborn child? Were we overreacting? Could she really be giving birth to the Antichrist? I did not even know whether I believed in such a thing—it seemed too bizarre to be true, and how could an innocent young babe hurt anyone? Perhaps we could physically force mother and child to follow us, to be led back to France and to justice, but Antichrist or not, I was no baby-killer. Even if this child were to grow up to be the most wicked human ever to live, for the time being, it was just an unborn child. Even the Christ, to my knowledge, worked no miracles as a babe. To kill the mother would be to kill the child, and then we would be more akin to King Herod slaying innocent babes than Christians or heroes of any sort.

My eyes scanned the road, looking far ahead for sight of her as all these thoughts tumbled about in my mind, but the village appeared in the distance before we found her. Was it possible she could have made it into Bethlehem so quickly?

And then I heard Roland, just a hair's breadth behind me, shout, and by the time I looked around, he was galloping off the path and into a field below a hill. As I turned my horse around to follow, I saw a donkey tethered to a tree, and then two women's covered heads kneeling on the ground, and they were shouting at one another.

"Give him back to me!" screamed one woman. Roland was reining in his horse to a halt just feet from the women as I heard the woman's cries, and then I saw the other rise to her feet, clutching a babe.

"He's my child," said the first woman, struggling to stand, exhausted from her labor. She was clearly the mother—my stepmother—but who was this other woman?

I came to a halt beside Roland, who was dismounting his horse.

"What is going on here?" I demanded, not understanding the situation.

The unknown woman, clutching the babe, said, "Roland and Ogier," stunning me that she knew our names, "you need not have rushed so, for never would I allow any grandchild of mine to be the cause of such evil coming into the world."

I did not know what she meant until I heard Roland gasp and say, "Do you mean? Are you my grandmother?"

"Yes," she said, "and this is my grandson, the future Count of Lusignan, and someday from his line will spring the Kings of Jerusalem and Cyprus and many other noble houses, and great and good things shall result from them, despite the tainted blood this woman gives to him."

"Give him back," screamed Gudrun, suddenly swinging her fist at the head of the woman I now understood to be the fairy Melusine.

But Melusine was too quick for her. She sprang up into the air, hovering there with the child safely cradled in her arms. As she turned sideways to continue speaking, I saw wings had sprouted up through the back of her robe.

"I will return the child to Lusignan, where the castle steward will care for him and I will watch over him," Melusine said to Roland and me. "In the meantime, do not let this evil one escape."

Before we could respond, she darted up into the sky like a hunting falcon and disappeared, becoming but a speck within a few seconds, and then being completely gone in the next.

I was stunned, and Gudrun let out a bloodcurdling wail, but Roland still had his wits about him. With drawn sword, he stepped toward Gudrun. He lifted his blade and prepared to swing it, but then he paused, as if respectful of her grief.

Finally, she looked at him. Then, scoffing, she said, "You are no true knight if you threaten a woman with violence."

"You are no mere woman but an evil witch," he replied, "and, therefore, undeserving of chivalry's courtesies. You are a thief, for you stole my Uncle Geoffrey's ring. Give it back to me now before I cut it from your finger. If you cooperate, I may let you live."

I also drew my sword, but before I could close in on her, a great gust of wind sprung up and blew sand into my and Roland's eyes, momentarily blinding us.

Over the roar, I heard her shriek, "You fool mortals; you stupid children of Adam and Eve!" And then placing my hand over my face and peeking between my fingers, I saw how the sand swarmed about her like a colony of bees, and then it seemed to pick her up into the air and carry her from our sight, as if she were a veritable tornado, and as she whizzed away into the sky, she screeched, "You shall never conquer me!"

We stood, peeking between our fingers, watching her disappear, and though she left only half as quickly as Melusine, nevertheless, we were amazed.

"She controls the very elements," Roland said in awe.

Then a burst of thunder warned us that she had not completed her revenge upon us; in another moment, we found ourselves soaked to the skin. Quickly, we climbed back onto our horses, unable to do anything more but seek shelter from the storm in Bethlehem.

As we rode into the village, I felt uncertain that we had succeeded in our mission. The child was safe. The fairy Melusine—I still could not believe I had seen her—had assured us the child was safe, but the evil one still lurked out there, and she still had Roland's family ring.

That night at an inn, as we discussed the day's events over our wine, I asked Roland, "Is it the ring, perhaps, that gives her power?"

"I had never heard that the rings had power other than to protect the wearer in battle or in law," he replied. "Certainly, my ring has never left my finger since my mother gave it to me as a keepsake of my father, and in all that time, I have never known anything magical to happen to me because of it. If she truly is an ancient evil spirit, who knows what powers she might have, regardless of the ring."

"I don't know then," I replied, "that I believe the ring is so important that we need to get it back from her when she already has such great power."

"No," Roland objected. "Merlin told me we must collect the ring, and also, we must bring the Holy Lance back to him at Montserrat."

"The Holy Lance?" I said. "What is that?"

"It is the spear with which the Roman soldier Longinus pierced Christ's side during the Crucifixion. Because Christ's blood flowed onto it, it is of great power."

These Christians and their holy relics, I thought. But then, we Norsemen had our holy wells and trees and whatnot, if you believed in that sort of thing.

"And where, pray tell, is this magical spear?" I asked. "And why is this the first I have heard of it?"

"It is in Jerusalem," said Roland. "We will collect it before we return to France, but first we must get back the ring. Didn't Morgan le Fay explain all this to you?"

"Then we will worry about the Holy Lance later," I said, not sure I had paid attention to everything Morgan le Fay had said, I being uninterested in these Christian stories—and too much under the spell of her beauty. "But how do you propose we get back the ring if, whenever we get close to Gudrun, she can just fly away, leaving us not even knowing where she has gone?"

"I don't know," Roland admitted, pausing to swallow the last of his wine, "but we will search for her until we find her."

I scowled, annoyed by the difficulty before us, although I dearly wished to capture and even kill my stepmother, if only to pay her back for causing me to lose my father's affection. I felt I would be justified in such a killing, and her having murdered Roland's uncle only made my desire all the greater.

"Fair enough," I said, rising to my feet. "I don't know how we'll get back that ring, but we'll get a good night's sleep, and then we can continue our quest in the morning."

CHAPTER 12

G REAT CALIPH, I will not bore you with all the many incidents of our journeys in search of the evil Gudrun, and I beg you not to be alarmed by our desire to carry away the Holy Lance from Jerusalem, for we never did achieve that part of our quest.

I can tell you that it was far from easy to trace Gudrun after her disappearance near Bethlehem. If she even remained in the Holy Land, then because she was no longer pregnant, she must have blended in well with other women, for except to say she was a fair woman from northern lands, it was difficult for us to describe her, and Jerusalem was always filled with pilgrims coming from France and England and other parts of Christendom who had fair skin, so she would have easily blended into the crowd. For all we knew, she could have returned to France or Denmark, but since she was now a known murderess, we thought that unlikely; perhaps, instead, she had traveled to the steppes of Russia or to far off Cathay or some other distant land. In truth, we had little hope of finding her, much less of capturing her and bringing her back to France for justice.

Yet Roland insisted we search. He was certain we would find her, and so we traveled throughout your domains, Great Caliph, from one end to the other, covering thousands of miles and spending seven years in our search. Everywhere we went, we asked about her, giving her description, and now and then, we received word of a sighting from someone who had good skills of observation and had noticed beyond her fair features and beauty that she was past her fortieth year and how she carried herself like a queen, or as was just as often the case, we met someone who had felt the lash of her sharp tongue.

We went into Egypt, to Alexandria and the ruins of Thebes, in search of her, and we went into Ethiopia and through the Arabian desert. We even visited Mecca, seeing the streams of pilgrims who worshipped at the great black stone in a manner we could not understand. We crossed the Tigris and Euphrates rivers and entered the lands of India and far off Cathay, as far as the Great Wall itself. We saw many strange and wondrous sites, enough to fill many storybooks, and I do not doubt it would amaze you to hear of all our adventures, Great Caliph, even though many of the places we saw lie within your vast empire. We had so many fantastic and unexpected experiences that it would take me a fortnight of evenings to relate them all to you, and so, because I know you wish to hear the end of this tale, I will skip over them and instead tell you solely of the last leg of our travels, which ultimately resulted in my arriving on a marvelous flying carpet in your glorious capital of Baghdad, as you yourself saw.

As I said, we searched for Gudrun for seven years, and finally, having been unsuccessful, we found ourselves in Anatolia. We had not yet acquired the Holy Lance, but we were now closer to Constantinople than Jerusalem, and we feared that trying to obtain the Holy Lance would prove extremely difficult on our own, so we hoped that if we traveled to Constantinople, we could have an audience with its patriarch and perhaps he could give us permission, or even get permission from the Pope for us, to obtain this holy relic and aid us in sending emissaries to you, Great Caliph, so that you would eventually agree to present it to us. That said, we knew that if we did obtain it, surely the Holy Church would want it for itself, and Roland said we could not tell anyone that we were to acquire it to give to Merlin, for no one would believe us that the great wizard yet lived, or even if they did, they would say he had not been a Christian but a pagan, so they would not surrender such a relic to him, nor have it in a place other than where Christian pilgrims might yet venerate it as a holy relic, for though we were to bring it to Montserrat, we did not know whether Merlin would leave it there. Roland and I discussed all these details at great length. Of course, we also considered stealing the Holy Lance, but we had no doubt we would be caught and killed if we did, so we traveled toward Constantinople since we were already in Anatolia.

Initially, we had gone to Anatolia in search of Gudrun. We had heard rumors of a powerful woman who resided in a cave not far from Mount Ararat. But after determining that this woman was not Gudrun—in fact, this supposed wise woman had been dead for several years by the time we reached her former location—we decided to go on to Constantinople, truly weary of our attempts to find Gudrun. We determined now to focus on the Holy Lance. After all, we thought that if Merlin wanted the Holy Lance, perhaps Gudrun also would desire to possess it, for she clearly sought any sacred relics or magical tokens to enhance her power. Therefore, we thought if we obtained the Holy Lance, we might find that she had been following or spying on us all these years, and then she would make her presence known in an attempt to take it from us. Very little would have surprised us, and so we decided to journey on to

Constantinople to see how the Holy Lance might be acquired.

As we traveled west through Anatolia, we came to the region known as Cappadocia, famous for its amazing geological formations created by volcanoes that erupted in ancient days before man's memory to form all manner of curious and oddly shaped hills, enormous rocks, and small mountains. Many of these large rocks had been carved out to become the homes of monks, and some of them even housed whole villages of people, but on this particular day that I speak of, we saw no one about even when we passed rocks in the distance that appeared to contain caves. The absence of people was not surprising to us, however, for it was winter, and that afternoon, it had begun to snow, creating one of the most beautiful and striking scenes I had ever seen as the white flakes covered the tower-shaped caves. But nature's beauty does not prevent its danger. Before long, Roland and I found ourselves caught in a blizzard, and within seconds, we could no longer see the rocky cliff homes; soon we had lost all sense of direction and knew not which way to turn to seek shelter.

Rather than ride now, we dismounted from our horses and led them on foot, hoping to prevent them from having an injury because we could not see the ground well when mounted. We traveled slowly in this manner for several minutes until something spooked our steeds; before we knew it, Roland and I had both lost hold of their bridles and they had bolted off into the storm, taking with them everything we owned, save the clothes and armor on our backs. We had no hope of pursuing them in a blizzard, but while we sought shelter, we also knew if we did not go far, perhaps we would find them when the storm was over.

We had not walked more than a couple of hundred feet from where we had lost the horses when I heard Roland, just steps in front of me, cry out. Before I could ask what was wrong, I found out for myself when the ground dropped out from beneath me; instantly, I was falling through the air, and then I landed in a rocky pit, cushioned by the snow.

Roland was lying beside me.

"Ogier, are you hurt?" he asked, quickly rising to his feet to shake what snow he could from him.

"No, I'm all right. The snow is soft," I said, struggling to stand.

Looking about me, I first wondered how we would climb out of this great hole in the ground, but after a few seconds, once my eyes adjusted to the darkness, I was able to see a cave's mouth in the pit.

"I have heard," said Roland, "not only of monks dwelling in this strange land's caves, but also of entire underground cities dating back to ancient times. Perhaps we have stumbled upon a cave leading to one."

"Perhaps," I said, "but regardless, that opening will shelter us until the snow stops."

I stepped into the cave's mouth, followed closely by Roland, who drew his sword in case it contained unfriendly inhabitants. At first, I truly thought the cave might lead to an entire underground city, for it branched off in several directions and into various chambers, but after we had ventured inside for several feet, it was clear to us the dwelling place was completely deserted.

"We should not go farther," I warned Roland when we had retreated far enough that we had lost what little glimmer of daylight existed amid the storm. "We cannot risk getting lost in a maze of tunnels."

"True," said Roland. "Hopefully, the storm will stop soon, and perhaps then we will be able to see whether the cave might provide us a way out of this pit."

But the storm did not let up. It quickly grew completely dark outside, and we found ourselves longing for beds rather than the cave's hard, cold floor, but a hard floor was better than facing nature's fierce elements on such a night. Still, I thought we should perhaps try our luck in climbing out of the pit. It could not be more than twenty feet deep, and if one of us stood upon the other's shoulders, perhaps he could find a foothold and scramble out to seek help in rescuing the other.

But before I could suggest such a plan, Roland was snoring on the cave floor. After watching over him for a while, I became convinced that no danger threatened us from deeper inside the cave, so I fell asleep beside him.

That night I had the strangest dreams. Long had I thought of Morgan le Fay, of how she had been present in my life since I was but a few days old, of how she had appeared to guide me at different times, stopping me from taking the crown of Denmark, and later rescuing me from death to show me a passionate night like no man before had ever experienced with a woman. She had even told me I had gotten her with child. But now seven years had passed since that encounter. Where had she been all this time? Had she forgotten me? I could not believe that. Had she given birth to my child as she had intended? Doubtless the child—I did not know whether it were a boy or girl, though I most frequently envisioned a boy—was safe at Avalon with his mother, but why did she keep him from me? She knew I could not find Avalon on my own. Or did she no longer need me once I had tracked down Gudrun? But she had not even needed me then, for after all my searching, Melusine had appeared to resolve the situation, and how could Morgan le Fay not have known she would? Why then was I being led on this long quest? Tonight, trapped in a cave in a snowstorm, all these thoughts raced through my head, as they had many nights previously, but now they manifested themselves in visions like never before.

In my dream, Morgan and I were together again, not just together, but caught in the throes of lovemaking. I was telling her—whenever I was able to pause long enough—how much I loved her, how much I desired her, how much I missed her and longed to be with her forever, but she only said, "In time, Ogier, my love, in time; we have nothing but time. We have all the time in the world, and time even beyond that."

I could not stop to ask her to explain what she meant because I was so enjoying her favors, finding it unbelievable that we were together again. I was marveling at her luscious breasts, enjoying the scent of her silky hair against my face, delighting in the feel of her hands stroking my broad back, and then just at that moment when I thought I could stand it no longer, she laughed—a hideous cackle of a laugh—and I suddenly felt her legs wrap themselves around my own until my whole lower body was aching, as if locked within a vise, leaving me unable to move, and soon my legs were growing limp and numb. Lifting myself up on my elbows, it was all I could do not to scream as searing pain ripped through my back. And then I saw her face, and before I could say a word, my eyes must have asked why she was torturing me. She cackled with delight, and then her face changed to that of my evil stepmother, Gudrun, and instantly, my whole body turned cold, as if a snake were slithering all over it, and unable to do anything but shout in fear, I woke myself up, cold sweat covering my body.

"Ogier! What's wrong?" shouted Roland, jumping up from beside me.

It took me a moment to realize I had been dreaming, and then relief swept over me as I found my legs working again. I rolled over onto my back, looking up to find Roland standing over me with his sword clutched in his hands because I had startled him awake.

"Are you bewitched?" he demanded.

"No," I said, struggling to my feet and looking about me for my armor. "Just a bad dream."

"I've had bad dreams this night too," he said, setting down his sword to reach for his own armor.

"It's morning," I said for the light was now gray and a peek of sunlight was trying to creep into the cave. "Let us leave this place."

We helped one another on with our armor and then proceeded toward the cave's opening, but while we had seen the sunlight and the direction from whence it was coming when we woke, now we found ourselves moving into darkness. Thinking we had taken the wrong path, we turned back and continued to seek the cave's mouth, but no matter which way we went, we found ourselves still unable to locate any sort of opening to take us back to the surface.

"This is very strange," I said, feeling the cave walls, for somehow we had turned inward and the cave continued to grow darker rather than lighter, even when we backtracked.

"I think it must be witchcraft," said Roland. "Why else did we both have nightmares here last night?"

"We had nightmares," I said, "because we were cold and hungry and fatigued, and we have been on a fruitless mission for seven years. We're bound to have nightmares now and then."

But Roland was not convinced, and soon I began to think like him that we were in an enchanted cave of some sort. Still, I told myself, an enchantment might work to our good as well as our ill, for if a witch or evil creature were about, I still had hope that Morgan le Fay and her fairies were watching over me.

The darkness continued to grow until neither Roland nor I could see each other, nor even a hand before our faces. Not until then did we begin to grow deathly afraid, although I am almost ashamed to admit it, for we were the two bravest knights in all of Christendom.

"Do not forget," said Roland, "that we fell into this cave's pit because we could not see last night."

"Yes," I said, "but while we could have waited out the storm, we can't wait for the daylight—it has completely vanished. We just need to walk carefully."

Before I knew it, Roland had slipped his hand into mine. "We cannot allow ourselves to be separated or we may never find one another again in this darkness."

And then he crouched down and pulled me down with him, and we proceeded on our knees, feeling with our hands to make sure there was ground before us while every couple of seconds, we reached over to make sure the other was near.

I don't think I was ever so terrified in my life as I was in that dark, treacherous cave, for when you cannot see your enemy, you cannot fight him—or her—or it. We knew not if a giant bat would come rushing at us, or a dragon, or my evil stepmother herself. I thought of asking Roland to tell me what his nightmare had been about, but I was afraid that to know would only frighten me more, and I sensed he felt the same way in terms of inquiring about mine.

I can't tell you how many hours we went on like this, never having found a drop off in the cave's floor to threaten us, but neither having seen any light, much less an exit. At times, we felt small twists and turns in the cave; sometimes, the air grew cooler and we could sense we were in a larger chamber; sometimes, we were in such a narrow tunnel that we had to move single file, which was truly the scariest experience, for we were large men and feared being trapped in a narrow passage. We moved about for so long, sometimes even up and down inclines, that we believed ourselves in a veritable maze of rooms without any entrance or exit. How had we gotten so turned around? Or had we been intentionally tricked and trapped by someone unseen?

Eventually, exhausted, hungry, thirsty, and thinking a whole day must have now passed, we decided to stop and rest, and hope our situation would by some miracle improve in the morning. We had no idea whether it was night or how long the night lasted, for the darkness seemed timeless. But our fatigue and our scraped up hands and knees caused us to sleep soundly, without any nightmares this time.

In the morning, I woke to Roland nudging my shoulder. "Ogier, look!"

Opening my eyes, I saw a shaft of daylight streaming through the cave.

This time, we would not risk any delay. Already fully clothed in armor—Roland and I had both decided not to remove it from fear we might lose it in the darkness or have it stolen from us by whoever may have tricked us into this dark cavern—I jumped to my feet and quickly stepped toward the light, Roland shoulder-to-shoulder with me.

When we walked around a curve in the cavern, we came upon a feast for the eyes. Daylight—the open sky! And in a few more seconds, we found ourselves standing at the cave's mouth, unable to believe what lay before us.

CHAPTER 13

THE LAND WHERE Roland and I now found ourselves seemed to be a very paradise of delights. As we stepped out from the cave's mouth and into the sunlight, we discovered we were on a high ledge overlooking a lush, green valley filled with all manner of fruit-bearing trees, from olive to orange, and including many I did not recognize, as well as towering oaks and evergreens beside palm and eucalyptus trees, and all manner of strange and flowering bushes my eyes had never seen before, despite my many travels over most of the known world. This strange configuration of vegetation and verdure was quite marvelous to us, considering we had just emerged from the rocky and largely barren Anatolian plateau in the midst of a snowfall. Now the sun shone brightly upon everything, and the season seemed to be the very beginning of summer when everything is at its greenest. And in the distance beyond this strangely diverse forest rose a glorious dome bigger than even Hagia Sophia in Constantinople—and far more stunning in its golden appearance. This breathtaking structure was surrounded by a massive walled city filled with impressive residences, businesses, and temples, each covered with a mixture of emeralds, sapphires, rubies, onyxes, pearls, and all manner of ornate decorations; to describe it makes it sound gaudy, but it was beautiful beyond words and as intoxicating to the eye as to the nose was the fragrance from the various flowers growing everywhere around the trees—roses being the least beautiful among them, yet the only flower I recognized—so you can well imagine—or rather, perhaps never imagine—the scents that filled the air.

"Is this Paradise?" asked Roland.

I heard his question, but I found myself unable to answer, awe having equally overcome me. I knew if it were not Paradise, it was the closest place to it that the earth could contain.

To add marvel to marvel, we saw elephants roaming about in the valley beside camels, and lions lying down in a meadow while sheep grazed peacefully beside them.

"How are the lions not eating the lambs?" Roland asked.

"I know not," I replied.

"It is the Garden of Eden; it must be Eden," said Roland, "where the lion lies down with the lamb as the Scripture reputedly says. I thought it had been washed away in the Great Flood, but here it is before my eyes."

"Let us go down and explore," I replied, for my curiosity overpowered any fear I had of lions.

Roland came back to his senses then and joined me in seeking a way down from the ledge. We could find no path or easily scalable descent, and we were a good fifty feet above the valley, but after a minute, we determined that some vines creeping up the cliff's side were strong enough to bear our weight, and so with great care, we grabbed on and rappelled ourselves down the mountainous wall onto the lush green grass below.

After congratulating ourselves on our safe descent, and hoping we would find some other means to return up the cliff if need be—though neither of us wanted to get lost in the maze of caves again, and already I felt stirring in me a desire to remain in this land forever, whatever adventures might come—we began to look about us.

Little could we expect what we were to find. After a few minutes of walking among the strange shrubbery and towering trees, while seeing monkeys jumping about above our heads amid the forest canopy, Roland spied a path leading through a forest of tall pine trees like those I had seen in Denmark and Saxony. We immediately ventured down this path, hoping it would lead us to the great city with the gold-domed palace that we assumed belonged to this strange land's mighty ruler.

We had not walked more than a few minutes when we heard a great stirring and trampling sound in the bushes behind us. It quickly grew louder, and fearing it was some great beast, a lion or a bear, we swung around with swords drawn to defend ourselves.

In a second, we found ourselves surrounded by men on horses— no, men who *were* horses.

"Centaurs!" exclaimed Roland.

"It can't be," I said in disbelief, but that's exactly what they were. A good dozen of them were around us, their lower bodies as large and powerful as Morgan le Fay's own horse Papillon, and their upper bodies as powerfully built as the greatest warriors in Charlemagne's kingdom, and every one of them, I could see, was a worthy match to Roland or me. Realizing it was pointless to try fighting so many and risk being trampled by them, I placed my arm in front of Roland, bidding him put away his sword, and then I put away mine.

"What do you want of us?" Roland asked the creatures.

But he who appeared to be their leader merely pointed toward the path we had been taking anyway. Assuming he did not speak the Frankish tongue, and too intimidated by him to try another language, we slowly turned our backs to these curious beings and resumed walking in the direction of the palace we had seen. We spoke no further words to the centaurs or to one another, and they spoke not to us, but they allowed us to move forward. With this unlikely escort, we came in another few minutes to the forest's end and into a meadow filled with lavender. In the center of this meadow stood a beautiful marble fountain, and upon it were inscribed many strange symbols and words in languages we could not read. Sitting on benches, one on each side of the fountain, were two men of saintly appearance, both dressed in white robes, and even their beards and hair were white as a dove's breast.

Roland and I approached until we were within ten feet of these men, and then they rose and bowed before us. We returned the courtesy.

Then one stepped forward and asked, "Art thou Believers?"

"We are," said Roland, making the Sign of the Cross.

I, however, did not answer, wondering what we were to believe, but neither did I contradict Roland, whose Christian sign seemed acceptable to these venerable old men.

"Wouldst thou be healed of all thine infirmities, both of body and of mind?" asked the other.

Roland replied, "Nothing do I desire more greatly, but I have a broken heart; my betrothed, Alda, has died, and so I fear my pain can never be healed."

These words surprised me, for Roland had never told me that he still mourned Alda, who had died of grief when she believed him dead at the Battle of Roncesvaux Pass. Apparently, the pain had been too great during all these years for him to speak of it.

The first old man replied, "It can be healed if you believe in the afterlife, for then you must know that you will see her again."

"I do believe," Roland replied, bowing his head.

"And do you, Sir Ogier," asked the same saintly man, "also desire healing?"

I was astounded that he knew my name; it only further confirmed for me that we must be in Paradise, whatever Paradise might be. These men accepted Roland's Christian Sign of the Cross, so it must be the Christian Paradise, but if so, was it then confirmation that Christianity was the true belief?

"Do not fear," said the old man, watching me hesitate how to answer.

"I do not feel infirmities," I replied honestly. "I am young and strong, and I wish only to fulfill my mission to protect from evil those who are unable to protect themselves. That is why we are here, seeking to right wrongs, to return to my friend Roland a ring stolen from his family, and to stop an evil woman before she can harm others."

"You are honest, Sir Ogier, though no Christian," replied the first sage, "and your sincerity will not go unrewarded. Nevertheless, your body and soul are weary in ways you refuse to acknowledge, and after your years of searching, being reinvigorated will not harm you."

"Come now, and bathe in this fountain," the second man invited us. "I promise you that it will lift your spirits."

I looked about, wondering what good taking a bath would do us, and yet I had not had one in weeks after walking many a dusty road, so the thought was appealing. But I hesitated, looking about me, wondering whether I dared to remove my sword and do what the old men bid. Once unarmed, would the centaurs take me prisoner? But when I turned to look back at them, I saw that they had all lain down in the fields as horses would do, with their arms crossed before them and looking peaceful and patient.

Roland did not need a second invitation. He was already removing his armor, and in another minute, completely naked, he was stepping into the fountain where he submerged himself. I feared some trick—perhaps one of the presumably saintly men would try to drown or otherwise harm him—but they did neither, and when I saw them look with gentleness upon him, I realized how foolish were my fears.

"Come, Sir Ogier," said the first, "wash thyself of thy fears and faults."

But still I hesitated, finally saying, "Thank you, but I will remain here."

They did not reply, so I waited patiently for Roland to climb back out after he swam around in the fountain like a fish, reminding me of the legend that his grandmother had possessed a mermaid's tail. After a few minutes, he reemerged, and when he did so, I admit he looked as young and fresh as if he were eighteen again. I even noticed that a scar upon his torso, which I had once myself accidentally given him in swordplay, had completely healed and vanished. I was amazed by this miracle, yet I still resisted entering the fountain for reasons I could not explain—not from fear, but perhaps a sense of my own unworthiness, if nothing else.

"Go now, Sir Roland, and may no evil thing betide thee," said the two saintly men in unison once Roland stood again upon the grass. I now stepped forward and helped him on with his clothes and armor.

"Why won't you bathe, Ogier?" Roland asked me, looking deep into my eyes, but I turned away from his gaze.

"It is not for me," I muttered, feeling troubled. And then regaining my composure, I turned to bid the holy men adieu, only to discover they had vanished—and so had the centaurs.

Instantly, I felt my spirits drop, for I could have joined Roland in the fountain, but now I felt the moment had passed and it was too late. Not wishing to delay our journey longer, I said, "Come. It is not far now," and I started once more toward the domed palace, which was clearly in view and almost blinding in the sunlight. In a moment, Roland was beside me, but I soon could scarcely see him, for we both had to place our hands over our eyes to ward off the blinding dome as we approached it.

When we drew closer to the magnificent building, I was overwhelmed with awe by its splendor—and that it was not solely a palace but an entire city with the domed palace in its center. The city walls were of the purest white marble; the gates were made of ivory, and even their bolts were fashioned from gold. "Surely, this is the Celestial City," said Roland, "the very Pearly Gates of Paradise." I assumed he was making some sort of reference to Heaven, and without pointing out to him that I saw no sign of pearls, I admitted it was comparable to what I had heard of the Christians' Heaven, for such dazzling white and pure materials had never before been seen by mortal eyes. Above the gate, I could not help but notice the image of a great serpent, formed of brass with ruby eyes; I did not recall anything like this creature in Christian lore, and, I confess, it made me shiver and hesitate, but we had come too far now to withdraw, and already a man at the gate had spotted us.

We expected to be interrogated about our reasons for visiting this immaculate and incomparable city, but before we could prepare any words, the guard, or so I supposed him to be, though he wore a simple robe and bore no weapons, opened the gate and beckoned us forward.

"Do you not want to know our business before we enter?" Roland asked him.

"We only keep the gate closed to keep the wind and animals out," he replied. "All are free to come and go here as they please."

"Thank you," I replied, bowing in gratitude to him. "But can you tell us where we are?"

"You are where it is best for you to be at this point in your journey," he replied, and then smiling, he bowed and returned through a door in the wall that quickly closed behind him.

Roland and I knew not how to take this remark, but we passed through the gate, closing it behind us.

And then we first truly looked at the city and were rendered even more speechless. If we had thought the city's exterior walls beautiful, we were not at all prepared for the bejeweled mosaic-patterned walls on every building—so many emeralds, diamonds, and rubies were enough to overwhelm the eye and mind with their beauty and priceless value. And above them all rose a great palace covered in gold, with many floors and turrets, countless doors and windows, and numerous gables and balconies; in its center stood an enormous tower whose golden dome we had seen from afar, and now that we could see it clearly, I noticed it was topped by the statue of a giant golden apple—truly a strange choice for where usually there would be a cross or a flag.

When Roland and I arrived at the palace, we found no door but rather a tall arched entrance that led into a great hall. We then stepped off the city street made of gold brick onto an onyx floor broken only by the ebony pillars that upheld the diamond-encrusted ceiling of this magnificent indoor courtyard to the palace.

We soon realized, from the dozens of people gathered, that we were inside a large assembly hall, in truth a throne room, for on a raised platform sat a white-bearded king in a splendid gown of woven gold that would have made even the Emperors of Constantinople look impoverished. This mighty sovereign was surrounded by tapestries and rich carpets, and seated about his throne, apparently waiting to serve him, were beautiful maidens dressed in every color of the rainbow, and they looked as lovely as Aphrodite, yet as innocent as the Virgin Mary herself. Surprisingly, not a soldier was in sight to show this potentate's strength or to ensure his safety.

But most amazing of all was the sheer number of people present—until we realized the walls were every inch covered with magnificent mirrors that stretched all around the massive room, curving like a serpent. Later, we were to hear how the mirrors allowed this powerful ruler to see everything that occurred within his kingdom and indeed within all the world—and while I do not wish to get ahead of myself and spoil the wonder of my tale, nevertheless, Great Caliph, even you with all your splendor were never clothed like this veritable Solomon, and I say that with the greatest respect, for know that this man was no ordinary potentate and far more than a mere man, as my tale will quickly reveal.

"Welcome," said the king, extending his hand and beckoning us forward. "Be not afraid; all visitors are welcome in my kingdom, for only those chosen by God find their way here."

I was both surprised and yet strangely comforted by these words. Roland stepped forward eagerly when he heard them, but I hesitated a moment before following him to the king's raised throne. I had only the presence to kneel, but Roland made a grand and courtly bow before saying, "Sire, we are your humble servants, but strangers to this land. Please, we beg you, tell us your majesty's name and that of this beautiful country, which is like no other we have seen, for we are weary travelers who stumbled upon it accidentally, having been lost in the winding tunnels of a cave that opened here and led us to your kingdom."

"There are no accidents," this splendid potentate replied, "and there is no need to call me 'Sire.' I am simply, like yourselves, a humble man. Yes, I have been chosen to rule this land, but in doing so, I am a servant to God Almighty and my fellow man, and not deserving of recognition beyond that."

"I do not understand," said Roland, again bowing.

"Understanding is not something I can give you, good knight," the king replied, "but I can tell you that my name is Prester John, and I welcome you to my kingdom, the name of which I must keep from you for now until you are ready to understand, but you may remain here as my honored guests, and I bid you stay until that which you seek, though perhaps you do not realize yet that you seek it, will be made known to you, and then all understanding will be given."

This mysterious speech made me feel comforted even as it raised a dozen questions in my mind that I dared not ask. This king seemed all-knowing, yet he spoke in vague enough words that they could be applied to anyone who came to his land. I wondered whether he truly did know what we sought—of our quest to locate an evil woman, which had accidentally led us to his kingdom.

"We accept your gracious hospitality," Roland replied, "and if we can return your favors in any way, please do not hesitate to ask us, for we are honorable men. My companion is Sir Ogier, a Prince of Denmark, and I am Sir Roland, nephew to King Charles the Great of the Franks. We hope someday soon to return to our home in my uncle's kingdom, and then we will delight him with the stories of your country's splendors."

"I have heard of your uncle's great fame," replied Prester John, "but I would not have you depart until you truly have seen the wonders of my kingdom and acquired the knowledge you seek. You look fatigued and overwhelmed at the moment. Please, I will have my servants show you to a bedchamber where, as my guests, you are welcome to reside as long as you please. Once you have rested, I invite you to join me this evening for dinner, and in the morning, I will take you on a long tour of my kingdom where you shall see what you never could have imagined."

Great Caliph, how can I even begin to describe the marvels that were to be seen in the Kingdom of Prester John? We were shown to a sumptuous chamber that only those in the palace of Morgan le Fay could have equaled for splendor. We were drawn warm baths and given silken robes to wear. We slept upon the softest of beds, and wine flowed through a fountain in our room, the bubbling of which lulled us to sleep each night. In the days to come, we had everything that our hearts could desire, that could feast our eyes, and that caused our bodies to relax into a sense of safety, of rejuvenation, of sheer blissful nothing-necessary-to-do tranquility. We had been given everything we could want except an explanation of the name and history of this land, which Prester John, whom we frequently saw and dined with, graciously brushed away whenever we hinted at wanting to know it, bidding us, instead, not to worry but to enjoy ourselves.

We felt ourselves in Paradise, it is true, but we were far from idle during this time. Prester John's kingdom, perhaps because it was inside a valley surrounded by mountains, had no neighbors, and thus there were no wars, and so there was no need to train with our weapons save from the need to stay fit. Indeed, Prester John expressed his dislike for our practice with our swords, saying we could equally exercise our bodies by swimming or running, but he in no way requested us to disarm. We had no need to work because our every wish was granted by his servants, and they themselves did little work, as we soon discovered, because Prester John could make anything he desired become true simply by wishing for it. Wine cups refilled at the nod of his head, items floated across the room at the wave of his hand—had Roland and I not already been in the presence of Merlin and Morgan le Fay, we would have been astonished by all this—indeed, we were astonished—but we did not fear it, for we sensed Prester John's great benevolence, and we saw the love, respect, and very adoration that all his subjects gave to him.

And he was the most pleasant of companions. At times, he spoke of ideas we could not comprehend, but whenever his words failed to meet our understanding, our hearts nevertheless burned inside us with a sense of peace and joy. "It is like listening to the very words of Christ," Roland once said after we had dined with the king and listened to him talk. Afterward that evening, however, Roland became very quiet, and when I asked him why, he confessed that he feared he had been blasphemous in making such a comparison to his Savior.

Prester John was as good as his word in showing us the wonders of his kingdom. We went on many a grand tour with him, and yet we saw very little of his country, I believe, for though we could always see mountains in the distance and in all directions as its borders, yet no matter how far we traveled, they always remained in the distance. I have no doubt his kingdom must have stretched on for thousands of miles, perhaps as far as Cathay. Indeed, at times, we did not know whether we were in Europe or Asia or even in the very land of Atlantis itself, and yet while there were bountiful flowing rivers and magnificent lakes, we never saw the border of an ocean.

Now and then, we would come to a lone mountain, and it would always have a great arched tunnel, through which we would travel, and on the other side would be more exotic forests, with trees and flowers and all manner of verdure like none we had ever seen. We walked along crystal streams and watched volcanoes erupting in the distance. We saw glaciers on an inland sea that stretched endlessly beyond our vision, and we saw idyllic valleys filled with abundant crops irrigated by rivers formed from breathtaking waterfalls. All manner of beasts roamed all these regions—elephants and camels, crocodiles and antelope, boars and horses, cows and sheep, lions and tigers and white bears, and so many creatures I had never seen before but which Prester John identified to us by such strange names as llama and giraffe, hippopotamus and rhinoceros, buffalo and kangaroo. Strange birds— flamingos, toucans, penguins, hummingbirds—creatures never to be found in Christendom—flew alongside nightingales and storks, eagles and hawks, robins and bluebirds. We saw spiders as big as a man's skull and all manner of terrifying insects, and yet Prester John told us never to fear them, for they were all God's creatures and had their place and purpose in the creation.

Perhaps most marvelous of all were the number of beehives we saw about, literally running over with honey that often flowed into a nearby pool or river. "It is the proverbial land flowing with milk and honey!" Roland exclaimed the first time we saw a beehive as big as a Frankish peasant's hut, and while I had always thought such biblical explanations an exaggeration, now I realized their very truth.

And, Great Caliph, please do not accuse me of being a spinner of lies when I go on to tell you that the centaurs we had seen were only the beginning of this lands' marvelous creatures. In time, we came to know dwarfs and giants, then fawns and satyrs, mermaids, dryads, pixies, and even genies. I once found Roland in our room crying, and when I asked him what was wrong, he exclaimed, "Don't you see, Ogier, that all this wonder, all these fantastic creatures, are just the very most natural thing in this land? That means I am not some freak for having had a grandmother who was a mermaid or serpent or whatever people call her. It is such a great comfort to me. My tears are those of joy."

"How could you ever doubt it?" I replied. "I only caught a glimpse of Melusine the day she stole the babe from Gudrun, but she was beautiful and radiant like an angel. She could not be some freak of Nature; no, she must be some very special part of the Gods' great plan for this world."

"Truly, this is Paradise, Ogier," Roland replied, "and we are blessed to be here."

"Or it is Fairyland, or some other magical place," I said, "but its name matters not. I do not understand it, but I am grateful to be here as well."

Nor was Prester John's kingdom some isle of Lotus Eaters where we were to forget our troubles. We did not forget our mission, but neither did we do anything to further it, for we felt we had come to this mysterious land for a reason, though what reason we could not possibly guess. Yet as the days passed—or perhaps the seasons, for we saw no changes in the weather or climate to mark the passage of time—I wondered how long we would wait for that reason to become known to us.

I knew we had traveled for seven years before arriving in Prester John's land, and in all that time, I had not seen Morgan le Fay, but I did not doubt that if anyone had a hand in bringing us to this marvelous country, she had done so. In all our years of searching for Gudrun, I had wondered where Morgan was, but scarcely did I doubt she was watching over me, and if what she had told me were true, she was no doubt raising our child, who must be six or seven years old now, and whether that child be my son or my daughter, I was anxious to meet my offspring. But I knew that would not happen until the day Morgan le Fay saw fit, and so I resigned myself to being in Prester John's kingdom—but "resigned" is not the right word, for who would not be happy in such a veritable paradise? And so, Roland and I were happy for more days than we ever could have numbered.

CHAPTER 14

ONE DAY, ROLAND and I were walking together through the palace compound, long after we had come to Prester John's land, so long that now it felt like home to us as much as ever did France. As we were crossing a long porch along one wall of the palace, we saw a passageway we had never noticed before; despite having been in this kingdom now for weeks, months, perhaps years, for all we knew, and despite the unusual being quite the normal in this marvelous land, we never ceased to be surprised by such discoveries. The palace itself was built like a series of gigantic individual rooms connected by a maze of porches with porticoes and trellises and all manner of fountains and courtyards, and inner rooms branched off that led to more porches and sunrooms and libraries and more courtyards with fountains and rooms with pools to bathe in, and then there would be a sitting room, a cool room filled with an indoor garden, and then another pool, another library, and another courtyard with an orchard in the middle, and so on and so on, all in a never-ending labyrinth of beautiful confusion, and Roland and I had come to realize in our journeys how the Oriental world delighted in intricate geometric patterns, and that delight was never more evident than in this marvelous land.

Somehow, no matter how many twists and turns we took through the palace and its grounds, we always inexplicably managed to find our way back to our own suite of rooms, and we always found the throne room and the great dining hall, and yet I swear that sometimes what was there one day was gone the next. New rooms, new gardens, and new fountains seemed to spring up and disappear periodically without rhyme or reason. When I mentioned this to Roland one day, he replied, "It is not so wondrous, for I have heard that my grandmother, Melusine, was reputedly a great architect and builder and knew many secrets of masonry, including how to raise stones with musical vibrations and other such secrets known to the ancients but now forgotten by us today. I am sure an explanation exists for all of it." But to me, it remained greatly wondrous, whatever its explanation.

While every day we would see hallways, corridors, and trellised gardens we had not seen previously, somehow today, this new corridor off the porch beckoned me to explore it, and Roland, shrugging his shoulders, agreed to follow me since we had nothing else important to do; we were just out for a walk, always eager to explore this magnificent land.

And so we wandered down this new corridor. It initially appeared to be a short hallway turning to the right, but when we turned in that direction, it appeared to go on for a hundred feet with windows, looking out onto lush gardens on both sides of it. The corridor then twisted about so that we felt we were walking in circles, or rather squares, and even after we had walked for what seemed to be a mile, we had still not come to its end.

And then taking a sharp turn, finally, we came into a room where we saw a number of women—three dozen perhaps—sitting on velvet cushions, which were placed on silk rugs of intricate weaves, all facing toward us, or rather toward a tall woman dressed completely in black, who stood only about a dozen feet before us, but with her back to us as she instructed them.

Not wishing to interrupt, we listened for a minute or two as she spoke about the meaning of true wisdom in words so esoteric that I could scarcely understand them. Nor did I recognize the language in which she spoke, yet I inexplicably understood every word she said and its meaning. But I admit the full meaning of her argument was beyond my comprehension.

Finally, this woman ceased her teaching to ask one of her pupils a question.

And when the pupil did not answer, because by then all the women had noticed us and were staring our way, the teacher followed her silent pupil's gaze and turned to look at us.

And then I found myself staring into the face of my stepmother.

She took one second's look at us, and then she let out a shrill, intimidating hiss. Before Roland and I overcame the shock of seeing her, she next ran down the aisle between her seated pupils and disappeared through an arched door some twenty or so feet away at the room's far end.

"My apologies, ladies!" I shouted as Roland and I tried to run between the women without tripping on their silk pillows, but we did not get far before half a dozen of them, seated in the back, jumped up to block our path.

We could not fight women, nor could we get past or around them, for the women we had already passed now rose to their feet and surrounded us from behind. Those before us began to move forward like an army while those in the back slowly retreated, finally withdrawing so we were forced back toward the entrance from which we had come. Having no other choice, we stepped back into the corridor, and the instant we did, a solid gold door materialized before our eyes, sealing us off from the room where we had seen Gudrun and her pupils.

Defeated, Roland and I returned back down the corridor.

"What is she doing here?" Roland finally asked as we reached the outdoors in just another minute and arrived at a completely different location from where we had originally entered the mysterious corridor.

I barely had time to notice this astonishing change before Roland began to demand answers. Nor could I fully attend to his words, for my own brain was whirling with confusion over Gudrun's presence within Prester John's seemingly sacred land.

"Why is she here?" Roland repeated.

"I don't know," was the only answer I could give.

"Do you think those women are her slaves or minions?" he continued as we stepped into the sunshine.

"More likely her pupils," I replied.

"But I don't understand," he said. "Surely, Prester John knows she is here and that she is evil."

"No doubt," I agreed. "I'm under the impression that there is little Prester John does not know."

Feeling defeated, I sat down in the shade of an enormous orange tree, my head still spinning. Roland's repeated questions did not ease my frustration.

He stood and stared at me for a moment before saying, "We can't just sit here. We have to go after her. Those women had no right to stop us, or to protect her, and—"

"Perhaps they thought we were the ones in the wrong," I

interrupted. "They do not know us or understand our mission, and maybe they do not know her true identity."

"Their ignorance is not our fault," he replied. "They don't know what evil she is capable of, or what she's done. Just what could she have been teaching them? Witchcraft? Sorcery? If Prester John knew—"

"I don't know what she was teaching them," I interrupted, "but it sounded more like religion than sorcery."

"What does she know of religion?" Roland demanded. "Black magic is her religion, if she has any. How can Prester John allow her to reside here?"

"I don't know, Roland," I repeated, "but I am sure he must know she is here, for his knowledge appears beyond that of normal men. I can't imagine he would allow her to instruct his subjects without his approval."

"But why? He claims to be a Christian king, to—"

"He never told us he was a Christian king," I interrupted again. "That is only our assumption."

"But then how does he...? Isn't his power from...?"

Roland was at a loss for words, but I did not need him to complete the sentence to know what he meant. He was a Christian, so in his mind, any supernatural or extraordinary powers had to come from God; if they did not, they could have only one other source. While I thought it possible the world was far more complicated than the dualism of good and evil the Christians believed in, Roland had by now drawn his own conclusions, and he could not stomach the answer to which his religious beliefs led him. Deflated, he now sat down beside me.

As we quietly pondered our situation, two lovely maidens, their garments matching the luscious fruit of the orange tree under which we sat, passed by and smiled at us. I smiled back, but Roland ignored them.

"Who were those women she was teaching?" he asked again.

"I have no idea," I admitted. "Who are any of these women in this kingdom? Are they all here to be taught by Prester John? Are they his daughters, or his wives, nieces, sisters, servants—who knows? We have seen plenty of men here, too. They are his people. That is all we can say."

"But why were those women studying?" Roland persisted. "What were they studying? What I heard her say had the ring of truth to it, as if it were great wisdom; my heart burned within me at the highness of such thoughts, and for a moment, I felt as if all the world and the mystery of life made sense to me, and yet I cannot remember a word of it now. Did she cast a spell over us with her words? And was the spell broken once she looked at us? I just do not understand."

"It is the same with me," I said. "I never heard such words come from her lips when she was married to my father. She is far more than a mortal woman; Morgan le Fay warned me she is possessed by some evil being from ancient times. After all, if she were capable of giving birth to the Antichrist, of—"

"But Ogier," Roland interrupted, "if she were Ganelon's sister, and he was torn to pieces by wild horses, as you told me was his punishment by my uncle, then he was surely mortal, so how can his sister be otherwise?"

"I do not know," I sighed.

"Nor do I," said Roland. "I can only think that she is evil beyond our comprehension, perhaps a mistress of Satan, and if Prester John harbors her, then perhaps he himself and all this land must also be evil."

"I suppose that could be possible," I agreed, closing my eyes, feeling intoxicated by the heat of the sun in this beautiful warm country, so unlike the cold of my northern land. I did not want to think it a place of evil. "But Roland," I said, struggling to make my thoughts come together, "look at this bountiful, beautiful land. When we were in France, we never could have imagined that such a place existed, and yet we are here, proof that so much more is possible than what the human mind can conceive, and so I think for us to assume that Prester John, or this land, or even Gudrun herself, is evil is to simplify what we do not understand. Is Prester John evil? I somehow can't believe that. Is he good? I don't know. I imagine it is all much more complicated than that."

"What you say now," Roland replied, anger rising in his voice, "sounds like what I vaguely remember Gudrun just now teaching. You know that Morgan le Fay told you herself that Gudrun is evil. Yet you, who are not even a Christian, are questioning the validity of right and wrong, of good and evil. Ogier, in doing so, you are moving into the Enemy's territory."

"I am not on Gudrun's side," I replied.

"No," Roland clarified, "but by 'Enemy' I mean Satan, who twists men's thoughts so that what is good seems evil, and what is evil seems good."

"Or perhaps," I started to say, for a second seeing another possibility, but then I forgot what I meant to say because such thoughts were making my brain hurt in the warm sun.

"Perhaps what?" Roland demanded.

"Roland," I replied hesitantly, not wanting to vex him, yet realizing I could not hold back from saying what appeared as truth to me, "tell me: are you good, or are you evil?"

"I am on the side of what is right," he said, his nostrils flaring as if I had insulted him by questioning his moral certitude.

"My friend, you are not understanding me," I said, trying to soothe him, and closing my eyes to gather my thoughts as I spoke. "I simply mean: can you truly say you are good when you have made mistakes, or can you truly say you are evil when you have done many a good deed?"

I opened my eyes now to see him looking at me, uncertain how to answer. I think he was afraid to answer. The way he pursed his lips, I could see he did not like the conclusion he had reached upon considering my argument.

"Enough with words!" he barked. "I can't sit here while she is free and teaching others the ways of evil. There is no point continuing to discuss this when we can easily learn the answers."

He jumped to his feet and began to walk away.

"Roland!" I shouted. "Where are you going?"

"To find Prester John and demand an explanation!"

CHAPTER 15

I KNEW THAT allowing Roland to charge, hotheaded, into Prester John's throne room could not be beneficial to us, so I quickly sprang to my feet and raced after him.

"Roland, you are angry. You need to contain your temper before you speak to the king," I warned. "This is his land and we cannot demand explanations of him."

"He is not my king," Roland said, not stopping but marching on with determination. "My uncle is my king, and another of my uncles was murdered by that foul witch whom Prester John is harboring, and so yes, Ogier, I will demand answers."

I grabbed his arm, trying to persuade him by force, but he shook me off. Running after him again, I grabbed him around the chest, and in a minute, we were wrestling on the ground.

"Let me go, Ogier! It's been our mission all these years to find that witch and bring her to justice, so why are you trying to stop me now?"

"I'm not," I said, slowly loosening my grasp on him. "I just don't want you to lose your temper and say something you may later regret. If you promise to remember your manners and breeding, then I'll let you go, but we must be delicate about this matter. We can't just take hostage a former queen and carry her off if she is under Prester John's protection."

"No, we can't," said Roland, pulling himself out of my relaxed hold to kneel on the ground and face me. "But only because we do not know where she is. I always knew there was something not right about this land, Ogier. Think of the strange way we arrived—how the cave seemed to shift. Think of how what we see one day disappears the next and a new oddity takes its place. Don't you realize this may well all be witchcraft? I want explanations for exactly how all these strange events occur and what she is doing in this mysterious land."

"You, Roland, are the last one who should speak of witchcraft," I said, staring him in the eye to reason with him. "Consider your own family. You said before that your grandmother is much like many of those here who—"

"My grandmother never murdered anyone!" he shouted, "and you are no friend if you would insinuate such things of my family."

I was embarrassed by his words, especially because several young maidens who were walking through the nearby gardens began to stare at us after our wrestling match. Trying to maintain my dignity, I stood up, and Roland also quickly regained his feet. As he shook the dust off himself, I was tempted to place my hand on his shoulder and make my peace with him, but then he said, "Perhaps, Ogier, it is time for you and me to part ways."

Before I could think how to reply, I was startled by a male voice behind me, asking, "What is the matter?"

"You are harboring a witch, a harlot, in your kingdom, Prester John!" exclaimed Roland before I could even turn around to see who had spoken, and by the time I did, it was too late for me to thrust a hand over Roland's mouth.

"I see," said Prester John, nodding, his eyes filled with sadness. "Come, then. It is time you be told all."

I was stunned by his resigned tone as he turned around and walked toward his palace. A few women sought to follow him, but with a wave of his hand, he said, "Leave us. All is well." Then he looked back, beckoning us to follow him. Roland swiftly stepped to his side while I followed a few feet behind. We proceeded to a new door into the palace that I had never seen before. The front of this entrance looked like a great temple with a curious blend of architecture like that I had observed in Greece, India, and Egypt.

Roland climbed the steps beside Prester John, determined not to let the opportunity pass to get the answers he desired. I also sought answers, but I was not so adamant in my demeanor. I wanted Gudrun brought to justice just as much as Roland did, but I sensed more was happening here than met the eye, and knowing I had been sent on this mission by Morgan le Fay, and taking comfort in Prester John's words that "All is well," I entered the temple, feeling relief that perhaps now the reason for our being in this strange land would finally be revealed.

Once we were inside the temple, I saw it was empty, devoid of statues or altars, or any other signs of worship. Simply a collection of silk pillows was on the floor beside a placid and clear pool.

"Come; sit, one of you on each side of me," Prester John said, seating himself on the center pillow.

We did as requested, I hesitating for a moment, while noticing the furious look that remained on Roland's face.

Once we were seated, Prester John gazed into the pool, not saying a word.

A couple of minutes passed, and then Roland could hold his tongue no longer. "What is Gudrun doing here?" he demanded. "She murdered my uncle—perhaps you do not know that, but she is a horrible woman, a witch we believe—"

Prester John raised a hand and slowly placed it on the back of Roland's head, gently turning it to face the pool.

"Shh," said Prester John. "Observe."

Roland was fuming, but he did his best to calm himself and look into the pool. I followed suit and soon saw goldfish gliding beneath the water's surface. A strange fancy now struck me; I began to wonder what it would be like to be one of them, careless, enjoying the water's flow, the very flow of life, without a worry.

Prester John now reached into a pocket of his robe and pulled out a handful of breadcrumbs, which he sprinkled into the pool.

"These fish are loved," he said. "They know they are because all their needs are provided for." He paused a moment as we watched the fish eat, and then he said, "And so are all of your needs provided for, and so are you loved, and so is the woman you label so harshly. She is loved just as well as you or I by our Creator. Do you remember, friend Roland, the words of our Savior, 'Look at the lilies of the field; they do not spin nor do they toil, yet never was Solomon, in all his splendor, clothed in such glory.' Our Savior taught us not to worry. Why then are you worrying? If she has done wrong, it is for God only to judge her."

"But she is a murderer!" exclaimed Roland. "She has murdered my uncle, and she has tried to bring about the birth of the Antichrist, and—"

"Oh, yes, the Antichrist!" said Prester John, and then for a good minute, he could not contain his laughter. Roland and I exchanged surprised glances that he could find the term so amusing, but we did not speak until he regained his composure. Then he said, unable not to smirk, "The Antichrist...such silliness. What a lot of balderdash it is! In fact, it is blasphemy in itself, and, worst of all, falsely attributed to me in letters I did not even write; do you know that those letters and the Book of Revelation are one of the reasons why I came to this land? That and because once Our Savior's mother was taken up to Heaven, I had no earthly responsibility to keep me in Ephesus. And so I came here, to continue God's work, but only among those humans who were ready to receive it. I was too much in the midst of the busy world at Ephesus; I had to go out into the wilderness, to this place where those who truly seek God and His truth would make their way, and so I have lived here ever since, some seven centuries or so now."

I had no idea what he was talking about, but I watched as Roland's eyes widened until finally he asked, "What are you saying? You—Our Savior's mother. You—you cannot be...."

Prester John smiled at Roland, and then he turned to sprinkle more breadcrumbs upon the water and watch the fish come up to eat. After a moment, he spoke again.

"He told us we would be fishers of men, but there is more than one way to catch a fish. Most will try to trap it in a net, or to torture it cruelly with a hook, but you cannot fish in that way for a man. You cannot force a man to come to God, or scare him with sin and damnation and Antichrists. You must be gentle with him, just as I am gentle with these fish. See, I give them love and so they come to me. Our Savior understood this, but most men do not."

He placed his hand in the pool, and the second his fingers broke the water's surface, several goldfish swam up to brush against them, clearly reveling in his gently stroking their reddish scales.

"Are you...are you...Saint Jo..." Roland tried to say, in such disbelief he could barely form the words.

"The Beloved Disciple?" replied Prester John. "Yes, I am he, though I have taken the title of Prester here. Saint is a difficult word to live up to, but Prester is not since God has blessed me so that now I am older than almost any other creature upon this earth—a few turtles and other such beasts, of course, have known more years than me, and then there are a handful of humans, including a couple whom you know—your friend Merlin has a few decades on me, and then, of course, there is your supposed enemy, Queen Gudrun, as she is known to you."

"I don't understand," I said, baffled by his words and wondering how he knew so much, for we had never mentioned Merlin to him, nor Gudrun until this hour.

"No, you're not a Christian, Ogier," he said, as if reading my mind, "and so you would not know my story, though Roland does. But it matters not whether you understand, for many paths lead to God, or the Goddess, as some prefer; in fact, all paths must lead there for all is part of His-Her Creation, and it is impossible that it could be otherwise, but since you do not know your Gospel stories, friend Ogier, I will simply say that I was one of Christ's disciples, and upon His death on the Cross, He asked me to care for His mother, Mary. I did so, taking her with me to Ephesus for her safety and so that I might preach the Gospel to those who resided there. We lived in that land until the time when she went to join the Lord. As for me, I grew so old that people began to think I had died—and with good reason since I was a century or more old and prone to being a hermit in those years— so they began writing books and claiming I was their author to lend them false authority. Most of the books were abominably written and thankfully were quickly dismissed, save for that pesky text, the Book of the Revelation. People grabbed onto that because they always want easy answers—predictions—promises about the future—even when they are grim ones such as that book contains, and because it lends itself to many interpretations, too many people have tried to use it for their own purposes. I soon saw that no matter how I had preached a message of love, small-minded people could not be convinced otherwise than that damnation, destruction, and punishment would be the only end for the majority of mankind—for all save a chosen few, so the entrance into Heaven would be difficult, and fear of not entering would allow a few to control the many.

"Sad as it was, I knew that if I protested that book, humans would only find some other way to make themselves miserable, and then about the time the Emperor Constantine established Christianity as the religion of Rome and forced it upon people, I decided enough was enough, and after much prayer, I was encouraged in a vision to come here, to this earthly paradise—or perhaps 'otherworldly' is a better word, for only those prepared for their souls to evolve to a new understanding may enter here. That said, this place is not the only of its kind upon this earth—there is Avalon and Valhalla and others—but this is the one I prefer, modeled after the Garden of Eden, indeed on the very same land, created by God after the Flood. I see astonishment in your faces, but are you truly surprised? Did you not already in your hearts know that you were in Paradise?"

"This is too much for me to take in," said Roland. "It makes it sound like everything I have been taught is not true. For you to tell me that part of the Scriptures is false—it makes me fear that you are Satan tempting me."

"There in your words, friend Roland, is that common human predilection for fear, but do not worry, for we all have a tendency toward it. It has taken me many centuries to conquer it. Not all you have been taught is false. God exists; Jesus existed and continues to exist; there are angels, but no demons, and God fulfills Himself in many ways so that all His-Her creation is good and shall be preserved. Most importantly to you, you do have a soul; you have just been misguided in how to nurture it because you have been taught by other humans equally fearful, and their fear has led to their trying to control you and everyone else, by trying to simplify everything into good and evil and right and wrong. But why should it be simple? Such simplicity is so boring. The universe is abundant. It is glorious. It is infinite in its variety, and that variety is splendid in so many countless, countless ways; the world and the sea and the heavens contain more possibilities than Abraham had descendants, and do not forget that God told Abraham his descendants would number like the stars in the sky and the sands on the seashore. So why then must there only be one way to Heaven? For that matter, why must there be only one Heaven? The human mind is complex, yet it is simple compared to the complexities of God, so does it not make sense that all the universe is complex, without it being hard and difficult, without it being painful and rigorous? Instead, it is all a glory, all enjoyable, all fascinating, all invigorating, and all worthy of celebration. But sadly, man tends toward the ridiculous, and in thinking himself superior to all the other creatures of the world and in his never-ceasing toil, he only proves himself the most ridiculous part of the creation. That is why many come here—because they have had a glimmering of how ridiculous is man's version of God, and now they seek to learn how to cease their foolishness and instead grow wise in the natural rhythms of the universe and the ways of the Creator."

These words were more than I could take in, for I had never heard anyone speak so joyfully, so strongly, yet so calmly. I cannot convey to you, Great Caliph, how marvelous these words sounded when first I heard them. Yet I could see on Roland's face how he could scarcely bear to hear such words that shattered what he had believed was true. While Prester John's speech made me feel light, relieved of all my fears and burdens, it made Roland look fearful.

"Fear not, friend Roland," said Prester John, patting him on his knee. "You have much time yet to learn. You shall remain here with me for some time as a consequence of having drunk from the fountain when you first arrived in my land. Your decision to do so was a sign that, deep inside, you sought to purify your soul. Ogier's soul, however, held back, for he is willing to sacrifice for the good of others rather than seek his own needs first, and so he shall venture forth again into the world, while you remain with me."

Roland was speechless. His face first turned white, and then red, and then I was astonished to see him burst into sobs until the tears flowed down his cheeks. Without a second thought, Prester John took Roland in his arms and held him for the longest time, stroking his back and soothing him. I did not understand Roland's sudden outburst, yet I did not feel awkward or grieved. Instead, I had the strangest feeling, as if I were floating up out of my body, observing all that was occurring as if from some other, higher level of existence.

Finally, Prester John released my friend, and pulling a handkerchief from his sleeve, he handed it to Roland to dry his tears.

"Thank you," said Roland, and I understood that for him, the weight on his soul had been lifted, for deep down, he had desired nothing more than to stay here and learn.

"You understand now that this is a place of learning, a place where the soul can evolve and find comfort," Prester John continued, reaching out his hand to take mine so I would not feel omitted from the conversation. "And that is why Queen Gudrun, as you know her, is here, and why she teaches here. Understand that no human being's soul has grown and evolved for as long as hers. She is indeed far more than Queen Gudrun, and she is not evil as you so suppose. When the time is ready, her entire story will be made known to you, but if I were to tell it to you now, it might cause you to understand her, to pity her, and that would be the easy way; it would not lead to the full growth of your souls as needed. Instead, I am asking the two of you both to pray for her, to seek in your hearts to love and forgive her, whatever you deem her faults, and to trust that in love, in forgiveness, in prayer can be found all that is necessary to right any wrongs you perceive, whether those perceptions be false or true, for as a great poet shall one day write more than a thousand years from now, 'more things are wrought by prayer than this world dreams of.'"

Here Prester John concluded, and Roland and I knew not what to say in response. We were both embarrassed, ashamed even of our behavior, of our quickness to judge, for I realized now that we had never seen Gudrun commit murder, only been told she had. And then I realized that I had no proof that she had ever turned my father against me; perhaps instead, I had first turned against her; in fact, although I had not wanted to admit it, I had been against her from the start for replacing my mother, and so I had not helped the situation. Who was I, after all, to have judged her? Whatever her character flaws, I had seen her affection for my father, and she had clearly loved my brother.

"It is a heavy task I ask of you," Prester John continued, "but as our Savior said, 'Come on to me all ye who are weary and heavily burdened and I will give you rest.' As you become accustomed to it, you will find it easier to pray. It is a great task. It is a quest I give you, a quest of the soul you are to engage in. Are you, as knights, ready to embark on this quest?"

"I do not understand what the quest requires," I said, feeling as if I were speaking from another's body, feeling I desired to take this quest, whatever it might be, such that my insides glowed within me. "I admit I fear it," I added, "but I am ready to go wherever the quest leads."

"And so am I," said Roland. When I raised my head to look at him as he spoke, I saw the pain and confusion had vanished from his face. Instead, he smiled at me, and I smiled back, and I felt closer to him at that moment than I ever had before.

"Bid each other goodbye, then," said Prester John, "for your paths will be different from this day on. Roland, yours will be to remain here in this land, to learn and assist me in preparing for mankind's future when humans are ready to embrace it. Ogier, you are to stay here beside this pool and pray as long as is deemed necessary by God. Fear not; I suspect you will be so caught up in prayer that you will not know hunger or thirst during this time, and then you shall return into the world to complete your destiny and be guided anew by one who has always watched over you."

I nodded, understanding that he spoke of Morgan le Fay.

Then Prester John rose and extended his hand to Roland, drawing him to his feet.

"Peace be with you," Roland said to me, and I nodded, returning the wish.

Then they walked away in silence.

Once they were out of my sight, I did not know what I was to do, so I remained seated for a long time. Finally, I began praying, or at least trying to pray. I did not know how to pray, having only seen Roland and Duke Namon and other of my Christian friends kneeling and muttering prayers I had never bothered to learn. In my father's palace, we had never prayed, my father only occasionally engaging in rituals to put on a good show of worshiping Odin to please his people.

Finally, after what must have been many hours, since darkness had now descended upon the pool, I found myself quietly speaking from my heart and saying:

God, I know not how to pray. I do not know what I need to say. But I do believe that somehow You have led me here to this moment, whether You be the Christian God or Odin or Allah, or some being whose name I do not know. I know You are the Creator. I know I am part of You. I know You have always watched over me and guided my paths, including through Morgan le Fay, and I know You will listen to me now, for You have led me here so You must desire my prayer.

I know little of forgiveness or love or how to pray for the woman whom for most of my life I have considered to be my enemy. I know not how to forgive her. I ask You to help me forgive her. I ask You to forgive her, to forgive all her trespasses and bring her to Your glory.

I ask You to forgive me all my own trespasses. I know I have wronged many in my life, both intentionally and unintentionally, men I have been forced to kill or hurt in battle. I pray for the welfare of all their souls.

I ask You to soften the Princess Glorianda's heart toward me, for I fear she loved me as I loved her, yet I never returned to her. I ask that You help her find it in her heart to forgive me and that You give her peace and comfort.

I ask Your forgiveness for the hatred I felt toward Ganelon and toward Charlot, and for any other ill feelings I have had in my heart toward any person, even if I cannot recall them now, but most of all, I again ask that You forgive me for hatred toward my stepmother, and that You forgive her for her own crimes, if crimes she has committed, and that You bring her to reconciliation with Yourself.

I know that You can do all things for You are the Creator and the ultimate source of good. I know You are the source of all things, and I know, therefore, that all that exists is ultimately part of the good that is You—I know this because Prester John has told me there are no demons, only angels, and he has told me many other marvelous things I cannot understand, and I know I need not understand them. I know I only need to trust in You to make things right.

I ask You to forgive me for my anger, my hatred, and all my human weaknesses, and I ask You to heal the soul of my stepmother Gudrun, for Prester John says it is Your desire that I pray for her and forgive her and even love her. I ask that You receive my prayer and teach me how to do that which seems so hard when it comes to loving my enemies. And finally, I ask You to make all things work toward the greater good for all those for whom I pray.

Amen.

Oh, Great Caliph, I prayed these and many, many more words; I prayed for what must have been hours, perhaps days, yet it seemed like the time passed in just a moment. And I know not how to go on explaining what I felt then. I lost my very stream of thought—my soul leapt up in me with great love. I cannot say how it happened, or how it was possible. I only know I felt lifted out of myself; I felt as if my very heart were about to burst, as if somehow I was one with all the universe and floating in the air in ways I can never explain, and I learned then that nothing, save God Himself, can be greater than the power of prayer.

And when my prayer had ended, I felt like I had woken from a long sleep or at least a trance. I truly believe I must have prayed for forty days and forty nights, for I was astonishingly hungry and thirsty, and I found laid next to me, beside the pool, a veritable feast of food, and I broke my long fast and ate.

And when I had finished my meal, I noticed a carpet was a little way off on the other side of the pool, and I arose and went to walk around the pool's side to look at it, for I did not recall seeing it there before, but I had scarcely lifted my foot when the carpet flew over the pool's surface and directly under my foot, and in great surprise, I stepped upon it and found it as firm as stone, and lifting my other foot, in a second, I stood fully upon it.

And then I heard a female voice say, "It is time for you to complete your quest, Ogier." The voice had floated into the temple, softly on the wind blowing through the open arched windows near the ceiling. I did not doubt whose voice it was. "You must return to Jerusalem now," it continued, "to obtain the Holy Lance, but first, you will have one stop along the way."

And before I could answer, before I could even half-understand, I felt the carpet move beneath my feet, and in fear of losing my balance, I crouched down into a sitting position as it began to rise higher and higher into the air—and then it shot forth, through the arched window and out over the bounteous land of Prester John. It rose higher and higher until the palace, the city, the trees, and the mountains were but specks to me, and I was up higher even than the birds until all I could see were the clouds, and such was my journey for many hours until I descended here, in your great city.

And that, Great Caliph, is my marvelous tale. I promised you that it would be unlike any you have ever heard before. I swear upon my very soul that it is all true, and I do not fully understand it yet, but I do believe the time I spent in prayer did make some sort of difference, if not to the world or to my stepmother, then to my soul, for I have felt all fear, all anxiety, fall away from me, and I know only that all things work for the greater glory of God, and so I feel content for whatever may now come to me in my life because I sense in my very bones that a greater existence awaits me someday in a paradise of my own choosing.

CHAPTER 16

WHEN OGIER THE Dane had finished his marvelous tale, which had taken several evenings to tell, Haroun al-Rashid, ruler of half the known world, found himself almost speechless for several seconds. Finally, rubbing his chin, he said, "Prince Ogier, it has been indeed as marvelous and wonderful a tale as you had promised."

Ogier bowed and said, "I am pleased that it has given you pleasure, Great Caliph."

"It did indeed, and far more than pleasure. It has given me much food for thought, and I would wish that it be written down so all peoples might benefit from the wisdom of it, particularly those words that the saintly monarch Prester John said to you, but...."

Ogier anticipated the caliph's next words, although he thought it impolite to finish such a mighty ruler's sentences.

"But it sounds," finished the caliph, "like Prester John thinks it best that we not tell the secrets of his land to the world; am I right?"

"As for that, Great Caliph, I do not think he fears his land being discovered, for I stumbled upon it by accident and do not believe I could find it again. Rather, I think he realizes, as doubtless you do, in your great wisdom and from years of leading the multitudes of your people, that it is impossible to change people's thoughts and behaviors and expect that they will listen or follow you. Even if they do hear your words, they will often close their minds and their hearts to the wisdom of God's ways."

"It is true," said Haroun al-Rashid, "and while you have told this tale to me, it was at my request that you did so, but if people are not seeking, not looking for something, they are unlikely to see or find it, so it will do us no good to present your tale to the world if men are not ready to hear it. Furthermore, it sounds like only those who are ready to learn can come to Prester John's land, and only if he agrees they are ready."

"Yes," said Ogier, "but perhaps in ten or twelve centuries more, all the human race shall be ready so that all the world can be like Prester John's land."

"That is a lofty dream, but perhaps an unlikely one," said Haroun al-Rashid, "for when I sent a clock to your great King Charles, he wrote to tell me how he was astounded by it, and I understand there was great confusion at his court from the inability to understand its workings. If the Christians, and the greatest of their kings, cannot understand something so simple as the mechanical workings of a clock, we cannot expect them to know the deeper, finer points of the soul that a Christian king, once disciple to the Prophet Jesus himself, who has lived for over eight centuries, has come to understand. You and I, who are eminently wise and born to be princes and live above the common men, even we are having difficulty understanding it."

"You speak truly, Great Caliph," Ogier replied, "for as good and wise as I know Charlemagne to be, even he has his moments of weakness, as evidenced when he considered having me killed out of anger toward my father."

"Charlemagne has come far since then," said the caliph, "having won even the friendship of Pope Leo III so that he was crowned Emperor."

"What?" asked Ogier in surprise. "Has Hadrian died? He was pope last I heard."

"Hadrian?" said the caliph. "Hadrian has been dead about seven years now."

"Seven years? No, how can that be? What year is this?"

"One hundred and eighty-one."

For a moment, Ogier looked puzzled, but then he realized why Haroun al-Rashid had made such an answer.

"Forgive me, Great Caliph; I know you Muslims number your years from the Prophet Mohammed's journey from Mecca to Medina, but do you know what year it is by the calendar we Christians keep?"

"Eight hundred and three," the caliph replied.

"Eight hundred and three!" exclaimed Ogier, beside himself, unable to imagine how it could be possible. "But, but no, it was, why it was the year 778 A.D. when Roland and I fought at the Battle of Roncesvaux Pass, and then we were reunited in Jerusalem not so many months later and wandered for seven years until we came to the land of Prester John, so that was in 785 or 786 at the latest—I know I remember seven winters spent seeking Gudrun, and after that, we were in Prester John's land, but I do not think it could have been for more than a few months, and then I came here...."

"I have heard of such strange happenings," said Haroun al-Rashid, "of time passing in another realm, a realm of magic, what you call Faerie. Could it be that such was the case for you in Prester John's land?"

"Well," Ogier considered, "I suppose Prester John's land was like Eden, a paradise, so I could have lost track of the time. I was so happy there that I did not worry over time like we do in the ordinary world. But if it is the year 803, that would mean I lost something like seventeen years there. Do I look so very old?"

"You look not a day over thirty, hardly a day over twenty-five. How old should you be?"

"Why," said Ogier, doing the calculation in his head, "perhaps forty-eight or thereabouts if it's 803. I...I just cannot believe it. It...it is unbelievable."

"That so many years have passed," replied Haroun al-Rashid, "hardly seems unbelievable if you so expect me to believe your tale of fairies, an evil sorceress, a mythical king of paradise who must be some eight hundred years old, and that Roland's grandmother could fly and had a mermaid's tail, and did I not with my very own eyes see you arrive on your magic flying carpet? I am a few years younger than you, if what you say is true, Sir Ogier, yet you look over a decade younger than me. It is all considerably strange, but *unbelievable*? After all you have been through, I should say not."

"Tell me," said Ogier, shaking off his stupor. "What does it mean that Charlemagne is emperor. Emperor of what?"

"Emperor of Rome, or so he calls himself."

"But what of Constantine VI, the boy emperor—he was Emperor of the Greeks and Romans last I heard."

"Oh, yes, that empire remains, but the Pope was very displeased. It would be a long and complex history to tell of what has happened since Constantine VI reigned, and I have not paid as close attention to the Roman emperors in Constantinople, while Charlemagne and I now have become allies, you might say, against the old Roman emperors' continual corruption and weaknesses."

"But then has Constantine VI died?" Ogier asked.

"No. He was deposed, though even that word hardly describes it. His mother, Irene of Athens, that monster of a woman, she—why she would rival your evil stepmother for how she harmed her own child."

"What do you mean?"

"She had him deposed, blinded no less, and declared herself Empress, some six or seven years ago now. It does not surprise me—she was always difficult; when she served as regent for her son, she refused to pay me tribute, so I had to invade her land. Her people stupidly treated her like a heroine because she brought back their icons, which you know we Muslims consider a form of apostasy, but her people soon grew tired of her. Even Charlemagne, who thought about marrying her to combine their empires and restore the greatness that once was Rome, eventually thought better of it because he could not tolerate the stench of her wickedness. And then her people, perhaps from fear she would marry Charlemagne and make them his subjects, deposed her and sent her into exile on the island of Lesbos. Nikephorus, her former minister of finance, has been placed on the throne in her place. I tell you, those Romans are so full of evil, of fighting and foolishness, that Allah will not tolerate them long before Charlemagne and I divide up their empire among ourselves. Much as I hate war and politics, to end the centuries of corruption of the Eastern Roman Empire will be best for both Christians and Muslims."

"It is passing strange," said Ogier. "Such odd things have happened, and to think I have been gone so long, but I am glad to hear the good king I knew has now become a great emperor."

"Our kingdoms are on good terms," Haroun al-Rashid admitted, "and so I bear you no ill will in your having loyally served him. In fact,

I think I may be able to help you, for it seems your mission in coming to Baghdad is to obtain the Holy Lance, am I not correct, and to bring it back to the Christians?"

Ogier shifted in his chair, wondering whether the caliph would truly help him obtain a Christian relic that resided in his own lands.

"Not exactly, Great Caliph," he replied. "I will bring it to Merlin, not Charlemagne, nor the Pope. From what Roland told me, I believe Merlin thinks it best that he keep it safe so it does not fall into the hands of those who would use it for ill."

"It is, then, a most delicate matter," said Haroun al-Rashid, placing his hands together as if he were in deep thought. "I cannot allow the Holy Lance to be openly given to you—my people would be infuriated if they thought it were being given to the Christians. Nor can we allow it just to disappear, as if it were stolen away, for then fingers would be pointed in blame, which could cause severe problems among all the peoples living in and visiting the Holy City. I have no doubt that Jerusalem shall be a point of contention between Christians and Muslims for many years to come, and while it is my fond hope that someday Islam shall unite the entire world so all may know that Allah is God and Mohammed is His Prophet, still I am well aware that there are well-meaning Christians and even Jews, and by the same token, those who profess to be Muslims whose hearts are less than pure. Hence, I am convinced there is great purpose to your mission, that you are not simply some fanatical Christian since you do not even profess that faith, and if anyone can be trusted to keep the Holy Lance safe, I suspect it is Merlin, for the stories of his immense wisdom and how he counseled one of the greatest of Christian kings have even reached these lands so distant from his own. No, I will not quarrel with your desire to bring such a sacred object to Merlin."

"I appreciate your trust in me and in my mission, Great Caliph," Ogier replied, bowing his head in gratitude.

"I will ponder upon this matter further," said Haroun al-Rashid, "and will let you know in good time how my giving of the Holy Lance to you might be achieved in the most delicate of manners. But first, I ask you to grant me the honor of being my guest for one more evening."

"It shall be as you wish, Great Caliph," Ogier replied.

In the morning, Haroun al-Rashid called Ogier to him, following the breakfast hour, and then he told Ogier his plans.

"Hear me out before you object," warned the caliph.

Ogier knew better than to interrupt a great ruler, so he simply nodded in agreement.

"I will give you a commission," said Haroun al-Rashid. "I will set you up as my vassal, as the King of Jerusalem, so you may rule over Palestine and so you may know me as your overlord while you help to protect the pilgrimage routes so there is peace between Christians and Muslims."

Ogier was quite overwhelmed by this prospect—he had not thought to change his obedience to a monarch—yet in his heart, he knew he had been guided by those with more foresight than himself. Nor could he object to a change in residence since he had long since lost any desire to see France or Denmark again. Most of his old friends were by now either dead or they had forgotten him, and he had still to complete his mission.

"Go then to Jerusalem, where the Holy Lance is," continued the caliph, "and befriend the Patriarch there. I shall give you papers announcing you as my emissary, and I shall have you crowned King of Jerusalem before you leave, giving you an escort of five thousand men to serve as your standing army in Jerusalem, as well as enough gold to set yourself up as king."

"You are most generous, Great Caliph," said Ogier, bowing in obedience.

"I am, but it does not solve how to get the Holy Lance to Merlin. Still, I have many other worries taxing my brain, so I will have to leave it up to you," replied the caliph. "Hopefully, once you are in Jerusalem, a proper means will occur to you."

"I trust everything happens in its time," said Ogier, although he did not like the burden placed wholly on his shoulders.

"There is no rush to solve the matter—after all these years, I suspect Merlin is very patient," the caliph continued. "In the meantime, you will be a great asset, for you will serve both Charlemagne and me, being an intermediary for us—assuring peace between our empires and between Muslims, Christians, Jews, and people of all faiths. Is that not a worthy role to play for the remainder of your days?"

Ogier did not like the thought of spending the rest of his days sitting on a throne when he considered himself a man of action, but after all the years he had spent in Prester John's land, he knew he was not getting any younger, and he thought it better to oversee the protection of pilgrims than to get himself killed in further adventures, for already he was starting to feel the creak of old age in his bones. His heart felt not older than twenty-one, but his body was rapidly aging to catch up with his actual forty-eighth year. The youthful appearance he had retained when he had first left Paradise and arrived in Baghdad was now quickly fading, and even Haroun al-Rashid admitted that he had aged swiftly in the past few days. Ogier himself had never expected his hair to remain a crown of gold, for he remembered his father's head had grown hoary at a young age, so when the first streaks of gray appeared in his hair, Ogier told himself he would soon have a golden crown to wear, so his hair color mattered not.

And then, within a fortnight of his arrival in Baghdad, Ogier the Dane set off for Jerusalem with the army that Haroun al-Rashid had given him, and soon after, his entrance into the Holy City was heralded by great celebrations. His new subjects were easily persuaded to love him when he threw gold and silver coins to them and provided them with food and drink for a three-day celebration, and by year's end, Ogier was acknowledged and loved by Jerusalem's residents as a wise and noble king who kept the peace and whom none dared to offend. Even the Patriarch of Jerusalem was won over when Ogier made a sizeable donation to the church, causing him to send a favorable letter about the new King of Jerusalem to Pope Leo III.

But amid all this pomp and circumstance and approval, Ogier did not lose sight of his purpose. How was he to get the Holy Lance out of Jerusalem without creating an uproar? He had many ideas, but he always found a reason to dismiss them, and so in time, he had spent years considering the matter, and admittedly, often being distracted from it for months at a time as he rode about, surveying his kingdom, hearing the people's law disputes, and dining with all the finest families of Palestine.

During this time, not a few noble and wealthy families tried to arrange marriages between their daughters and Ogier, but each time, he managed to dissuade them, telling them he was too old to marry a young maiden, and then when the widows began to chase after him, he finally told them that he had long ago lost the great love of his life, and therefore, he could never consider loving any other. (He did not say who this great love was, whether it was Glorianda or Morgan le Fay, for from day to day, he sometimes wondered which one it was himself, although he knew Morgan le Fay would someday bring him to Avalon, as she had promised, but that had been many years ago now, and so he began to think again that perhaps she had forgotten him.) When the people came to understand that their king had lost his love and would not marry again, they thought him a very good and wise man—and the women found him all the more attractive for being so unobtainable—and many of his court remarked that they could see the suffering from a broken heart in his eyes, which they assumed had led to the cultivation of his great wisdom. Ogier knew his people loved him, and while he sometimes felt he had deceived them with his story of lost love—for he could not know for certain whether either woman had truly loved him—he also realized how important was public perception, so he used it to his advantage to govern wisely.

And now and then, Ogier's thoughts turned again to obtaining the Holy Lance and transporting it to Montserrat, though he wondered whether Merlin would even be there, still waiting for it after three decades had now passed since he and Roland had first gone on the quest to acquire it. And Ogier also sometimes wondered what had become of Gudrun; he wanted to believe she must be dead by now, but he also knew her evil would outlive her body regardless, so he tried not to think about her, save occasionally to say a prayer for her.

Time continued its endless march until in 809 A.D., the great Haroun al-Rashid passed on to Jannah, the Muslim paradise, and his son, Al-Amin, became ruler of the Abbasid Caliphate. Then in 813 A.D., Al-Amin was killed during an uprising in Baghdad. Ogier himself rode to the caliph's rescue, but it was too late. Next, the throne passed to Al-Amin's brother Al-Am'mun.

In these tumultuous years, Ogier was often visited in Jerusalem by Zubaida, the great Haroun al-Rashid's widow. She had first traveled to visit him because, as she told him, she wished to meet the man her late husband had told her was the only one in his realm whom he felt he could trust completely, especially after he had found it necessary to put to death the grand vizier, Giafar, for secretly daring to marry the caliph's sister.

Haroun al-Rashid had loved his wife greatly, and so from his lips, Zubaida had heard many of the marvelous episodes of Ogier's tale, and now, whenever she visited Jerusalem, she would ask Ogier to repeat his stories to her, for she was a great lover of strange and adventurous tales, and she had continually entertained her husband and her own ladies with her wonderful stories; in fact, many said it was her ability to weave a fantastic tale and always stop at the most suspenseful part that had made her husband fall in love with her. She told Ogier many of these stories—fabulous ones filled with genies and magic lamps, and even a few that were quite bawdy for a well-born lady to recite, but Ogier enjoyed them just as much as Haroun al-Rashid had, and a great friendship developed between them. Not surprisingly, more than once, Ogier suspected that perhaps Zubaida wished to marry him, based on their shared love of story, but before she could suggest a union between them, he made a point of telling her how his heart belonged to another, and Zubaida, having heard his tales of Glorianda and Morgan le Fay, understood his feelings and did not question him about which woman he truly loved most; she was content simply to have Ogier's friendship, for in truth, she felt that Haroun al-Rashid's love was also the only love that could ever completely fill her heart.

Then in 814 A.D., word came to Ogier of Charlemagne's death, which brought Ogier great sadness. Suddenly, he felt all the world he had known, all the glories of the past, had faded away, and he began to pray more and more, seeking counsel from the Patriarch of Jerusalem and many holy monks who resided in the hills nearby, although Zubaida was the only one he trusted with the entirety of his story. He also continued to pray for Gudrun, as Prester John had requested he do, until his faith in God grew deeper and stronger and he came to the realization that a reason must exist for everything and that reason must be working with a purpose, even if he could not foresee it himself, and since God was eternal, how quickly that plan unfolded really did not matter. All things would come in their time, and he did not have to see the fulfillment of them during his lifespan, even if that meant he would not live long enough to present Merlin with the Holy Lance.

Once Zubaida rejoined Haroun al-Rashid in 831 A.D., Ogier knew his days on this earth were few, for he was now well past his seventieth year. He began then to prepare himself for the day when he would leave the world, although he still pondered Morgan le Fay's promise upon his birth that someday he would join her in Avalon... and sometimes, as old age began to take over his mind, he wondered how much of his past life he had dreamt or simply imagined...had he really lived through all the marvelous experiences he believed he had? Had he ever even really known the mighty King Charlemagne who had restored the Roman Empire in the West, or his friend Roland, the hero, by now long renowned in song, or the great Caliph Haroun al-Rashid, once ruler of half the known world? Or was his old mind playing tricks upon him with all these adventures he thought he had known? But when he doubted all these things, he reminded himself that he was the King of Jerusalem, and he knew that could not have happened by accident.

CHAPTER 17

FOR THIRTY YEARS, Ogier had ruled as King of Jerusalem, and he now wondered how many more years he had left to reign. He was pondering this question one morning when the guard announced that a beautiful young woman, "like none I have ever seen before, my lord," had arrived at the palace from a faraway land she would not name, but she requested an audience with him.

Ogier was quite curious to know whom this visitor could be, and when he further questioned the guard, who could provide him with no additional answers, he thought it best to have her shown into his throne room. Then, upon second thought, he decided he would instead meet her in his private chamber where he would offer her refreshment after what must have been a long journey.

A few minutes later, when this mysterious young woman was shown into the King of Jerusalem's private sitting chamber, where a table of refreshments had been laid for her, Ogier was not surprised to see her dressed in the fashions of the Arab world with her face covered, but nothing could prepare him for the astonishment he felt when she drew back her veil to reveal such striking features that he instantly felt as young as a colt seeking its first mare, for her skin was soft and fresh as a newborn's, her eyes as green as the ripest olive waiting to be plucked, and her smile made his heart leap with joy while at the same time making his old knees feel even weaker. He so marveled over such beauty that he found himself unable to move or speak, until finally, like a dam ready to burst, his words gushed forth.

"Glorianda! Is it really you?"

Could it be possible, after all these years, that she could be standing before him, looking as if not a day had passed since last they had met? From where could such eternal youth spring? Not even in Prester John's land had Ogier seen the Fountain of Youth. He felt completely baffled by her appearance, a feeling only surpassed by his overwhelming desire for her—and surprise that Morgan le Fay had stayed away from him for so long, for did she not know that Glorianda would return and bewitch him with her beauty? Did this mean that Morgan le Fay had forgotten him? But no, he could never believe her capable of that, despite the decades that had passed since he had last seen her or heard her voice.

But all these thoughts soon turned out to be pointless when the visitor replied.

"No, my lord. I am Asalah."

Ogier heard the name, but it meant nothing to him. All he could do was continue to gaze upon her, stunned by how much she looked like his Glorianda. Finally, remembering his noble breeding, he stepped up to her, bowed, and kissed her hand, a European custom, not a Muslim one, for touching such a young woman would have been forbidden, but as King of Jerusalem, he thought he could get away with it, and he could not restrain himself from his desire to touch her.

She pulled back her hand, giggling like a small child.

"Forgive me, fair maiden," he said gallantly, "but you remind me of one I once knew—knew and loved—perhaps the comparison is just an old man's fancy, but do not think me unkind, for it is meant as a compliment."

"I think it sweet, your majesty," she replied, "and I am proud you see my mother in me."

"Your mother?" Ogier felt stunned, yet enticed by this response.

"Yes, my mother. I am Glorianda's daughter, and you will perhaps be both happy and sad to know she never forgot you."

"Tell me how your mother is, beautiful Asalah," he replied, unsure how he felt in knowing that Glorianda still remembered him, yet she had a daughter of her own—and by another man. And why now did that daughter seek him out?

"My mother is well, your majesty," Asalah replied, "and she has sent me to you for a special reason."

"If it is in my power to assist you or your mother, fair maiden, I will be more than happy to do so," said Ogier.

"Thank you," Asalah replied. "She and my father said your answer would be such. They send you their love."

Ogier now found himself wondering who her father might be. He realized he had probably never met the man, but he hoped it was not that horrid and ugly King Brunamont whom he had defeated in armed combat so many years before. Still, if the man spoke well of him, shouldn't he know him?

"Tell me," Ogier requested, with great curiosity, "how you came to me, beautiful Asalah, and what has become of your mother since last I saw her."

"I will tell the story, your majesty, for without telling it, you will not understand why I make the request I do."

Ogier asked her to be seated; then he poured them water, for she refused his wine. Finally, he nodded for her to begin her tale.

"I will tell the story, my lord," said Asalah, "and I think you will find it quite a surprising one, as I did when first I heard it. I never considered, until my mother told it to me just a few months ago, that she ever could have loved any man besides my father, much less that the man should be yourself. I will skip over what her life was like prior to her meeting you, save to say that she grew up a spoiled child, the apple of her father's eye. Because King Corsuble had no son, against all his counselors' recommendations, he decided his daughter should inherit his throne; therefore, he had her educated like no woman has been before or since, so as you know, she was proficient in languages, including being able to speak the Frankish tongue with you. I will begin by telling you in her own words how she described first meeting you and then what happened to her after you were separated."

Ogier bowed to show his eagerness to hear this tale, and so Asalah began, reciting the story of her mother as if Glorianda herself had been present to tell the story.

PRINCESS GLORIANDA'S TALE

When my father told me I was to wed King Brunamont, I cannot begin to tell you how my heart sunk within me for he was by far the ugliest man I had ever seen, even if he were big and strong and a great warrior, who had never been defeated, and, therefore, was greatly revered by my father and all his court. Instead, I longed for a young, handsome, and gentle man, one who would recite poetry to me, one like those I had read of in the ancient Greek scrolls in my father's library. I wanted a Paris, not an Achilles—and Brunamont was neither; in truth, he was more like a cyclops.

And then when Prince Ogier was taken hostage and brought to my father's court, I was instantly struck by his northern beauty and his manliness. Never had I seen a man with such golden hair, such strong, flawless, and chiseled features, and I had heard from my maid, who had heard from a soldier, who had heard from another, that he had a beautiful singing voice. Indeed, when first he opened his mouth and out came his Frankish words pronounced with his Norse accent, I thought I had heard the voice of a nightingale. And Ogier's gentlemanly grace was surpassed only by his courage, his great strength, and his noble countenance. In just the few moments I spoke to him, I felt he was perfect in every way.

And Ogier appeared even more perfect to me when he agreed to fight Brunamont for my honor. I had no doubt he would win, and, of course, he did.

But after Prince Ogier defeated Brunamont, my father forced me away, leaving Ogier behind. I was heartbroken, but I would not give up hope and envisioned Ogier coming in the dead of night to abduct me, to carry me away on his horse and bring me safely to the Frankish court. I waited, but he did not come, and I do not doubt his Frankish friends persuaded him not to until he felt it impossible that we could be wed. My father, knowing himself defeated, now had to leave Rome and all of Italy, and within a few days, we were sailing back over the sea to my father's kingdom in North Africa, and I was heartbroken. For days, I constantly looked over my shoulder, praying Ogier would return, that he would come after me, that he would marry me and thereby make peace between our peoples. Think what such a marriage could have done to ensure good relations between Christians and Muslims, but neither of our peoples ever would have allowed it.

And obviously, Prince Ogier had come to agree with them. What went through his mind, I could not know. I was convinced he was a good and noble knight, yet how good could he be if he were not sensitive to how he had broken a maiden's heart? How could he not have known my love for him, for I was sure every inch of my face had declared it when I was in his presence. Surely, he knew that I would have run away with him if only he had asked. But he did not ask. He was silent. And I never heard another word from him.

I cried many nights on the ship home, and once I was back at my father's palace, I cried in the privacy of my own room. For months, I wept and felt my very soul would expire with grief that Ogier could not be mine. My father never even noticed that my eyes were red; that is how little he cared for me; he thought of me as no more than a pawn he could use to further his kingdom's interests. He had spoiled me as a child, indulged my every whim, but to let me wed a Christian was more than he could stomach.

And what would I do the next time my father proposed a husband for me? How would I get out of it then? For if I could not wed Prince Ogier, I would have no other man.

But I had no need to worry over future marriage proposals, for I would receive none.

Instead, a few months after we had returned to my father's kingdom, I went one day with my maid and a palace guard to the bazaar in the town near the castle. I never went anywhere unescorted, but my father had little fear for my safety in his own kingdom. Who would dare to show disrespect to a princess? Who indeed?

On that day, I was talking to a shopkeeper when I turned to ask my maid for her opinion on a silk rug I wanted, only to discover she was gone—and so was my guard. I was surprised, but not yet alarmed.

I thought perhaps they had gotten separated from me in the crowd because the bazaar was teeming with people that morning. When I took a few steps around a corner to look for them, suddenly I found myself pushed into one of the shopkeeper's tents, and then the next minute, a blanket was thrown over my head. Before I could put up a struggle, I was being tied up, still wrapped in the blanket. I felt a knife against my face—fortunately, it was only used to cut a slit in the blanket for me to breathe through—and then a hand was over my mouth, saying, "We have your maid, and if you utter one word, we'll kill her and you both." Soon, strong hands lifted me up and tossed me over some man's shoulder, and I felt myself being hauled out of the bazaar like a used carpet.

I had no idea who had kidnapped me or where I was being taken, but it wasn't long before I could smell the sea air. When I felt myself being carried up an incline, I knew from my bearer's unsteady steps that we were on some sort of boat, and not long after, I sensed we had cast off from shore, for I could feel the rocking of the vessel upon the waves.

"We left your maid behind," said a deep male voice. "There are plenty of maids in my own land to serve you."

"Who are you?" I demanded, still entwined in the blanket. "How dare you kidnap me? Do you know who I am?"

"You are Glorianda, daughter to King Corsuble. You are the desire of my heart, and you will be my wife as soon as we arrive in my own kingdom."

Could this man be Ogier the Dane? I wondered, I hoped, but the voice was far from melodious, and I knew Ogier would never do anything so ignoble as to abduct me, though if he had wished to take me in such a manner, I would not have fought at all; after all, once he had taken my maidenhood, my father would not be able to oppose our marriage. But I could not fantasize about what could never be at such a moment. I had to stay focused on discovering whom my captor could be.

"*Your kingdom!*" I scoffed back at him. "Whom do you seek to fool? No king would treat me this way!"

"A true king knows what he wants, and he is not afraid to take it," he replied. "Here, see what king is to be your husband."

And then I felt fingers reach through the hole where my mouth was, and in a second, they ripped the cloth before my face. As my eyes adjusted to the bright sunlight, I was horrified to find myself staring at Brunamont, King of Maiolgre.

I was speechless. I had never thought to see him again. He was a coward—defeated by the man I loved—he had run and fled by diving into the river, and he had drowned, I had thought—indeed, had hoped. Now I was surprised to see him, but not at all pleased. Nor was I going to submit to marrying a coward—certainly not one defeated by the fabulous Prince Ogier, and definitely not one who had kidnapped me.

"You are surprised, Princess Glorianda," he said, "but you shouldn't be. Did you think I would allow the pinnacle of Muslim feminine beauty to escape my grasp for long?"

"My father will send an army after us," I declared, "to rescue me and to burn and destroy your lands!"

"Your father will not know who has taken you until after I have claimed your maidenhood for myself, and then he will acknowledge me as his son-in-law, for what other choice will he have, you being his only child and he needing an heir to his kingdom?"

"I will never wed you, and I will never love you!" I retorted.

"You may not love me," said Brunamont, "but I will wed and bed you nevertheless, even if it be by force, for I am used to having what I want, and my appetites must be satisfied."

And then he picked me up and handed me off, my wrists still tied, to one of his men, ordering that I be taken down into the ship's bowels to await arrival in his kingdom.

For hours I lay in the bottom of the ship in the dark, though finding it preferable there to seeing his face. At first, I refused all food and water, but then I thought better of it, knowing I would need my strength if I were to escape, and so I waited patiently for my opportunity. In time, the ship did dock, and then I was carried, again like a carpet, up the hill to his castle. Once inside, I was brought to a beautiful suite of rooms fitting my station, where I was kept watch over by a dozen guards.

Although we had arrived late at night, Brunamont had the audacity to come to my room as I was preparing for bed. My face then scrunched up as if I were ready to attack, despite the trembling I felt in my heart.

"I will not take you when you are tired," he replied, perhaps fearing my anger, or perhaps trying to make up for his crime by acting like a gentleman now, "but sleep well, for tomorrow we shall wed, and then I will show you what paradise truly is."

I glared at him, but he only smiled, then departed, leaving me more disgusted by him than I had been before. How could a king behave in such a manner and to another king's daughter?

Where was Prince Ogier? Where was my father's army? What hope did I have? If I had been the subject of one of the songs the great bards sing, then I would have been rescued by Ogier before Brunamont could force me into wedlock, but it was not to be.

The next day, Brunamont had a marriage ceremony performed. I refused to consent to it, but it mattered not. I was wed to him regardless, and then fighting and clawing at him like a wildcat, I was lifted and carried to what he termed our "bridal chamber," and there against my will, he took me, destroying my virginity. When the beast was finished, he left me upon my bed, bleeding, crying, moaning from pain and a broken heart. I lay there, numb, miserable for I knew not how long. Finally, one of the maids arrived to wash and comfort me.

Brunamont returned every night after that to rape me again and again. I cannot describe to you the horror I felt, how much I longed to die, and how I even plotted to kill him. Had he not ensured that anything usable as a weapon had been removed from my room, and had my maids not kept watch over me, as well as comforted me, and had there been no guards to watch my every move, I would have taken my own life—for what kind of life could I live as the wife of such a brute? I had been destroyed as only a man can destroy a woman, and he had proven himself no true follower of the Prophet, no respecter of Allah, considering the way he had treated me. He was nothing but a coward and a monster, and I despised him.

But then, after about a fortnight of his brutal nighttime visits, he had me escorted down to the banquet hall to dine with him. Prior to that, I had been fed in my room, though I was hardly willing to eat, but food was practically forced down my throat by one of my guards at Brunamont's command. That night, in the banquet hall, however, I did eat, realizing that whether or not I protested by starving myself, he would continue to rape me. I had no desire to eat, but I thought again now that I should try to keep up my strength, for if I were to be allowed out of my room, perhaps at some point I would be able to escape long enough to find a way to end my miserable existence.

"Come, my queen. Your tears and anger will do you no good," Brunamont said when I first sat down to the table. "Eat."

I did as I was bid, not speaking, but simply filling myself with meat and fruit while glancing about the room, trying to determine what chance I had to escape, although where I would go, I could not tell. And every once in awhile when Brunamont spoke to me, I would look at him and shudder over his ugliness.

For months, this situation continued. I found no means of escape while he continued to visit my bed nightly. Then one day, I realized I was gaining weight at an alarming speed, and the horror dawned on me that I was to bear the beast's child. The thought made me vomit, but my maids told me it was only morning sickness, and that I should rejoice, for soon I would be mother to a future king.

I did not want Brunamont's child, but if I were to give birth, I hoped it would be a son, for I would not wish to bring a daughter into this world when someday she might be subjected to the same abuse I had experienced.

Finally, the day came when I gave Brunamont a little boy. I wanted the child taken away from me; I wanted nothing to do with it, but Brunamont came rushing into the chamber as soon as he heard he had a son, and when I refused to hold the child, he nevertheless thrust it into my arms and told me, "You are his mother, and you will nurse him and love him, even if I have to make you."

And so I took the child in my arms, and then, I know not how to explain it, but despite my resistance, I felt love burst inside me like I had never known before, and I vowed that I would raise up this son to be a true prince, one who would know how to treat women properly.

For the next few days, Brunamont stayed away from me, sending word only that he was engrossed with matters of state. When I next saw him, he came into my room while I was nursing our son, whom I had chosen to name Hakim.

"A beautiful sight," Brunamont said, sitting down on the bed beside me, and for perhaps the first time when he came near, I did not flinch or pull away, not wanting to upset our precious little boy.

"You are a good mother," Brunamont continued. "I knew I had picked well. You realize I could have taken any other woman, but I did not want a whore. I wanted a queen. I want you to be my queen. You are such in name, but I want you to be in spirit as well, and I will love you and treat you as one if you will only let me. I do not wish to force you any longer. It is not satisfying to me. Not when I cannot force you to love me, nor would I wish to force you; I wish for you to love me freely. I will not think of you as my property. I will not even hold you here any longer; you are free to go if you wish, although Hakim must remain with me, but I will have a ship take you back to your father's land if that is your choice. Still, I hope you will stay because now you understand that all this while, my only true wish has been to win your heart; I just knew no other way to do so. I would gladly be your slave, Queen Glorianda, if only you would love me."

I looked at him with surprise, but I saw sincerity in his eyes. He was rough, and his ugliness none could deny, but I could see he sought my forgiveness from the way he looked at me. And when he reached out to stroke our son's head and he laughed when Hakim continued to suckle at my breast, more intent on his meal than attention from his father, I felt, no matter how I wanted to fight it, some sympathy for this ugly brute who was now showing me some tenderness.

"A boy after my own heart," Brunamont said, smiling, as he watched Hakim feeding, "but thankfully, not ugly like me; instead, he takes after his beautiful mother."

It would take a great deal more time before I felt anything like affection toward my husband, but from that day, the war between us ceased, and I did not feel that I had lost the war, but rather, I had made mutual terms of peace.

Brunamont did not tell me again that I was free to leave, and I did not bring up the subject, for I would not separate him from his son, nor separate myself from Hakim. A few days after this conversation, my husband sent emissaries bearing gifts and apologies to my father, and the following spring, we traveled to my father's kingdom to pay him a visit, and from that time, there was peace between our kingdoms.

I do not mean to condone Brunamont's behavior. It was unworthy of a great king to treat any woman, much less a princess, the way he had, although it has never been uncommon for men to treat women so. But in time, I came to forgive him, and he gradually became sweeter and gentler to me, showing me small kindnesses and being generous to me in every way until within a few years of our living together, I realized he was no longer the violent and roguish man I had first known. And to his people, he became known as the good and great King Brunamont of Maiolgre, and they loved him.

But despite the change in his behavior, I could not forgive the past. Brunamont had been brutal with me initially, rending me against my will from my home, and roughly and unlawfully taking my virginity. His people admired him because he was their king, but even though they thought him a good ruler, I knew that a truly great king was more than just strong and able to stand up against his enemies; he was also kind and protected those weaker than himself. To me, the man I would respect as king had to be as wise as Solomon, as handsome as Ogier the Dane, and ultimately, gentle with me; he had to be a hero, not just a warrior who knew only how to take what he wanted. And so, no, I did not love my husband; while I bowed to him and treated him with the respect due the father of my child, I did not hold him in my heart as my lord and master or seek to worship him as I had so longed to do with the man I had dreamed of one day loving.

Time passed quickly, and when our son was but a few years old, word arrived that my father had gone to Allah. Brunamont had been acknowledged by my father as his heir, with the throne then to pass on to our son Hakim. While I felt great sadness over my father's death, I could not travel with Brunamont to my father's kingdom. He must go so he could be crowned as king there, but I was forced to stay behind because I was now expecting our second child. And so, I remained behind in Maiolgre while my husband journeyed to North Africa, and although I protested, he took our son with him so my father's subjects would be assured there was an heir and no reason to fear for the succession.

My husband and son had not been gone more than a week when a fleet of ships appeared on our shores. They were from the Roman Emperor Constantine in Constantinople; he was seeking now to regain the kingdom that my husband's father had won from the Eastern Roman Empire.

For many days, we found ourselves barricaded within the castle, our people fighting bravely as the ships blockaded our harbor and landed men on our shores to hold the city and castle under siege. Messengers were sent to my husband in my father's kingdom, begging him to return with my father's army, but it was too late. The city was taken and then the castle, and I was forced to flee through a secret passage out of the castle and across the island to where I could take ship elsewhere.

Oh, the miseries that were then to befall me! I and a handful of loyal servants and soldiers made it to the ship and quickly set sail for my father's kingdom, seeking my husband's protection, but a great storm rocked our ship all the way there, and I, so close to my time, underwent horrible labor pains and gave birth on a rough sea that tossed us all about and caused my child to be stillborn. My maid later told me that she was certain she would lose me as well, but somehow I survived to experience the heartbreak of a lost child and more dangers yet awaiting me.

By some miracle, our ship survived the storm and we made our way to North Africa, only to find my father's kingdom equally besieged, not by the Romans, but by the neighboring Saracen king, who had long been my father's ally but now sought to take advantage of my father's death to claim the land for his own.

When our ship approached the harbor and we saw the enemy ships, we were forced to turn back, quickly finding ourselves chased for dozens of leagues before losing our pursuers. The kingdom neighboring my father's had been the only friendly one nearby until it had turned against us. Our ship now had nowhere to go. I wanted to sail back to my father's kingdom, in hopes of finding a way to get inside the city so I could be with my husband and son, but the sailors and soldiers with me refused to return until it was safe. So where could we go?

We drifted about the Mediterranean with nowhere to land our ship so that soon starvation and thirst became our state. Finally, I convinced the men to sail back to my father's land; by then, it had been conquered by the enemy. I knew not what had become of Brunamont or my dear son Hakim, but I thought that for me to be a prisoner with them, if they were still alive, would be better than to die of starvation.

When our ship sailed into the harbor of my father's former capital, we were quickly boarded by the conquering enemy. I did not reveal my identity, from fear I would be killed, but I was taken to a prison nevertheless. There, a few days later, I overheard the guards talking about how my husband had died from an arrow wound while trying to defend the city. As for my son, he had died from starvation during the city's siege. All whom I had loved had now been taken from me, but saddest of all, for me, was that I had never told my husband, because I had never realized until that moment, that I loved him.

When the prison guards saw my tears over this tragic news, they quickly realized who I was. I was then brought before the enemy king, who turned out not to be my father's old friend, but that man's son; this young king I had known as a playmate whenever his father had paid my father a visit, and at one time, he had been considered as a future husband for me until my father learned he already had a bastard child by a maid in his palace; while bastard royalty was not uncommon, my father, may he rest in Allah's peace, was wise enough not to wish his daughter to have a husband unwilling to wait until marriage to have his male needs met; therefore, my father had instead favored Brunamont, hardly knowing his true nature then, as my prospective suitor.

Now this boy I had known, styling himself as King Hasaan, mocked me for rejecting his love so many years before. "You sought yourself a great hero, but now I have killed him with a simple arrow, and from what I hear, he was not man enough even to kill a puny Christian when in Italy, but instead, he went running with his tail between his legs and then took you by force. Some husband. I would make you my wife now, but I will not have a coward's whore."

And then, before I could say a word, he spat at me and had me sent back to prison.

To make a long story short, I remained alone in that cell for several years. In time, I learned that the soldiers and sailors who had fled with me from my husband's kingdom were put to death. My maids also grew ill and died within a few months. Still, out of stubbornness perhaps, I lived on. The only pleasure I knew during this time was when I overheard the guards one day talking about how the Emir of Cordoba had invaded Maiolgre and driven the Roman Emperor Constantine from its shore.

And then one day—I can only think that it was an act of Allah himself—an earthquake struck the city. Fortunately for me, I was kept on the ground floor of the prison, so rather than being buried in the earth, I was able to escape when the wall of my prison crumbled. Without knowing where I would go, I seized the moment and fled before anyone could come looking for me. I ran and ran, though my legs could scarcely run after years of close confinement, but somehow, exhausted, hungry, thirsty, I made it to the desert. I knew the desert most likely meant death, but so would returning to the city, and so I began to cross the desert, praying that God would have mercy on me and send me some respite—perhaps a tribe of Bedouins would take me in, if only to keep me as a servant or even a slave, so long as they would feed me and treat me with some small degree of kindness and respect that would make life bearable again.

I wandered the desert during the cold nights to keep from freezing, and during the days, I rested under the hot sun, getting what sleep I could on the hot sands, praying I should not die in a sandstorm. I lived this way without food or water for three days until I cried out to Allah to deliver me or show me mercy and swiftly take my life rather than let me suffer the miseries of thirst and hunger.

And then, when I was certain I must be hallucinating, I saw an oasis marked by a cluster of date palms and a well, and two elderly men were sitting at the well, and one of them said to me, "Welcome, Glorianda. Drink and be forgiven all your sins." My thirst was so intolerable that

I did not ask their names or how they knew mine. I simply drank long from the bucket I drew up from the well. And when I had lowered the bucket, I saw that I was no longer at the desert's edge but in the midst of the most vibrant, lush, and colorful land I had ever seen.

At first, I thought I must be hallucinating—that my thirst was making me dream of water and verdure. The look of astonishment on my face must have made that thought visible to the men, for one of them laughed and the other said to me, "You do not dream. You are in an earthly paradise."

I then felt my soul quake with fear, but the first man took my hand and said, "No, you are not dead. Welcome to the Kingdom of Prester John."

I had never heard of this king, but I was in such awe that I allowed the man to lead me away from the well and toward the great gold-domed palace that you, Asalah, have seen all your life, so you cannot imagine how magnificent a sight it seemed to me.

You can, however, imagine what my life was like from that moment, living here in the land of Prester John. Here I studied, here I grew spiritually, here I learned to make sense of my sufferings. One day, finally, I found the courage to ask Prester John how it was that I had come to his land, for he said only those worthy or who sought worthiness could come here from the outside world. I will never forget his reply: "There are two reasons you are here, Glorianda. First, because you have learned forgiveness; you learned to forgive and love your husband, Brunamont. Secondly, because another has sought your forgiveness; Prince Ogier was once here, and he prayed deeply that you forgive him for he feared that he had wronged you by never returning to share your love, and it was in the same hour that he sent up his prayer that you first saw the palm trees and made your way to the well."

I was overcome by these words. Ogier had loved me after all. I asked then to see him, but Prester John told me it was not to be. "Ogier has returned back into the world of men," he said, "but there is another, a dear friend of Ogier, who resides here. The two of you will find a great love for each other through your mutual love for Ogier." And it was then, Asalah, that Prester John took me to meet your father, Sir Roland, nephew to the—"

OGIER INTERRUPTS

"Roland!" burst out Ogier. "Your father is Roland, and your mother is Glorianda!"

"Yes, King Ogier," said Asalah, "and that is the end of my mother's tale, for she and my father married not long after and remained in Prester John's kingdom where I was born."

"You have certainly taken your time in telling me this wonderful news!" Ogier said. "But I welcome you, daughter of my bosom friend and of the most beautiful mortal woman I have ever known."

"You speak well, Ogier," said an unexpected voice above them.

Startled, Ogier and Asalah looked up, where through a high window, Morgan le Fay came floating into the room.

"You speak well," repeated the Lady of Avalon, "in saying 'mortal' woman, for I will not have you deriding my own beauty."

As Morgan le Fay's feet touched the floor, she smiled, causing Ogier and Asalah to realize she was teasing them, and yet they were so awestruck by her beauty, by the glamour of her appearance, the glow about her, that they knew not how to respond.

For a moment, Ogier felt the impulse to rush to Morgan and clasp her in his arms, but she immediately turned to speak to Asalah, saying, "I, Asalah, am Morgan le Fay, whom I'm sure your father has mentioned to you. I have waited for you to finish your tale so your request may be granted. Tell Ogier what that request is."

Asalah hesitated. She who had grown up a child in the land of Prester John, who had seen more wonders in one day than most mortals see in a lifetime, nevertheless felt intimidated by this immortal woman's presence.

"I dare not, milady, for though my parents are well-intentioned, I feel now it is much too bold a request."

"It is a request based upon what has been planned since time began; not predestined—for humans are given Free Will—but what it has been the natural evolution of your ancestors' desire and your own desire to make happen. It is well. Speak."

But rather than speak, Asalah held out her hand, palm up, and there upon it, Ogier recognized Melusine's ring, which Roland had previously had in his possession.

"It is my wedding ring," said Asalah after a moment, "the wedding ring of my ancestors, Adam and Eve, the ancestors of all the human race."

Astonished to see it again, Ogier could only ask, "Who is your husband?"

"She has none yet," said Morgan, "but her chosen one will now join us," and she stepped aside, and inexplicably, there, where a moment before Morgan had stood, was the most handsome golden-haired youth whom Ogier had ever seen. Ogier could not fathom how anyone could be as powerful yet beautiful as this veritable giant of a man for he stood a few inches taller than Ogier and was broader in the shoulders, meatier in his forearms, and thicker in his chest, and he wore a simple white garment akin to a Roman toga.

And then this glorious youth spoke the most wonderful word Ogier had ever heard.

"Father."

And Ogier found himself in the youth's embrace.

"But...but how...you are hardly more than a boy," said Ogier, stepping back. "Morgan, we, why it's been years and years since—"

"Our son Meurvin is past his fortieth year," said Morgan le Fay slowly, allowing his son's name to register in Ogier's brain. "He appears in the prime of his youth, beauty, and strength because he has dined all his life on the royal jelly of Avalon, as Asalah has drunk all her life from the living water of Prester John's land. Now that they are here in the human realm, they will begin to age, but they have been allowed to have extended lives so they could gain the wisdom required for the mission that lies ahead of them. Together, they will be sacred keepers of Melusine's ring and of my and Arthur's lineage."

"They are to be wed?" Ogier asked, wanting to be certain he understood all her amazing words.

As he spoke, Ogier saw Meurvin first look upon Asalah and then draw her to him, and she went willingly until their bodies fit perfectly together in an embrace.

"You need not fear, Ogier," said Morgan. "Your time in this story is nearing its end, but the next generation will carry on your good work."

Ogier looked upon the young lovers as they separated yet continued to hold hands and gaze into one another's eyes. And then Morgan le Fay reminded him, "You have known such passionate love, yourself, Ogier. It has not been so long since you and I felt the same way about one another, and now the time approaches for us to rekindle our romance."

"Will they rule my kingdom when I am gone?" Ogier asked.

"No. Someday in the future, the Kingdom of Jerusalem will be ruled by Melusine's descendants, but through the child Count Geoffrey conceived upon Gudrun. That time is many generations in the future, and I'm afraid it shall be short-lived. No, our children's line will continue, but hidden from those in power for some time. More to the moment, it is time now for you to complete your last quest by bringing the Holy Lance to Montserrat as Merlin wished, and then I will take you with me to Avalon."

Ogier was greatly stunned by all this—having all his life waited for Morgan le Fay to return and take him to Avalon. But he had never been with his son until now, so he did not wish to part from him so quickly.

"We shall spend a week feasting, celebrating our son's marriage," Morgan le Fay said, as if reading Ogier's thoughts. "And you will never be far away from him; you will always be able to watch him in the pool at Avalon, through which all that happens in this world can be observed, and someday, he and Asalah shall also join us there."

Ogier nodded in acceptance of it all, but one problem yet troubled him. "How," he asked, "will I bring the Holy Lance to Montserrat? If I take it from Jerusalem, the people will possibly riot, for they hold it as sacred and believe it belongs to them."

"You have worried over that for many years," said Morgan le Fay, "and your worrying has served you not at all. All things work out at the best time and in the best way; worrying does nothing to make things happen sooner—if anything, it only hinders their completion. Come; let us now prepare to celebrate the wedding and trust that, in the meantime, a way will be found to achieve this quest, for sometimes the greatest thing we can do to make something happen is to do nothing at all."

CHAPTER 18

AND SO A great feast was held that lasted for an entire week. Meurvin and Asalah were wed in the tradition of the Muslim people, for Ogier did not wish to upset the new caliph, al-Mu'tasim, the third son of Haroun al-Rashid, who had recently ascended the throne. At the same time, Ogier wondered whether, despite what Morgan le Fay had said, the caliph, upon learning Ogier had a son, might not want to make the kingship of Jerusalem hereditary.

But Ogier tried to dismiss these concerns from his thoughts since Morgan le Fay had instructed him to focus on enjoying the feasting. Most of all, he enjoyed the time he spent with his son, who was so stunningly handsome, so wise, and so strong that Ogier found it difficult to believe Meurvin was his grown child, despite his own great fame as a knight; Ogier could only think Morgan's ancient blood of Avalon was the cause for why Meurvin excelled all other men. Indeed, Meurvin's appearance left in awe all who saw him, and the people of Jerusalem were quickly willing to embrace him as their prince, despite his fair skin, which they associated with Christians. His marriage to the beautiful Asalah, whom it was understood was of royal Saracen blood, made all those of any status in Jerusalem very pleased, and many a toast was made and a prayer said for the young couple's happiness.

Morgan le Fay had told Ogier that seven days feasting would take place, but during that time, she hid herself away from the celebrations. She did not want people to suspect witchcraft or magic was afoot, and she had forbidden Ogier to reveal whom Meurvin's mother was. Nevertheless, she often came to Ogier in the privacy of his bedchamber to discuss with him his past and what he was to expect when the time came for him to join her in Avalon. What concerned Ogier most, however, was how he could complete his mission to bring the Holy Lance to Merlin, and he also wished to understand what had become of Gudrun. But he sensed Morgan would chide him for his impatience if he were to ask her questions, so he remained silent.

Then on the morning of the seventh and final day of the feasts, when Ogier felt he could not withhold his questions any longer, Morgan was no longer to be found in the palace. After several hours and after he had called for her in private several times, without her appearing, he began to feel dejected, little suspecting that during that same afternoon, all the answers he needed would be given to him.

Not long after the midday meal, messengers arrived from Caliph al-Mu'tasim, bringing congratulations to the bride and groom, but also proclamations and instructions that would change the course of Jerusalem's history. Meurvin and Asalah were very pleased with the sumptuous gifts they received from the caliph, including an entire caravan of camels carrying gold plates and cups, expensive silks, priceless rugs, ornate jewelry, and enough spices to last for years to come. But they were not half so pleased by these gifts as Ogier was by the message the caliph sent to him. After gazing upon all the rich gifts his son and daughter-in-law had received, he carried the caliph's letter to his personal chambers to read it in privacy.

Greetings to Ogier, King of Jerusalem, from al-Mu'tasim, Caliph of the Abbasid Empire, Commander of the Faithful by the Grace of Allah.

Peace be to you, Ogier, faithful servant of the empire and of my late father Haroun al-Rashid.

It has come to our attention among our late father's papers that there exists a document in our father's own hand requesting that the sacred relic known as the Holy Lance be given to you to carry to the Patriarch of Constantinople, or rather, the accompanying spear, which we have sent with our men and which is a fair replica. It is our understanding from our late father that you were to bring the actual Holy Lance to a place of safekeeping as appointed by those immortals who watch over all earthly realms, both Christian and Muslim, and work for the good of all humankind.

Because the absence of the Holy Lance might stir up trouble in Jerusalem, save for it leaving by the caliph's own permission, and because any differences in the Lance would be noticed should it be replaced in Jerusalem, it is our wish that your newlywed children, Prince Meurvin and Princess Asalah, journey to Constantinople to take this replica with them and pass it off as the original, which the Patriarch of Constantinople, having never seen the true Lance, will not notice as false. The people of Jerusalem, furthermore, will simply have to rely upon and respect the wisdom of their caliph in this matter, or feel my terrible wrath.

As for the original, you are free to take it away in secret to that place where it shall be safe and known only to you. We have reason to believe that certain people in our kingdom are not trustworthy and likely to attempt treason against us, and if this move is not made now to protect the Holy Lance from falling into the wrong hands, it may be too late, so we urge you to make haste in the matter. There are those in our realm who are no friends of fair-skinned people from the North, be they Christians or not, so I fear what might result if you and your family should remain as Kings of Jerusalem.

Therefore, I wish you to make your departure with haste. I have appointed a new king over Jerusalem and the outlying lands of Palestine who will arrive within a fortnight of your receipt of this letter. Treat him as you would treat my own self; make him welcome, and leave the Kingdom of Jerusalem in his hands as quickly as it is possible for you to depart.

I apologize for the haste of this communication and its obscurity of content, but I have reasons for my actions. Furthermore, based on all that my father continually told me of you during his lifetime, I know you were the most trusted of all his vassals; therefore, follow my commands, which are in keeping with what I believe are in your own best interests as well as desires.

I give you my sincere affection and gratitude for your long service to our family.

May the peace of Allah be with you and your heirs.

al-Mu'tasim, Commander of the Faithful, Caliph of the Abbasid Empire

Ogier was stunned by this letter, but he had the forethought to destroy it immediately. Then he rushed out to the caravan to inquire whether it contained a special gift solely for him.

"Indeed, there is, my lord; it has been entrusted to me completely," said the caravan leader. "I did not wish to present it until you had read the caliph's letter. Even I know not what it is, save that it is in a large and bulky wooden box that has caused us considerable trouble to transport all this distance."

Ogier had this box taken to his private chamber where he opened it in solitude. Inside, he found wrapped in a great carpet an exact replica of the Holy Lance that resided in the Church of the Holy Sepulchre; the difference between the original and this false lance none would ever know. Ogier was astonished by this turn of events, and yet he had no time to question how such a replica could have been made. He knew only that he must now obtain the true Lance while he had this false one sent to Constantinople. He rolled the false lance back into the carpet and enclosed it in the box. He failed, however, to notice that the carpet in which it was wrapped was the very same carpet upon which he had once flown through the air from the land of Prester John to Baghdad. Over the years, he had occasionally wondered what had become of that carpet—he had forgotten it when he departed from Baghdad, leaving it behind in the guest bedchamber of the caliph's palace—but now so many years had passed, and he had seen so many beautiful carpets in his time, that he no longer remembered the pattern that had been upon it. After all, he had only ridden upon it for what had seemed no longer than an hour, and his thoughts now were for the Lance, not a flying carpet, however marvelous it might be.

In the silence of that same night, Ogier took Meurvin into his confidence about the Holy Lance and its replica, and Meurvin, having been raised in Avalon, was not surprised, although he was very pleased by the caliph's cunning. Together, they made their way to the Holy Sepulchre, and under cover of night, they removed the Holy Lance and carried it back to the palace, leaving in its place the false lance fashioned by order of the caliph.

At the end of the fortnight, the new governor of Jerusalem arrived, and with him he carried an official proclamation from the caliph that the Holy Lance was to be brought to Constantinople and given as a gift to its Patriarch so it should never fall into the hands of those who might show disrespect to such a revered Christian artifact; furthermore, by this act, he hoped to bring about peace between his caliphate and the Eastern Roman Empire—and death be to him who should object to his making such a gift.

Within a few days of the new governor's arrival, Ogier embarked on a ship with Meurvin and Asalah to Constantinople with both the legitimate and the false lance. Upon their arrival in Christendom's greatest city, Ogier presented the false lance to the Patriarch of Constantinople. As a result, for many centuries to come, the lance would be seen within Hagia Sophia, the Church of the Holy Wisdom.

During their time in the imperial city, Ogier and his children were begged by the current Eastern Emperor to remain in Constantinople and make their home there. Meurvin and Asalah graciously accepted this offer, and in time, their children would marry into the highest houses of Constantinople, their descendants blending in with the lineages of the emperors themselves, including the last Constantine who would hold the city before the conquest of the Turks. And through various dynastic marriages, Meurvin and Asalah's descendants would also spread across Europe, until in time, one of those descendants would make his way over the English Channel in 1066 to fight beside William the Conqueror at the Battle of Hastings, and upon that battle's success, be named the first Baron Delaney.

Ogier the Dane, however, did not remain in Constantinople to see the birth of his grandchildren. He still pondered what had become of Gudrun, and why he had failed in his mission to capture her, or whether he had failed at all, for he continued to marvel over Prester John's words concerning her and the strange transformation his own soul had experienced when he had prayed for her wellbeing. Nor did he know how to complete his mission concerning her—or even if a mission yet remained—but he did know he must still bring the Holy Lance to Merlin.

And so one day, a few months later, the hoary-haired hermits of the holy monastery of Montserrat were surprised to see an old man, nearly eighty years of age, dressed in pilgrim's garb, but with the bearing of a great king, walk up their mountain. The visitor was barefoot and carrying a long wooden box, which he told them contained a sacred relic. When the hermits asked him how he could have the strength to walk up the mountain carrying such a large and awkward object, he told them that despite whatever hardships he had faced on his long journey, the relic had given him strength to endure until he reached their holy dwelling. He then asked to speak to Merlin, but none of the hermits understood whom he meant, for he did not speak well the local Catalan tongue, and none of them were believers in legendary wizards who were not akin to their Christian beliefs.

Then Ogier—for, of course, the visitor was he—drew the spear from the box. The holy men all marveled at the glow emanating from it, and then Ogier told them, "This is the true Holy Lance that pierced the side of Christ, the Savior. I have brought it here to be kept in safety until the time when it shall be called for by King Arthur or Christ Himself or whoever is the one meant to possess it at the end times."

And the abbot, bowing his head in gratitude, came forth and accepted the spear, feeling its power course through him as he touched it, and then he said in the Norse tongue, surprising all those who had known him for decades and never heard him speak any tongues but Latin and Catalan, and who, it need not be said, did not understand what tongue he spoke, "It is well done, Ogier the Dane. I have waited many decades for you and Roland to fulfill the quest I sent you upon, and now it is complete. Know that I am Merlin, and that you have completed your mission, and now, finally, has come the time for your reward."

And then this man, clothed as an abbot, turned and carried the spear into the chapel, and all the monks, still not knowing what he had said, followed him, but Ogier remained behind, wondering what he was now to do, for that which he had spent a lifetime pursuing had been fulfilled. Ogier waited as the last monks entered the chapel, but neither the abbot nor any of the monks turned back to beckon him to join them, and Ogier felt no need to follow them.

After a little while, when no one returned outside to fetch him, Ogier shrugged his shoulders and turned to walk away. He started back down the mountain, wondering where he should sleep for the night, for the sky was growing dark. Then when he was halfway down, it began to rain. Noticing a cave in the mountain's side, he decided to take shelter there. When the rain did not let up after an hour, he was uncertain what to do next; perhaps he should return to Montserrat, for the night was descending. Merlin had said that he had now completed his quest, and it was the time for his reward, but what had he meant by such words? *Perhaps*, Ogier thought, *I should have gone into the chapel and questioned Merlin further.*

But Ogier was tired and cold and did not wish to venture back out into the rain to climb halfway up a mountain again. He was old, and he had all his life been on a quest, or so it had seemed. Perhaps all he wanted to do now was to sleep.

He was just thinking about lying down in the cave when he saw a dancing light on the interior wall that made him realize the cave must go back farther than he had suspected. And taking a few steps toward the light, he realized it was a shadow, a reflection, of falling water. When he explored further by walking around a curve in the cave, he suddenly found himself in a great interior chamber filled with a pool and a waterfall flowing down from the chamber's mountain roof.

And then from out of the waterfall, and walking upon the water, stepped Morgan le Fay.

"Long have I waited for you, my love," she said, walking to him where he now stood on the pool's edge. When she took his hand, he felt a tingling sensation run up his arm, and looking down, he saw that his wrinkles were gone; his skin was as firm and fresh as it had been when first he had been made a knight. Looking with astonishment into Morgan's eyes, Ogier saw in them great shining crystal seas that stretched on and on like the life that was yet to come for him.

"Fear not, Ogier, my love," said Morgan, leading him now over the pool, his own feet barely touching its surface. And then, as they stepped into the waterfall, she added, "We have all of eternity for explanations."

EPILOGUE
ENGLAND AND SEATTLE, WASHINGTON
1995

ADAM OPENED HIS eyes. For a moment, he lay on the bed in the jail cell, trying to wake up, trying to come to grips with returning to the late twentieth century after all he had seen. Then he slowly sat up, feeling dazed, and looked about the room. As far as he could tell, he was alone in his cell. But perhaps Merlin was hiding in the top bunk, waiting to surprise him. Adam swung his feet to the floor and was about to stand up when he heard footsteps. In another second, a police officer appeared and held open the cell door. Adam stood up, quickly glancing toward the top bunk and seeing it was empty, as the officer began to speak.

"Your lordship, bail has been posted for you by your solicitor. We will be in touch regarding a hearing date. You are not to leave England before the hearing."

"Thank you, officer," Adam replied. "I understand."

"I'm sorry it took so long," added the officer, more kindly this time, "but at least you got a good night's sleep. You must have been asleep for fourteen hours. I was about to come in to check whether you were still breathing."

"Really?" said Adam, having thought it was still the same day, but considering that his dream had covered decades of history, he could well imagine a full day had passed. And what a dream it had been! Flying carpets and mysterious caverns, shipwrecks and fairies—all of it would have been unbelievable, and yet...the unbelievable had now almost become the expected in his life.

Adam waited for the officer to unlock and open the cell door. Then he followed the officer to the lobby where Devin waited for him.

"Am I glad to see you," said Devin, immediately hugging his cousin.

"Thanks," Adam said, still feeling sleepy and almost in shock over all that had happened—it would be hard to say whether his mother's death, his children's kidnapping, or a journey back to the time of Charlemagne had been the most shocking for him. And now he felt like he had so much to do, so much to resolve, and yet he did not know what he could do. As usual, he wanted explanations, and knowing Merlin, they would be coming...but not until Merlin felt it convenient to give them.

"This whole thing is ridiculous," Devin said once they were in the car and on the way back to Delaney Castle.

Adam was largely silent; he almost wished he could disappear back into the dream where he had been a silent observer, not a participant in tragic events. He had not forgotten the evil that Gwenhwyvach, or Gudrun or Lilith or whatever name she went by, was going to unleash upon the world in his own time—an evil that would be far worse than anything she had done in Ogier's era, yet somehow, from something he only half-remembered of what Prester John had said, Adam felt that perhaps he need not worry.

"Aren't you angry?" Devin finally asked, surprised by his cousin's silence as they walked to the car and climbed in.

"Yes," said Adam, "but the police were just doing their jobs. I don't like being a suspect in my children's kidnapping, but knowing my mother is dead is so horrendous that everything else seems minor by comparison."

"Yes, it does," said Devin, "but we can't do anything to help your mother now. We can still hope the twins are safe."

"But how is Grandma?" Adam asked. "She must be devastated by my mom's death."

"She's holding up better than I would have expected. She apparently knows more about the family's past than she ever told us; she knew the danger your mother was in all these years as Gwenhwyvach's keeper. I am really amazed by her. I think she's spent more time trying to comfort Anne than grieving herself."

"That's her way of coping," said Adam, wishing he knew how to cope better himself. He had not cried yet, but he thought he was still in too much shock for his mother's death to have sunk in—and when it did—but no, he had to hold it together for now, he told himself, crumpling up his face to hold back any tears.

"Are you tired?" asked Devin, looking at Adam and seeing that he seemed to be squinting.

"No, I slept like a rock, and after a cup of coffee, I'll be up for whatever comes next."

Neither said anything more, and a few minutes later, they were pulling up to the castle. The car hadn't even come to a stop yet when Anne came running out of the house. Adam was in her arms a split second after Devin put the car in park.

After the longest hug he had ever received, Adam entered the house with his wife; then he hugged his grandmother in the hall before they all went to the dining room where Cook had breakfast awaiting them on the table.

Anne went to fetch the coffeepot, and in another minute, the four family members began a hearty meal, knowing they had to keep up their strength, despite their grief and exhaustion.

After a few minutes of conversation, it was clear to Adam that the rest of the family had nothing new to report since he had left. He decided then to tell them an abbreviated version of the dream he'd had, letting his food grow cold as he spoke, and only pausing to sip his coffee.

"What an amazing story," said Elizabeth when he had finished. "I've heard the basics of it before because some of it's been passed down in the family, but I never heard it with so many details."

"But what does it mean?" asked Anne. "What are we supposed to do with it?"

"I don't know," said Adam. "Obviously, it tells us more about the history of the rings and what became of them, but it feels like nothing was resolved—Ogier and Roland never did get the ring back from Gudrun or know what became of her. Still, somehow the ring ended up in Cedric's family."

"I don't think it matters what Gudrun did after that or how Cedric's family got the ring," said Anne. "What's important is that we know where the rings are now—or at least we did, until the one Cedric had was stolen."

"Actually," said Elizabeth. "We don't know where either of the rings is because we don't know whether Mary retrieved the ring she had from the safe-deposit box before she died, and if she did, how do we know Gwenhwyvach didn't take the ring from her before or after she...." Here Elizabeth began crying at the thought of her daughter's death.

Anne put her arm around Elizabeth, while saying, "That's true. Gwenhwyvach could already have both rings, but it could also be possible that Mary gave my father the ring—maybe we haven't heard from him because he has it, but he's hiding from Gwenhwyvach."

"Or maybe he's also dead or her prisoner," said Devin, "and she has both rings now."

Adam shot Devin a glance that showed he was perturbed at his cousin for upsetting his wife with such a suggestion, but Anne saw the look and said, "It's okay, Adam. I'm still hopeful, but I know my father also might be dead. I think with Gwenhwyvach freed, we have to be prepared for the worst."

Elizabeth squeezed Anne's shoulder, returning the comfort she had given. Meanwhile, Adam, seated across from his wife, reached out to hold her hand across the table.

"What I don't understand," said Devin, his mind more intent on working out the puzzle than giving in to fear or grief, "is if Gudrun had the ring, how it ended up with the Counts of Lusignan to be passed down in Cedric's family line. I know Adam just said those details don't matter, but I'd still like to know. Adam says his dream ended with Morgan le Fay telling Ogier that all would be explained, but why did the dream end there when the explanation hasn't been given to us of what became of the ring?"

"I don't know," Adam replied. "We don't know what Gudrun did after Ogier and Roland saw her in Prester John's land."

"Well, it got back into that line somehow," said Elizabeth, wiping the tears from her face.

"Yes, but...." said Anne, but she did not finish.

"What is it, dear?" asked Elizabeth.

"It's just," said Anne, breaking into tears, "just that I hate to think that my father is from an evil line."

"Don't focus on that," said Elizabeth. "It's not exactly true. There have been good and bad Counts of Lusignan, and your father's ancestors branched off from the Lusignan line centuries ago. There are good and bad people in all families, and there are so many thousands of people now descended from Arthur and Morgan le Fay, as well as from Geoffrey and Gudrun, and Ogier and Morgan le Fay. Out of all of them, only a few have carried on this battle all these centuries, while the vast majority of humankind have forgotten about it. To say any of us is from a good or an evil line is to oversimplify it all."

"My father is a good man in many ways," said Anne. "He's never been anything but kind to me, and he loved the twins."

"Of course," Elizabeth said. "We all have good in us, and even when Cedric did what was wrong, such as commit adultery, good has come of it. You wouldn't be here otherwise, dear. That just shows that when bad things happen, or even when people intend bad things, it all turns out for good in the end."

"I hope so," said Anne. "But it just makes my head hurt. I think I need another cup of coffee."

Anne got up and went into the kitchen while the rest of them sat in silence, trying to make sense out of the puzzle they all faced.

"I just had a thought!" said Anne, returning. "What if—well, what was the point of Ogier praying so hard? What if it somehow did make a difference? What if Gudrun had a change of heart, and so she gave the ring to her son by Geoffrey, not so she could pass down evil through her line but because the ring rightly belonged to Melusine's descendant, and Gudrun's son, after all, was Melusine's grandson."

"Are you saying that Ogier's prayer may have caused her to have a change of heart?" asked Adam.

"It's possible," said Anne. "Don't you think so—I mean, otherwise, we weren't told what effect, if any, Ogier's prayer had."

"Yes, why not?" Devin agreed. "After all, didn't Prester John tell Ogier and Roland not to judge Gudrun—maybe she isn't evil or at least not all evil. Maybe Ogier came to understand that—I mean, how do we know she really did kill Count Geoffrey—he could have died from a heart attack for all we know, and how do we know she really turned Ogier's father against him—we have only his word for it. We can't really know what was in her heart."

For a moment, they all felt better at this thought, but then Anne's smile began to droop as she said slowly, "But...it's so contradictory then. We can't think Gudrun became good after Ogier prayed, even if we want to. She killed Adam's mother and—"

"We don't know that," said Devin. "We just know that Aunt Mary is dead."

"She had to have been killed," said Elizabeth, her tears springing forth again. "How else does one fall from the top of the Space Needle?"

"I suppose," said Adam, "it could have been an accident...."

Elizabeth began sobbing again at the thought of her daughter being dead, so Adam got up and went to find her a tissue box. When he returned, he said, "I think Devin is right. I want to blame Gwenhwyvach or whatever this witch's name is, and she's the most likely suspect in my mother's death, but we don't know for sure what happened."

"It's all so contradictory," said Devin. "That's what's so confusing because we can't forget what Prester John said—"

"But it's also in contradiction to what Merlin told us," Adam interrupted. "Merlin hid away our children to protect them because he believes Gwenhwyvach is going to unleash great evil upon the world. That doesn't sound like a woman who had a change of heart."

Anne began sobbing now too. "Where is my father? Why haven't we heard from him? If I could know the answer to just one thing now, it would be that."

Adam was more inclined to want to know where his children were, but he got up from his chair and walked over to Anne, kneeling beside her chair to wrap his arm around her. "We just have to be strong and hope for the best. I'm sure Cedric will contact us as soon as he can, or that Merlin will show up any minute now to tell us what to do."

"I wish Merlin had a cell phone so we could contact him," said Anne, her sobs turning to anger. "Why do we always have to wait for him to come to us? It's like we're just chess pieces in his and Gwenhwyvach's game."

"No, dear," said Elizabeth. "Merlin may not communicate with us the way we would like, but we are not pawns. I know that much. We have Free Will and shape our own destinies."

"Well, it sure doesn't seem like it," said Anne. "I sure didn't use my Free Will in any of this—I mean, I love you, Adam, don't get me wrong, but I didn't even choose to be with you initially—Merlin manipulated all that, and I didn't choose to have my children taken away. If he had explained to us sooner about Gwenhwyvach, maybe I would have agreed to his taking our sons away and hiding them to keep them safe, but he did it without asking, so I can't help it if I feel like just a pawn being played with."

Adam continued to hug her as all of them felt the same frustration. All they could do was just wait to see how it would all play out and hope for the best.

TWO DAYS EARLIER....

As Cedric buckled his seatbelt on the plane bound for Seattle, with Mary in the seat beside him, he realized how marvelous everything had suddenly become. After years of failure, now everything seemed to be turning out how he had always wanted.

All his life he had desired to have Mary—to make her his own, his wife, to control her, and to make himself and his descendants powerful through her. Ever since his father had first told him about their family's past and he had first heard Mary's name and learned of her special bloodline, although he was but fourteen years old at the time and had never even seen a picture of her, he had lusted to possess her, fantasizing about her night and day. His father's stories had inspired him into believing it was his duty to breed a new race of superhumans—to make Mary his wife so he might create powerful children who would regain the ring not in his family's possession; then they could be restored to their rightful place above the rest of mankind—the place their ancestor Lilith had once held with her husband Adam before Eve had dispossessed her. Cedric had been determined that the evil of Eve's descendants, Mary's own ancestors, would be suppressed once he married her and possessed the ring. Then he would control her and break the power her family had held for so long; then all the power would belong to him and his children.

The only thing he needed besides Mary was the other ring itself, but that was in the Delaneys' possession. For that reason, he had befriended Bram Delaney, not knowing where the Delaneys kept the ring, but thinking that in time he would gain access to it. He had never suspected that Bram would take possession of Mary and plant his seed in her before he could himself; enraged by this turn of events, he had taken out his frustration on Mary's sister, Martha, then tossed her aside, for she was not Mary, not the oldest sister, the one who should have been his bride. But once Bram had taken Mary, it had seemed too late.

Still, when he and Bram had returned to England, he had done the only thing he could. He had hired private detectives to keep an eye on Mary. He had learned of her son's birth, but then she had mysteriously disappeared without a trace. Now and then he had checked up on the boy, ironically named Adam, but in time, he had grown complacent, focusing rather on his revenge upon Bram, making sure the newly made earl never again connected with Mary, arranging for Bram's wife Sarah to meet him so he could forget Mary, and then seducing Sarah after she had wed Bram so he could impregnate her with his child, and so she would give him access to the ring. Only, Sarah had been completely clueless about the ring when he had subtly questioned her about it. And then she had died, and Cedric had used her death in childbirth—it was all so perfect he almost wished he had planned it that way—to apologize to Bram for betraying him and to renew their friendship through the illusion of their mutual grief. And he pretended to have Anne's best interests at heart, convincing Bram not to reveal the secret of her parentage.

And because of this elaborate charade that Cedric had concocted, Bram had never suspected that his "friend" did not feel the slightest bit of remorse. Oh, Cedric knew he had played it all so well, winning Bram's affection back through the child, infiltrating his way into Bram's heart and home so he could keep an eye on the daughter who was truly his. Bram had been a smart man, a good man, an honorable man, and for those reasons, Cedric had delighted all the more in keeping him wrapped around his finger in a way that made Bram clueless just how thoroughly he was being played by the man who could sleep with his wife and still continue to be his best friend.

And during all those years, Cedric continued to seek the ring, convinced that Bram still had it, and in time, he would tell Anne about it, and through her, Cedric would gain possession of it. It had only been in the last few days that Cedric had finally learned the truth—that Bram had given Mary the ring all those years ago. He had waited a long time to possess that ring, but now, traveling to Seattle, he would finally have the chance to obtain it.

But unexpected developments had begun to change Cedric's plans. He had never realized he would love Anne or adore his grandsons, or find, in the last few days of getting to know Mary, that he would no longer lust for her, but rather, realize what an amazing woman she was—yes, he thought maybe he was even falling in love with her. And neither of them was much over forty—it was still possible they could be united and have a child of their own—perhaps a daughter he could mate with one of Adam's sons. Oh, fools would call that incest, but he knew it was really genetic engineering—something the Church frowned on only to keep a master race from developing so it could retain its own power, its hold of fear over mankind. He would still find a way to make it happen—to restore the balance of power that had been lost all those years ago in the Garden of Eden. Just because he loved Mary did not mean he had to alter his plans, and once the two of them had possession of both rings and brought the rings together, think how she would admire him all the more for what they had accomplished.

All Cedric needed now was that ring in the safe-deposit box in Seattle because he already had the other ring. Yes, he had told Adam and Anne the one he possessed had been stolen, but that was only to throw them off the scent. In time, they would forgive him; after all, he would make sure they were well taken care of when he came into his power. And he would know exactly what to do once the rings were reunited. He had spent years studying the secrets of extended life that the descendants of Avalon knew; he had pored over the many research files his father had left him, and he knew he had almost perfected the secrets, the recipes, so that he might eventually live for centuries and have plenty of time to bring all his dreams to fruition. Sometimes, the thought of the power and the long life within him being so within his grasp almost made him think he was crazy—could such things really be possible? And yet the possibility was enough to drive him on in his quest to achieve such power.

Sometimes, Cedric also almost regretted that he had arranged his father's death when he had. He did not regret murdering his father—just that he had been so impatient that he did not wait longer so he could have gained more information from the old man. But his father had been a control freak, a hard taskmaster, and Cedric had grown weary of being under his thumb, plus he had become overly anxious to have his inheritance. He had despised his father—despised his old-fashioned ways—and shown it by calling him "Old Man" to his face, even though his father had always appeared strikingly young—he had been well into his forties when he died, yet he looked young enough to be Cedric's older brother by just a year or two—all the more reason why Cedric had been convinced that the old man knew the secrets of extended life, though he would not share them with him or even tell him much about his past. But the old man had a room he kept locked up. Once or twice Cedric had seen through the door—when his father entered the mysterious room—his father's stack of secret books, and

Cedric was certain that the knowledge he sought lay in those pages, so he was intent upon possessing it.

When Cedric had turned eighteen, he could wait no longer to claim his inheritance. He had then toyed with the brakes to his father's car, not enough to cause them to fail completely, but enough for them to work sporadically so that his father crashed into another vehicle and was killed instantly—as was the innocent driver in the other car...but that was a small matter when Cedric had succeeded in his purpose. The police had thought it just a mechanical brake failure and told him his father's body was terribly mangled—Cedric feigned grief and paid the minimal costs required to bury the old man, but he had not bothered to arrange a funeral.

And when Cedric realized he had successfully gotten away with murder, he became confident and took to manipulating others. In time, he built up a fortune by taking advantage of Bram's friendship to embezzle his money as his solicitor. He had manipulated Anne's mother Sarah into sleeping with him. And as recently as just a few days ago, he had feigned great remorse for his deeds of the past to win Mary's sympathy and trust as a means eventually to winning her heart. And serendipitously, that had resulted not only in his being present when she revealed not only that she had always possessed the other ring he had sought, but that she was the keeper of his powerful ancestress, Gwenhwyvach, and now he had the opportunity to go with Mary to recover the ring.

Yet one aspect of these recent events still worried him. Gwenhwyvach might be his ancestress, but she was also incredibly powerful. Yes, he hated Mary and Bram because of the family feud between their ancestors, but while that feud meant he had been denied his rightful inheritance, it did not mean he was ready to hand over what was rightfully his to a woman who should have been dead long ago. Yes, she had once ruled over the Garden of Eden, and once been Queen of Britain and Queen of Denmark, too, but now it was his turn to acquire power—to regain the throne of England that had belonged to his ancestors—to control the very world itself, to rule as its rightful king, as one of Lilith's descendants should have done long ago. He had not worked all these years to hand over everything to Gwenhwyvach now. He admitted that he feared her, but if he could gain possession of the other ring before she could, he should be able to defeat her, and if she gained it first, as her descendant, he believed he could manipulate her into believing he was on her side—after all, did he not have the other ring she wanted? Nor did he believe for a second that she was as powerful as Merlin claimed. Cedric was not at all impressed by Merlin—after all, what kind of fool wizard appears as steam from a teapot? Perhaps the wizard knew the secret of eternal life, but beyond that, he was clearly incompetent or he would have finished off Gwenhwyvach long ago.

But it would all work out. Let Merlin and Gwenhwyvach have their showdown. Meanwhile, he would get the rings, and then he would figure out how to exterminate whichever of the two immortals remained to threaten him. Yes, it was all going to work out. He was certain of it. After all these years, Gwenhwyvach's ancient wrongs would be redressed, and he, her descendant, would achieve it, but he would also ensure that he was rewarded with all the power in the end.

These thoughts filled Cedric's brain all the way to Seattle while Mary caught up on her sleep. Finally, the plane landed late in the evening. After they entered the airport and collected their luggage, Mary quickly called Adam on her cell phone to let him know they had arrived while Cedric used the airport restroom. The sun was setting by the time they found a taxi to take them downtown to a hotel. Once the driver dropped them off at the hotel door, however, Mary had picked up her suitcase and begun walking down the street. Cedric had followed, wondering where she was going. She offered no explanation, so he did not ask for one. When they were within a few blocks of the Space Needle, she stopped before a locked garage door and entered a security code. Cedric watched with curiosity as the garage door opened.

Nothing surprising lay inside the garage—just a truck and some trashcans and other ordinary items one would expect, but Mary entered regardless, then turned around to face Cedric.

"Come on," she said.

He quickly ducked inside as she pressed an automatic garage door button; he just barely made it inside before the door closed.

"Where are we?" he asked.

"We're not wasting money on a hotel room. We can sleep in the compound. Besides, the safe-deposit box is there. I only told Adam and Anne it was in a bank in case Gwenhwyvach was listening."

"The compound! Do you mean...where you kept—"

"Yes, Gwenhwyvach's prison," said Mary.

To say Cedric was surprised by this information would be an understatement. He had known the compound was in Seattle, but he had not realized they would be staying there.

Mary walked through the garage to a back door. When she opened it, only a brick wall was revealed. Then she uttered some words Cedric did not understand, though they must have been the equivalent of "Open sesame!" for suddenly the wall disappeared. But Cedric figured it was not magic, but some sort of voice activation, that had caused the illusion of the wall to vanish.

He and Mary passed through the door into a hallway that looked like a Jetway to an airplane. It inclined gently downward for several hundred yards, turning once or twice in the process, until they came to the end of it—in front of a large gate.

Mary fumbled in her purse, then drew out a card that she inserted into a slot beside the gate. In a moment, the gate rose and allowed them to pass beneath it before it closed again. Now they were in a dark stone hallway that resembled a narrow basement chamber; after some twists and turns and branching off halls, it led them to an octagonal room with eight doors, one per wall. Cedric was about to ask which door they should go through when suddenly the walls seemed to grow—no, not grow, but pass by them; he and Mary were actually descending—they were in an elevator without walls of its own, and they descended many floors past numerous more sets of eight doors. Cedric lost count of how many floors, but he guessed they went down at least twelve or more before they came to a stop, this time on a floor with only one entrance, an arched doorway in front of them. Mary stepped through the arch as soon as the floor quit moving.

In a few seconds, Cedric found himself in what looked like the lobby of a luxury hotel, complete with a clerk at the front desk—only the clerk was wearing what looked more like a *Star Trek* costume than proper business attire—it was some sort of military uniform, and it instantly made Cedric feel uncomfortable.

"Keeper Morgan," said the woman, nodding to Mary. "How was your flight?"

"Just fine, Keeper Weir," she replied. "This is my son's father-in-law, Cedric Harker."

"We have been expecting you both," Keeper Weir replied. "We have rooms available for you, and Keeper Stewart is awaiting you whenever you find it convenient."

"Thank you," said Mary.

Cedric simply nodded at the desk clerk and then followed Mary down a hallway to what had every appearance of being the door to a regular hotel room. Mary again inserted her key, and they entered a suite of rooms, complete with a living room, kitchenette, and two bedrooms, each with its own bathroom.

"I can put my stuff away later," said Mary. "If you're tired, you can stay here and rest, but I need to go talk to Keeper Stewart about Gwenhwyvach's escape."

"I'll go with you," said Cedric, exhausted and longing for a cup of tea, but not wanting to miss out on any information that might be valuable to him—he never knew what that might be, and he did not want Mary to acquire the ring when not in his presence.

After they set down their suitcases and quickly used their individual restrooms, Cedric followed Mary through a maze of rooms until they came to what appeared to be a boardroom; at the far end of the room, which Mary and then Cedric approached, was a full wall of glass windows overlooking some sort of subterranean jungle with a good-size ranch-style house in its center.

"This was where Gwenhwyvach was kept," said Mary, looking at the house. "It's a beautiful yard with a garden—about the size of a football field—plenty of room so she would not feel too trapped, and a ten-room house. She had everything she needed to live, including her meals delivered and people to guard her for her own protection as well as the world's, so she would not desire to hurt or free herself."

"It sounds like she had everything except human companionship," said Cedric, feeling somewhat sorry for her. After all, she was his ancestress.

"To some degree, we all felt sorry for her," said Mary, as if reading his thoughts, "but we knew that if we showed her any sympathy or compassion, it would give her the ability to control our minds. We don't think that happened—that she used her will to make one of the keepers weak enough to give in to releasing her—but that is why I must meet with Keeper Stewart and the others, so we can—"

"You should not have brought him," interrupted a female voice from behind them.

Cedric instantly felt threatened by the words as he saw the woman's reflection in the glass. He expected it was Keeper Stewart since he could not see the reflection very well, but he knew better the moment he heard Mary gasp as they turned around.

"How? How?" Mary stuttered.

"*How?* Did you think you could keep me trapped forever?" demanded Gwenhwyvach. She was dressed in the same *Star Trek* type uniform as the woman at the desk, but her words and her face made her identity clear to Mary. "Don't bother with the 'feeling sorry for me' speech," she continued. "I don't buy it. Not after how you have cruelly treated me all these years."

"But how—"

Before Mary could finish her question—the same one Cedric had: Why was she dressed like a keeper?—Gwenhwyvach interrupted.

"They all think I'm Keeper Stewart. I have brainwashed them all. Trust me; it was not terribly difficult."

"What do you intend?" asked Mary. "You—"

But then Mary grew silent for a second. And a second later, she let out a scream. Gwenhwyvach had momentarily allowed Mary to read her thoughts. "No, you can't!" Mary cried. "Cedric, she intends to—"

But Mary never finished her sentence. She was lifted off the ground by an invisible force—lifted, tossed backwards halfway across the room, and then, like a cannonball, she was sent flying forward at an alarming speed into the glass window.

Cedric was almost as shocked not to see the glass break as he was to see Mary fly through the air, then crumple to the ground.

"It's so much more fun," said Gwenhwyvach, turning to Cedric, "to take over their brains via concussion than just brainwashing them."

"Yes, Mistress," said Cedric, fear now taking possession of him. He quickly got down on one knee and bowed his head in submission to her. He did not know what instigated such behavior in him, but this woman was his ancestress, and he felt a deep longing to pay her homage. Had she brainwashed him too, he wondered, or was it just some primeval instinct within him to obey her? She was all powerful; what other choice did he have, even if he wished to do otherwise?

"I told her she shouldn't have brought you," Gwenhwyvach continued, "but only because it hurts her. You are of my blood; your presence strengthens me."

"I am pleased to hear so, Mistress," he replied, amazed to hear the words flowing from his tongue.

Mary now woke from her stupor on the floor and rose to her feet.

"What is your will, Mother of the True Race?" she asked, almost robotically.

"Lead me to the ring," Gwenhwyvach replied.

Cedric, still on one knee, looked with amazement as Mary turned and headed toward the door.

"Come along, whimpering dog!" screeched Gwenhwyvach, turning toward him before she followed Mary out of the room.

Cedric jumped up and scurried after them, passing through a maze of rooms and hallways, until finally they came to a large metal door. Mary took the card from her pocket and placed it into a slot in the wall, causing the metal door to swing forward. Then Cedric saw— in the center of the room, in a shaft of light and suspended in the air by what he could not tell—the ring.

Gwenhwyvach rushed forward, pushing Mary aside, reaching out to clutch the ring in her hand. In another second, it was on her finger. She then grinned a more hideously evil grin than any Cedric ever could have imagined, revealing the great gap between her teeth.

"Do you love me, my many greats-grandson?" she asked him.

"Yes, Mistress," he replied.

"Then prove it!" she roared.

He dropped to his knees in fear because her voice was like thunder ripping through the sky and her eyes flashed like lightning.

"Anything you wish, Mistress," he whimpered.

"Very good," she said, her face now changing from that of a demanding queen to one possessing the sweetness of a kitten as he dared to look up at her awful beauty. "We'll go upstairs then."

Before Cedric knew what had happened, Gwenhwyvach had grabbed Mary's wrist in one hand and his own wrist in the other, and suddenly, they were soaring up toward the ceiling. Cedric prepared himself for the pain of crashing through the roof, but he felt not a thing, and in a second, he looked down and saw they had flown upward through all the subterranean chambers and were now out in the open air and heading into the sky.

In another moment, he realized they were soaring alongside the Space Needle, and a minute later, they had landed on its observation deck.

Then, as Mary stood there like a zombie, Gwenhwyvach gave Cedric his orders.

"Push her off."

For a second, Cedric could not comprehend the words.

"Mistress," he begged, "I don't understand. I—"

"Are you not my descendant?" demanded Gwenhwyvach.

"Yes, Mistress, I—"

"Then kill her. She is the enemy of our kind. Kill her now, or I will kill you."

And then Cedric felt hatred soar up inside him, hatred like he had never felt before, and all for this evil creature. He had hated Mary Morgan and Bram Delaney and all of King Arthur's descendants since he had been a child, and now finally, he was able to have his revenge, but strangely, he did not want to do it. Instead, he wanted to run and hide, and even more, to protect Mary. And most of all, he did not want to bow to anyone who threatened him. He wanted power for himself—not to be another's minion.

"Kill her!" Gwenhwyvach shouted. "Throw her off the deck!"

Mary leaned against the observation deck's railing, silent, numb, perhaps so brainwashed that she did not know what was happening.

Cedric now felt rage pulsing through him, but he knew he must control it if he were to survive this moment. And he felt another strange feeling, a desire to see Mary live; perhaps he and she could still....

"I...I...Mistress," he said, "is it necessary? Couldn't you—"

"Coward!" she screamed. "Is this the lily-livered milksop race my descendants have become? Must I do everything myself?"

Before Cedric could reply, an invisible force raised Mary's body above his head, and then, by equally invisible hands, the woman he had begun to love was thrust over the observation deck's barrier. For a moment, Mary hung suspended in the air as Cedric felt panic, and then he watched in disbelief as Mary fell through the air. He leaned over the edge of the barrier just in time to see her splatter onto the pavement below, the noise so loud that it made him jump.

It was night now, but Seattle was lit up enough that several passersby saw Mary fall, and as soon as she hit the ground, a crowd ran toward her bloody mangled corpse.

"Fool!" Gwenhwyvach screeched at Cedric. "Your incompetence has made me angry. I was ready to reward you, to give you what you desired after all your years of service to me, but now I see that you are not deserving to be called my descendant."

Cedric fell to the floor in a fetal position, sobbing, certain she would now kill him.

"Give me the ring," she said.

He did not know how to reply. He tried to think, tried to say, "Mary already gave it to you," but he knew she was reading his mind.

"Give me the *other* ring."

He reached into his pants pocket, pulled out his wallet, and opened it. After a second, he pulled out the ring that he had hooked inside it that morning—the same ring he had told Adam had been in his safe-deposit box and then stolen, presumably by Gwenhwyvach; he had lied so no one would suspect that he desired to obtain both rings.

"The greatest plans of mice and men," said Gwenhwyvach, clearly reading his thoughts. "You thought you could become some type of superman. You thought you could convince Mary to give you the other ring so you could rule, but you are more like Adam's descendants than mine, for like my husband Adam, you are easily won over by a pretty, dithering, mindless female whose breasts aren't even as large as my own. You fool men are all the same. Give me the ring."

For a moment, he considered slipping it onto his finger—perhaps it would protect him, but she grabbed it from his hand before he could stop her. She slid it on the ring finger of her right hand, while the ring that had been in Mary's possession was now on her left hand.

"You haven't seen the end of me, you pathetic little mouse," Gwenhwyvach said, hissing like a snake about to swallow him whole.

Then a glaring light appeared, and in a flash, she was gone—gone with both of the rings. And Cedric was alone on the Space Needle's observation deck.

He remained there, shivering in the cool night, watching the police and ambulances arrive below to clean up Mary's remains. Then he realized the police would be coming up the Space Needle any minute to investigate, and if he were found, he would be a suspect in Mary's murder. He pulled himself to his feet and tried to open the doors back into the interior of the building. Finding one unlocked, he entered inside and managed to hide in a storage area, even squeeze into a vent, just before the police arrived to investigate the floor. He hid there for two days, cramped, famished, exhausted, but not daring to leave from fear he would be arrested and placed in a jail cell.

In truth, the safety of a jail cell would have been preferable to facing Gwenhwyvach again, but Cedric knew he had to remain free so he could get back to England somehow, to help Adam and Anne in the fight against this evil creature. He had always thought himself justified in hating the Delaneys and the Morgans and all of King Arthur's descendants, but now he understood for the first time just what evil was—and he shivered to think he had always been on its side, and he had always been wrong. He decided now that if he could do anything to reverse the deeds of his past, he would. But how could anyone fight the power of this ancient evil and supernatural woman, especially now that she had both rings? What did all his years of hating the Morgans and the Delaneys matter now when Gwenhwyvach was just as likely to destroy him as them? She was his enemy now, and his former enemies had become his allies.

But how could they fight Gwenhwyvach when even Merlin and Morgan le Fay did not seem to have the power to defeat her?

After two nights of hiding, Cedric finally dared to make his escape, assuming observation of the Space Needle by the police had now ended and Mary's death had been ruled a suicide. In the dark, he made his way down through the Space Needle, all the while fearing an alarm would trigger and he would be captured. He could not let that happen—he had to find some way to help his daughter and his grandchildren. He did not know how, but he had to get back to England and save all those he loved, for he realized now that there was love in him for Anne and his grandchildren at the very least—that even evil intentions could not overcome the human heart's inclination toward love.

Finally, Cedric stepped out of the Space Needle into the darkness of the night. He had not walked fifty feet when he heard footsteps behind him.

He was afraid to turn and see who was following him until he heard his name spoken.

And when he turned, he expected to see a policeman.

Instead, standing before him, in the glow of the streetlights, was a tall, handsome, dark-haired man dressed in a long black coat that looked like a cape.

"You know me, do you not?" asked the man with an Eastern European accent.

"Father!" exclaimed Cedric. "But it's...it's impossible!" He was nearly as shocked by the man's presence as he had been by Gwenhwyvach's.

Quincey Harker simply smiled at his son.

"I...how...why, you still haven't aged. Are you a ghost?" Cedric felt terrified, yet unable to resist stepping closer to see the man's flawless complexion, as if his father were but twenty-one years old.

"I have aged in my soul," Quincey replied, "but my outer appearance does not reflect it."

"What...where...what—"

"I have come to help you," Quincey said. "Who else could aid you in getting out of this mess that you have helped to create?"

Cedric could not think what to reply. Days of fear and exhaustion and now this added shock simply overpowered him. His brain and body could handle no more. Suddenly, his world went black.

Quincey Harker rushed to his son's side, catching him just as he fainted. He lifted Cedric in his arms, hailed a cab, and the two men disappeared into the night.

AUTHOR INTERVIEW

TYLER, *OGIER'S PRAYER* links the Arthurian legends to the Charlemagne legends, as did *Melusine's Gift*. Were the legends always linked, or was doing so your idea?

The Charlemagne legends already made mention of Merlin and Morgan le Fay, no doubt because the Arthurian legends were so popular, but from a character standpoint, I always wondered why these Arthurian characters were in the Charlemagne legends. Especially, why is Morgan le Fay interested in causing trouble in France centuries after Arthur's time? I wanted to develop the backstory behind those reasons, which is why I further linked the legends together. Plus, Morgan le Fay's attraction to Ogier in the legends was never really explained, but I gave her a motive for her behavior—to help to continue Arthur's line by producing a child who could marry the child of Roland, who is already Arthur's descendant in my stories.

While you created a backstory to connect all these legends, you also weaved historical people into the novel, especially Charlemagne

and Haroun al-Rashid. Why did you want to use historical people as characters in a fantasy novel?

Inserting historical people just makes for good historical fiction because it makes the fictional story feel more real, and I think that technique is even more important for historical fantasy. I am not a big fan of fantasy that does not have some attachment to the real world. By weaving these legends together with real history, it raises the possibility that these legends could have been true. If that's the case, I could even be descended from these legendary characters, and why not? As an avid genealogist, I already know I'm descended from Charlemagne in more ways than I can count—in fact, DNA and mathematical calculations prove that everyone of European descent alive today is likely descended from everyone who lived in Europe prior to 1200 A.D., and if we go back to 800 A.D., it's likely that many of us can claim descent from Haroun al-Rashid as well—after all, he is said to have had dozens of wives and concubines, so I don't think it unlikely at all.

So when we consider the vastness of the past and its possibilities, historical fantasy becomes not quite so fantastic but rather a portal through which we can enter and feel connected to the past. And I feel it's fun to have that connection and ask ourselves, "What if these legends aren't fictions? What if they were true, and what would that mean to us today? Would it inspire us to be better, kinder, or wiser people if we knew the truth of King Arthur or Melusine's stories?" To go a step further, "What if by believing that this could have been the past, we can change the past and also the future?" That's sort of a quantum physics idea, with a little Law of Attraction added in. If we decide to believe King Arthur was a real person, who's to say our thoughts can't bring that about and alter the past? Rather a mind-blowing idea, isn't it? And that's why I enjoy historical fantasy so much. It allows us to create the past we want.

Nevertheless, while you have the license to create a fictional past in a novel, you clearly did a lot of research. How did the history itself influence your writing, and did you find any surprises in researching this time period?

In writing this novel, I learned a lot more about history than I expected, filling in details of the bigger historical moments I was already familiar with. Perhaps the biggest surprise to me was to learn that Charlemagne was crowned Holy Roman Emperor in 800 because the Pope could not stomach a female emperor, namely Irene of Athens, who was then the Byzantine empress. No one teaches you that in high school Western Civilization classes. In fact, efforts were made to arrange a marriage between Irene and Charlemagne to add to Charlemagne's legitimacy as Roman emperor and possibly combine their empires.

I should clarify that at this time, the Byzantine emperors styled themselves as Roman emperors and the Greeks of that empire called themselves Romans since they were Rome's heirs. The term "byzantine" was not used until the sixteenth century and not commonly applied to describe that empire until the Victorian period, which is why I have avoided the word in this novel. But when Charlemagne and his successors started styling themselves as Holy Roman Emperors, the Byzantines became distinguished from them by calling themselves Greeks and the emperors often styled themselves as basileus. The details of how these people all referred to each other is more complicated than that, but you get the general idea.

Another real issue in writing the novel was understanding the languages of the period. There was no French or Spanish to speak of. Characters in Spain spoke several languages, including Catalan. The Danes spoke Norse, and the Franks spoke Frankish. Names of countries were also an issue, though I finally decided just to call Charlemagne's kingdom France to make it easier for readers.

Overall, this whole time period is fascinating to me. Charlemagne was really responsible for laying the foundation of what would become modern Europe, and his empire eventually became France and Germany as we know them today. And the Byzantine Empire has always intrigued me, as will be obvious in the next book where it plays a more significant role in the story.

Are there any books you would recommend to people who wish to know more about this period of history?

There are countless books, both about the historical time of Charlemagne and about the legends surrounding him, so I'll just name a few. The most famous work about Roland is the eleventh century French epic poem *The Song of Roland*, although it was not a major source for me in creating this work. It deals solely with Roland's death on the battlefield. My primary source was *The Story of Roland* by James Baldwin. I also consulted stories in Bulfinch's mythology. As for scholarly works, I recommend Derek Wilson's *Charlemagne* and, perhaps my favorite, *Becoming Charlemagne* by Jeff Sypeck, which gave a wonderful overview of the period and what was going on in Charlemagne's empire as well as in Haroun al-Rashid's caliphate and in the Byzantine Empire. *The Arabian Nights* also influenced me in creating the scenes with Haroun al-Rashid and his vizier, who accompanies him on his disguised wanderings through the city in the stories. The vizier's historical counterpart really was put to death for marrying Haroun al-Rashid's sister without his permission.

What about the main characters—Ogier and Roland—are they purely legendary or do they have some historical basis?

I tried to ground both characters in history, but they both appear to have been fictional. There is no record of an Ogier in Danish history or of a Roland in French history. That said, they may still have lived. In fact, I even found a genealogy of Roland's descendants which gave me the idea to give him children. It turns out that he supposedly had a son named Faralando d'Angleria. There is no mention of who Faralando's mother was. This son lived in Spain and married a woman named Flora Valdez and they had a child named Diego Valdez. In turn, Diego's descendants are said to include Alfonso V of Leon, who is historical, although most of the generations between him and Diego are questionable. Alfonso V of Leon's descendants measure in the thousands if not millions today and past descendants included King George I of England and all his descendants, plus Otto Bismarck, and Winston Churchill. As for Ogier and Morgan le Fay, one story says they had a son named Meurvin. Of course, if I wanted these lines to intermarry, someone had to have a girl, and Meurvin had his own medieval romance, *Lhistoire du preux meuruin filz d'Oger le dannoys* (*The History of the Valiant Knight Meurvin, Son of Ogier the Dane*, published in 1531), but Faralando did not, so I decided Roland would have a daughter instead; I made up Asalah so she could marry Meurvin, and thus, the bloodline could continue.

What about Asalah's mother, Princess Glorianda? Is she historical or a regular figure in the legends?

I doubt she's historical, but she does appear in the Charlemagne legends and the scenes in my novel of her in Rome and the battle between Ogier and Brunamont are all based on the legends. What happens to Glorianda later is all my own creation—her marriage to Brunamont, journey to Prester John's land, and marriage to Roland—to make her a key player in the genealogy of Arthur's descendants.

I chose for Glorianda to play a major role in the novel so there would be a Muslim heroine (and hero, which Karaheut is). I wanted to show that love surpasses barriers of religion, skin color, culture, etc. For centuries, Muslims and Christians have fought and misunderstood one another, though I've never understood how anyone could kill in the name of religion. In the novel, I tried to depict good and bad people and show that they are found among Christians and Muslims alike. Furthermore, at the center of the novel, I placed Ogier, intentionally choosing a hero who was neither Christian nor Muslim, so he would have difficulty understanding what all the squabbling was about. Of course, I grew up in a Christian culture so Christianity influenced me, but I hope I have shown respect to all peoples, races, cultures, religions, and genders in my novels. And if Glorianda had lived, I would have loved to meet her.

How about Prester John? Is he in the Charlemagne legends?

Yes. In the Charlemagne legends, there are varying accounts of both Roland and Ogier visiting his kingdom, although my depiction is more elaborate than those stories.

Prester John's legend has many versions, but I chose to go with the supposition that he is the Apostle John, who went to Ephesus with the Virgin Mary and who may have written the book of Revelation (although I've always thought that book a greater problem than solution for Christianity, so I've had him deny its authorship). In the Bible, Jesus hints that the Apostle John might remain on the earth until his return. Sometimes, the Apostle John is also equated with the Wandering Jew, although so is Joseph of Arimathea, so I've allowed Merlin to reveal himself as really being Joseph of Arimathea in this novel while Prester John is the Apostle John.

Of course, Prester John is fictional. The first reference to him in history was in the twelfth century when reports were made of a great Christian king in the east, probably in India. Unweaving his legend and its origins is a fascinating task, but much of the legend was probably made up by people of the time, or it was hearsay from stories told to Europeans who visited India and probably misunderstood or mistranslated what they heard. And, of course, as is usual with these legends, what is fictional is far more fun than what is probably true, but once again, what if it were true? What if there were a kingdom like the one in this novel that Prester John ruled, where earthly people could find sanctuary from the world if they were deserving and willing to learn and seek wisdom so their souls could evolve? Perhaps there isn't a kingdom of Prester John, but there should have been; the world would be a better place today if there were, just as it would be if Camelot or Avalon existed.

What about Gudrun? How much of her story is legend?

In the Charlemagne legends, Ogier has a stepmother who seems to be against him. I chose to give her a name and add a backstory for her of being Ganelon's sister and also of her marriage later to Roland's uncle, Count Geoffrey. It only made sense to me that if this supernatural evil woman could reincarnate herself, she could have been many of the evil women throughout history and in legends. Stay tuned to learn more about her past as Lilith and also her lives after her incarnation as Gudrun in the next novel. I think you'll be surprised as more light is shed on her character.

Considering the novel's title, Ogier's prayer is obviously intended to be a pivotal moment in the plot, but is it really effective since in the epilogue, Lilith/Gwenhwyvach is still evil?

I intentionally left the effects of the prayer somewhat vague because I don't believe we can always know the influence of our prayers. Sometimes, prayers are answered in ways we don't expect, and while Ogier's prayer may not change Gwenhwyvach, more importantly, it does change Ogier. And as Prester John tells Ogier, quoting Tennyson's lines that would be written a thousand years in the future, "More things are wrought by prayer than this world dreams of."

I'm a firm believer in the power of prayer—today many of us call it positive thinking; it's the same thing because for a true prayer to be effective, it needs to be positive. People who pray with fear and worry tend to block the prayer from being effective, but when we pray with the vision that what we ask for will be answered, we present God or the Universe with a clearer understanding of what we want so it is more easily presented to us.

Akin to how the Law of Attraction works, true prayer allows us to use the power of our mind more fully, and that's what happens for Ogier. When he ceases to hold negative thoughts about Gwenhwyvach, he frees himself from the pain and unhappiness he has been holding onto. Gwenhwyvach might not change because Ogier wills it, but I think perhaps she could sense that his feelings toward her have changed and that helps to break down the wall between them, and perhaps that is why she need not be seen by him again. By comparison, Adam, Anne, Mary, and the rest of the modern day characters are living in fear of Gwenhwyvach, and she may well feed on that fear, which allows her to grow more powerful because they perceive her that way—it's positive thinking in reverse then, but nevertheless a testament to the power of human thought. I encourage people interested in understanding this concept better to read many of the classic books on positive thinking and the Law of Attraction, including *Think and Grow Rich* by Napoleon Hill, *The Power of Positive Thinking* by Norman Vincent Peale, and *Ask and It Is Given* by Jerry and Esther Hicks.

I'll just add that in writing this series, I didn't want to write yet another story of good vs. evil. I really dislike that format, besides it being such a cliché, because I don't believe fighting a war against evil can have positive results. Instead, I believe that when you change your thoughts, you change your world—and by extension, others' worlds through your influence. When Ogier stops feeling hate for Gwenhwyvach, he opens the way for a better world for himself, if not for her. Fighting evil doesn't work; it just leads to more fighting, but loving our enemies does work. Jesus knew that. Gandhi knew that. But most of us are still waiting to learn that. I hope reading this book will help someone else come to that understanding.

The epilogue also introduces Cedric's father, Quincey Harker. What more can you tell us about him?

Ah, if you were a reader of Gothic literature, you would already know all about him and the legend he is tied to. But I won't give that away now. I'll simply say that all will be revealed in my next book.

What will you tell us about the next book?

It will be called *Lilith's Love*, and a lot will be explained in it. It will begin with a prologue set in 1453, the year Constantinople fell to the Turks. How that event ties into the story will be made clear as the book progresses. You can expect some more characters based in old legends to make appearances. The place where Adam and Anne's sons have been hidden away will be revealed, and there will be a showdown with Lilith. The only other thing I'll say is that I hope my readers like vampires.

Be sure to visit my website, **www.ChildrenofArthur.com**, for updates on when the rest of the series will be released.

ACKNOWLEDGMENTS

I WOULD LIKE to thank those friends and fellow writers who read in whole or in part the rough draft of this novel.

Diana DeLuca and Rosalyn Hurley read the entire rough draft as it was written chapter by chapter, and they have followed me on this galloping, twisting, and turning ride through the entire series, giving me feedback on characters, motivations, and where along the way they were lost by the complexities of the stories so I could make straight the path.

Lee Brown and Gene Stroobants of the Writer's Ink group listened to me read aloud several of the chapters and gave me their immediate feedback and reactions as well as the encouragement to carry on.

Jenifer Brady read the final draft with an eagle eye and an accomplished writer's expertise. I appreciate all her suggestions and comments almost as much as her enthusiastic support.

Scott Pavelle shared with me, through the Internet, his own interest in Charlemagne, including maps and timelines he had made to try to make sense out of the inconsistencies in the legends, versus in history.

Dana Perrow Moran listened to me discuss the book and offered me feedback and invaluable encouragement.

Larry Alexander, with this and all the books in the series, took my ideas and created the novel's stunning cover as well as its interior design.

Finally, I wish to thank my literary predecessors, especially James Baldwin for his book *The Story of Roland* and all authors and others current and in the past who continue to keep the Arthurian legend alive and before the public's eyes. May it never be forgotten.

THE CHILDREN OF ARTHUR SERIES

continues in

LILITH'S LOVE

THE CHILDREN OF ARTHUR, BOOK FOUR

BY
TYLER R. TICHELAAR

EIGHTEEN YEARS HAVE passed since Adam and Anne Delaney's twin sons were kidnapped, ostensibly by one who wished them well. Now, after a string of useless clues and years of doubting their own sanity, the couple arrive in Istanbul where they have been told they will find the answers they seek... and hopefully the infant boys who—if even alive—would now be grown men and strangers to them.

Lilith's Love, the fourth volume in Tyler R. Tichelaar's revolutionary historical fantasy series, The Children of Arthur, brings together diverse legends to create a new human history that both surprises and reveals how powerful the imagination can be. With an impressive cast of historical and legendary characters that includes Merlin, Emperor Constantine XI, the Wandering Jew, Dracula, and Lilith herself, this tale takes readers from the Fall of Constantinople to a New World Order in the twenty-first century, rewriting a past we thought we knew to create a future far more fabulous than we ever dreamed.

Be sure not to miss any of The Children of Arthur series:

ARTHUR'S LEGACY: THE CHILDREN OF ARTHUR, BOOK ONE

MELUSINE'S GIFT: THE CHILDREN OF ARTHUR, BOOK TWO

OGIER'S PRAYER: THE CHILDREN OF ARTHUR, BOOK THREE

LILITH'S LOVE: THE CHILDREN OF ARTHUR, BOOK FOUR

ARTHUR'S BOSOM: THE CHILDREN OF ARTHUR, BOOK FIVE

and you might also enjoy Tyler's nonfiction study of the Arthurian legend:

KING ARTHUR'S CHILDREN:
A STUDY IN FICTION AND TRADITION

For the latest information, release dates, and to purchase books, visit:

www.ChildrenofArthur.com

A Sneak Peek at Lilith's Love: The Children of Arthur, Book Four
the next volume in
The Children of Arthur series:

LILITH'S LOVE

PROLOGUE

CONSTANTINOPLE MAY 29, 1453, JUST AFTER MIDNIGHT

"The city will be both founded and lost by an emperor Constantine whose mother was called Helen."

— Ancient Byzantine Prophecy

FOR FIFTY-THREE DAYS, the siege had held. He had never thought he would be able to hold off the Turks for as long as he had. Had Pope Nicholas V and the rest of Europe come to his aid, it might have been different; even so, his people had been remarkable in their determination not to surrender to the enemy. But any day now, even any hour, it was bound to end.

And he would be the last, he Constantine XI, the last Emperor of the Romans. For fifteen centuries, there had been an empire, and for more than eleven centuries, the capital had been here in Constantinople, but now all that would come to an end. He had done everything he could, trying to negotiate peace with the Turks, striving to get the Orthodox Church to concede to the Pope's demands that they become Catholic, imploring the rulers of France, England, Hungary, Venice, whoever would listen, to come to his aid, but it had all been to no avail. The Turks far outnumbered those in the city.

And the city was not even worth taking; Constantine knew that. Its wealth had diminished to almost nothing in the last two centuries, ever since the Latins had used a crusade to the Holy Land as an excuse to sack the city and then rule as its emperors for most of the thirteenth century. Although the Romans had regained the city and the throne in time, the empire had continued to shrink and weaken; continually, Constantine and his imperial predecessors had sought to keep the Turks at bay, the emperors wedding their daughters to the Ottoman sultans and doing anything necessary to ensure the empire's survival.

And as the last emperor, Constantine knew the blame would lie upon his head, without regard to how little chance he had to stop his enemy or how all of Christendom had abandoned him and his people to their fate. What would they call him? His first namesake was Constantine the Great. Would he be called Constantine the Defeated, Constantine the Failure, Constantine the Unworthy? Perhaps the best he could hope for was to be killed in battle so he would be remembered as Constantine the Martyr.

He stood alone now on the battlements, his soldiers knowing he wished to be alone with his thoughts. He looked out at the vast hordes of Turks encamped around the city. Even now they were battering at the walls, hoping to topple any one of them, not even seeking sleep as the night moved toward dawn.

How had it come to this? To some extent, Constantine could understand the reluctance and ignorance of his fellow rulers to come to his aid. Even the Pope, the supposed leader of the Christian world, he could forgive for his stubbornness when he considered that they were all men, full of weaknesses, but how could God Himself turn His back on them? How could the Holy Virgin to whom the city had been dedicated, desert them?

And there was no doubt they had been forsaken. The Holy Virgin had shown she would no longer protect them. The city had been dedicated to the Virgin since its ancient days. In desperation, the people had cried out to her ever since the siege had begun, and just three days ago, her most holy relic, the Hodegetria—an icon of her, believed to have been painted by St. Luke the Evangelist himself, which had saved the city on numerous occasions—was brought forth from Saint Sophia and carried in a procession through the streets. It had been mounted on a wooden pallet and lifted onto the shoulders of several strong men from the icon's confraternity. The people followed as the Hodegetria traveled through the city, while the priests offered up incense, and the men, women, and children walked barefoot to show their penance. Hymns were sung, prayers said, and the people repeatedly cried out to the Virgin, beseeching her protection: "Do thou save thy city, as thou knowest and willest. We put thee forward as our arms, our rampart, our shield, our general: do thou fight for thy people."

Then, before anyone realized it was happening, the Hodegetria slipped from the hands of its bearers. They struggled to grasp it, but it was too late. The people ran forward to pick it up, but it was as if it were weighted with lead, refusing to be raised. Eventually, when it was raised again, the procession had barely restarted before thunder burst through the clouds and lightning split the sky. Then the heavens poured down rain, soaking the procession and all the penitents. The downpour became torrential so that the procession had to halt; water, inches deep, filled the streets, making them slippery, and the flood soon threatened to wash away the children in the procession. Struggling, the icon's bearers eventually managed to return the Hodegetria to Saint Sophia as gloom settled over the city, less from the weather than the omens that clearly stated the Virgin had refused their prayers and penance.

Worse, the next day, God's grace had left the city. Since its construction by Emperor Justinian in the sixth century, Saint Sophia had held within it the Holy Light as its protector. But that night, a great glow was seen in the sky. First, the sentries on the walls and then people in the streets had cried out in fear that the city had caught on fire. All the sky lit up, but the flame was located only on the roof of Saint Sophia. The flame shot forth from the window and circled the entire dome several times before gathering itself into one great and indescribable flash of blinding light that shot up into the heavens. Clearly, the Holy Light had returned from whence it had come, no longer offering God's protection to the city. The sight had been so overwhelming to Constantine that now, two days later, it still made him sick to think of it. Had he himself lost favor with God? At that fatal moment, such a thought had caused him to go numb throughout his body and collapse to the ground in a faint, remaining unconscious for hours.

When Constantine finally woke, the people had begged him to flee the city before it was too late, but he had insisted he would not do so. To leave his people solely to save his own life would be to heap immortal ridicule upon his name. And even if he did leave, what life would remain for him, without a throne, marked as a coward for not standing by his supporters in their hour of greatest need? Better he stay to fight, and if need be, die with his people.

He had seen both these catastrophes with his own eyes, but the most shocking event he had personally experienced. Early the next morning, when he had gone out walking in the palace gardens, he had come face-to-face with an old man with a flowing white beard in a tattered black robe. Constantine had never seen the man before, and he could not understand how the man had entered his private gardens. But before he could accost the man, the stranger looked him square in the eyes, his eyes piercingly gray, and without showing fear or deference for Constantine's station, he said, "Greetings, Constantine, last of the Romans."

Constantine had frozen, feeling himself unable to speak or move. His mind went blank for what seemed the longest time as the question "Who are you?" struggled to rise to his lips. His first fear was that the man might be an assassin, sent by the Turks—who but an assassin would dare to enter his private garden at dawn? But then slowly, the answer came to his lips in a whisper.

"The Wandering Jew."

Before the words fully escaped Constantine's mouth, the man turned and disappeared behind a clump of trees. Constantine ran after him, so stunned that he pursued him into the bushes, scratching himself on their branches but unable to see anyone. After a couple of minutes, he calmed himself and returned to the walkway, fearing his people had seen his frantic behavior. Had he dreamt it, or had he truly seen the man? But he could remember those words clearly; they yet rung in his ears: "Greetings, Constantine, last of the Romans."

He knew such a meeting forebode great ill. The Wandering Jew— he whom Christ had cursed to wander the earth until His return—had long been rumored to appear at pivotal moments in history. Stories claimed he had been seen in the city once before, back in 1204 when the Latin Crusaders had sacked Constantinople. He had also been seen at the surrender of Jerusalem to Saladin in 1187, amid the mob during the Peasants Revolt in England in 1381, and most recently in the crowd when the Maid of Orleans had been burned at the stake in Rouen, France in 1431. Constantine had heard rumors in recent days that the Wandering Jew had been sighted in Constantinople's streets, but he had dismissed such rumors as folk tales. Now, he could not imagine who else this man could be who dared to address him as "last of the Romans"—an ominous reference, indeed.

The next day, Constantine knew his death was certain when twelve Venetian ships arrived to aid the city, bringing with them the news that no larger fleet nor other enforcements would come. Twelve ships would be of little help against the incredible Ottoman navy and the hordes of Turkish soldiers preparing for the final assault they all knew was coming. No one could accurately tell the numbers, but a city of just over fifty thousand souls—a city that in its glorious past had been home to a million residents—was being protected by an army of less than twenty thousand against some one hundred thousand Turks, plus their allies. Surely, the situation was hopeless.

Constantine had little doubt that tonight was the last time the sun would set on the city before it was taken, and pillaged, and perhaps even destroyed. The walls could well be broken through before dawn. The Turkish cannons had already damaged them beyond repair. The conquest would happen as soon as Sultan Mehmet II led the next charge.

Nothing was left to do but offer prayers, though prayers now seemed of little help. Nevertheless, Constantine had spent the last day at service in Saint Sophia, on his knees before his people and God, begging forgiveness for their transgressions. Afterwards, he had spent time here on the ramparts with his longtime friend and advisor Sphrantzes. And then he had sought some time alone, time to prepare himself for what he did not doubt was his imminent death. He would do so nobly, as Emperor of the Romans, and in a manner to make his ancestors proud, but he would be dead nonetheless, and he had his doubts that God would have mercy upon his soul after the signs he had already seen.

"Your majesty." He turned to hear himself addressed and found the captain of the guard speaking. "The Turks are about to break through the wall. You must return to the palace. You must look to your own safety."

"You know better," Constantine replied, already in his armor. "Come; we will fight together, and may God have mercy on our souls."

The Turks were firing their cannons. It was almost half-past one in the morning. Just as the emperor joined his army before the St. Romanus Gate, a cannonball came ripping through the wall, sending stone and men flying, and by the time Constantine and his men recovered from the shock, three hundred Turks had poured through, their voices roaring as they entered the city. In panic, some of the Romans fled into the streets, desperate to see to their own and their families' safety, but most stood fighting beside their emperor and the officers.

The Romans fought violently, but they were far outnumbered, and while the battle raged at the great crumbling opening in the wall for several minutes, eventually, the Romans were cut down as the Turks began to spread and pillage throughout Constantinople.

Constantine found himself covered in blood as his sword continued to slice at the Turks before him, but within a few minutes, he was surrounded by his enemies. He had taken care not to wear anything to make the enemy suspect he was the emperor, for he knew if they discovered his identity, his life would be spared, but only because the sultan would want to hold him as a prisoner. No, he would much rather die here with his people than be forced to go down on bended knee before Mehmet II, or worse, be paraded through the streets by his captors.

Suddenly, Constantine felt a great pain in his back. He immediately became dizzy; for a moment, he felt his knees buckle and he thought he would collapse, but then he experienced a great lifting feeling, as if he were floating into the air. He could only think that his soul was leaving his body. Had he been slain? Was he now dead? Was he being taken to Heaven—could death be this quick?

Looking up, bending his head all the way back, he saw he was in the arms of a great winged man, a beautiful gorgeous man, a man a good couple of feet taller than him—no, not a man but an angel.

And then all went black.

When he opened his eyes, Constantine found himself lying on a cot inside a barren room all built of stone. He could see the sky, but nothing else from the window, making him assume he was quite high up. All he heard were birds chirping and a breeze rippling through the trees. No screams of his people. No cannons booming. And most surprisingly, he felt no fear.

Was he dead? But, surely, Heaven did not look like the barren room of a castle.

For a moment, he relished the quiet, but his curiosity overcame him. He sat up and continued to look out the window. From his sitting position, he could see what appeared to be a marsh, and beyond that a river, and then just a green row of trees and a lush countryside. He appeared to be in the middle of nowhere. Certainly, he was far from Constantinople.

"Where am I?" he muttered, about to put his feet on the floor when the door opened. In walked a man whom Constantine had only seen once before.

"You!" Constantine gasped.

ABOUT THE AUTHOR

TYLER R. TICHELAAR holds a Ph.D. in Literature from Western Michigan University, and Bachelor and Master's Degrees in English from Northern Michigan University. He is the owner of his own publishing company, Marquette Fiction, and of Superior Book Productions, a professional book review, editing, proofreading, book design, and web design service.

Tyler is the author of numerous historical novels, including *The Marquette Trilogy* (composed of *Iron Pioneers, The Queen City*, and *Superior Heritage*), *Narrow Lives, The Only Thing That Lasts, Spirit of the North: a paranormal romance*, and *The Best Place*. He has also authored non-fiction titles that include *My Marquette: Explore the Queen City of the North, Creating a Local Historical Book, The Gothic Wanderer: From Transgression to Redemption*, and *King Arthur's Children: A Study in Fiction and Tradition*, and he has written the play *Willpower*. An avid genealogist, Tyler has been fascinated by the Arthurian legend and medieval history since childhood.

Visit Tyler at:
www.MarquetteFiction.com
www.GothicWanderer.com
www.ChildrenofArthur.com

www.ingramcontent.com/pod-product-compliance
Lightning Source LLC
Chambersburg PA
CBHW020636020726
47494CB00001B/214

* 9 7 8 0 9 9 9 6 2 4 0 0 1 7 *